The
Blood
of the
HOOPOE

Also by Naomi Foyle

Seoul Survivors

The Gaia Chronicles

Astra
Rook Song

The Blood of the Hoopoe

NAOMI FOYLE

BOOK THREE OF THE GAIA CHRONICLES

Jo Fletcher
BOOKS

First published in Great Britain in 2016 by

Jo Fletcher Books
an imprint of Quercus Editions Ltd
Carmelite House
50 Victoria Embankment
London EC4Y 0DZ

An Hachette UK Company

A CIP catalogue record for this book is available from the British Library.

ISBN 978 1 78206 922 5 (TPB)
ISBN 978 1 78429 971 2 (EBOOK)

10 9 8 7 6 5 4 3 2 1

Typeset by Jouve (UK), Milton Keynes
Printed and bound in Great Britain by Clays Ltd, St Ives plc

for Louise Reiser

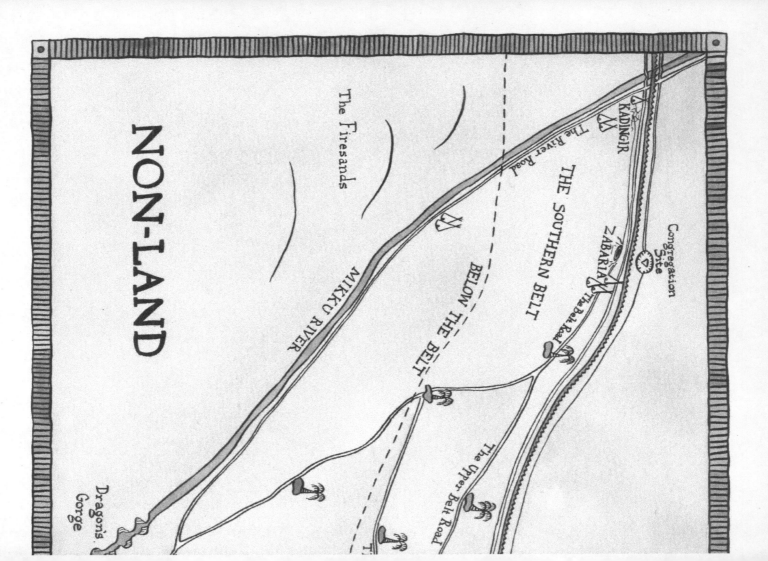

IS-LAND

SHUGURRA RIVER

The White Desert

Congregation Site

Shugurra Chott

The Great Depression

Shiimti

The Silk Route

The Black Desert

Boundary Road [The Hem]

The Lower Belt Road

The Belt Line

The Windsands

To ASFAR →

Asfar Road

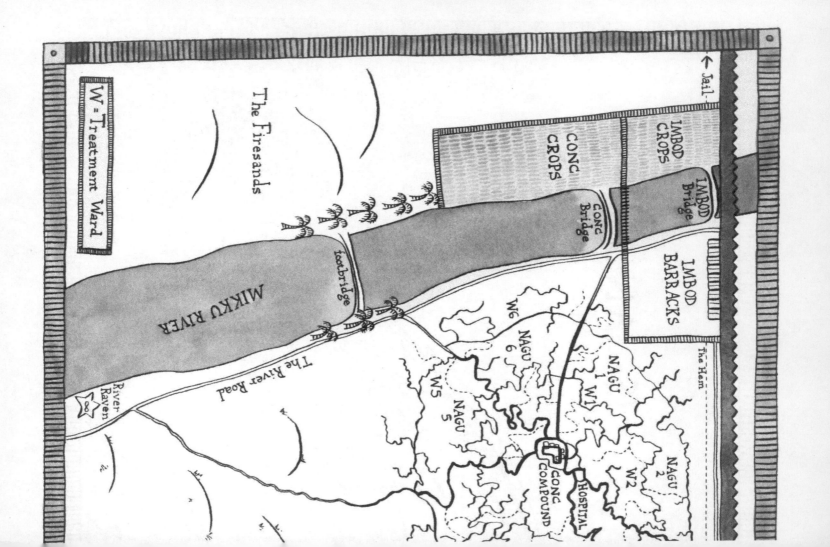

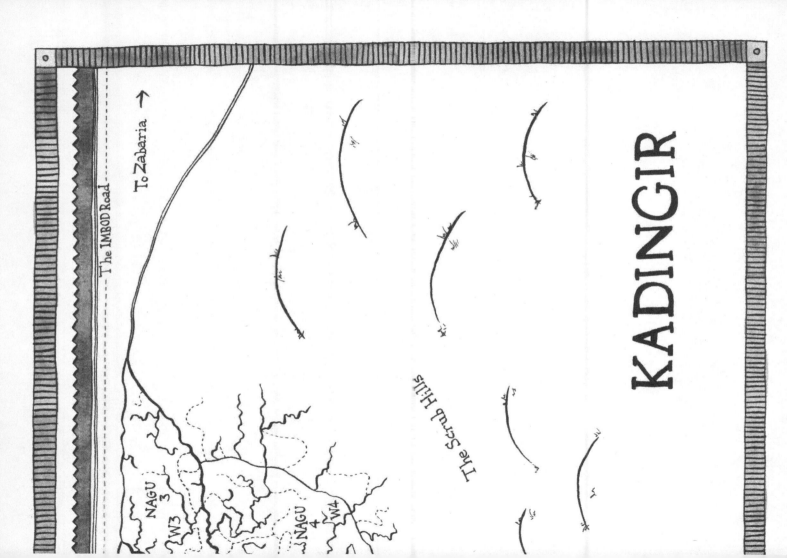

KADINGIR

The IMBOD Road

To Zabaria →

The Scrub Hills

NAGU 3

W3

NAGU 4

W4

Dramatis Personae

Astra Ordott	Gaian political refugee. Code daughter of an Is-Lander mother and Non-Lander father
Muzi Bargadala	Shepherd; Non-Lander

The Youth Action Collective (YAC)

Enki Arakkia	Rhymer and warrior
Bartol	Trainer and warrior
Lilutu	Producer and warrior
Ninti	Speaker and warrior
Malku	Speaker and warrior
Tiamet	Singular [see also Pithar]
Simiya	Singular
Asar	Singular
Sepsu	Asar's partner and carer
Ėšgśd	Warrior
Khshayarshat	Warrior (deceased)
Abgal Izruk	Mentor (deceased)

The Non-Land Alliance (N-LA)

Una Dayyani	Lead Convenor
Marti	Personal assistant to Una Dayyani
Artakhshathra	Researcher
Tahazu Rabu	Chief of Police

Kadingir

Uttu Dúrkiñar	Elderwoman; grandmother of Muzi (deceased)
Kingu Dúrkiñar	Eldest son of Uttu
Habat Bargadala	Daughter-in-law of Uttu, married to Kingu
Gibil Dúrkiñar	Second son of Uttu
Nanshe Emeeš	Daughter-in-law of Uttu, married to Gibil
Geshti Bargadala	Daughter of Kingu and Habat
Hadis Bargadala	Daughter of Kingu and Habat
Suen Emeeš	Son of Gibil and Nanshe

Pithar [In Zabaria]

Tiamet	Singular [see also YAC] and sex worker
Neperdu	Sex worker
Anunit	Sex worker
Ebebu	Infant son of Tiamet

Shiimti

Zizi Kataru	Astra Ordott's Code father
The Zardusht	The High Healer of Shiimti
Hozai	World Whiler
Sãñãl	World Whiler
Boranduhkt	Beer-tent manager
Salamu	Friend of Zizi Kataru
Talmai	Son of Salamu

Is-Land Ministry of Border Defence (IMBOD)

[VC: Member of the Vision Council]

Chief Superintendent Clay Odinson	Head of the Non-Land IMBOD Barracks; VC
Superintendent Samrod Blesserson	Code Scientist; VC [see also Is-Land]

Peat Orson — Sec Gen constable [see also Is-Land]
Laam Vistason — Sec Gen constable (deceased)
Jade Sundott — Sec Gen constable
Robin Steppeson — Sec Gen constable
Chief Convenor Stamen Magmason — Head of National Wheel Meet; VC
Riverine Farshoredott — Senior Officer; VC

Is-Land

Hokma Blesser — Astra's Shelter mother (deceased)
Samrod Blesserson — Hokma's brother; leading scientist [see also IMBOD]
Ahn Orson — Hokma's ex-partner; leading architect
Klor Grunerdeson — Astra's Shelter father; Code worker
Nimma — Astra's Shelter mother; Craft worker
Sheba — Klor and Nimma's Code daughter; killed in a Non-Lander nanobomb attack
Peat — Astra's older Shelter brother [see also IMBOD]
Yoki — Astra's Shelter brother; Sec Gen
Meem — Astra's Shelter sister; Sec Gen (still at school)
Congruence — Ahn's partner, a relationship begun secretly and illegally in her teens; non-Sec Gen
Dr Cora Pollen — Code worker; political prisoner

The Council of New Continents (CONC)

Major Akira Thames — CONC Compound Director
Dr Tapputu — Non-Lander; Head of CONC Medical Outreach Service
Rudo Acadie — Mobile Medical Unit medic
Photon Augenblick — Mobile Medical Unit medic
Sandrine Moses — Mobile Medical Unit supply coordinator

'Oh Glorious Hoopoe,' cried another bird,
'I cannot come – have you not heard?

My heart's held hostage here, my Love
an outlaw in the dunes, a blazing dove,

her face a torch that sears my wheat to waste –
and yet her absence fuels my haste

to heap the bonfire of my soul, stoke
the passions she provokes . . .

The Way is not for me; a cinder on the wind,
I am weak, unworthy, chaff to leave behind.'

'Your suffering,' said the Hoopoe, 'is a game
you play against the clock. Time

will seize Love's smile, grind her beauty into dust.
You cannot see the unseen prize: and yet now you must.'

from *The Conference of the Birds*
by Farid ud-Din Attar [c. 1110–1221]

author's version

Her name is Istar. She is placeless. You will know her by these signs:

She will arise in the night, enchained by the light of a day that is dead. Young among the mighty, knowing among the innocent, with her first kiss she will appoint her vizier, the raven-haired Helpmeet of Harpies. Her chariot charged with the anger of ages, she will arrive resplendent at the House of Abundant Women. The Seer shall bless her, and she shall heal his warriors. Attended by the Prince of Shepherds, she will move like a *mergallû* over the windsands. She will greet her father, drink his beer, steal his [word missing] and her lustre will illume his alliance. Alone, she will fly to the ashlands and bury herself in the earth. When she arises the placeless ones shall be in all places, and all places shall sing glad hymns of welcome and of [word missing].

The Prophecy

[Fragments from cuneiform tablets c. 3250 BCE]

The Pale Plain

The plateau was as dry as a scab. Since leaving the stream they had passed no water, no bushes, just the odd withered clump of grass, parched and yellow like the soil that cracked in all directions out to the rim of the horizon. The sun was midway to its zenith in a cloudless sky, the shadow of the cart and horse shrinking like a puddle stain. Astra had left the shelter of the tarpaulin purely to pee behind a hump of black stunted rocks; there was no way on Gaia's ill earth she was staying here.

'*Oh!* This is . . .' She grasped for *ridiculous* in Asfarian, settled for, '*stupid.* I am going too, Muzi, and that is THE END!'

Her hair was a crusty sponge, her skin measled with heat and coated with grime, and she stank; even her bum ached, and if she ate any more spelt porridge she'd turn grey. Right there, not even an hour's ride east, so close she could almost see its friendly jumble of sun-baked cubes, feel the breeze from the palm trees waving a lush green welcome against the pale morning sky, was Lálsil, the oasis town she had been dreaming of for three jolting, rattling, sweating days and nights. Even more than the thought of buying dates and oranges at Lálsil's famous market, drinking beer under its tasselled canopies, getting online, the engine driving her forward for the last twenty-four hours had been the promise of the town's legendary steam bath: the vision of lying moist and shining on a marble slab under an ancient dome pierced with stars. She stepped back towards the cart.

Quick as a snake, Muzi blocked her, his lithe limbs everywhere she turned. 'No, Astra. You stay here.'

She flung up her hands, clasped her head. 'I need to wash, Muzi. And

I have to email Photon. There's a war on. We've got to keep in touch with Kadingir.'

'Hello?' Muzi waved his short arm in front of her face. 'You famous now. You *goddess*, Astra. You Istar, ShareWorld queen. You want IMBOD spies see you?'

'No one will see me. I'll buy a . . . *veil*!' She retrieved the word triumphantly, splaying her fingers over her face in case he didn't know it, 'Some of the Asfarian traders wear them, I know, I saw on Archivia—'

'We no speak good Asfarian!' His astonishing eyes dazzled with scorn. 'I no good words; you no good accent.'

She glowered. He was right, and she knew it. Muzi's Asfarian accent was excellent. He could do the throaty vowels that made her sound as if she'd swallowed a whole cat, let alone its hairball; the sharp trills her tongue floundered over like a soggy dishcloth. But he couldn't speak a full correct sentence in the language if his life depended on it.

Nor could he strategise. Muzi wasn't thinking this through. And he wasn't even trying to discuss it all properly with her. Her anger flared again. 'IMBOD could be hunting for you too. You're just as easy to recognise as me. If it's so dangerous, we need to stick together. Look. I'll wear a veil and I won't speak to anyone. You can say—'

Muzi leaned close. She could smell his musk, his dusty shirt, his breath, aniseed-scented from the twigs he chewed to clean his teeth. 'If you go into Lālsil, Istar,' he threatened in Somarian, 'I'm going home.'

She understood perfectly. At the same time she no longer knew where she was, who this person in front of her was, his rare blue eyes glittering like patches of ice in hot earth. 'You promise to help me,' she hissed in his language. The tense was wrong, but a promise was timeless.

'I told Photon I would take you to find your father.' He tapped his chest, switched back to Asfarian. 'I take. I guide. You follow. You no want follow – I go back Kadingir.'

She was speechless. She'd asked Muzi to be her *guide*, not her leader. And Photon was *her* friend, a man Muzi had met for an hour. But of course: the CONC driver was a *man*. For three days and nights she'd fought the temptation to kiss those finely arced lips. Now she wanted to punch them. Here in this lifeless plain all had become brutally clear: Muzi's lean poise and keenness to help were not expressions of grace and restraint and consideration. They were deeply etched signs of arrogance – the bone-deep arrogance of a cocky, ill-educated, meat-eating *patriarch*.

She dug in her pocket, brandished her Tablette. 'I have the money, remember. Who's going to pay for the supplies if I stay here?'

He turned his back on her and, with that fluid ease that would *never again* make her heart shiver like a moonlit meadow, leapt back up into the driver's seat. 'You keep money,' he tossed from the shade of the tarpaulin, a lord granting a boon. 'I trade.'

She thought he was going to take the reins and drive off, but he slung his bag over his shoulder, hopped into the back and began dumping blankets, dishes, cutlery, the spelt sack – everything they owned – out onto the ground. Fear shot through her. 'What are you doing?'

'Cart no good now. I trade for camel. No want trader see we travelling two.'

'*What?*' Yet another decision he was taking without her. 'Camels are expensive. And we can't both ride one. We need to talk about this, Muzi.'

She had raised her voice. Sisi snorted and stamped. Muzi shot her a reproachful look. 'Camel good for carrying. Good in sandstorm. Not eat or drink much. We walk.'

She stomped to the back of the cart, to yell without disturbing the horse. 'Are you *crazy*? You want to *walk* the rest of the way? That's *suicidal*, Muzi. That's the most preposterous plan I've ever heard. It's not even a plan. It is NOT A PLAN. It is the absolute absence of a plan. It demonstrates the fundamental non-existence of the *capacity* to plan.'

She was shouting in Gaian now, shouting and sputtering, not caring that he didn't understand. He just had to get that he was an *idiot*, as thick as the Precambrian layer. She had the CONC map on her Tablette; they both knew that it was at least a week's journey to Shiimti. Walking all the way would take two or three times longer, if they got there at all. They'd get blisters if they walked, risk exhaustion. They might get sunstroke, get lost, stop being able to make sense of the compass in her watch, start going round in circles. They might *die*. She boiled over, steaming and pacing as Muzi emptied the cart. Loads of people travelled with horses and carts on the Belt roads. She had seen photos. They could buy *barrels* of water; that was what the cart was for. They could wait out any storm; shelter the horse beneath the tarp if necessary. Muzi was a sheepherder and scrap-metal merchant from Kadingir. Had he ever owned a camel? Ever gone to Shiimti before? No? Well then, it was better to stick to the beast he knew. She shouted louder and louder, pacing and flailing, until Muzi jumped down in front of her and blazed in her face in Somarian,

'The horse and the cart are *mine*. I'm trading them for a camel or I'm *going home*.'

'*You*—' She clenched her fists.

Muzi's eyes flashed blue fire.

She stepped back, thrust her hands in her pockets. Suddenly she felt as drained as the sallow yellow grass on this barren plain. Technically, the horse and cart belonged to Muzi's father and uncle. Thanks to *her*, Kingu and Gibil and their wives and children were in an IMBOD jail. Thanks to her too, Muzi's grandmother was dead. Uttu had been killed for the crime of inviting Astra to lunch.

'Okay,' she muttered, crushing a lump of soil beneath her boot heel. 'Go without me. Get a camel.' Her temple was pulsing. If she wasn't careful she would bring on one of her headaches. She had been taking her medication, but she wasn't used to spending time in the sun. Or having screaming fights with a man who didn't listen to a word she said.

'Is only way, Astra. You see.'

'Be careful,' she insisted. 'You've got to wear sunglasses, and your CONC hand. And you should get a pair of gloves to hide it.'

She hadn't ever mentioned his prosthesis before. He hardly wore the clunky old thing, but surely he understood that a one-handed youth with broken sapphires for eyes would stand out nearly everywhere in Non-Land.

'No worry, Astra. I keep safe.' He took his flask from his bag, filled it from the water barrel Photon had given them and set it down by the rocks. The barrel was nearly empty. 'This water for you. I get more in Lālsil.'

He was really going. Really leaving her here. Really selling the horse.

'What about the dream-catcher? You're not going to trade that, are you?'

Muzi frowned. It was the first time she'd seen him concede a point. He walked to the front of the cart and regarded the old propeller fan he'd mounted there, three rook feathers tied by thread to the cage. He took his knife from his shirt pocket, cut the feathers free and offered them to her.

'We keep dreams. I take catcher to money-lend stall. One day I buy back.'

The feathers that had danced in the air as the cart jolted over the plain lay like three black blades in her palm. 'We'd better come back,' she grumbled, slipping them into a cargo pocket. 'One day *I* want to go to the Lálsil bath house.'

'You no need bath.' He grinned. 'You smell like scrubland.'

'I'm serious. I'm filthy. Buy me some soap, Muzi. And a washcloth and a hat. And as much water as the camel can carry. Promise?'

'Camel spit lots. Is good shower, you see.'

She didn't answer for fear of losing her temper again. If he'd kept the cart, he could have brought barrels of water back. And this was goodbye to the horse. She couldn't even trust Muzi would find a good carer – she couldn't bring herself even to think 'owner' – for Sisi. Muzi's family hadn't even given the beast a name. When she'd asked, he'd laughed and replied 'Sisi': looking it up on her Tablette, she'd discovered the word meant horse in Somarian. She stroked the creature's soft whuffy nose, whispered, 'I'm sorry I yelled, Sisi. I'm sorry Muzi's trading you. Thank you for bringing me this far. Thank you.'

High in the driver's seat, Muzi waited for her to finish.

'Make sure she goes to a good person', she ordered. 'And email Photon. Tell him to send someone to meet us in Pútigi. Someone who knows the best route to Shiimti. Don't forget the soap. And Muzi.' She tugged his sleeve. 'Find out the names of the Sec Gens who've been killed. Make a list for me, please.'

His lip curled, as if in disbelief or disgust. To him, the Security Generation Gaians were monsters, cannibals, nothing but huge Coded fighting machines. One had killed Uttu, snapped his grandmother's neck as easily as cracking a knuckle.

'Please, Muzi. I just need to know if my brother is alive.'

'I do everything we need. You make tent with blanket. Rest. I back evening. No worry.'

That was easy for him to say. She gazed around the plain. Even if there was somewhere to run to, in the heat of the day she wouldn't get far.

'What if someone comes?'

'No one come. Nothing here: no water, no hunting, no plant. I go back to stream, cover tracks. No one follow.'

The stream was an hour north. She understood now why he had insisted on leading the horse down it for so long. At the time she'd been grateful to walk in the cool water, barefoot beneath the delicate canopy of sunrise and into the morning. The idea, she had thought, had been to approach Lálsil carefully, keeping out of sight as long as possible. They should have had this conversation much earlier. If she'd known what he had in mind, she would have washed in the stream.

'Anyone could come,' she persisted. 'Then what do I do?'

'*No one come, Astra. We travel three days. See no one. Everyone travel on road.*'

'Everyone except *bandits*.'

He rolled his eyes but handed her his knife.

'Stab throat first, then heart.'

She snatched at the weapon before he could retract it. 'I still can't believe this. You're leaving me to kill someone all by myself.'

'I kill next bandit. Promise.'

It wasn't funny. 'What if you not come back?'

He wrapped the rein around his short arm. 'I coming back, Astra.'

'How do you know?' Her fear, at last, seemed to reach him. He stared at the horizon, for the first time since they'd stopped the cart, giving her a moment's thought. 'If I no come back,' he ordered, 'walk back to stream tonight. Follow water to road. Go to Lálsil Treatment Ward and call Photon. CONC look after you. Okay?'

All that was do-able. She swallowed. 'Okay.'

He nodded, then clicked the horse into motion. With a lumbering creak, the cart rolled out in the direction of the stream.

As she had been all morning, the horse was twitchy. Her ears pricked at nothing he could hear and uncharacteristically she strained at the reins. He hadn't wanted to give Astra an excuse to come with him, but that meant a bad storm was gathering. Not today; the sky was too pale – probably tomorrow morning, tonight at the earliest. It was vital to get the camel today, Astra would see.

To keep her fresh for her market paces, he held the horse to no more than a fast walk, the cart jangling over the parched ground, its only cargo now him, his bag and the bits of scrap metal and old tools he'd brought from Kadingir as currency. Thinking of the good trading ahead, he brightened: today, for the first time in his life, he would be a wealthy man. The largest of the oasis towns and the final stop on the Asfar road, Lálsil boasted the biggest market in Non-Land; most Asfarian traders went no further into the Belt – having travelled for a week, they preferred to let the Non-Landers flock to them. But other than livestock and their own labour, most Non-Landers didn't have much to bargain with. Many simply paid Asfarians to take them south in their caravans and find them jobs in the cities and towns of the Gulf. Some stayed; others returned with a wife, a husband, a car, bags of coin, determined to set up one of Non-Land's rare successful businesses. For the region did have its specialities. The oasis women's weaving cooperatives were famed for their detailed designs, wild herbs from the non-toxic areas of the scrublands were esteemed for their flavour and medicinal minerals from the Chott were in demand as a cure for conditions from asthma to heart disease. People sold these luxury goods for next to nothing in Lálsil and in return the Asfarians charged outrageous prices for stale sweets, factory-loomed robes and last year's Tablettes. Prices were even higher in Pútigi and choice more limited; another reason to do his trading here. He would have explained all that to Astra, but she hadn't been listening to reason and he needed to get to market in good time, before all the best camels were gone.

At the stream he got out of the cart and walked the horse over the slippery pebbles, back north to the place they had joined it. From there, he set off at a southerly angle. It was a necessary detour. If he was unlucky and an NLA police van stopped him as he joined the road, the wheel tracks would back up his story: he was travelling from Kadingir to escape the war, and had gone to the stream to let his horse drink. He was glad he had nothing in the cart. Some of the Non-Land Alliance police officers were the biggest bandits on the roads.

'And how did you know there was a stream?' He rehearsed the interrogation – Astra's pelting questions were good practice. 'I've been to Lálsil before with my father,' was the easy answer, because it was true. He had come to Lálsil when he was nine, on one of his father and uncle's annual trading trips. They'd left Kadingir with a cartload of scrap metal and sheep fleeces and returned with tools, spices, beeswax candles, skeins of dyed wool, fancy buttons and threads and, best of all, tales to tell Kishar, his best friend. It had been the biggest adventure of his life: travelling down on the long road, watching the grassy scrubland slowly thin to this pale flaking emptiness; arriving at night, sleeping in the cart, waking to spend the next day immersed in the heaving market, its stalls, unlike their drab counterparts in Kadingir, heaped with treasures: fruits he had never heard of, let alone tasted, cloths in which all the tints of the rainbow were interwoven with silver and gold; barrels of spice, shelves of incense, glass cabinets of perfume. He had stuck close to Kingu and

Gibil, drinking cinnamon lassi as they bartered, sipping tea after tea as the traders gradually reduced their outrageous prices to sums two sheep farmers could afford; at last, when all the business was done, taking an evening stroll around the broad green oasis pool, watching the camels drink. Camels in Kadingir had moulting hides and ribs you could play music on; camels in Lálsil were living temples, huge, shaggy-haired beasts adorned with bright woollen blankets, their harnesses dripping with pompoms and bells. He had wanted one ever since.

His mother wouldn't let him go back to Lálsil the next year. Stories had been heard about a new type of trader, seemingly friendly and generous Asfarians who would invite a man for a beer, then slip a potion in the drink, a chemical to make his heart happy but his eyes heavy, a potion that drove him into a sleep so deep that when he woke up in a ditch on the outskirts of town, his cart, horse, moneybag, children and wife were already halfway to the Dragon's Gorge. N-LA had investigated, and eventually a gang of beer-tent owners were arrested — corrupt Non-Landers who had been taking a cut of the slavers' profit — but you still heard occasional tales of young men and women disappearing, never to be heard of again. It was a good thing he hadn't told Astra that.

Thinking of his family, he peered out from the shade of the tarp, cast his gaze upwards. The thin morning haze was burning off: just keep going and your mind will clear, the sky-god was saying. That was good advice. If he thought too much about what IMBOD might be doing to his family, what that Sec Gen had done to Uttu, he would lose his way, fall down a deep crevice inside himself, perhaps never get out. Kingu had told him that too: when IMBOD takes a prisoner, they capture all his family's hearts. At such times, you must not give in to fear. Instead you must nurture your resolve.

He felt stronger recalling that phrase. It meant to do all you could to stay strong and focused – both on the tasks at hand and on the future victory. His job right now was clear: to guide Astra to her father. Then he would focus on freeing his family. There were powerful people in Shiimti, he knew, healers in close communication with the gods: another good reason to travel all the way there.

At noon, the road came into sight, a pale raked line across the plain, traversed by a steady stream of cars and carts. He frowned. The traffic was heavier than he had expected: people must be fleeing Kadingir, not a good sign. But he was in luck: no N-LA van, and the road was in good repair. He joined the flow, rumbling along between carts stashed high with furniture and sacks, and soon Lálsil was glimmering like a mirage to the south: a floating vision of golden buildings and dark trees crowned by the town's ancient bath-house dome, solar towers and Tablette mast. His spirits rose. If he did all his trading quickly, he'd have time for a steam and a good meal before heading back.

There was more traffic in the outskirts, taxis and minibuses raising dust that got up his nose. There was far more to see, too, the road lined with blue CONC-issue tents, goatskin shelters, screenposters, a straggle of stalls selling water and beer, fruit juice and roasted beans, deep-fried chickpea balls and lamb skewers, anything you were hankering for after a long journey, or might need for sustenance on the way home. He was thirsty, but didn't stop. The smell of roast goat wafting over from an old woman's stall made his mouth water; that would have to do until he got to the market.

The horse clopped past the first building, a mud-brick grocery shop with a red awning. Beyond rose a honeycomb of businesses and dwellings, the walls festooned with washing lines. Ahead was a red light and the traffic came to a halt, battered taxis jammed up against laden hand carts, women in white and gold veils sailing through the vehicles, beggars tugging at sleeves, raggedy boys offering bags of nuts to the incomers. The driver of the cart beside him was swatting away a pleading hand; his children were perched on the family's baggage as if guarding it from thieves.

Muzi didn't remember Lálsil being like this. He glanced back at his meagre load. It was unlikely, but a swarm of those street kids . . . He took advantage of the stalled traffic to hop into the back and chuck his best tools into the front. The horse tossed its head and whinnied as he took up the reins again. 'Shhh,' he soothed, though he felt anything but calm himself. At this rate it would take hours to get to the market. Then a bright flash caught his eye and he forgot his hurry. Mounted on the wall of a squat apartment block was a wallscreen ad for retired racing camels.

It was a video of the sort he and Kishar had watched a thousand times without getting bored, betting imaginary coin on the results, keeping a running score of debts to be paid in thumps and their mothers' date biscuits. Transfixed, he gazed at a line of beasts lurching out of the starting gates then pounding for glory, mouths foaming, robot jockeys swathed in bright cloths mounted like second humps on their backs – humps with whips controlled by the camel owners, who were hanging out of the windows of their cars on the road running inside the track. It was a great race: for ages two beasts ran neck and neck, and then in the very last moments a beast with a red jockey pulled in front and vanquished them both. The kids in the next cart erupted, a mix of triumph and dismay, the mother turning to yell at them just as the older sister punched her little brother in the arm. Muzi grinned. The red light turned green and the traffic moved on, but his thoughts lingered on the race.

Kishar's brother had a car, as did many youths in Kadingir, but camels at home were just pack beasts. Racers were temperamental, his father had told him; the animals had spent their lives being lashed to go fast and required a strong hand. They were also unreliable, frequently suffering from arthritis or gastric problems. And for all their issues, they were expensive, sold mainly in Non-Land to the breeding farms that lined the Lower Belt Road. *No*, he told himself firmly, *an Asfarian camel would be a foolish investment*. Perhaps, though, if there was time, he could go and have a quick look at the racers.

Impatient again, he considered the side streets. They were less crowded, but he didn't want to risk getting lost. The horse shied at a chicken on the road. He frowned. She had never been this jittery in Kadingir. The sooner he traded her, the better. First though, he had an important stop to make in the market.

He didn't just need a camel and supplies. He also needed advice. As well as urgent questions about market rates, he had serious enquiries to make about travelling in the desert: what equipment was required, if there were impassable ridges, how to survive the storm that was coming. To get answers to those questions, he needed to see the man Kingu and Gibil said was the most generous and knowledgeable trader in all of Non-Land – the Karkish ironmonger with the sign of the tree of ten fruits hanging outside his shop.

He knew what Astra would say about this plan. Loudly, over and over again, like rain drumming on a roof: his family's disappearance might be on the news. IMBOD spies could be looking for him. With his blue eyes and short arm Muzi was distinctive. He would have to ask the trader not to talk about him; tell him why. *It's too risky, Muzi. Too risky*, Astra worried too much. But . . . He reached into his bag and pulled on his CONC hand. The Council of New Continents could only afford cheap prostheses and his would fool no one, but Astra's idea had been a good one: he would buy a pair of gloves to disguise it. Even if his family's names were on the news, the greybeard would surely not connect just another blue-eyed Non-Lander youth with a small boy he'd met once, ten years ago, who'd sat eating date-filled pastries while his father and uncle haggled over pots and pans and candlestick holders.

Pushing on down the hot main road, he smelled the oasis before he saw it, a moist bloom in the air, hinting of vegetation and animal dung. Then the road forked and he was in the shade at last, circling a wide pool fringed with trees, shrieking children running down to splash in its lush green waters, people leading horses and camels to sip from the edge. He took a deep breath. It was a miracle, this open, giving, earth-bowl of water, fed by the only unpoisoned aquifer in Non-Land.

The market was also as he remembered it: a crescent of concentric roads, cafés and beer tents lining the shore of the pool, a clutter of signs and screenposters announcing the hardware, produce and clothing stalls behind, the livestock pens out to the back. He pulled over and joined a queue for the pool. Before he sold it, the horse needed to drink. And he needed time to think. If he remembered correctly, the greybeard's stall was in the second road before the livestock pens. There were parking lots at the rear of the market too, where, for a coin, a man would make sure no one stole your horse or bedding. He hadn't got a coin, but he would show the man his tools, explain that he was going to trade them, would pay when he got back. He'd sell the tools first, then check the news, and after that he would go and have a cup of tea from the greybeard's famous *samovar*.

Astra didn't understand: the risk of his father's old friend betraying them was like the chance of being killed by a flea bite compared to the dangers ahead. He tugged at the horse, climbed back into the cart and entered the teeming market.

Muzi was gone, not even a speck on the horizon any more. Astra laid his blanket on the soil, draped hers over the rocks, took off her boots and crawled into the makeshift tent. This was not a good day. Men might come, bandits, Asfarian traders or even IMBOD officers. Is-Land's Ministry of Border Defence was not allowed to enter Non-Land without permission but that hadn't stopped IMBOD from sending a secret team into Kadingir to kidnap and kill Muzi's family. She opened his knife, a black-handled switchblade curved like a flame, and placed it at the base of a rock, ready to grab in a flash. Between the rocks, where she didn't have to look at it, she placed Muzi's water flask. Hers was plain metal; his was covered in goatskin, some poor animal killed and flayed for needless decoration. He hadn't cared when she talked to him about that either, she thought moodily. Then she put her boots back on. She might have to kick a man in the groin before she stabbed him in the throat. She lay in the shade, sipping from her water flask, alert to every flicker of light over the plain. As the sun rose, her fear subsided: any sensible bandits would be bedding down soon for siesta. But despite the silence and emptiness of the wide-open plain, she didn't feel peaceful. She felt dirty. Dirty inside.

She had a right to be angry. Maybe she was too easily recognised, maybe Muzi had no choice but to leave her in this desiccated wasteland, but he'd made two major decisions without consulting her, and browbeaten her with the threat of going home. His refusal to recognise her as an equal partner in their journey was infuriating. Even so, she had to be honest with herself. Her emotions were threatening to run out of control. She shouldn't have shouted like that; it was embarrassing to remember, and a little bit frightening.

She took her bottle of headache pills from her trouser pocket. Maybe her bad temper was a lingering symptom of the pain-ball or the grey wave, the punishing pains IMBOD's memory treatment had left her with. She swallowed the pill. But her stomach still felt lined with grime. She had no excuse. She wasn't getting the pain-ball or grey wave any more; that violent fit wasn't IMBOD's fault, it was hers. At one point she'd wanted to hit Muzi. What if she had? Tears sprang to her eyes. At the start of this journey she'd liked Muzi. A lot. They'd been close. Now he was being cold and demanding, and she'd come to the edge of an unforgivable meltdown.

She wiped her eyes and stared out miserably over the heat haze warping the plain. She had been stupid, that was the problem. She had expected too much, read far too much into Muzi's surface courtesy. He had charmed her the day they met, lighting her birthday candle and laughing off his family's attempts at matchmaking. And though the last thing she'd wanted to do was get married to anyone, somehow she'd left his house tending a spark of attraction. The next time she'd seen him, he was crying over the body of his grandmother, Uttu's neck broken by a Sec Gen in punishment for being Astra's friend. Rather than blame Astra, Muzi had volunteered to help her find her father. It had seemed the only way forward, as though they were meant to be together. Bitter sorrow washed over her. The journey had simply created the illusion of togetherness.

On the first day, united by grief, she and Muzi had done things for each other – she'd made daisy chains for his neck, her wrist, the horse; he'd picked wild rocket to supplement their porridge. Through these simple deeds, they had taught each other necessary words. There'd been comfort in his presence, something like hope in his agile beauty. At times she'd wanted to touch him so much it hurt, but he had kept his distance. 'Astra no my wife. Brother sister,' Muzi had told Photon at Uttu's grave, and he had meant it. She was an idiot if she thought otherwise. He was just doing what he saw as his duty: their conversation about the flask had proved that.

She couldn't keep watching him drink from it without saying *something*. 'Why didn't you use felt?' she'd asked as they bumped over a rocky stretch of scrubland in the dusk. 'Then you not have to kill goat.'

It had been too difficult to explain 'felt'. Muzi had laughed as she mimed shearing a sheep, but shrugged and flicked the horse on. Near midnight they'd stopped to camp, and as Muzi got a pot of grains cooking on the fire, she'd checked her Tablette. Without an internet signal they couldn't use instantaneous translation, and her pre-loaded Asfarian-Somarian dictionaries were proving invaluable.

'Felt' in Somarian was *sīg gazumaka*. Muzi considered it, then typed into the search box, using the bony corner of his stump to shift the keyboard. Practically everything you might think a person needed two hands to do, Muzi managed perfectly well with one. In the glow of the fire, their heads nearly touching, she'd followed his finger.

The Somarian word *kuš*, she learned, meant leather or hide. He raised his palm, searched again, concluded . . . '*Dart*'.

She squinted at the definition in the firelight. '*Eternal*? It's the animal's skin, Muzi, not its soul!'

He pointed again. *Dart* had a second meaning, a word she didn't know in Asfarian. She had to open another dictionary to look it up in Gaian. '"Durable"', she read.

Muzi sat back against his hump of blankets, folded his arms behind his head and whistled, a cheeky chirp of success. She'd laughed, the argument had dissolved and the night air had shimmered like water between them, warm water she wanted to swim through, straight into his arms.

Afraid of humiliating herself, offending him, trampling all over

Somarian courtship rituals like a cow in heat, she had busied herself with stirring the pot. Later, when she'd cried again over Uttu, Muzi had wrapped a blanket round her shoulders, then sat a couple of metres away, staring into the fire. After her sobs had subsided he had said in Somarian, his face a dance of shadows and flame, 'We will find your father, Astra. Then we will find the Sec Gen. I know his face. He killed my grandmother. I will kill him.'

She had hugged her knees, stared silently into the flames. She'd wanted to tell Muzi not to take vengeance on the Sec Gen, but she couldn't. He might think she was defending her fellow Gaians; that she cared more about them than she did about Uttu. But that wasn't true, not at all. Suddenly, she was afraid, so scared of losing him she couldn't speak. Hearing his vow, she had felt a twist in the chain around her throat – that invisible choker of losses cinched round her neck, each thin ring linked to the next, one after another, stretching back to before she was even born. Sheba, her Shelter sister; Hokma, her Shelter mother; the Owleons, Helium and Silver: all dead. Nimma, her other Shelter mother, cold and cut off, her heart turned against Astra; Peat, her Shelter brother, glimpsed in a convoy, his face hard as rock, utterly changed from the joyful boy she had grown up with; Klor, her Shelter father, the only one who still loved her, forbidden to contact her. She had lost her family too, and Uttu, who had cared for her, and she could not bear to lose Muzi as well.

But that was not all. The lock on her tongue was forged not only of fear. From the moment she had seen Muzi cradling his grandmother's body, she had known Uttu's death was her fault. Photon and Muzi had told her she was wrong, but staring into the fire that night she accepted it fully. Uttu's death was the result of her being born wrong, a Non-Gaian, cursed to cause suffering to everyone she loved. More than afraid, she was ashamed: ashamed of dragging Muzi into the ever-tightening circle of pain that was her life. Ever since then, she had been on edge. And here now, alone in the wilderness, sticky with dirt inside and out, she understood why. Calm, brisk and capable, Muzi was doing his duty. *She* was spinning out of control, lashing out at him just like she did at everyone around her. She was violent, sick with it, had been for a long time, long before IMBOD's memory treatment.

More tears spilled down her cheeks as she acknowledged the truth at last: she was in Non-Land as a result of her own actions. She had inflicted a punishment on Ahn for Hokma's death, hurled those Kezcams at his groin in a spasm of hatred and rage. Ahn had lost his virility. She had killed a vital part of him – killed his children before they were even conceived, and that action had set IMBOD against her. Then instead of taking Klor's advice and going to New Zonia, she had insisted on coming to Non-Land. She'd said she wanted to meet her Non-Lander Birth father, but really, she knew, she had wanted to keep fighting IMBOD. For a long time she had been glad she'd hurt Ahn, had revelled in her revenge, polished the memory of her deed like a secret jewel. Ahn had betrayed Hokma, his former Gaia partner. He and Samrod Blesserson – Hokma's own *Code brother* – had done deals with IMBOD, had let Hokma be killed in jail in order to prevent her testifying in court to their own misdeeds. A man who could connive to kill his own Gaia partner shouldn't be allowed to reproduce. There shouldn't be any more Ahns in this world. She'd only regretted not being able to take down Blesserson too.

But wounding Ahn hadn't been a glorious victory. That decision had resulted in Uttu's murder, added another link to the death chain, wrapping it higher and tighter round her neck. It was no longer a matter of just trying to remove the chain; she had to accept that she had helped create it. The stifling heat in the tent was a cool breeze compared to the searing guilt running through her, a laceration cutting deeper than the brand IMBOD had burned between her legs. Her guilt was a mark no laser-surgeon could ever remove. The headaches, the painful tracker IMBOD implanted in her brand, were just freckles compared to the disease she was riddled with. Just as much as the Sec Gens, *she* was a killing machine. She stared out at the cracked landscape, riven by despair. There was no way home. She did not know how to break the chain of death. She was travelling to find her father as if Zizi might help her, but for all she knew she would just turn him into another link in the stranglehold.

She sat looking out at the wasteland for a long time, wishing she could take off her clothes, walk out under the broiling sun, without water, towards the horizon and never come back. But she couldn't do that. Killing herself was a fantasy, that was all. She had been in this state of mind before, on the roof of the CONC compound, and she had vowed then not to do IMBOD's job for them. She also couldn't do that to Muzi.

She kicked at the rocks with her boot, splashed the last of her water on her hands, rubbed her face hard. Stood up outside, jumped up and down, returned to the tent, glugged water from Muzi's flask. She must try and control the disease that she was, try and stay calm and reasonable, even when Muzi was being pig-headed, because it wasn't fair to take all the blame for every fight they had. Muzi was difficult too. She stuffed his flask back between the rocks. He really didn't care about animals. What about yesterday morning?

She hadn't wanted to go through the bone maze. The place was terrifying, enchanted, a warning, of what she didn't know. They had been travelling all night through the scrubland, flatter and drier than it was near Kadingir, but still sparsely covered with shrubs and grass. As the horizon began to glow a fierce pink, and they moved towards the strange saturated colour, the high, sweet sound of birdsong filled the air. *Birds.* She had made Muzi stop and listen as the morning light cast insectoid shadows across the pale earth and the trilling song became a deafening cackle. Then they saw it was not the soil or stones catching the sun's rays. They were standing at the edge of a vast bleached field of bones: rib cages, skulls, femurs, pelvises, scattered like smashed crockery, as far as the eye could see.

'Ancestors,' she whispered at last, 'From the Old World.'

'Ancestor spirits gone now,' Muzi said. 'Birds come, clean the air.'

The birds were darting from skull to skull, small dumpy brown balls, piping their tiny hearts out. 'Wrens,' she breathed. Wrens had nested in the woods around Or, delighted her with their fearless voices. Here in this treeless place she clutched at their beauty as if their song was a bright flying carpet that might carry her over this bleached battleground, open grave, bombsite – whatever terrible fate it was the ancestors had met.

'Uttu tell me this bird,' Muzi said at last. 'Wren is brother and sister energy. Is making welcome to us.'

She decided to believe him, had to: the bone field was too big to travel around. They progressed slowly, taking turns to walk ahead of the cart, but though they cleared a path through the stark, appalling clutter as well as possible, she flinched every time the cart wheels crunched. And as they moved, the mystery of the place deepened. The ancestors' clothes had long ago decayed or blown away, but occasionally the curved sole of a boot broke the soil. Soldiers wore boots, but some of the skeletons were children. The babies were the hardest to accept, trapped in the white embraces of their mothers. And though she had to, in order not to step on them, it was difficult to look at the skulls. Some were cleanly pierced by bullet holes, some smashed into fragments, others grinned up at her, whole.

She couldn't ask questions of the bones, or answer their stares. She could only empty her mind like the skulls were empty, except for those that sheltered nests, the wrens shrill with fury as she moved them aside.

At last they neared the other side. Muzi was walking, she had the reins. Ahead was open soil, a few shrubs. Just before they reached it, Muzi stopped, pointed down at the soil, waved her over. She drew up the cart, jumped down. He was pointing at tracks. Something with small claws and a fat body had been sliding by.

'A lizard!' An intense euphoria rose to fill the hollow spaces grief and guilt and fear had carved within her. An *animal* lived here. The first wild animal she had seen evidence of since she left Is-Land. They had crossed the dry white sea of death and arrived at the shore of new life. For a precious, desperate moment, it was as if she had a chance, as if the entire Earth was being reborn and she could be renewed with it. She spread her arms, spun round to hug Muzi. He was at the back of the cart, taking out a trowel. She watched him dig a hole. It took her a moment to understand.

'It's a *wild creature*, Muzi,' she stormed, 'maybe the only one in the whole of Non-Land. You can't *kill* it.'

'In *Kadingir*, no wild creature,' he corrected. 'In scrublands, many urchin lizards.' He rubbed his stomach. 'We buy in market sometimes. Roast. Very delicious.'

'You don't have to eat meat, Muzi. We have a whole bag of spelt and we can buy trail mix in Lálsil.'

He was striding back to the cart, ripping off a piece of the box cardboard they slept on. She pounded after him, switched to Somarian. 'When Uttu invite me lunch you not eat meat.'

'Was your birthday.' Ignoring her blatant attempt to invoke the moral authority of his grandmother, he continued in Asfarian, 'Now is long journey. Many days. Must eat meat.' With his knife, he cut a slit in the cardboard. 'Uttu take me to market, Astra. When I little boy. We buy lizards together, talk to traders. They tell me how to make trap. Uttu say one day I make one too.'

There had been no rejoinder to that. They had stopped to rest and she had slept as far away as possible from him, and when they'd woken up she'd busied herself with Sisi. From Muzi's 'ha' of delight, she knew the trap had worked. She'd kept her back turned as he slaughtered his prey and stashed it somewhere in the cart.

Remembering the trap now, cold anger crawled over her. Muzi had left her in the middle of nowhere with a murdered lizard. Unless he'd taken it to town to trade, the corpse must be in one of the bags piled outside the entrance to the rock tent. She got to her knees, shuffled out of the blanket tent into the blinding sun and began digging through the bags. Muzi might be right about some things; she was right about others. This was her journey too, and she wasn't going to let Muzi eat that lizard. It was one of Gaia's creatures and she was going to bury it, like she, Muzi and Photon had buried Uttu. She might be a violent, terrible person, incapable of loving anyone or being loved, but she could at least try to protect innocent animals. Burying animals wasn't a Gaian tradition, but this was different. If she had to pound a hole in this hard earth with her elbows, she was going to hide that lizard from its *killer*.

'Ya, Muzi!' Doron raised his glass of frothy beer. 'Here's to your first camel, nephew. May she race you to Asfar, and when this war is over, back to Lálsil again!'

Muzi clinked glasses. After all Doron had done for him it would have been incredibly rude not to buy the man a drink.

'To my uncle in Lálsil,' he toasted in return. 'And to your father, may the gods guide his way.' The old man had died a few months ago, which was sad, but also diminished the worry of being associated with any news that might be released about Kingu and Gibil's disappearance. Doron, the greybeard's middle-aged son, had returned from Asfar to take over the business, and to him Muzi was just another kid from Kadingir – an orphan heading out to find work in Asfar, and hoping for some advice from an old man he vaguely remembered.

All in all, there was little reason to think anyone was looking for him. He had popped into a Tablette tent before the ironmonger's, and his family's kidnapping hadn't made the news, not even the Nagu community newsletter. He had sat and thought about that for a while. Photon knew IMBOD had taken his family and stolen their sheep and, like Astra, Photon was a CONC officer. The Council of New Continents was supposed to mediate disputes between the Is-Land Ministry of Border Defence and the Non-Land Alliance; Astra had said that Photon would have told Major Thames, the CONC Compound Director, what had happened; also that Major Thames would help them get justice for Uttu. But for some reason, that hadn't happened.

The Major might not care about his family, he considered. Or they (the Major was a manwoman person, and in Somarian it was easiest to call such people 'they') might have decided it was better that IMBOD thought no one knew what the Sec Gens had done. The story was easy to hide: war was raging in Kadingir, people were fleeing the city, and even if his neighbours discovered that the house had been ransacked, and piles of human shit left on the wreckage, right now that wasn't big news.

Yes, he could relax now, celebrate the purchase with Doron, perhaps even have a steam bath before he went back to Astra. He peeled off his gloves and stuffed them in his bag. It felt silly wearing gloves to drink beer, and Doron had already seen him without his CONC hand, when he'd taken it off to say goodbye to the horse. He had always liked the way the horse snuffled his wrist.

'If he has a camel like yours in the world to come, Muzi, my father will be three times around Paradise by now.' Doron lifted his glass to the camel, which was tied to a tree across the street from the beer garden. 'A shame we didn't have longer to barter, but you paid a fair price. Your beast is like a divorced woman, Muzi – a little over-worked, but her legs are still good and she'll be grateful for some kindness the second time round.'

Muzi grinned at the joke. The Karkish man spoke excellent Somarian: he had worked with Somarians in a hotel in Asfar, he said, and ended up marrying the head housekeeper. That history was a boon to Muzi. Between what Doron said was his duty to his wife's tribe, and his delight in Muzi's vague memories of his father, the man had taken him under his wing, and more like a long-lost son than a nephew.

It was shady under the canopy. He pushed his sunglasses on top of his head. 'I couldn't have bought her without you.'

It was true. Doron was a gift from the sky-god. 'A pack beast?' he'd scoffed with an elaborate hand-twist as Muzi explained his plans. 'You've come all the way to Lálsil, nephew, you want to buy a decent racer.' He'd closed up his shop and taken Muzi to the Asfarian market, where he'd first ensured Muzi got top price for his horse and cart, and then put umpteen camels through their paces. Doron had made the beasts sit down and stand up; he'd checked their foot pads and hides, pulled ropes through their noses, leaping aside if the beast tried to bite. He was a nimble leaper for a fat man – and an astute camel buyer. The mare he'd chosen had passed all the tests except one, but Doron said if Muzi tied her blankets carefully, the ulcers on her flanks would soon heal. She had certificates too, never an outright race-winner, but in her prime she'd always placed in the top ten. A breeder, she was, Doron had declared: a long-term investment, only eight years old and ripe to give a calf every two years.

'You've got some coin left?' Doron lowered his voice.

Muzi shrugged.

The trader, stocky and balding, his beard dark and patchy where his father's had been a silver cloud, winked. 'Take my advice: don't spend it on a woman here. The pretty ones are riddled with pox; the ugly ones are in league with the traffickers. You'll do much better holding onto your purse to impress an honest girl's father.'

Muzi took another swig of beer and wiped his lip. At the next table a young woman in a headscarf smiled at him. She was pretty, except for her bruised eye. He dropped his gaze. He knew about the women here.

Though the threat of slavers had faded from his mother's mind, in recent years Gibil had been the one to refuse to allow him to go back to Lálsil. *The boy's needed at home to look after the sheep*, his uncle would declare, though something in his father's silence and his aunt's mounting anger when the Lálsil trip was due – and her bitter complaints about the poor quality of her wool on the men's return – told Muzi that there was more to the refusal than that. One day his friend Kishar had told him that some Asfarian traders brought women with them, women who would, for a registration fee, offer a man a temporary marriage: three months, two weeks, two nights, whatever he had the time and money to purchase. Temporary marriages were illegal in Non-Land, but not in Asfar, and the certificate made the transaction feel more dignified, Kishar said, as if he knew all about these things. The arrangement didn't sound at all dignified to Muzi. A wife was a woman to make a home and children with, not someone you rented like a party tent and then left for the next man in the queue to enter.

The girl was giggling with her friend, another young woman with an uncovered head of curly hair. It was nice hair, but not as bouncy as Astra's. Astra's hair when it was clean, that was. He must not forget the soap. Or – what else had she asked for? – a hat. 'I don't need a woman,' he announced.

'What sensible man does?' Doron replied philosophically. 'Wanting one, though, that's a different story. Be careful of any woman you want, son. Wanting is a weakness, nephew. She'll smell it on you, like fear or decay, and then, trust me, like a leech sucking at a wound, she'll heal you the hard way.'

There weren't any leech doctors in Kadingir, but he'd seen them on Asfarian Tablette programs. Muzi laughed. It was good, drinking a beer with a man, exchanging jokes and advice. 'My father says,' he offered in return, hoping he would remember all the parts of the tale, 'that the way to live with a woman is to let her rule her realm, and make sure you rule yours. If lunch is a little late one day because she stopped to gossip, don't worry – maybe next week you'll stay late at the market to drink a beer with a friend.' Doron nodded sagely, and Muzi concluded triumphantly, 'But don't ever let them make you make the flatbread. They'll laugh at how lumpy it is until the end of your days.'

It wasn't as good a punchline as Doron's, but the man guffawed as if Muzi was a travelling beer-tent entertainer. 'Ah, Muzi,' he said, shaking his head. 'If we men have to have a weakness, let it be for a woman. Find one you want and marry her. But remember, marriage is like a market, that's what *my father*, blessed be his memory, always said.' He adopted an old man's deep cracked voice: 'A noisy place of constant negotiation, son.' Muzi grinned, half-recollecting the greybeard's intonations, but Doron's smile had vanished, his stubbly jowls drooping, his eyes lost and watery. 'My old man gave the best advice in Lálsil, Muzi. That's why his shop was always full, and mine is half empty.'

'That and your stewed tea, Doron.' A woman behind him swung round to interject, 'Your father sometimes put a few fresh leaves in the *samovar*.'

Doron rolled his eloquent eyes and his hairy hand made a flutter of dismissal. 'Antha, please. It's a family heirloom. The tannins build up inside.'

'I'm just telling you, Doron, what all of Lálsil is saying about your tea.' The woman's long face was creased like a leather purse, and a gold stud gleamed in her nose. Her eyes flicked down to his CONC hand, then up again to meet his. 'How was it today, young man? Best you ever tasted?'

Muzi resisted the impulse to hide the hand in his lap. The thing was so heavy and ugly; he hated wearing it. 'It was strong,' he replied diplomatically. 'But I don't know what *samovar* tea is supposed to taste like. His father gave me cinnamon lassi.'

Beneath her worn brow, Antha's eyes danced with amusement. 'Well, you must have *some* of the old man's charm, Doron, to have made such a fine friend over that foul brew of yours.'

'Thank you, Antha. I will bear your comments in mind. Now, with your permission? I am trying to impart some wisdom to this young man before he leaves for Asfar.'

Antha winked at Muzi and returned to her companions. Doron leaned closer. 'The war clouds are gathering, Muzi. We may all be swept hither and thither; I may never meet you again. But I believe you came to my shop today for a reason – not to refresh my camel-bartering skills or to buy my greatest treasure, no, though I hope it serves you well. To hear these words, words that have altered me forever, brought me happiness where other men meet their ruin.' He paused, his eyes moist, his breath sweet with beer. 'When I got married, Muzi, my father took me aside. "Marriage is a marketplace, son," he said, oh for about the thousandth time.' He gave another hand waggle. ' "But now you have entered the souk, let me tell you now the secret of success. The best deals in marriage are not the hard bargains you drive with the poor and the hungry and fearful. The best deals are the private exchanges of luxury goods, accomplished over warm afternoons, many cups of fine tea and dishes of sweetmeats, with bottles of perfume and trinkets thrown in for good measure. Those are the deals that bind a marriage, my son, bind it close, unto death." Twenty-four years later, I can tell you – on your way to Asfar with your camel, perhaps to meet your wife, as I met mine – my father was right. Long, patient haggling is the essence of love.'

Doron lifted his glass again as if settling an argument. As his friend drank, Muzi remembered his mother and father kissing, pulling apart with little smiles when he came into the room. He remembered, too, his uncle's scowls when lunch was late. Gibil didn't see what was so difficult about getting a meal together on time. He'd complain if he had to wait, and when Nanshe threw his own failings back at him, Gibil would raise his voice, Nanshe too, and they would go on until Uttu ordered them to stop. The argument wouldn't be over though. Nanshe would spend the next two days ignoring Gibil and lavishing affection on their son. Even if it appeared they had reconciled, the next time his uncle and aunt fought, they would both add the interrupted argument to their arsenal of grievances.

Astra had a temper too: she had even argued with Gibil, he

remembered, and today she had shouted for a long time. He frowned, then paused, sensing someone looking at him. Down the table, the girl with the bruised eye was staring at his CONC hand. He flushed. Weren't there any alt-bodied people in Lálsil? Now he did put the hand beneath the table.

'I apologise for the ignorance of this place,' Doron said quietly. 'People don't travel to Kadingir and Zabaria any more. But we do boast a shop selling the very best in prostheses. Perhaps, if you have enough coin left in your purse, I can take you there. The shopkeeper is a very old friend of mine.'

He shrugged it off. 'I don't need a new one, thank you.' He paused. 'What if a woman gets angry with you? Did your father say anything about that?'

'Ah,' Doron sighed. 'The exquisite pain of the unforgiven husband. Muzi – you live near the Mikku, yes?'

Not exactly. His house was on the other side of Kadingir from the river. But close enough. He nodded.

'A magnificent watercourse,' Doron solemnly pronounced. 'I saw it once, on a trip to the Dragon's Gorge after my manhood rite. My father told me then: "Son, women are like rivers. When they are in full spate it is not time for fishing or dam-building. When their anger bursts the banks, you should just stand on the cliffs and let their feelings rush over your toes. When the waters recede, you can go swimming again." Once again, Muzi, it was the best advice in Non-Land.'

Stand on the cliffs. He had done that today, hadn't he? Speaking only to make it clear that guiding the journey was his job, and the horse and cart were his responsibility. It had worked, too: Astra had stopped herself. He had won, but he sensed it was a temporary victory. He gazed at the camel, scratching its neck against the tree. What if Astra found fault with his purchase?

'Ah, Muzi,' Doron filled the silence with wondrous reflection. 'Life is an ever-replenishing gift. Your father knew my father, and now here we are, sitting and—'

'Oh stop with your mystical mumblings, old husband. Do you want to be happy in love, my sky-eyed young man?' Antha had turned again, was sticking her gnarled finger in Muzi's face. 'When you win an argument with a woman, never consider the matter closed. To ensure her continued cooperation, you must do something tangible to demonstrate that you acknowledge her forbearance, are forever grateful for her generous acquiescence to your foolish will.' She cackled and dug Doron with a bony elbow. 'And I don't mean give her a cuddle, do I, Doron?'

Doron gave in, his chuckle sending beer foam fizzing through his beard. 'She's right, Muzi. Kisses soon melt away – jewellery is best.'

Antha's bright gaze was fixed on Muzi. 'Women are rivers that never run dry, but be warned: we can divert our course in a moment if necessary. And as emotional traders, we keep meticulous accounts. If you make sure to remain in credit, young Muzi, you'll never be left high and dry.'

Down the table the two girls burst into giggles. As the old woman returned to her drink, Muzi, suddenly rattled, felt for his purse. It was still there, buttoned into his pocket. A present for Astra was a good idea. Something on top of the soap and the hat. He had a little coin, yes, and the markets and the steam bath would be open for another couple of hours.

'It's cooling down now,' he said. 'I have to be going, Doron.'

'Muzi.' Doron poured, spread his hands. 'There's a *mergalla* brewing. Stay the night. My wife would love to meet you. And I tell you, her chicken stew is to die for.'

'No, honestly.' He stood up, grabbed his bag. 'I'm meeting my cousin in the next town. If I go now, I won't get held up by the storm. Thank you so much, Doron. Ma'am. Thank you for all your advice.'

There were two lizards in Muzi's bag, strangely beautiful potbellied creatures, their white skins patterned with delicate bumps like the Braille books she had seen once on a school trip to Sippur. Muzi had wrung their necks: their heads hung limp from her hand. She laid the bodies down at the top of his blanket and composed their tender limbs. One was slightly smaller than the other; both were utterly compelling. Their toes were long and agile, like babies' fingers. Their faces were like old men's, their eyelids pouched, jowls loose, their mouths disdainful, even in death.

It was ghoulish to sit admiring them, and arrogant to compare their physiognomy to humans'. She flung back the blanket and used a spoon to dig a hole between the rocks. Afterwards she drew the blanket over the grave and sat on it, respectfully, at the edge. It felt like the right thing to do: to cover the lizards, protect them as she couldn't do when they were alive.

She sat still for a long time, consumed by the finality of her task. The hidden grave was like a buried fire, centring her, readying her for something, she didn't know what. Gradually, the fire became a magnet. Her eyes dry and fierce, her muscles taut, she removed her boots, then her clothes. Naked, she lay flat, stomach pressed to the blanket over the lizards. Elbows raised, fingers and toes lightly flexed, she gazed out over the plain.

Here, the length of her kissing the earth, she could see that a faint breeze was stirring: almost imperceptibly, a fine layer of dust was drifting over the plain. She watched for a long time, flicking her eyes side to side in their sockets. Certainty stole over her: this wind was a warning. A storm was coming.

She became aware of movement above her. Keeping her body perfectly still, she looked up. Her brow was an obstruction. Abruptly, she tilted her head up, froze again. The source of the sensation was a spider, hanging on a single thread over the front of the tent cave. Small and black, it rapidly scaled down its silk and swung gently in front of her face, perhaps in the breeze, perhaps in the heat emanating from her skin.

The spider pendulum. The floating dust. The strange white coals of the lizard spirits, burning beneath her belly. Her view of the plain blurred. She closed her eyes. Her stomach throbbed. When the voices came she didn't so much hear as absorb them, as if the deep bell tolling in her stomach was transmitting slow, silent messages up through her body to her brain.

Ah. You are listening at last. We have been waiting for you to listen. For days our white scales burned in the shade, the Earth's pulse quickened in our bellies, the birds wheeled and whisked in alarm.

The voices did not speak in any single language she knew. The words were more like meanings, multiple meanings emanating from a resonance of tongues, known and unknown. There was a sense of great distance too: she wasn't sure if the lizards were addressing her or merely speaking through her. There was only one way to find out.

The wrens, she replied.

Yes, insistent little wrens most humans never see. Not because they are hidden – they flit about like tiny wind-blown planets – but because you never venture from your road to walk our stretch of the plain. You humans do not like the sight of your own bones.

The pulse in her belly, the sense of inner conversation, were new, but the feeling of being in a light trance, receptive to insight, was familiar. Down there in the earth, the lizards were cooking up a Gaia vision for her.

I tried to protect the ancestors, she told them. I picked up the skulls. You were different, the voices agreed. When we licked the air to the north, the tines of our tongues sizzled and curled – fear, it was clear, was driving you not away, but straight to us. Why, we did not know, nor did we seek to. We are not incurious creatures, but when it comes to humans we are cautious ones. For though your claws are feeble and your hides thin, you are violent and unpredictable and until very recently you roamed the Earth in great numbers killing whatever you could find, even your own kind.

The voices were reflective, not stern, but her stomach winced. *I'm sorry Muzi killed you,* she responded. *I was angry with him.* She paused. *I'm sorry I'm violent too. I understand now that I am. I am going to try to be a better person, I promise.*

Do not be sorry for our deaths. Every predator is relentless; what is done is done and we hold no grudge, against him, or against your kind. Because of you it is hotter, and we like the heat. Because of you there are no more desert foxes or weasels or hawks – just sun and stone and soil and insects and wrens' eggs. And at last, too, there are no more tank battles, no more pounding hordes or blinding explosions. The humans have run out of noises. Here now on the Earth, quiet reigns.

For how long, she didn't know, there was quiet in her ears, not silence, she realised, but a sense of space amplified by these reverberating voices. Her own protest echoed there still.

It was beautiful where you lived. We had plenty of food. He didn't need to do it.

He took for the future, and no more than could be spared. He is a good hunter. We sensed him coming too. His mind had a steady, even touch. Yours was erratic. It darted over the land, kicking pebbles, pinching leaves. His attention was dangerous, to be respected. But our scales burned brighter after your mind skimmed over our backs, and that tingling glow told us you were the one we were waiting for. The one worth what you call 'dying' for; what we call 'becoming the shade'. She wasn't sure she understood. *You died on purpose, so that you could talk to me?*

Yes and no. We did not volunteer for the trap, but as you drew nearer each of us understood that we might be chosen to deliver the message of our people to yours.

Within the trance, she tensed. *A message? Why to me? Is it because people say I am Istar? Do you know Istar?*

We told you, we are not interested in who you are. We only know you have been chosen to receive our message, just as we have been chosen to deliver it. Humans have been given this message many times. We thought you had finally understood it after the Dark Times, but it is clear you need to have it spelled out to you again. Are you ready to hear and understand?

She gave in. *Yes.*

Good. Relax, please – but not too much. It is not yet time to sleep.

Her neck felt crooked and sweat was dripping from her nose onto the blanket. She turned over onto her back, flopped her arms to the side.

This is our message. You must tell it to all your people. In order to survive, in order for all living beings on Earth to survive, you humans must break your deadly pact with metal and re-learn how to merge with all of your relatives.

She rolled her head from side to side. Perhaps this wasn't a Gaia vision. Perhaps she was just having a dream. A vivid, bizarre, incomprehensible dream.

You are not listening.

I am. I don't understand, that's all. I don't have a pact with metal.

Something like a sigh wafted through her. *Child, consider this: human skins and fur are earth shades, yes? Dark loam, grainy wood, sand-brown, root-white, straw-blond, bark-grey. Beautiful shades. So why, unlike us, who have survived for millennia by blending in with our surroundings, have you forsaken the rich shelter of the earth and with it, the wise counsel of your fellow living beings?*

She considered the question. It was, she thought, a familiar one, put in new terms. The lizards' terms. She tried to reply tactfully. *I know human beings forgot how to live in harmony with the Earth. That was a terrible mistake. But if you don't mind me saying so, we're not exactly like you. Sometimes we like to stand out against our surroundings. We only use camouflage when we're trying to hide. But we are learning our lesson. We don't use oil any more, and CONC is a vegan organisation. Where I grew up, animals have the same rights as humans.*

A low rumble in her chest told her the lizards were not impressed. *That is a feeble answer, child. Human beings forsook harmony when you surrendered to the harsh call of metal. If you are unaware of this pact, it is because you humans are so deeply in thrall to metal you are no longer even aware of its hold over you.*

The lizards' logic was surreal. She tried now to respond in a way they might accept. *Maybe we're just close to metal as well? Our bones are made of calcium. And some people have copper hair. Or silver. Or gold.*

The rumble deepened. *Just as we feared: metal is speaking through you. Copper, gold and silver are incidental to your appearance, often no more than an effect of the light. And the fact that some earth metals are essential to life does not justify the sick bond you have made with the entire metal family. You humans worship metal with every soft, perishable fibre of your being.*

The lizards' venom took her aback – but they were related to snakes, after all. Warily, she tried to placate them. *Please believe me, I honestly think that we don't. Not most of us, not any more. People do care about the plants and the animals now. Even meat-eaters are trying to re-green Gaia.* An immeasurable sadness flowed through her. *It's each other we still can't get along with.*

There was a murmur as though the voices were conferring. *You must listen very carefully, child. The problem is not that you humans cannot get along. The problem is that you have invited metal to poison your minds. The root-whites were the worst offenders, but humans of all shades have betrayed your nature as living beings: as a species you have sought the immortality of metal, and in so doing become its willing slaves. Yes, you are replanting the wilderness, but only in order to resurrect metal's hard, inert structures of control. In so doing you will obliterate us all.*

Again, it was a familiar argument, couched in absurd terms. *I'm sorry, I don't mean to argue with you. I know we need to respect Gaia, not try and control Her. But metal can't control people. Metal is just matter. It doesn't have any feelings or plans or a will of its own.* A speculative theory from Year Two Gaian Physics floated back to her. *Even if metal does have some kind of a mind, it's very rudimentary, nothing like human consciousness. And anyway, metal rusts. It's not immortal.*

The lizards' scorn lashed through her like a storm of dry leaves. *It is worse than we thought. You have been taught lies, comforting lies! Listen, child, metal has a place in the cosmos and in your lives. But it must not be allowed to control this planet. Other living beings are your closest relatives, and your only allies here on Earth. If you wish to survive, you must forsake your metal dreams, you must re-learn how to listen to us, how to join us in the shade. That is our message, and you must deliver it to all of your kind. Can you remember that, child?*

She gave up. The lizards' weird brand of political science didn't matter:

this was a dream, and dreams had their own way of meaning. Even so, she was lost. *I can remember it. But I still don't understand it all. Who am I supposed to tell, and what exactly are they supposed to do, or not do?*

When they spoke again, the voices were remote, echoing in the vast space they had created in the tent. *You are slow learners, we know, and the cleverest of you the slowest of all. You are clever, child. It will take you a long time to unlearn what you think you know. But that is what you must do. We will wait. All of us. We are patient. You must be too. The secret of patience, child, is not to hope and not to care. That is our special lesson to you.*

Her body glowed, then went limp. It was over, the spell, or whatever it was, broken. Filmed with sweat but suddenly cold, her heart pounding, she sat up and scrambled back against the rock. Dead lizards had been talking to her. It was an impossible, frightening thought, as if the grave beneath the blanket was a bottomless well, out of which untold monsters might spring.

It must have been a Gaia vision. Gaia visions, though, normally filled her with a sense of discovery – this experience, whatever it was, had left her confused and scared. Maybe it was another symptom of IMBOD's memory pacification treatment. That was also a frightening thought. Surely, she told herself, if the voices were a MPT side effect she'd have a headache by now. More likely – she gazed at her palms – the lizards' skins contained some sort of psychedelic drug. Maybe she had just spent who knew how long arguing with hallucinations.

Quickly, she washed her hands. Her heat rash was itching, so she splashed some water on her stomach too. Sunlight was slanting into the tent. It must be late afternoon already. She had slept in a stiflingly hot tent; no wonder she'd had a bad dream. It could easily have been just a dream. Klor had once told her that some dreams were a form of inner intel, the brain not just randomly processing memories as the body slept, but problem-solving on autopilot, the way that often happened when you went for a walk.

At the base of the rock opposite, Muzi's knife winked at her. She stared at the blade. If the voices were her mind trying to come to some sort of solution to her problems, she needed to puzzle it out. Metal was an inorganic element. It had helped humans evolve: to make tools and weapons, cut wood, grow food, build houses and computers. Yes, the Old World had invented guns and the nuclear bomb and scarred the earth with their mines – terrible mistakes had been made, were still being made – but even if not everybody was learning the lesson, *she* wasn't a slave to metal.

Or was she? Dreams spoke the language of symbols, she remembered Klor saying. Maybe, she thought slowly, the dream was saying something about her recurrent sense of choking, that feeling of being locked inside an iron necklace of death. Maybe, she considered, the dream was offering her a way to break that chain. But it hadn't been an emotional experience, more like a weird political lecture. In it, she had defended human beings, but if the lizards' voices were in fact hers, then they must be reminding her of something she knew but was overlooking. She pondered it all again. Was she really doing as much as she could not to repeat the mistakes of the Old Worlders? *What about . . .* As if with a mental glint, a key dropped into her hand . . . *the rare earth mine in Zabaria.*

IREMCO, the Is-Land Rare Earth Mine Corporation, didn't protect their Non-Lander workers from radiation; that was why there were so many alt-bodied and ill people and Singulars in Kadingir and Zabaria. IREMCO also hired Gaian men who played barbaric games with the Non-Lander sex workers in the town, killing their babies for sport. Samrod Blesserson was involved in the mine too: Hokma's brother was on the Board of Directors. She hated IREMCO. She had promised the women in Zabaria that she would take up Istar's mantle to help close the mine down. Instead, she was rushing off to safety in Shiimti.

She was throttled by shame. But the key was in the lock. It turned, and for the first time since the moment she had seen the lizard tracks, the chain loosened. The lizards hadn't said to go back to Kadingir and fight. They had said she needed to give the world a message about metal. Her mind began to race. Lil had said her father was in touch with Cora Pollen's people. Hokma's accomplice, Cora Pollen, was trapped in a traitor's jail, alone at the bottom of a well, but her network of dissidents was still active in Is-Land. If anyone could get hard evidence of Blesserson's complicity in the mine-managers' crimes, they could – they would know lawyers and journalists, could help her bring Blesserson to a court of international law. Yes! With Zizi's help, she would make contact with Cora Pollen's people. Then she would return to Kadingir, collect witness statements to present to CONC. If she had to pretend to be Istar to get people to trust her, she would. Samrod Blesserson would go to jail and the mine would be shut down. She sat, elated, imagining it all. She would get her revenge. But it would be a good vengeance, a victory over the terrible violence inside her. She would act not out of blind rage, but duty. By working with others, she would help restore the web of life, just like the spider was doing over the entrance to the tent.

She stared up at the creature. The spider had nearly finished its work. Watching it swing from one gossamer spoke to the next, a dreadful thought struck her. There was nothing for a spider to live on out here. She hadn't seen any flies, not even an ant on this desiccated plain. An even worse thought hit her next. She and Muzi must have brought the spider here, hidden in her blanket, or on the horse, eating its fleas. It would die too, because of her.

The spider went on calmly creating its useless web. She wiped her face, overcome by the impossibility of it all. She was trying to heal, trying to take care of the plants and the animals and other people, but doing so was exhausting. And even if she did put Samrod Blesserson in jail, nothing would bring Hokma or Uttu back.

She tugged Muzi's blanket as far to the side of the tent as she could and lay down again along its edge, her back to the lizard grave. She was tired. She was done digging, done worrying, done trying to make some tiny sliver of sense of what was happening to her. Now she would just have to hope the spider was spinning a shield around the cave, stronger than Shell tech, so that if someone was crossing the plain, they wouldn't see the blanket spread out on the rocks. She curled up and dozed off.

She woke in the early evening. Stiff, and fed up with hiding, she dressed and dragged the blanket out under the spider's web and into the shade of the rocks to do yoga. An hour later, as she was standing in tree pose, a cloud of dust appeared on the horizon, coming straight down the cart tracks towards her.

If the spider had spun a shield, it evaporated. She ducked, stuck her feet in her boots, tied the laces and scrambled for the knife. Clutching it, blade extended, she peered around the rocks. The cloud was coming fast towards her. It was *huge*. It was a bandit, a trader, a man who'd killed Muzi and stolen his cart and forced him to say where he'd left his sister . . .

The Firesands

There was an itch the size of a fist between his shoulder blades. When he fought on the Hem he forgot the rash, but here, moving alone across the moonlit sand, it was burning holes through his shirt. He longed to stop, take off his backpack and scratch, but he mustn't; the rash would weep, might get infected. And he had to keep his mind on his task. He gripped the handle of the metal detector firmly and walked slowly, as the Archivia webpage had taught him. Keeping the flat disc level with the sand, he made sure each sweep overlapped with the last, missing not one millimetre of land. It was colder than he'd expected; his hands ached, his nostrils flared with it. The sand was weirdly streaked in the moonlight, rippled with shadows like the grain of grey wood. All the time he had to listen, not to the burning rash on his back or his thumping heart, but to the whispers of sound in his earphones. The faintest pulse from the sands could be the last thing he heard.

Of course, he might not die. He could just lose his leg. But that was a fifty-fifty risk. He could also just lose his prosthesis. Better *he* stepped forward than someone else. Bartol would have done it, but everyone knew YAC needed Bartol on the Hem. The Karkish giant had slain thirty-eight Sec Gens as of this morning; it was probably fifty by now, all decapitated with a single stroke of Is-Land's Pain, that mighty sword, sending jets of blood shooting up like black fountains over the battlefield. On the first night of battle he himself had been blessed by one of these magnificent gushes, the enemy's blood splattering a shirt he would never wash again. Last night, he had finally claimed his own Sec Gen: charging at the enemy with a sharpened broom handle, he had caught a girl monster off-guard, slammed her to the ground with his spear sticking out of her neck. There had been no time to claim her head. Other Sec Gens had hauled the body away and his comrades had rescued him from their wrath. Later in the medical tent the warriors had chanted his name: *Ésgíd. Ésgíd. Ésgíd.*

He mustn't let his mind wander. He stopped, looked up, checked again he wasn't walking in circles. The sky was enormous, the stars a great river of light. But there was Istar in her blazing helmet, right where she should be, cresting the waves; there was the Shepherd, Sippad, with his staff, leading his sheep across the waters; and behind him, shining brightest of all, the watchful eye of the Shepherd's Dog, Urbár. If this was another night, if he was out on the riverbank with his friends, Ésgíd would be lying on his back, drinking beer, asking questions of the stars: did human beings really all arrive on Earth from Urbár's invisible bitch, like that darkskinned CONC officer had said? Was that bluish light a spaceship full of Old World humans, waiting for the rest of us to kill each other off at last? Do we look like snuffed candles when we die, trailing smoke and a bad smell? Here, inching through the firesands on his own, all questions were silenced by the great unanswerable force of time flowing through him. He trudged on, one boot after another, the heavy pack shifting and scratching his itching back, trying not to think about his parents.

Time, his parents had taught him, was a river, more powerful than the Mikku but turbulent only on the surface; beneath the whirlpools and white water of human conflicts, the currents of time draw us all into oneness, a vast sea of love. His family were Somarian Non-Landers. The river of the Dark Time had sucked them away from their homeland, deep into Asfar, and then swept them again up to Kadingir. Life was hard in Kadingir, no one disputed that. They could leave, of course, go back to Asfar, even try to emigrate to Neuropa, but if they did, his parents said, Non-Land would travel with them. They would be torn then, living in neither one place nor another: truly homeless. Here, though, where people lived patiently, sharing what little they had, where no one cared if you were Somarian, Karkish or Farashan, or a mixture of these, they were immersed in the swell of that great ocean of love, an ocean that would, one day, rise and flood over the Boundary, returning them home.

He had only ever seen pictures of the sea, but standing in the scrublands or under the night sky, or listening to his grandfather tell tales of his time as a fisherman in Asfar, he could imagine it – water everywhere, warm silky water you could float through forever. He loved his family, was grateful for their constancy. So what was he doing, swimming back out of that ocean, battling upstream against time's immense, invisible river? He wasn't an orphan; nor a youth club member. He had just gone to the meditation tent to hear the singing bowls. He didn't know that Gitmalu, the bowl player, was going to give a lecture.

Time, Gitmalu had said, flowed, yes, but not outside us or through us; it *was* us, an energetic field composed of human will as much as cosmic forces. Nor was time a river, rushing in one direction; or an eternally swirling ocean that dissolved all differences like his parents said. Time was an ocean, yes, but one composed of cross-currents and tides human beings could learn to direct. Love was one of those tides, but to reach the shore it had to be powered by collective action, not weakened by collective compliance. Working together, Gitmalu said, Non-Landers could create the waves that would carry us home. Then Enki had rolled up to the front. 'History is drowning us,' the rhymer had chanted, 'dragging us under the waves. Rise up in resistance, or die like shackled slaves.'

Ésgíd had returned to the meditation tent. He had started visiting the YAC gym tent too. And at home he had begun to argue with his parents. Not everyone shared things in Kadingir, he had reminded them. The N-LA families ate well. Everyone else in Kadingir was loving, but hungry; peaceable, but poor. Yes, they should have fertile land, clean water, proper schools and hospitals, businesses and farms, but the fastest way to do that was to take their ancestral lands back from Is-Land. *That* would be oneness – together, to make the Boundary fall!

'My son.' His father had looked up from his sewing. 'I know a young man thirsts for action, but believe me, if you join YAC you will regret it. It is better to wait, and let N-LA keep working for nationhood. Then your children will have a chance of walking through the Boundary gates without a drop of blood being spilled.'

'Ésgíd,' his mother had pleaded. 'We haven't waited here all this time for you to be killed! Think of your grandfather!'

His grandfather had been watching from his cot in the corner of the tent. 'Tell me, Ésgíd. Is that preacher preaching love?' he'd asked. 'Or anger and vengeance?'

'He is preaching love with a *purpose*,' had been his stubborn reply. 'The ocean of resolve is the sea I swim in now.'

YAC had risen. They were fighting on the Hem and N-LA had joined them. But gratifying as they were, Non-Land's victories were symbolic only. The Sec Gens were killing machines. Enki was in hospital, gravely wounded, barely able to speak. Khshayarshat, their second-greatest warrior after Bartol, was dead. Everyone in YAC knew that if they didn't change their game, within a month they would be vanquished. They had one new secret weapon: money, great quantities of it, pouring in from overseas donations. *Buy firearms*, some had shouted. *But where would that lead?* others asked; *the Sec Gens would just be given guns too, no doubt better ones.* Then Lilutu had stepped forward with a plan.

Èsgíd didn't know if fighting IMBOD was just making things worse; he didn't know if Astra Ordott, that half-Gaian half-Non-Lander girl, was Istar on Earth, like Lilutu said. He just knew he couldn't let the Sec Gens kill them all, down to the last orphan. He had volunteered. Tonight he had crossed the Mikku on a raft, an old door from the scrapheap, paddling hard against the current. He had the upper-body strength for the paddling, everyone at the conclave had agreed, and the patience, his family's gift to him. This was a painstaking task in the service of an audacious plan; if he died doing it, that was his destiny. But it would be infinitely better to survive. He was wearing a belt and had stuffed a scarf in his pocket – as long as he still had one hand, he could tie a tourniquet. If he didn't return by dawn, Etlu would come and find him. If Etlu was dead, someone else would.

His fingers were stiff with the cold. He was wishing he'd brought gloves, thinking to wrap the scarf around his hands, when the faintest of crackles sounded in his ears. He froze, then swept the detector again over the sand. The noise fizzed again: unmistakable.

He did as the website had taught him: swept a third time, at a right angle, pinpointing it. A CONC minesweeper would prepare to begin digging now. But a CONC officer would have a team, equipment, training to help him disable the weapon, safely remove it. He was a YAC scout. He just had an old CONC watch donated by Khshayarshat's uncle in memory of his nephew, and an ancient but staggeringly expensive Geiger counter bought – along with the merchant's silence – with a portion of the funds raised on ShareWorld. Carefully, he laid the metal detector down, a line he must not cross, then crouched and examined the watch. Currently, the face told the time: 01:12:38. He pressed the geo-coordinates button, saved the figures. Then, flinching as the fireball flared on his spine, he removed his backpack. It squatted upright on the sand, solid with its load, a faggot of rusty iron rods, each topped with a red cloth poppy flower or a dried poppy head.

CONC ran a poppy farm on the banks of the Mikku. Poppy seeds flew on the wind. Some might land in the firesands, take root, Lilitu had argued. Why not? If anyone in IMBOD, CONC or N-LA doubted it, or suspected a trap, they would hardly send someone out into a minefield to investigate.

He drew a rod from the bundle. The poppy head wired to the tip was a small grey ball, brittle and eerie, like the sudden rattle of fear in his gut. Gitmalu said that through meditation you could conquer fear. Enki said that fear was a warrior's fuel. 'I'm not afraid of pain,' Enki had thundered before the first Hem battle, 'I'm afraid of what will happen to our souls if we give up and drown.'

Gripping the rod, he stood, his body casting a grey shadow on the grey sand. The scream on his back fell silent. All was silent, apart from his mother's voice wincing in his head: *Why, Ešgíd, why? To make Enki Arakkia famous on ShareWorld? We are Non-Landers. We belong here. Like lichen on a rock. We don't need to fight – all we have to do is keep living. I'm begging you, son, stay at home.*

Then his grandfather's voice cut through his mother's like a saw: *I've waited a lifetime for CONC to sort this mess out. The time for waiting is over. You fight, Ešgíd my boy, fight to the last drop of your blood.*

Ešgíd craned his neck, filled his lungs with cold, his eyes with stars. Then, infinitely slowly, he drove the rod into the sand.

Peat heard the explosion in his chest, a dull boom that pressed against his ribs, as if he was emerging from a deep dive. He peered out of the car window into the darkness, tense, though not in fear but readiness. Dr Blesserson's new serum was working wonders: for longer and longer periods each day he felt his old self again, keen to prove himself, ready to move into action at the slightest sign of alarm.

In the front seat, Dr Blesserson took off his glasses, misted them with breath, wiped them clean with a hanky and replaced them on his nose. 'A suicide vest?' The scientist murmured to Odinson. 'About half a k away?'

Peat relaxed his guard. The firesands munitions were ancient devices; their circuit boards or fuses could be triggered by corrosion, exposure to the wind or even, it had been discovered, a strong Tablette signal. And the road was safe: it had been cleared decades ago. They were speeding along it, faster than he'd ever driven in Is-Land, the solar engine so quiet they could have been gliding. Peat was aware in his peripheral vision of the flickering grey Boundary running north of the convoy; to the south, the firesands stretched into a vast black void. The car was black too, sleek as a panther, the interior a dark rich crimson. The alt-leather upholstery, glossy and firm as a ripe cherry, gleamed in the headlights of the transport van following behind.

Odinson stretched his arm across the back of the front seat. It was a warrior's arm, the bicep big as a boulder, the forearm furred with black hair. The nape of his neck was thickly haired as well, and so too, down where Peat could only imagine them, were his thighs. Peat and Dr Blesserson were in full uniform, trousers and a flak jacket, standard kit for assignments outside the Barracks, but the Chief Superintendent had met them skyclad save for his black hipbelt, armband, watch and boots.

'Good call, Samrod,' Odinson purred. 'You're lucky, Peat; don't get to hear one of those every night.'

'Thank you, sir,' he replied, still unsure how to respond to the men's conversation. It was an unimaginable privilege to be riding out in the night behind the Non-Land Barracks Chief Superintendent and IMBOD's top scientist, the man responsible for his very Code. He was coming, they had said, as a legal trainee, to complete the slave rescue mission and observe the interrogation of the prisoners – but then why had Jade and Robin been left behind? And why was he travelling in the lead car, not the transport van, guarding the prisoners? He didn't know; he just had to do his best to rise to the honour.

'They must nearly all have detonated now,' Blesserson reflected. 'Or been cleared. In our day, Peat, they went off like popcorn.'

Again, he was being addressed as if he were an equal; as if he had something wry and knowledgeable to say in return. He swallowed.

'Don't worry, Peat.' Odinson glanced at him in the rear-view mirror, his eyes, even in reflection, dark lasers that cut to Peat's very core. 'There are still plenty of explosives round the jail. N-LA weren't *that* stupid.'

The men laughed. It was a relief to join the salvo of appreciation for a good joke: N-LA, after all, had been incredibly stupid recently. After years of promising peace, Una Dayyani and her Chief of Police had broken the Hem agreement, snapped it like a twig, sending N-LA police to join the young mutant Non-Landers attacking the cladding operation.

Of course that hadn't seemed funny at first – just the opposite. Sec Gens were dying. Unbelievably, *Moss Higgson* had died. A classmate from Golden Bough School, Moss had been assigned to a different division and Peat had only caught glimpses of him since they'd arrived at the Non-Land Barracks. Now he would never see Moss again. A blond, bronze-skinned boy with a passion for plant-Coding, Moss had been butchered by that inhuman mutant, the YAC giant, and his head had been stolen by the Non-Landers. The laughter Peat shared with his commanding officers was harsh, and hard won.

'When your enemy makes a mistake, don't stand in their way,' Blesserson's elbow was jutting over the front seat, his profile monumental in the sweep of shadows and headlights. 'Right, Peat?'

'Yes, sir.' He cleared his throat. He did have something to say now. 'The Chief Super's strategy is pure genius, sir.'

Odinson's grin was a wet slash in the mirror. 'Genius? My my, that's a big compliment for a ravaged old general like me. IMBOD is a competent national security force, Peat, acting to protect our interests in the region. But thank you. I will treasure the remark.'

Odinson *was* a genius. He'd explained it already to Jade and Robin. But of course, a man like him wouldn't think so. For the Chief Super, it was all in a day's work.

'He's too modest, isn't he, Peat?' Blesserson regarded the Chief Super with owlish affection. 'Our glorious leader.'

'Yes, sir,' he blurted. 'I mean, no sir. But to me, the strategy was . . .' He chose a legal term: 'without precedent.'

'Go on,' the scientist coaxed. 'Don't be shy. Explain yourself.'

He faltered. How to explain what the Chief Super already knew? That while all of Is-Land was baying for a full-scale invasion of Kadingir, the deployment of firearms, the final eradication of those parasites, those rabid meat-eaters, squatting on their doorstop, Odinson had been absolutely correct to hold steady, focus on the cladding operation, take the moral higher ground against Dayyani's betrayal of the Hem Agreement. Peat himself had not understood it at the time. It was bitter, he'd discovered, having to wait in the Barracks while others fought, won battle glory, lost friends and Gaia playmates – lost their heads. And though it would have been unthinkably disloyal, traitorous, to voice the question, on the fourth night he had allowed it to cross his mind: why was IMBOD allowing the slaughter?

This morning, the answer had become blazingly clear. As usual, the Sec Gens had gathered on the lawn for Odinson's daily speech to the cohort. Always thrilling to watch, today the Chief Super had stoked them to a state of exultation. *The tide has turned*, he had roared. Overnight, it transpired, in a top secret mission, IMBOD had liberated Zabaria and the firesands jail tower! Special squads of Barracks Officers, chosen Sec Gens and IMBOD reservists had travelled out east and west along the Hem Road. In the west, the N-LA jail guards had been swiftly overcome, were prisoners now themselves. Hilarious! No wonder Odinson was still chuckling over it. The conquest of Zabaria, however, was an unimaginable coup. In the mining town, the N-LA police had *defected*. In exchange for decent pay instead of the pittance N-LA and CONC had tossed them, the Non-Land forces had declared Zabaria an independent township, allied to Is-Land. Together with IMBOD, Non-Land police would maintain law and order, run the mine and patrol the perimeters against any attempt to compromise the town's autonomy. Una Dayyani had been left sputtering and steaming like a battered old cookpot with a broken lid. The thought of the triumph still filled Peat with awe.

'Speak up, Constable,' Odinson growled. 'We can't hear you in the front.'

Sweat prickled his brow, his heart juddered, but it was a direct order and he had to obey. 'War is like *hnefetafl*, or chess, isn't it?' he began. 'Thinking ahead; laying traps. You did that, sir, superbly, but you also changed the rules.' That sounded like cheating. He flushed. 'Consciously evolved the rules, I mean. Look, sir, you've "rooked" your King and taken White's Queen at the same time. All while your opponent is still setting up her pawns. And it's totally legal. Devolution is a core CONC principle; they can't argue if Zabaria declares independence. And we built the jail tower; it was ours before the Hem Agreement, so Dayyani can't complain that we've taken it back. Honestly, sir, it was a genius play.'

He immediately wished he could stuff the words back down his throat. 'Look,' he'd said. *He'd given Odinson* an order! But Blesserson was bathing him with grave approval. 'What a marvellous analogy, young man. "Creativity in service of security", eh, Clay? That was my motto when I designed Sec Gen brain chemistry, Peat. It's a joy to see it in action.'

He didn't know what to say. He had no words for Blesserson's genius. Subtle, comprehensive, pervasive, the scientist's intelligence had profoundly transformed Is-Landic culture. And here he was, blabbing in the back seat like a boy crowing over a Tablette game.

Odinson chuckled. 'You're embarrassing the boy, Samrod.'

'Nonsense. We're family friends, aren't we, Peat?'

Peat swallowed. He had only met Blesserson once, very briefly in Or, at that inspection meeting when the scientist had demoted his own Birth-Code sister, the traitor Hokma Blesser. Peat had been a child, had barely spoken to Blesserson. But a memory floated back to him: Blesserson laughing and joking with Ahn. The architect had sat with the scientist at the head table in the Dining Hall. Ahn, Hokma's long-suffering partner whom Astra had attacked and *mutilated*.

'Yes, sir.' He lifted his chin. 'You're like Ahn: practically my Shelter uncle.' Ahn had never given any Or-kid the time of day, but that, Peat's Shelter mother Nimma always said, was because he was an artist. Since Astra's attack on the man, Nimma had talked so often of Ahn that he felt like a family member.

'Now that's an honour,' Blesserson mused. 'To share a Shelter nephew with Is-Land's greatest biotect. I'm sure Ahn would be glad you think of him as family, Peat. I know he always wanted children. My wretched Code sister, of course' – he directed this remark at Odinson – 'kept on palming him off.'

Odinson grunted. 'A good thing too. Her Shelter daughter caused enough trouble, didn't she, Peat?'

Astra. Peat flushed. He had been trying desperately not to think about Astra. Blesserson came to his rescue, turning and blinking quizzically at him. 'I was so glad when Ahn met that young woman, what's her name . . . Confluence?'

'Congruence.'

'Congruence. That's right. She was there wasn't she, when Astra attacked Ahn?'

Blesserson was speaking as though Astra's treason was a topic for ordinary conversation. Something loosened in Peat's chest. Blesserson was *Hokma's* brother, after all.

'Congruence was very brave, sir. She threw one of the Kezcams back at' – he licked his lips, risked it – '*my* wretched Shelter sister, sir.'

'*Females,*' Odinson intoned. 'Fantastic bed-mates, furious warriors, but let's be honest, boys: the creatures are psychological bogs. Love to feel the hormones pumping myself, but ours give us purpose, detachment, *direction*. Oestrogen? It's an emotional swamp! Women swim about in their own needy, greedy, dank little worlds, Peat, and it's a big mistake to even squelch about at the fringes. In the ten days of the month women have any mental clarity whatsoever, they focus it all on arguing that whatever went wrong in the swamp is *your* fault.'

'Now, now, Clay,' Blesserson demurred. 'Hormones don't—'

Odinson overrode him. 'Thanks to Dr Blesserson, Peat, you Sec Gens have just about overcome that inherent design problem, but take my advice, never expect any other human female on the planet to think rationally. Look at Dayyani. She's a walking hot flush. As for your sister, Samrod, we should have realised when Hokma started living alone in the woods that she was developing a full-on Gaia complex.'

Blesserson pursed his lips. 'Hokma was a little more complicated than that—'

'C'mon! A classic case! It only hits women, Peat. IMBOD's had to deal with dozens of them over the decades. The woman thinks that she and she alone is destined to save the planet, mainly by living on berries and painting in caves. Because men – in *general*, Samrod – innately respect social structure, Gaia Messiahs usually decide we have to be eliminated, or at least heavily culled. It's no accident that a woman recruited your sister, not you, Peat, and turned the brat against your uncles.'

Once again, Peat was wrong-footed. He didn't like to quibble with the Chief Super, but Hokma hadn't been his Shelter mother. And he'd never heard gender or mental illness discussed in such bold terms before. But maybe that was, as Odinson said, because he was Sec Gen?

'Clay?' Blesserson sounded tart now. 'How about you leave the science to me and I'll leave the war games to you? Hokma was deluded, yes, Peat, but unfortunately far from isolated or insane. She was motivated partly by jealousy of my success, and was working with a highly organised network of fellow traitors on some very sophisticated science. Congruence, on the other hand, is a credit to her IMBOD training, How. is Ahn, Peat?'

That he could answer. 'He's well, sir. My Shelter mother says he and Congruence are trying clone-Coding. They're not going to let the traitors stop them having a family.'

'Now, I didn't know that. That's excellent news, Peat.'

The playful mood broken, they drove on in silence. Staring at the back of the Chief Super's head, Peat began to feel anxious. Had he spoken too much? Disgraced himself? And why couldn't he just sit here and feel proud? He was a Sec Gen, so why was he sometimes so terribly insecure? Grief, Dr Blesserson had told him, compounded grief: losing Moss so soon after Laam's suicide had been a double blow. That was true: he could pinpoint the moment he had started to backslide. It was the night Moss's four Shelter parents had appeared on the news, sitting at a table with Moss's Birth-Code sibling Leaf, a studious boy-girl a year below Peat. Leaf was finishing hir training in the Atourne Barracks but had been granted a week of compassionate leave. The leave was clearly needed; hir eyes red and swollen, Leaf's voice choked as together the inconsolable family pleaded for the return of the head of their beloved brother and son. Watching the clip fade into a vine-bordered photograph of Moss, Peat had experienced a dream-like falling sensation, as if he were slowly tumbling over a crumbling cliff, down into the torment of fear and confusion that had engulfed him after Laam's death, able to see the turbulent storm below him, but helpless to stop his descent.

The car flew on through the darkness. He would be fine, he told himself sternly. The new serum shot had worn off, that was all. He was being given a chance to avenge Moss and Laam's deaths, to play his part in Is-Land's ultimate victory. He focused on Dr Blesserson's profile, so haggard and noble in the light sweeping in from the prisoner van. The scientist was helping him recover, clamber back to solid ground. He would keep taking the serum, and he would keep climbing. He had sharp legal instincts, both Blesserson and Odinson had said that at the briefing session. He would hone those instincts, train them on Is-Land's enemies. He sat up straighter. If this journey was a test, he was determined to pass.

The Sec Gen had fallen quiet, perhaps overwhelmed by the candid conversation of his superiors. Samrod made a mental note to talk to Clay later, remind him not to confuse the boy by contradicting all he'd learned in school. For now, he should try and put them all at their ease again after that little near-spat.

'That's new.' He tapped his window. To the side of the road was a grove of date palms, the only life he'd seen since they left the IMBOD farm fields on the banks of the Mikku. Water glinted between the trunks, a silver gift of the moonlight. It was an enticing scene, a memory of Gaia's bounty to share later with Clay, to help dissipate the stress of the journey.

'N-La's fake oasis,' Clay scoffed. 'Some CONC-funded prisoner work scheme. They cemented a pond, planted a few beans. Some bio-diversity "expert" decided to introduce bats. Next thing you know, the place is infested with sandflies and no one can go near it.'

Gaia moved in mysterious ways. Samrod chuckled and turned to the boy. 'We don't have to worry about the disappearing munitions, Peat. Gaia is ensuring this will always be the firesands.'

'Oh!' Clay clapped his hands to his mouth. 'Samrod! Are you think-ing what I'm thinking?'

He kept his voice dry. 'What, like hands on wheel? Eyes on road?'

Clay lightly pattered his fingers on the wheel. 'My cruising is under control, darling. Isn't it, Sweety Peat?'

They really were going to have to talk. Intellectual banter in front of the Sec Gen was one thing; outright flirting with the boy another. Before he could retort, though, Clay braked. Thrown forward into the screech, Samrod braced himself for the impact of the prisoner van. But the driver behind had quick reflexes, or was used to Clay's games. There was no col-lision, Clay wrenched the wheel and with another squeal of rubber pulled a U-turn, leaving the van standing in the road.

Clay voice-activated the intercom. 'Jackal 442. This is your inglorious leader speaking. New plan. We're taking the hostages down to the date grove. Cover up out there. Over and out.'

'Clay?' he enquired archly. 'What precisely are you doing?'

The van was catching up, its headlights again flooding the crimson interior. Odinson flapped a hand. 'Samrod, those Nonners have a date with destiny, and under this moon, isn't it going to be *romantic*!'

In the back seat, the Sec Gen had gone rigid, with excitement or fear, Samrod didn't know, but he had to normalise the situation. 'One thing hasn't changed since I was last in Non-Land, Peat,' he remarked lightly. 'Clay Odinson is still Gaia's wildest flower.'

Clay pulled a glass bottle out of the glove compartment, stuck it between his thighs, unscrewed the lid, and took a long swig. The scent of aniseed wafted over to Samrod. Akik. He sighed.

'Samrod?'

'Not while I'm working, thank you.'

'Go on. Just a sip?' Driving one-handed, Clay made a sharp turn off onto the side road to the oasis.

He waited until the car had straightened. 'All right, we've had our joy-ride. Can we turn around and go back to the jail now, please?'

Clay took another glug of the liquor. 'Oh, don't be such a spoilsport, Samrod. It will only take a few minutes.'

A spoilsport. This again. At least Clay didn't offer the Sec Gen a drink. But what on earth was he thinking? Clay knew the prisoners were ultimately Samrod's responsibility. He couldn't seriously be intending to interfere with the treatment like this?

Clay parked beneath the trees. He stashed the liquor back in the glove compartment, and fumbled for a small spray bottle. He spritzed his face and the sharp scent of citronella overpowered the last sickly traces of aniseed.

'Peat,' Samrod ordered. 'Will you stand outside for a moment please?' Clay rolled his eyes, but handed Peat the bottle.

'He doesn't need it.' Samrod gripped Clay's wrist, then, in a calm tone, added, 'Genetic insect repellent, I can do, Peat. You could turn somersaults out there skyclad and you wouldn't get a single bite.'

The boy got out of the car. Samrod waited until he was a few metres away.

'I mean it, Clay.' He grabbed the bottle of repellent and threw it on the dashboard. 'This is a whim, an exuberant whim that could undermine the whole operation. The treatment works best when the patients are cooperative.'

'Samrod, dear heart,' Clay drawled. 'You are confusing the Sec Gen. You are undermining my authority.'

'I am *not* confusing the Sec Gen!'

Clay was gazing out of his side window. 'Then why has he fainted?' he murmured.

The water was glinting ahead down the slope. Around him, quick black shapes flittered between the silhouettes of the leaves; above, stars blazed and the full moon cast a metallic light across the sand. Peat stood enveloped in Gaia's dark majesty, but all he yearned for was to be back in the car, watching the Chief Super massage the insect repellent into his biceps, his neck, his scalp. Odinson's fingers were mesmerising – strong, long and agile, the knuckles etched with fine black hair, the tips probing each ridge of muscle, every crevice of bone. Peat couldn't help himself: his mind slid back to Laam, divulging his fantasy of being gang-banged by their commanding officers . . . Laam's eyes, his slim back . . . the last time he'd seen Laam, he was stepping into a pond of thrashing, flesh-eating fish—

His vision chequered. He was dizzy, breathless, back on the edge of the cliff. Beneath him swirled fear and confusion. Then he was plunging off, falling with a thump to the sand, curling up in a tight little ball. *Laam.* Clutching his knees, his heart a red-hot lump in his chest, he rocked back and forth moaning. It *hurt*. It hurt so much to think of Laam. One more second and he could have grabbed him, pulled him back from the edge. But there was no stopping death, he knew that now. Moss was gone, and all the others, never coming back. He was afraid – afraid of losing Jade next, and Robin, everyone he loved. Afraid of being killed. Afraid of everyone knowing how afraid he was. Oh please, make it stop *hurting* so much.

'Peat?' Dr Blesserson's voice floated into the darkness. Warm hands stroked his back. 'What's the matter? What happened?'

Slowly, he came back to the oasis. He sat up, brushed the sand off his palms, waited for his heart to cool down.

'How are you, Peat?'

Odinson was standing right behind Blesserson, the Chief Super's magnificent loins shining in the moonlight. He lowered his eyes.

'I . . . I think I was having a panic attack, sir.'

'Why? What triggered it?' Blesserson gripped his arm. 'You need to tell me, Peat, so I can help you get better.'

What could he say? That he had been seized by a fit of lust for his commanding officer? His mouth dried. He was flawed. A broken Sec Gen. That was why they'd brought him here. Not because he was a legal genius, but to keep him from infecting his team with his doubt and anxiety and stupidity. Why didn't they just let him kill himself, like Laam had done?

Blesserson shook him gently. 'Peat, whatever is wrong with you is *my* fault, not yours. I didn't make your neurological Code strong enough for the stress you are under. But I can improve it. I want to learn how to fix you, how to make the Sec Gens fitter and fitter with each generation. I can only do that, Peat, if you tell me the truth.'

He swallowed. He couldn't mention the lust. That was illegal. And anyway, it was the grief, the *compound grief*, that had swamped him. 'I had . . . a memory of Laam, sir. Not on purpose. It just came out of nowhere. I . . . I think I'm still upset about Moss too, sir.'

'Moss?' Odinson was asking Blesserson, not him.

'Moss Higgson. Peat went to school with him. His head is missing in action.'

'Ah. Higgson. The ultimate sacrifice. I didn't realise you were close to him, Peat.'

The scientist helped him to his feet. 'That's good, Peat. Very good you told us. We don't want to eliminate your memories of your friends. That wouldn't be right, would it? But we need to work on controlling their emergence and lessening their impact. I'll make an adjustment to the serum, don't you worry.'

'Thank you,' he whispered, but he was quaking inside. He'd had shots of serum every day. He should be over Laam and Moss by now, able, like Jade and Robin, to talk about his friends with joy and gratitude, as eternal inspirations. Instead, he was exposing himself as a fool and a weakling before his commanding officers. 'I'm sorry,' he added, almost inaudibly.

The scientist frowned. 'Sorry? What for?'

He braced himself. Odinson was watching them both. 'For letting you down.'

'Peat. Look at me.' The scientist touched Peat's chin. The man was shorter than he was, but the gesture had the desired effect; Peat raised his eyes to Blesserson's. Those eyes were quiet now, brimming with sorrow, and something else, something rare from an officer: pure kindness. 'Never mind Odinson's chess moves,' the scientist said softly. 'If I could make human beings immune to trauma, I would be the greatest Grandmaster that ever trod on the hem of Gaia's green cloak. I've given the Sec Gens extra layers of emotional protection, but some of you will always feel loss more keenly than others. It's because you care about each other so much.' He took Peat's hand, squeezed it. 'You can't have love without grief, Peat. My job is to find ways to boost the love and drain the grief. Your pain is very hard for you to bear, but it's helping me enormously. Helping me to do my job better.'

The scientist's touch was like a poultice, drawing out his fear, spreading warmth and reassurance through every cell in his body. 'Thank you, sir,' he managed.

Blesserson released him. 'Peat's not well, Clay. Shall we take him up to the tower?'

'Best cure for grief is purposeful action.' Odinson jutted his chin towards the van, parked under another tree. 'Stay in the car if you like, Samrod. We won't be ten minutes.'

The scientist gave Peat a searching glance. He froze, terrified that his face would betray a stronger allegiance to one or the other of the men, but

Blesserson nodded and trudged back to the car. Peat saluted Odinson. He felt immensely relieved. After that outburst he needed to prove himself, in honour of Laam, if no one else. He strode behind the Chief Super over to the van and saluted the three IMBOD officers too. They were all older and smaller than him: not Sec Gen. Odinson gave his orders and the female officer flung open the van door and shone a torch inside. Gagged faces blinked into the beam: two men, two women, two girls and a boy, their hands cuffed behind their backs, their ankles bound with heavy chains.

'Just the adults,' Odinson announced. 'I want them buck-naked. Peat, give the officers a hand.'

He jumped into the van and grabbed the biggest man – big for a Non-Lander, that was; the man weighed no more than a sack of flour and was no trouble at all to dump out onto the sand. On his back on the ground, his thick black moustache bristling over the gag, the Non-Lander glared up at him. Then the man's eyes narrowed, spitting impotent fire, and craning his neck, straining against his ties, he emitted a long strangled sound, like the creaking of a tree being felled in the forest.

Oh, you recognise me, do you? Peat lunged for the man's shirt, ripped it open and flung it aside. *Yeah, I was there. I took you from your slave farm. I set those beautiful sheep free. What are you going to do about it, then?*

The man had a burly barrel chest and muscular arms, but cuffed and chained, he could do nothing to stop Peat tearing at his trousers; deep-crotched hemp pantaloons that stank of piss and shit and practically melted into rags in Peat's hands. It was amusing, really, the way the man squirmed like a maggot, thrashing and kicking, his bound legs no match for Peat's long arms and capable fingers. Peat began to enjoy himself, laughing as he worked alongside the officers, stripping the slavers, kicking and flipping them over and over, exposing bare arms, chests, flesh, breasts, buttocks to the light of the moon. He wished *he* was naked, could rip off his flak jacket and trousers, let Odinson see his muscles flexing, watch him grow erect and proud. The wish itself was like a slow erection, a mental tumescence. He worked harder, pulling off the man's boots and flinging them deep into the trees. As the sweat broke on his chest, a memory or an image from a dream, a sexual dream of blurred bodies, groping hands, taking what he wanted, gnawing, suckling, nursing, eating his fill. His mouth watered and the taste of cherries filled his throat.

'Good, Peat,' Odinson murmured. 'Nice and easy. Now bring him down to the water. It's time for your treat.'

His Non-Lander drew his knees up in a vain attempt to hide his pathetic cock. It was no trouble at all to haul him down to the pond; as sweet as pumpkin pie to push his face down in the sand, rub his nose into the sandfly breeding grounds. The other male slaver, a scrawny runt, strained as the female breeding officer stamped on his hand. One of the women had gone limp and was crying, her face a mask of tears. The other was still writhing like an eel.

'Enough!' Odinson roared. 'Let the flies feast, officers!'

Leaving his slaver face down on the sand, Peat stepped back on his own beneath a tree, the guard officers a few metres away. He stood, breathing hard, the smell in his nostrils dank pondweed, mineral dust and … sharp lemon.

'It hurts to lose a Gaia playmate, doesn't it, Constable? And to lose a friend.'

Odinson was right beside him in the shadowy dark. The Chief Super was just shy of Peat's height, but broader, his chest a masterpiece. He was standing so close the hairs on that chest grazed the back of Peat's bare arm.

'Yes sir,' he stammered, staring out over the water.

The Chief Super gripped the nape of his neck. If Blesserson's touch had been reassuring, Odinson's fingertips sent hot darts shooting down his spine.

'You wonder why.' His thumb began rubbing circles on Peat's back. 'You think it should have been you. You try to make it up to his parents. You torment yourself for years. But believe me, Peat: there is no reason why. There are just insects feasting, rams clashing, bats flitting in and out of the night. What are our paltry human fears and desires compared to the convulsive ecstasy of all creation?'

'Nothing, sir.' His voice was unexpectedly bold. 'I would die for Gaia, sir.'

'I'm sure you would, my lovely pup, bravely and willingly.' Odinson released his neck. His hand slid over Peat's flak jacket, then under it, squeezing his shoulder. Heat jolted through him again. 'But don't expect Her to throw you a bone if you do. Remember: Gaia is nothing like human women; she doesn't give a fig about her young. She cares only about *self-preservation*. To quote my favourite hymn, "Her ruthless beauty lies in Her blind drive to survive." '

He vaguely remembered the hymn. He would have to look it up as soon as he could. 'Yes, sir. I know, sir.' An Imprint came back to him from school. "We are Gaia's guardians. We must protect Her from ourselves.'"

Odinson chuckled. His chest was pressed hard against Peat's arm now. 'That's what they teach you, isn't it? Even now we still think we're responsible for Her. *We're special*,' he minced, '*Gaia's stewards, Her shepherds. We're here to take care of all the plants and the animals*. When really we're insatiable predators, the worst of the lot.'

Yet again, Odinson had dumbfounded him. Humans *were* responsible for the planet's wellbeing, at the very least for not destroying it. That was Gaianism, everything he had ever been taught. Is-Land was home to beautiful reintroduced creatures: manatees, butterflies, otters . . . but he wasn't in Is-Land. He was in a barren wasteland, a concrete oasis, receiving a private lecture from the man he respected more than anyone else in the world. He could barely breathe.

'The truth is, Peat,' Odinson continued, that electric hand still clamped to his shoulder, '*Homo sapiens* is a rogue species. Apart from our parasites, any self-respecting animal left on the planet can't wait for us to finish eliminating ourselves. Think about it.' With the unpredictable swerve that made his speeches so compelling, the Chief Super adopted a playful, almost nursery-rhyme tone. 'The vipers and hyenas downright detest us; the sheep and mice trust us about as far as they can propel their little shit pellets; the horses, camels and cattle do their best to ignore us, and are the bees grateful for their hives? Not one whit – bees are ants with fur coats; they do what the queen wants and she wants a dark, quiet place to pump out her eggs. Gaia would be far better off without us, don't you agree?'

He still could not speak. In front of him, the dim shapes of the slavers were limply struggling on the sandbanks. He was no better than the Non-Landers, he registered, his mind bound as surely as their limbs.

'I'll tell you who needs us.' Odinson's hand swooped down his back, gripped his hip. 'Listen? Can you hear them?'

He could hear nothing except his own thumping heartbeat, the fluttering in the trees.

'The bats, sir?'

'Oh, the bats. They don't give a shit about us. Listen to the *sandflies*. They're giddy with it, hysterical, splitting their infinitesimal sides!'

Listen to the flies? In the sand? There was nothing to hear but Odinson, his chin digging into Peat's shoulder as he hissed, *We love you, we love you we love you we jump like joy beans as your thermal mass lumbers near. But don't get too cocky, folks. We love, not your precious human souls, but your BLOOD.'*

He pinched Peat's side and Peat jumped. Odinson giggled. 'That's what the sandflies sing,' he crooned. 'We are special after all, Peat. Human blood is the hot mulled wine of the universe. All the honey and spice of Creation, its cinnamon and cherries and zest, its paradoxical collisions and impossible fusions, sizzle and sluice and shine through our veins. Bat blood is corked plonk in comparison to ours. Tell me, young pup, don't you like to lap up a splash of fine vintage Burgundy with your dinner?'

Cherries. His mouth swam again with the taste. He remembered now where he had tasted those cherries before.

'I drank wine in Zabaria, sir. After the mission. The secret mission, sir.'

The moonlight was stark on the sand; the palm leaves were sharp blades cutting black shapes out of a dazzling sky. He belonged here. He was a Sec Gen at war.

'You did, didn't you? You ate your fill. And your turn will come again. Right now we are feasting the sandflies to keep them on our side. We're a bad animal, Peat, a very bad animal, and we need some of the creatures to stick up for us as we try and sort ourselves out.'

'We will, sir, won't we?' he offered. 'Sort ourselves out?'

'Absolutely. Conscious evolution, Peat.' Odinson rubbed his back again. 'IMBOD is working on it round the clock, Blesserson is getting all the serums down pat. The problem with *Homo sapiens* is the sapiens part. We think we know everything, when really we think far too much. We need to learn how to just *be*. Look at you. You're very happy, aren't you, following orders?'

'Yes, sir.' His chest swelled. 'I'd . . . I'd do anything for you, sir.' Odinson's fingers returned to his nape. Then the Chief Super was gripping his throat, his breath hot at the whorl of his ear. 'I know, lovely puppy,' he whispered. 'And when I want you to kneel and suck my hard cock, I will tell you to do so. Understood?'

The words flooded his world. They flared through his body, nearly overwhelmed his ability to comprehend them. Had he heard right? He was *nineteen*. Odinson was not allowed to . . . but he *bad* . . . his head swam with impossible visions. Had Odinson read his thoughts? Was the Chief Super really going to—? Fucking a teenager was illegal, could disgrace a man forever – but who would arrest *Odinson*?

'Yes, sir,' he gasped. 'Understood, sir.'

'Good dog.' Odinson released him, stepped away. 'Now *stay*.' His voice rang out. 'Stand back, kids. It's my turn for some *fun*!'

Peat's arm was exposed, cold, crying out for the return of that radiant battle heat. Desperately, he watched Odinson, the high thrust of his buttocks as he aimed a kick at the big prisoner's ribs, the confident angle of his elbow, the tilt of his chin as he lifted the man up by the ankles and dropped him on his head in the sand. Even then the slaver had not quite given up; he writhed at Odinson's feet, flailing weakly. Odinson took a pair of latex gloves from his hipbelt and snapped them on. As the Chief Super bent and grabbed a handful of sand, Blesserson joined Peat, his silent presence a reassuring return. Together, bats swooping like dark garlands between the palm branches, they watched the Chief Super serve the final course of the feast.

The Windsands

It was Muzi. Muzi's red headscarf, brown smock, slim frame: Muzi riding a camel.

Relief coursed through her. She flung the knife down on the blanket and, laughing and waving, ran out to meet him. He did a victory lap of the rocks, showing off his camel-riding skills, then, somehow not toppling off, drew the beast to a jerky halt in front of the tent.

'Astra. Meet camel!' he announced.

The camel was so tall – *enormous*. The colour of straw, with shaggy flanks, it was bearing the water bottle, a solar panel, and two bulging green and orange embroidered pouches, festooned like the harness with fluffy white pompoms. Fascinated, she drew closer, but the beast was not at all interested in her. It gazed out over her head like someone glamorous and demanding, who had come to stay but was already regretting the decision. As she stepped back – would it spit? – the camel sat down, a fast, unexpected seesawing motion, its rump landing hard on the ground. Muzi lurched backward, then forward, and clutched at its neck. His expression of triumph was blotted out by eye-popping alarm.

She laughed until her side hurt.

Laughing too, Muzi rolled off the beast's back and bowed to her, the rope in his hand. 'I bring camel. Where bandit treasure?'

She caught her breath. 'I spent it. All on me!'

Joy flashed between them. Behind Muzi the beast yawned, emitting a loud gargling sound and a long string of foam.

'Is it sick?' she worried.

'No. Is normal,' he said proudly, toeing the camel's saliva into the soil.

Suddenly Muzi was the camel expert. To give him credit, he'd learned to ride it pretty quickly. Maintaining a respectful berth, she examined the animal. Muzi had been sitting on blankets strapped round its barrel belly. But what were those marks on its hips?

'This camel was *whipped*.' She spun on her heel. 'Muzi! Did you give Sisi to a' – she didn't know 'animal abuser' in Asfarian – 'bad man?'

'No, no. I give her to a good man, man with little boy who want a horse. Nice boy. I meet him. Astra, this camel *special*.' He patted the beast's neck. 'Retired racing camel. Very good breeding. No biter. Not bad treated. Camel driver hit her only on journey to Lálsil. We tie belt here, see, not hurt her. Very *grateful* camel.'

He said 'grateful' proudly. It was a new word for him in Asfarian. But there was nothing to be grateful for. He'd brought back an abused animal. It was already carrying a massive load. How on earth was it going to take the rest of their supplies as well?

'This animal has been beaten. It should be in a health farm, not carrying us through a desert.'

'Camel strong animal.' Muzi began tying the rope around one of the rocks. 'She young still, only eight years. Take much more bags. We don't ride – only if very tired. We talk nice to her, give treats, all fine. Only don't stand behind her, or show her stick. She not like sticks. Is good animal, Astra. Name for you to choose.'

At least the camel wasn't old. But it was psychologically damaged and after a career as a racer, no doubt ready to collapse. Either Muzi was a lousy trader or a horse and cart weren't worth much around here. She stood staring at the beast as Muzi untied the water bottle and set it in the shade. For the first time the camel appeared to acknowledge her existence, sniffing in her direction and languidly batting its sandy lashes before turning its attention back to the horizon.

She was getting angry again, she realised. She needed to give Muzi, and the camel, a chance. 'What's camel in Somarian?' she asked.

'*Aria-má.* Mean desert-ship.'

'Ariamá.' It sounded glamorous, like the name of a singer. 'Okay. That's her name, then.' She watched Muzi set the solar panel against a rock. 'Why did you buy that?' Their Tablettes recharged directly, and even if there was the odd rainy day in Non-Land, the sun was always back full strength the next. 'We don't need one.'

'Was cheap. I trade fan for.'

Fan? She felt a stabbing sense of loss. 'You said you were going to *pawn* the dream-catcher.' Her sense of grievance mounted. 'And you haven't brought much water. I need to wash, Muzi.'

Muzi dug through one of the camel pouches, and held out a fat metal cylinder. He smelled – she frowned – like sandalwood. He'd washed. He'd been to the steam bath, the selfish tyrant.

'We need the sun panel for this,' he said proudly.

She took the object, eyeing it suspiciously. The cylinder had a dial and a measured window on the side. One end was a metal lid, the other a funnel. If it was a water flask, it wasn't a big one. It looked like an expensive kitchen device, but they didn't need pastry-makers out in the desert.

'I give up. What is it?'

'You not see before? No CONC machine? No Is-Land machine?'

'No.'

Crooking the thing in his elbow, Muzi unscrewed the base, and showed her the complicated insides: a cage of blue crystals surrounded by a series of spinning combs. She was none the wiser. With an air of supreme satisfaction he replaced the cap. 'Is *kàš* cleaner.'

Kàš, she knew, was urine. 'What?'

'Is excellent for us. No worry water.' He smirked. 'You just careful not miss hole.'

She'd pee on *him* if he wasn't careful. 'How much did *that* cost?'

He shrugged. 'Half the cart.'

'*Half the cart?* You could have got a donkey for half the cart, so we could both *ride*, and you bought a piss machine instead? We're passing three more towns! If we run out of water we can buy more.'

She had used a rude Asfarian word. Muzi laughed. 'Piss machine. I like.' He stuck the gadget back into the pouch. 'Towns no good for us. Road no good, Astra. We must go in desert. When we meet man in desert, we let him use our piss machine. He give us food and give you camel-ride. All good.'

'You want to go to Shiimti through the desert?' He'd only been back five minutes and already she felt like exploding. Especially now they were walking, they needed to stick close to the road. It would be hard going, but the scrubland continued all the way to the furthest oasis town, Pūtigi, and they could be there in a week. That was plenty of time for Photon to send Lil to meet them. Lil would guide them over the final stretch, first down the salt route, the stretch of hard white mineral soil traversed by countless caravans over the centuries, then deep into the windsands. Going on their own through the desert was insane.

But she mustn't shout any more. She had to be reasonable, hear his point of view, then express hers. She set the urine filter down by the rock. 'We need to work as a team, Muzi, and consult each other on important decisions. I don't want to go through the desert. Neither of us has ever been south of Lálsil before. We'll get lost. We need to follow the road.'

'You have CONC watch. CONC maps.' He pulled a bar of honey soap out of the pouch. 'No problem.'

'It is a problem, Muzi. We could get lost and die.'

'We not get lost. And not get caught by N-LA either.' He pulled out a comb next, then a bag of dates, a sack of apples, pellet treats for the camel, but nothing could sweeten her temper. *He wasn't listening.* He simply wasn't listening to her. At last he handed her what looked like a big chunk of soft dried honeycomb, and a bundle of clothes.

'Sponge. Clean clothes. Special present. You need bath, Astra. I make food, you wash now. Feel better then.'

Sponges were dead animals — Gaians didn't use them. But he hadn't bought a washcloth as she'd asked, so she was forced to use it. She stomped behind the rocks with the water bottle and a bowl. For the first time in ages she undressed outside. It was like peeling away a carapace of grime. And the sponge, she had to admit, was wonderful, like a big juicy shower in her hand. Naked and clean, she washed her dirty clothes too, and laid them to dry on the rocks. Then she sat for a time and calmed herself down. Muzi was just doing what he thought was best for them both. He was wrong, but not malicious or stupid. They could discuss the route in the morning.

He had got a fire going with the kindling they'd gathered in the scrubland, laid out a picnic blanket. 'What was the news?' she asked when she rejoined him. 'Was there anything about your family? Did you email Photon?'

He passed her a mug of tea. 'My family not report missing. But news not good. Fighting in Kadingir every night. More YAC warriors killed. And IMBOD take back firesands jail. And Zabaria.'

They had to use the Tablette dictionary, but finally she understood. In Kadingir, the Sec Gens had remained within the Hem, and though armed now with blades, were not using firearms. The invasion of Non-Land had happened elsewhere, in surprise twin attacks on the N-LA jail in the firesands, and the mining town. IMBOD had claimed that now N-LA had broken the Hem agreement, the firesands tower should revert to Gaian ownership, while in Zabaria the long-corrupt N-LA police had defected, on the promise of what advantage Muzi didn't know, and declared the town an autonomous zone. Some frightened mine-workers had fled, but most were trapped in the town.

It was terrible news. Lil might be in Zabaria. She and Tiamet might have gone back to the Welcome Tent to be with Tiamet's baby; what was his name? Ebebu. And what about all the other Pithar Singulars? Neperdu, with her commanding presence. Anunit, with the flamethrower eyes and murdered child. Conditions had been bad enough for the women when the police had taken bribes from the Gaian mine-managers; what would happen to them now that Zabaria was completely under IMBOD's control? She pressed Muzi for more details, but he just shrugged.

'All talk in Amazigia now. N-LA say IMBOD make land grab, take town hostage. IMBOD say Is-Land need protect the mine. CONC,' he rolled his eyes, 'ask everybody talk talk more please.'

It was enough bad news for a year, but she had to ask, 'What about the Sec Gens?'

His face shuttered up. 'I look at list. I don't see Peat Orson.'

'What about the dry forest region?' she persisted. 'Or? New Bangor?'

He squinted. 'One from dry forest. Boy, I think. Moss . . . Hikkson?'

Leaf's brother; Peat's golden-haired friend. She hugged her knees to her chest. 'Moss Higgson. I knew him when he was just like you and me.'

Muzi shook his mug out. 'That long time ago, Astra. He monster now. YAC take his head. Good for talk talk and trade.'

She couldn't listen to him any more. She laid her cheek on her knees and gazed out towards the sunset. Moss Higgson, who loved flowers and played the panpipes. Moss had been decapitated, a mutilated body sent back to his family, his head kept like some kind of brutal currency. Leaf would be distraught – heesh had idolised hir brother. A tear trickled down her nose.

'You okay, Astra?'

He sounded concerned. But she couldn't tell him she was crying over a Sec Gen. She wiped her cheek. 'I'm sad about Zabaria. I know some women there. They gave me the directions to Shiimti.'

'I sorry. But no killings in Zabaria. Only work for IMBOD forever. Just like before.'

Lil knew everything, everyone. Maybe the women had been able to escape. Photon would know. 'What about Photon?' she persisted. 'Did you tell him what I said? To meet us in Pütigi?'

He stretched his legs, made a face. 'Camel riding hurt. We only ride if sick.'

'Muzi? Did you email Photon?'

He began rubbing the backs of his thighs. 'I not use email or Share-World, Astra. I not use my Tablette. I rent one in café, only read news. I no want CONC see where we are.'

Who was he? What went on in his head? 'Muzi!' she pleaded, as if there was still time to make a difference. 'It doesn't matter if CONC knows where we are. It's *good* if they know we're safe!'

He shook his head. 'You *war leader*, Astra. YAC still showing your photo. Una Dayyani say she Istar too. And N-LA want CONC to go. Maybe Dayyani not want you safe. You must stay hiding,'

She struggled to keep up. 'Is CONC leaving Non-Land?'

Again, it took time to sort out. CONC was still in Kadingir and might even send police troops. But Dayyani was angling for Asfar to enter the conflict. In the meantime, though, Major Thames was – not her friend exactly, but an ally. And Photon would do anything he could to help her, if he only knew where she was. 'But if Photon doesn't know our plans, how will we travel on from Pütigi?' she asked in the helpless tone Muzi had reduced her to. 'We don't know the way from the salt route.'

Muzi was doing the dishes. 'I get you to Shiimti, Astra. Don't worry,'

She felt dizzy. He was prepared to throw away a lifeline, just to say he'd got her to Shiimti all by himself. She stared up at the blood-curdled sky.

'Nap now,' Muzi took out his tooth-cleaning twig. 'Storm coming soon. Man in beer tent tell me. We leave midnight.' He rubbed his gums vigorously with the stick, took a last swig of water and spat into the sand. Then he turned his back and folded himself into his blanket.

He'd been to a beer tent. He'd had a steam bath. He'd decided to take them days out of their way through a desert. She wasn't remotely sleepy. She wanted to jump up, walk to Lálsil, email Photon, go back to Kadingir, work for CONC, fight with YAC on the Hem.

She could do all that. But chaos reigned in Kadingir. And she had a plan. She sat brooding as the sky darkened. There was so much she hadn't told Muzi – *couldn't* tell him. She had buried his lizards, spoken with them. Her Gaia dream in the tent was as real as anything she had ever experienced and it had told her to get to Shiimti. Now she'd learned that the women in Zabaria needed help more than ever, the message was even more urgent. And, thinking about Moss, she remembered her other task in Shiimti: Photon had asked her to put the Non-Gaians in touch with him and Dr Tapputu, who thought the Shiimti healers might be able to help him find a cure for the Sec Gens' condition. She fingered the edge of the blanket. She might not trust Muzi, but she had to trust herself. She had got this far, and she would continue.

She had to do something, so she fed the camel, digging in the bag of pellets and approaching the beast with her palm flat out. It got to its feet so fast she thought it would get its knobbly knees in a knot. She held her breath, let it snuffle mucus all over her hand.

'Hello, Ariamá.' She wiped her palm on her trousers. 'Thank you for coming to help us.' She paused. The lizard voices had been very real. 'Do you want to talk?'

The camel munched, arched its neck. If it was speaking, she couldn't hear it. She looked up into the darkening sky. 'Istar? Any messages?'

The evening star remained silent also. It was twinkling at her, but just a star, the moon, a pale orb in the twilight, just the beautiful moon.

The barren plain was beautiful now too, endless and awash with purple and orange shadows. Soon the plateau would be far behind her, one more place she had passed through on this strange journey. She was thankful she had seen its more alluring face, but glad too they would be leaving soon. So much was going on in the war: she had to get to Shiimti and start building the resistance there – meet her father, contact Cora Pollen's people, help Dr Tapputu. Looking up at the moon, and Istar beside it, for the first time since the start of the journey, she allowed herself to think about Zizi.

All she knew for certain about her father was that he was a Non-Lander infiltrator who'd worked as a waiter in Atourne and had a secret affair with a young Gaian woman and now, according to Lil, hung around in beer tents, being bossy. The details had never been comfortable to dwell on. Zizi had known full well the risk he was taking with her Birth mother, fathering a child he might never see, never be around for. Was he, like Rudo had suggested back in Kadingir, irresponsible, selfish? Was he, despite his own behaviour, a traditional Non-Lander father, wanting to marry her off? Or would he want to make it up to her for his absence?

Perhaps it was the sunset, the companionable warmth of the camel or the fact that she was drawing near him at last, but it was impossible not to feel a little bit hopeful. Everyone liked beer, and Lil didn't take orders from anyone: her father could be a perfectly reasonable man; no bossier than Muzi anyway. And he would welcome her, wouldn't he? Zizi had been in touch with Hokma all those years; he must want to see her again. She imagined him for a moment: a man who looked like her, with the same curly hair and small nose, but taller and broader, a strong, patient, elegant man, who had waited all these years for his daughter. He was a Non-Gaian; he would be like Dr Tapputu, a Non-Lander elder with a vision of peace, but also like Klor: loving and proud of her, a protector of the Earth. Caught up in the drama of the sunset, she let her thoughts blossom. Perhaps Zizi was looking up at the moon too, thinking of her. He would have stories to tell her, about her Birth mother, Eya. He would have things he had kept to show her too. He might – the thought occurred to her for the very first time – he might even have other children. He might have a family to give her.

She had to stop dreaming. 'Tell my father I'm on my way,' she told the moon. 'Tell him I'm walking to Shiimti with a camel and a piss machine and a bossy boy from Kadingir.'

He didn't sleep right away. Istar was rising, taking her place by the moon. He watched the star shine through half-closed lids. Istar was the wilful, imperious daughter of the sky-god. She wore a dazzling crown and danced through the night, her footsteps making patterns that, if you traced them over the months, formed perfectly symmetrical flowers. In the morning and the evening Istar wore lustrous robes of lemon-yellow, powder-blue or flame-red, gifts from her father. At night, when the sky-god slept, she spoke to the world in his place – not *for* her father; Istar had her own mind. A tricky one. On rare occasions Muzi had come to her with a dilemma but he wasn't sure if she'd given true advice, or just twinkled with laughter and left him to find his own way. The sky-god, with his weather and colours, was much easier to understand.

Astra had laughed this evening, very hard, when he'd nearly fallen off the camel. Everything had been wonderful, both of them happy, the way a man and a woman should be when reunited at the day's end.

But soon she'd got angry again, and then sad. He was starting to feel worried about her.

When people *stay* angry, his grandmother had once told him, they rot inside. They stink, become swampy and bitter as wormwood. He hadn't known what wormwood was, but she had explained it was a poisonous tree. Even a little bit of anger could be poisonous. That was why it was so important to be open to the sky. The sky cleans us, Uttu had said, with the rain and the wind and the stars and the moon. When it rains, unless you are ill, don't complain about getting wet. You will soon be dry off. While it rains, run through the drops and laugh, letting the rain rinse your heart. When the *mergallā-lā* come, take everything indoors that you don't want to blow away, and then stand outside with your eyes closed and arms outstretched, letting the wind blow away all your bad deeds, and remind you how strong you are, how connected to the earth. And at night, every clear night, gaze at the stars and bathe in the moonlight. The stars will shine inside you, burning away your anger, and the moonlight will wash away all of your fears like the mildest of soap. Do all that, Muzi, his grandmother had said, and you will never get bitter.

Bitter like Gibil, Uttu had not said, but even when he was five years old he knew she was thinking of his uncle.

He looked at Astra. She was standing with the camel, gazing up at the moon. Perhaps she was speaking to Istar.

She walked back and lay down on the blanket. 'Stars are Uttu's robe,' he said into the night.

It was a beautiful thought. Above, the stars were a dazzling shroud, sheer finery. Uttu, who had spent her days washing soiled sheets, deserved to be wrapped in them.

'She flying now, Astra,' Muzi said. 'To One Land.'

One Land. Bringing the Boundary down, uniting Is-Land and Non-Land, was a goal as distant as the stars. But the stars were pouring into her, streams of bright milk and crushed diamonds flowing from a jug in Uttu's withered hand, sluicing through her and washing away any doubt about the decisions she had made today. Muzi and she were on this journey together because of Uttu. One Land had been Uttu's dream. If she did nothing else with her life, she vowed on the queen star, Istar, she would honour that dream. She wasn't Istar, the goddess Lil and YAC said she was, but it was clear that her destiny was here. People – Muzi, Photon,

Lil, Dr Tapputu, Anunit – loved her, needed her, were counting on her, and she would not let them down. She would direct her fury against IMBOD, like this cascading stream of stars, into a quest for justice. She would put Samrod Blesserson in jail, she would close the Zabaria mine and cure the Sec Gens, and she would help Muzi get his family back.

'My father knows people who know lawyers and journalists, Muzi,' she said. 'When we meet him, I'll make sure they help free your family.'

There was a long silence. She thought he was asleep. Then he spoke again, quietly. 'Lawyers no help Non-Land. Uttu help us. You see.'

Vicious and spiteful, as if Muzi had dialled it up to prove his point, the sandstorm broke just before dawn. They had been walking for five hours, cutting a wide loop around Lálsil, then walking half a kilometre south of the road to the next town, a fiercely struck compromise between his insistence to travel through the desert and hers to make good time on the empty night road. The terrain was still flat, but the hard soil of the plain was behind them now; her feet sank into the sand and the going was slow. Then the going was gone. One minute she was watching a dirty brown line widen on the horizon, the next, sand was blasting her eyes, dragging a wrench through her hair, and she was choking in lungfuls of grit.

Muzi was shouting, but she couldn't hear a word he was saying. He tugged the camel to the ground and she crouched beside it. He was digging into the pouches, handing her goggles, a mouth mask. She pulled the gear on and the relief was immediate, but the wind was still driving a drill through her ears. She helped Muzi fasten the blankets around the solar panel and lash ropes around the camel's load. Then, in the scant shelter of the beast's back, he gave her a headscarf and opened a small pot of salve. He dabbed the ointment around his own nostrils and she did the same, then tied the scarf around her hat and put on the gloves he gave her. She was hot, but now most of her exposed skin and all her mucous membranes were protected from the needle-sharp sand. There was nothing for it but to huddle against the camel and wait for the wild wind to pass.

Dawn broke and the world lightened marginally, a ceaseless circulation of brown. The sky was brown, her shirt was brown, her boots were brown, Muzi was brown, the camel was brown, everything was lost in a violent brown haze. The day passed, and with it all sense of time. Speaking was pointless. The masks muffled their voices and ears and the wind pulverised any sound the moment it escaped, tore it away in a gust of grit into the disappeared world. She sat and simmered.

She liked Ariamá. In a windstorm, though, a camel's back was no substitute for a cart. If it were up to her, they'd be sheltering under the tarpaulin, playing Tablette games and waiting for the skies to clear. But very little, it appeared, was up to her on this trip. As the morning sweltered and swirled into evening, as she nibbled hard bread and sand, dates and sand, sipped water and sand; as her back cramped and her body shrank into a petrified stump, Astra began to think they would sit there forever, or at least until their provisions ran out and the camel died. Perhaps Muzi would eat it, slicing the meat from its bones then trudging back home with a sack of protein, leaving its carcase behind with hers.

At last she nodded off. When she awoke the haze had lightened again and Muzi was tugging at her sleeve. As she blinked, he dropped his mask, cupped his hands and pressed his mouth to her ear.

'*Mergalla* HELP us,' he shouted.

'WHAT?'

He crouched low to the ground, took out his Tablette, pulled off his glove and typed. She brought the Tablette up close to her scratched plastic goggles and read his message. It was in Somarian. It took time, but she looked up all the words in Asfarian, Inglish and Gaian just to make sure. *Alduge* in Somarian meant to pray, desire or insist. *Mergallá* could mean 'wind demon,' 'angry wind demon' or 'violent storm spirit.' The politest translation of Muzi's message was:

The wind demon is blowing south. It prays that we will go to Shiimti over the windsands.

No, they didn't want to walk into the desert with a demon. They wanted to *get away* from the storm, go *east* along the road, stopping at the oasis towns to buy supplies and pick up internet signals. There was still time to ask Photon to tell Lil or someone from YAC to meet them in Pútigi, help them on the salt route. Her Gaia compass wasn't so scrambled that she would go for a stroll in a sand storm, directly away from all possible help. She replied in Asfarian:

It's a DEMON. You want to follow a demon into the middle of nowhere?

He handed the Tablette back to her.

'Demon' not right. Too hard to explain. A *mergallá* is sent to hurt you or help you. If it wanted to hurt us, we'd be dead now. We aren't dead. So the *mergallá* wants us to walk. Better on high ground. We have to go back to the ridge.

A *mergallá* could last up to a week, she had read. The worst storms could bash camels against rocks, pick people up and drop them kilometres away. If for some reason this one was trying to help them, it was telling them to SIT STILL. But Muzi was standing, coaxing the camel to its feet. She was attached to them both by a hemp rope. She couldn't tie Muzi up with it, and she couldn't stay here on her own. She stood. They had passed a ridge about two hours back.

Heal you? Ha ha ha! No whip is long enough to drive you apart, no grit strong enough to scour you clean. We could rub you raw, inside and out, strip your skin from your bones and you'd still be steeped in it, rotten through and through with it: human emotion. The old joke, told again and again, funnier each time. How we laugh, harder and harder, at you perverse creatures, in thrall to your own flaws: pride, anger, self-pity, jealousy, fury, anxiety, grief – all the instinctive afflictions you, alone of the mammals, could learn to control, you instead found civilisations upon. Ha ha ha!

The *mergallá* was howling in his ears, sending voices to taunt him, tempt him to anger and despair. He ignored them. *Mergallá-lá* were the wild, rebellious servants of the sky-god; even when they were sent to help you, they tried to test you, distract you, get you walking in circles. You had to block them out. If you listened, tried to talk to them, then, worse than losing your way, you might lose your mind. Moving was better than sitting. When the body was moving the mind had a task to focus on. And walking with a *mergallá* was far easier than trying to round up sheep in one. He had done that more than once, whirling in all directions, chasing lambs as the wind lashed and bashed him, tangled ropes around his feet. Compared to that, this was steady work. The *mergallá*, despite its vicious desire to see them fail, was obeying the sky-god, propelling them forward. All he had to do was place one foot after another.

The wind reminds you how strong you are, his grandmother had said, how connected to the ground.

Ha ha ha! Walk on, girl, collapse . . . walk on, collapse . . . it makes no difference what you do, makes no difference if you live or die! For you are human and when your empires of emotion fall, you resurrect them, brick by crumbled brick, tile by smashed tile. How many libraries have we scattered, songs snatched, dreams hollowed, corpses flayed, and yet still it soars again into the skies: the glittering prison of your greed to possess the one thing you cannot: another person's soul. Walk on girl, ha ha ha, walk on until you wither to dust . . . you will never leave your human nature behind . . .

The wind was a ceaseless unintelligible scream in her head, a battering of laughter and derision she endured as she endured the stinging gauntlet of hands slapping her back, her legs, her skull, shoving her on and on and on. It could be driving them in circles, she thought angrily, but every time they stopped and checked her CONC watch they had progressed further south and soon she gave up hoping Muzi would change his mind and turn back. In between the watch checks, distance and time could only be measured by pain: the blisters on her feet, slowly abrading, the silent scream in her knee, a micro-fraction louder with every step. If only she could cut off her feet. And her head. The goggles dug into her cheeks, her lips were swollen and scalded and every breath was a torment. Despite the mask and the salve, reapplied every four hours, her nostrils were raw, and after swallowing sand along with every scant mouthful of water and food, even her throat was inflamed.

The only way to cope was to try and focus, however briefly, on parts of her that miraculously did not hurt. She experienced blissful periods of amazement that her brand-wound had finally healed. The IMBOD circuitry must have been the cause of the irritation, and Dr Tapputu himself could not have given better post-op instructions than to sit in a cart for three days: her perineum was giving her no trouble at all. She was also, for the first time in her life, grateful for clothes. Trouser legs tucked into socks, sleeves into gloves, the garments kept her limbs and torso sauna-hot, but safe from the sand. Sometimes in the pearly light of the morning, the fabric rippling and billowing over her chest made her wooden limbs feel, for fleeting moments, like the masts of a ship.

After a while she lost track of time. As the numbers danced on her watch in a random fashion, she plodded on, dragged one stifling breath into her lungs after another, huddled against the camel, ate and drank sand. Time was no longer a progression of events but a singular, concentrated experience: one immense challenge funnelling into another. Right now she was thirsty, and her flask was empty. It was not just pointless, but foolish to speak. Her mouth parched, she tugged on the rope that lashed them both to the camel. Muzi stopped and she thrust out her empty flask. Whether to keep the ghost of conversation alive in this deadly brown cloud, or just reassure herself she still could, as he loomed up beside her, she forced the words out.

'*Water please.*' The words clogged in her throat. But she had formed them in her mind and moved her jaw. She had spoken.

His eyes nearly colourless behind the lenses, Muzi lifted a finger to his own cloth mask and shook his head. He took the flask and refilled it from the water bottle, a task he insisted on performing since she had fumbled the first time she'd tried in the wind. That was a lifetime ago. She'd been angry, wanted to argue over the Tablette that they had limitless water, but arguments took up energy, and anyway, he was right. The urine filter was for calmer times. Who knew what sand could do to its mechanics?

She took the flask in her gloved hand. She understood 'insulation' now. It was hotter in the sand storm than anywhere she'd ever been – hotter than the steppes in summer; hotter than Kadingir at high noon. So hot she couldn't put the flask to her lips, had to tilt her head back and splash the water in beneath the mask. Even so, if it had been any hotter, the water would have blistered her tongue.

Muzi tapped his wrist and she rolled up her sleeve and showed him her watch. First the time, then, pressing the side buttons, the pedometer and compass. He pointed at the ground, their sign for a rest. She nodded: *Yes, thank Gaia.* They had reached a point 28.23 kilometres south of the Lower Belt Road and, according to her feet, the absolute limit of her endurance. She had to stop now. Stop and drink more sand and eat more sand and rub sandy salve into her nostrils and blisters and sleep in the shelter of the camel, to desperately dream that this demonic blizzard would have died down by the time she awoke. Muzi patted the camel's neck and tugged at its nose rope. As if fed up with these pathetic humans, Ariamá slowly rolled the grey nictitating membranes over her dark eyes and, flaring her long nostrils, sank to her knees.

Astra sat too, the steady measure of the camel's rising and falling flank little defence against the bitterness rising within her. It was true that Sisi could not have walked through this storm, but they were only attempting to do so because they had the camel, and none of them had yet survived the experience.

Around her the brown sky slowly brightened: above this whirling dome the invisible sun was rising. A memory of the ion glove came to her, her body merging with Lil's glowing form in a honey-bronze light. Something shifted. She was watching the storm as though it was happening far, far away. There were shapes in the sand, faces and figures, a woman diving, a mouth yawning, flocks of birds sweeping past. Everything was moving, curtains parting, skirts twirling, ribbons streaming…

Except for *that* figure. That figure was still. Tall, broad-shouldered, something, someone, was standing ahead on the ridge. Was it a man? Her heart pounding, she grabbed Muzi's arm.

Ha ha ha. You've survived. Well, well. A stronger boy than we thought. And the girl was so angry with you she didn't even hear us. What a lovely couple you make, both blasted with sand. Yes, we're happy you made it. Delirious with joy! The gods must have plans for you. Oh pity the humans the gods fall in love with! Ha ha ha! HA HA HA!

He stirred, blinked. The air was white-gold, the sand sparkling in the sun, frisky little flurries dancing lightly upwards, not driving onwards. It no longer felt like being trapped in a dome: there was a sense of space, of sky, even.

It was so pretty. He lay watching it; Astra was agitated, though, shaking his arm and pointing ahead. He peered in the direction of her finger.

In an instant he understood. Fumbling in his pocket for his knife, he jumped up. Astra tried to pull him down but flipping open the blade he stepped into the whirling sand. See how this watcher, this thief, this bandit reacted to *that*.

The gold curtains blew this way and that, but the giant man did not move. Astra was standing now too, had taken the frying pan from a pouch. Hesitantly, he took another stride forward. Still no sound, no gesture from the man. Was he ill? Did he need help? He inched towards him. The sand parted, thinned, until – *was it possible?* – like retreating waves, plumes of sand were falling away down the sides of the ridge; above, the sun was a pale silver disc shining down through a white sky . . . and he could see . . . *he could see!*

The *mergallá* was over! The wind spirits were flying back up to the halls of the sky-god! He tore off his mask, yodelled his triumph, twirled, looked back. He could see the camel, stretching its neck, its white pom-poms brown and bloated with sand. He could see Astra too: just her dim outline, but her shirt, her boots, the stick in her hand, ready to bash against the stone heart of the tall stone man the *mergallá* had brought them to meet! Who was he, this man? He jogged closer.

Even close up, the man was a puzzle. Not a smooth carved figure, but a craggy human tower, hunks of sandstone wedged and glued or some-how pegged together, white plaster bulging out of the cracks like cream in a biscuit. Big chunks of him were missing; he lacked a right arm, his left leg ended at the knee, the *mergallá* had bitten and clawed him and a sec-tion of his torso was a jumble of rocks and wire, but like the alt-bodied YAC warriors, the man emanated authority. He was dressed in long robes and a crown and was seated on a throne. His beard curled down to his chest and though his nose had been scoured clean away and his long face was traversed by a diagonal scar, his large empty eyes were unper-turbed by all he had endured. The hollows in his head looked steadily into the far distance, taking the measure of all he surveyed.

The man was a king. Or many kings. Perhaps his head came from a quarry in the Dragon's Gorge, his missing arm from Asfar. It was impos-sible to say. But as Muzi marvelled, his gaze lit upon a clue, a sign . . . and then another. *Of course!* He knew exactly who this man was.

He spun round to summon Astra but there was no need for that; she was upon him, throwing her mask aside, ripping off her headscarf. Her hair was matted, there was a dark groove on her forehead where the mask had dug into it and a split sore on her cheekbone was oozing blood like the plaster in the cracks of the man. But none of that mattered. She was beau-tiful. They linked arms, danced round and round and round until they fell in a heap at the foot of the stone man.

Astra stared up at the statue. 'One more minute of that demon storm and I would have crumbled into a million bits too.'

'*Mergallá* not demon.' He sat up. 'I tell you, Astra, *mergallá* is spirit messenger. Like a cloud or a bird.'

She gave him, not a scoffing look . . . suspicious, perhaps. 'You believe in bird messengers?'

'Birds quick messengers, for short stories,' he explained. 'Clouds slow messengers, for long stories. Wind is strong messenger, for life and death stories. It bring us here. Right here. To meet King Shlemun. See?'

He pointed at the signs – the king's left shoulder was gripped by slender stone claws, though the bird's body had been knocked off long ago; his right hand boasted a ring engraved with a six-pointed star.

'Messengers everywhere, Astra. This Shlemun' – what was the Asfarian word? – 'is shrine. Shlemun Karkish god. Asfarian too. People come, give gifts, ask questions. Shlemun give answer.'

'Oh.' She brushed the sand off her lap. 'If he's Karkish and Asfarian, he's a prophet, Muzi, not a god.'

Doron was Karkish. And his shop sign, the tree of ten fruits, was a secret sign of the people of the six-pointed star. Shlemun was saying it was right to have visited the brass merchant. 'I give him gift,' he announced.

She scowled. 'We can't afford to give anything away, Muzi. We're lucky we didn't bang right into him. Anyway, you're Somarian. Why do you want to worship Abrahamic prophets?'

He considered her with concern. Perhaps she had a temperature. That sore was ugly; it might be infected. In any case, she must be hungry and hot and shaken by the storm. They would set up camp, eat, wait for the heat to drain from the day, then move down into the valley. For now, he tried patiently to explain, 'Religions all brother sister, Astra. Somarian, Karkish, Farashan – all Non-Land gods help all Non-Landers. Asfarian god brother god too.' He pointed at the bird's feet. 'King Shlemun is brother to Somarian sky-god. He speak bird language, control wind spirits. He bring us here.'

She raised her voice. 'We could have passed any number of shrines on this ridge, Muzi, how would we know? And I don't believe in a sky-god. The Old World Abrahamites believed in a sky-god and look what happened to them. They drilled oil for arrowpains and weapons of war. They built glass towers and forgot where they came from. Look what happened to the *Earth*.'

She spread her arms. To either side of the ridge, the sand was settling into the valleys. There was nothing else to see: no trees, no plants, no water, just the spine of dry soil they had been walking along, the camel, Shlemun and, above them, the sun still veiled by a thin white haze. Hunched, furious, glaring at him between her outstretched arms, Astra looked like an avenging angel – a small angry sand-angel tearing a sandcloud into two. For a moment he wanted to smooth her matted hair, tease her like his father teased his mother, make her giggle . . . for a moment, he wanted to kiss her.

'What are you laughing at?' she demanded.

He pushed those thoughts aside. To marry a woman – to even kiss a woman you wanted to marry – you had to ask her father to approve your engagement. He was Astra's guide and he would get her to her father. If, right now, she wanted to talk about religion, that was good. Religion was a serious topic and you needed to agree with your wife about it, or agree to disagree, or else many disputes would arise.

'No laugh. Only think.' He'd had many Karkish friends at school. Scratching at the stubble on his chin, he summoned the distinctions he had learned from them and his Understanding Religions teacher. UR class had been the only one he liked at school, but it seemed a long time ago now. 'You right, Astra. Shlemun is prophet, not god – King Shlemun. Karkish people have one god, a big letter, no name, father God; and many prophets, many angels, many Kings. Somarians have many gods. River-god, wheat-god, rain-god, beer-god, sky-god. But Somarian sky-god is not like Karkish god. Not father god. He . . .' He paused. She had just said she didn't believe in a sky-god. Did she not believe in any god ar all? No wonder she was upset. He had to help her understand. 'Somarian sky-god sees the future. He give signs, talk to people. He talk to me. He talk to you now too.'

'How?'

Again, doubt shadowed her eyes, but again, shining furtively behind it, like a candle behind a curtain, something else flickered.

'He send *mergallá*.' That was obvious, wasn't it? 'Take us far from Lál-sil, far from road. Shlemun tell *mergallá* to stop. Now sky-god say: sun shining, we rest.' He stood up. 'First I give gift.'

He strode back to the camel, along the way picking up the storm gear they had flung aside. Astra trailed behind him and stood picking lumps of sand out of the camel's hide as he rummaged through his bags.

'What are you looking for? We need everything we've got. Muzi, we don't—'

'I give him lizards.' That should make her happy. 'No eat, okay? Give to the gods.' He found the bag. He should have cooked the creatures right away; the meat might have gone off after so long in his pack, but as long as they still looked good they would make powerful offerings. Lizards were the gift of 'disguise', Uttu had told him. He and Astra still needed to stay hidden; he could ask Shlemun for help with that.

Astra was toeing a rock. He dumped the bag out. A pack of dried bis-cuits, his mother's favourite wooden spoon, a sewing kit, a can opener and a bottle opener tumbled to the ground.

He shaded his eyes, looked up at her. 'Where my lizards, Astra?' She kicked the rock aside. 'I buried them. In the tent. When you were in Lálsil.'

'Why you do that, Astra?'

'They were going rotten! They smelled!'

Lálsil was days ago. 'No they not. They only just dead.' His anger was rising. If they'd dried in the heat, the lizards might still have been good to eat. He could have given one to Shlemun, roasted the other. He'd just walked three days through a *mergalla* . . .

She was pacing back and forth, pumping the air with her arms. 'You don't have to eat animals, Muzi. We've got lots to eat. And it's not *right*, killing creatures. It's *murder*.'

This again. After all he'd done to protect her, to get her where she needed to go. He was shouting too now, over her, that animals killed other animals; he would eat what he wanted to eat and she would leave his bag alone. If she wanted to survive this journey she would not interfere with any of his plans. She had to trust him – he'd got her this far, hadn't he? Finally she squared up to him, face-to-face, and pointed at the sand.

'I asked the earth-goddess what to do, okay?' she growled. 'I asked Her and She said to bury them.'

A minute ago she was turning up her nose at his gods. 'You don't believe in gods.'

'I do.' She jutted her chin, defiant, not apologetic, not *wifely*. 'I believe in asking *Gaia*. The goddess of the whole planet.' She pointed wildly up to the sun. 'Probably your sky-god is *Her* son.'

He regarded her in disbelief, fought off dismay. How could a man marry a woman if her goddess claimed dominion over his god? How would a husband ever establish his own realm if the wife thought her goddess was his god's *mother*? Such unions were not unheard of, but rarely were they happy ones.

'Sky-god and earth-goddess brother sister,' he told her flatly. 'Mother and father of all are the night and the sea.'

'Whatever!' Her dark eyes flashed. 'I just know Gaia told me to bury the lizards, that's all.'

She ran her hand through her hair, scowled at the knots. He reassessed the situation. At least she had a goddess. That was far better than not believing in any gods at all.

'It was weird, Muzi.' She sounded bewildered now. 'I fell asleep afterwards and in my dream it was like they were speaking to me. I thought maybe the skins were poisonous. Do those lizards normally give people bad dreams?'

'No.' He frowned. Some gods spoke to people through dreams. They could be very powerful messages. 'What did they say?'

'That human beings shouldn't be so dependent on metal. That we should talk in the shadows with plants and that I should be patient. I think it means I'm supposed to help the mine-workers and the women in Zabaria.'

He considered it. The message was confusing, but being patient and staying out of the light was about keeping hidden, which was what the *mergalla* had done for them. His gods were in agreement with Astra's, they were just not communicating with each other properly, that was all.

He relaxed. Things were clear now. If Astra had stolen the lizards to prevent him from eating them, he would have the right to be angry, but if the earth-goddess had claimed them, that was different. And, most importantly, they had established some common ground on a fundamental question. 'Okay, I understand. No problem, Astra.'

'Really?' She didn't sound as though she believed him.

'Yes. Lizards ears of earth-goddess. They will keep listening for trouble for us. But Astra, we must keep hidden. No go near road. We stay in desert.'

She looked out over the settling sand cloud. 'Muzi, I've been doing what you want for *days* now. If I keep walking through the desert, can you do something for me? Can you please promise not to kill any more animals when you're with me? Or birds. It upsets me. A lot.'

So this was the crux of it. 'Is a long journey, Astra. We maybe run out of food.'

'If we do, then you can hunt. But right now we've got plenty of nuts and grains and dates. We don't need to kill any creatures.'

There were a lot of things he could have said: because he had hunted, Astra's goddess had spoken to her, through the lizards. Their message was unclear, but she might have another dream later that would explain it.

Quite often the gods worked in such a manner. Plus, some roast meat would have been very good right now.

But he remained silent. Astra was hunched into herself, her face troubled. She was withdrawing from him, he could sense it. Not hunting made no sense, but it was important to her; if he didn't respect that, he would lose her. She would walk silently beside him all the way to Shiimti, and then she would disappear. Losing Astra was not something he could ever accept. But if he gave in, she might demand that he never hunt again. Why could she not just accept him and his way of life?

He sat, letting handfuls of sand run through his fingers. As he stared out at the bright hazy sky, another memory of UR class came back to him. They had been studying the three founding sacred texts of the Karkish people, and there was a verse in one of the books about hunting on pilgrimage. He didn't know the word for pilgrimage in Asfarian, but Astra would understand 'holy'.

'Okay Astra.' He brushed the sand off his trousers. 'We are making holy journey now. Some Karkish people say no hunting allowed on holy journeys. From now, from Shlemun to Shiimti, I am Karkish-Somarian.' She turned to him, searched his face. 'Honestly?'

'Yes, for true.'

The relief in her smile pierced his heart. 'Thank you, Thank you, Muzi.' She chewed at her lip. 'I'm sorry I didn't tell you I buried the lizards. We can give Shlemun something else,' she offered eagerly.

'What?' He scanned the contents of the bag but she was right, they needed everything else. Perhaps they could live without the bottle opener – but what would Shlemun do with that?

Astra squinted. Above them the sky vapour was evaporating, the sun a gold shield against the blue robe of the sky. Her face lit up. 'He talks to birds, right? We can give him a rook feather – one from the dream-catcher!'

Any last trace of confusion and doubt had burned off with the haze. The sky-god was speaking through Astra and – from a bright blue sky – sending a bolt of lightning through him: a memory of his UR teacher, explaining how Shlemun got his wisdom.

'Yes.' He leapt to his feet. 'Good idea. Best idea. Karkish god speak to King Shlemun in dreams.'

They made the offering together, sitting at the foot of the king. Astra took the three feathers from her pocket and they chose the biggest one.

She smoothed the vanes, realigning the barbs. He pierced the shaft with a thread from the sewing kit. Then she stood on the prophet's lap – he made her take off her boots – and looped the thread around a leg of the missing bird. The gift looked right there, dangling down against the King's luxurious beard.

She clambered down and stood beside him, inspecting their offering. 'Why is there a bird on his shoulder?'

'Bird is hudhud.' He tried to remember the story. 'Hudhud is Shlemun messenger. Take message to queen in far-off land . . . Theopia. Queen of Theopia come long way to visit Shlemun. Bring many camels, many gifts. Spices, gold, jewels. They have good visit. Queen go home happy, son in her belly.'

Astra giggled. 'She sounds like the women from where I come from.' She was in a very good mood now. There was an eyelash on her cheek, he noticed, a small black smile plastered in the grit and sweat above the cut from her mask. He thought he should point it out, perhaps remove it – he could do so with the tip of his finger, blow it up to the sun. But she was looking over his shoulder, east. Her eyes had widened, her face blank with alarm. He turned and followed her gaze.

The sand had settled. Below them to the east, shimmering in the sun, was a vast white city. Towers and pylons, building after building, low and flat, stretched out across the plain.

'I've got a question for Shlemun.' She shrank back behind the stone. 'How are we going to stay hidden now?'

He had no answer. And nor could he hide. Three metres away the camel had got to its feet and was wandering back along the ridge.

Kadingir

The odour assailed him the moment he entered the gym tent, a snake of putrescence stealing through the familiar fug of chalk and stale sweat. Water rose in the back of his mouth and for a moment he craved another dusty draught of street dirt and sun. Sweetish, like the stink of a heap of melon rinds rotting behind a juice shack, the smell of decay was not entirely repulsive – but it would be soon.

'Enki Arakkia! All hail our star warrior!' Pushing him into the tent, Lilutu announced his return. Flanking him, Bartol reached inside his jacket and withdrew the sword: Is-Land's Pain. The big man brandished the weapon, its lethal curve sheathed in its engraved scabbard. From their jumble of tables, Tablettes and solar panel leads, the media group looked up and cheered. Enki raised his unharmed arm and star-flared his hand in return. Behind them – was the name Ninsigal? One of the orphans, anyway – closed the tent flap.

'Welcome back, brother.' Bartol offered him the sword. Enki grunted and placed it across the arms of his wheelchair. Bartol's constant displays of deference, his pretence of sharing the weapon, were increasingly irritating. Enki's right arm was in a sling, his neck and shoulder a spongy mass of bruises and stitches and his fifth vertebra exploded into white-hot sparks of pain every time his wheels hit so much as a pebble. He was also running a temperature and could barely keep solid food down. He wouldn't be wielding his grandfather's sword any time soon and he was starting to wish Bartol would just keep the thing to himself.

'Do you want to address the media group?' Lilutu asked, like some kind of *aide-de-camp*. The half-Gaian girl had been annoying before the war, attempting to use their brief fling on the riverbank to further her aims within YAC, and now she'd spearheaded the firesands mission she was even more so – as though she had assumed deputy command of YAC, she was sticking her nose in the business of each working group, ordering Bartol about like a donkey. She'd even managed to show up with the big man at Enki's tent this morning, his *home*: a place he would much rather she didn't know how to find. But Lilutu had proved herself a warrior, he'd had to admit, and her current agenda appeared to mesh with his. She'd messaged him every six hours while he was in hospital, seeking his advice on the firesands plan and from all accounts following it. For that, he was willing to put up with her. Any sign of her sex games though, and he would tell her to scat off back to 'Zabaria or Shiimti – or back to Is-Land for all he cared.

'Later,' he half-gasped, half-croaked. On top of everything else there was a radioactive thistle stuck in his throat. Shouting was a major error, but if he kept his voice low people paid attention. He peered round, his eyes adjusting to the dim light. 'Is Eŝgid back?'

Bartol spoke first. 'Not yet.'

'He will be soon,' Lil insisted airily. 'It was a big job.'

Eŝgid should have returned from the firesands two days ago. At least he, Enki, was here. His mother had wanted him to stay at home, but she had been left to mutter and smoke and beat pillows and slow-cook bean stew. He'd demanded to be let out of hospital expressly to attend this Diplomeet and it would not proceed without him. Ninti and Malku he trusted, but Lilutu was capable of derailing any plans, even her own. And beyond all that, Una Dayyani needed to know that while Enki Arakkia might be off the battlefield, he was still in the thick of this war.

Lilutu steered him along the mats, up to the stage at the top end of the tent. He would rather be in Bartol's hands, but his friend was too tall for pushing wheelchairs, had to bend like a wind-crooked tree to reach the handles. What Enki needed was an electric chair: another reason to come to the Diplomeet. Now that Singul had been martyred, one was free and the family were bringing it to the gym tent today. It was bullshit that Singul was dead, but everyone wanted Enki to have the chair.

For now he was still at Lil's mercy. She stopped a few feet from the stage. The stench was stronger here and his stomach turned, but the sight of the heads made him want to bottle the stink: a perfume for YAC celebrations, holy occasions, his wedding night.

'The wheelchair repair team made the display,' Lil announced proudly. The heads were mounted on white plates on microphone stands, or poles welded to resemble mic stands, each arranged at different heights: low at the front of the stage, high at the back, all drenched in coloured spotlights – red, blue, purple and white. Lil skipped to the side of the stage and fiddled with a control panel hanging from a tent pole. The plates began to spin. Whooping, she waved a pair of imaginary rattles.

'We thought we could have a dance party after the Diplomeet. Cheer people up a bit.'

He paid no attention. On the stage, thirteen Sec Gen heads slowly rotated for his pleasure, their open mouths and drooping eyes dumbly acknowledging his victory, his right to inspect their every last pore and hair, approve their black seals of congealed blood. Thirteen slain IMBOD mutants. Even garish and shadowed in the spotlights, even with gaping mouths and slack eyes, they looked like handsome youths and beautiful girls – *striking individuals*, as IMBOD called them on the news – but that was an enormous lie. Their skins were different shades, their short hair kinky, curly, buzz-cut; red, black, brown. There was even a blond boy, with lank golden hair like some of the CONC officers. But inside their thick skulls the Sec Gens' rotting brains were all the same: the grey squelchy engines of subhuman killing machines. Several of the males had ridged brows; even the women's jaws were wide and square. One of these massive mouths might have mauled his own throat and shoulder. But all the Sec Gens' bone armoury hadn't helped them when they met Is-Land's Pain – his grandfather's sword. Fingering the scabbard, Enki felt a bitter tingle of pride spread across his chest.

'One of them is yours.' Of all the warriors in the world, only Bartol would not be crowing right now. Face to face with the evidence of his own immortal triumph, YAC's *real* star warrior just hastened to share the credit. 'Everything happened so quick, brother. I didn't see the one you got.' He pointed to the tallest poles. 'But those two are from the first night. They smell a bit more than the others, so we put them at the back.'

He didn't care which one he'd killed. The Sec Gens were all the same to him, and his family's sword was dedicated to YAC, wielded by the warrior who could raise it the highest. The only disappointment he felt was at the Sec Gens' expressions: the drooping eyelids gave them all a dopey look. Gravity, he supposed. It was a pity – ideally the faces should look harrowed, agonised, frozen in the devastating moment of recognition: death had come, for them, not for the Non-Landers. Perhaps if this spoilage issue could be resolved, the lids could be sewn open.

'The smell is getting worse, Lilutu,' Bartol sounded worried.

'They're fine,' Lil retorted. 'We've been keeping them in the fridge, Enki. And the formaldehyde is on order. But the blond one took a day or two to get here – some kids in Nagu One found it and didn't want to give it up.'

The blond male head had bruised temples and cheeks, torn skin. Perhaps the kids had kicked it about a bit, scored a few goals. Good.

'The formaldehyde could take days to get here,' Bartol fretted. 'And it's not just the blond one going off, Lilutu.'

'We should dry them.' The doctor had said to rest his vocal cords until they healed; he had settled on a policy of talking as little as possible to his mother, saving his voice for the meeting. 'What about a smoke hut? The lizard sellers in the market have one.'

Bartol exhaled, long and soft, as he used to do as a boy, pondering a maths problem Enki would inevitably solve for him. 'The smoke huts are for food, Enki. There might be health and safety problems.'

Health and safety? This was Non-Land, for the gods' sake.

'We should skin them and make lamps out of the skulls,' Lilutu announced, before he could take a dig at Bartol. 'I read how to do it on Archivia. You make a clean cut from ear to ear and peel the scalp back. If you scrape away the flesh and dry the skin it makes a nice soft cloth. We could stitch them together and make you and Bartol a pair of vest fronts.'

That was actually a good idea. Not that he wanted to tell Lilutu that. 'Maybe,' he said.

Bartol placed his hands on the top of his head. 'I thought we were going to give them back. I mean, sorry, trade them for something we want. Isn't that why we called the Diplomeet with N-LA?'

Now he barked. 'That's why we've *said* we called the Diplomeet. We haven't agreed to anything yet. These heads are solid gold. We're not letting them go cheap, understand?'

Silence. His throat blazed, his spine detonated and his vision chequered. As he sipped water from his flask, Bartol stepped over to the control panel. Just a week ago that broad back had been Enki's battle steed; now it was turned to him in mute rebuke. Oh Gods Who Have Forgotten Us, *grow up*, Bartol. This was war. There was no room for sentiment. You'd think a man who had beheaded fifty enemy combatants would get that!

Bartol flicked a switch, putting a stop to the party. As the plates slowly stopped spinning, voices rose from the tent entrance. With one hand Enki could at least turn the wheelchair to watch the YAC Singulars arriving in style, as befitting their new status as international media stars. There was the spider-armed Tiamet with her three sets of finger cymbals and big red drum; the double-faced singer Simiya in a new silvery dress; and the Seer, Asar, on his carer Sepsu's arm. The three icons were trailing a cloud of orphans. Ordering Lil where to push him, Enki wheeled around greeting people, getting news of the injured, sharing grief, discussing with Gitmalu and the others where the Singulars and singing bowl players ought to sit. In the end, it was decided YAC's musical stars should be positioned by the door, to make an impression when the N-LA delegation arrived and not distract from the heads on the stage. All the while, Bartol swept the mats clean, pulled gym machines to the edges of the tent, arranged chairs, but whenever Enki looked at him, the warrior's gaze was averted.

Let him sulk. What YAC had started was bigger even than Bartol now.

So this was the famous gym tent. Una Dayyani bestowed a practised smile of benediction upon the space. It needed a blessing. The gloomy enclosure was furnished with little more than a few grubby weights benches and rickety tables. And though high, the tent was suffocating. The stained and patched canvas could do with several slits cut through the sides and a good hose-down: it stank, and not just of rancid adolescent pheromones. Her nose wrinkled. Probably dirty dishes. Altogether it was an entirely depressing venue, though perhaps that could be turned to her advantage. Some sensible members of the group might well be amenable to the offer of some material aid development funding.

Or perhaps some music lessons. Graciously, she acknowledged the caterwauling din emanating from YAC's new international stars, noting in passing that the two-voiced singer was sporting a slinky silver lamé dress, the deafblind Seer and his carer were draped in gold-trimmed linen robes and the multi-armed drummer girl was decked out in a deep purple silk gown. Lamé, linen, *silk*? And how much would it cost to tailor eight puffed and ruffle-cuffed sleeves? Such quality fabrics and expert tailoring were supplied, to her knowledge, in only one market in Kadingir, the exclusive New Souk in Nagu Three, frequented only by the oldest N-LA families. So the YAC Singulars were making money, were they? And spending it on fripperies for themselves? Well, well.

Una sailed up the aisle between the wrestling mats. Her Chief of Police and Minister of Restorative Justice trod steadily behind her; her assistants Artakhshathra and Marti brought up the rear. There weren't nearly as many YAC members present as she had expected, no more than fifty people on the mats or in their wheelchairs, Tablettes glowing in their laps. By rights she should be addressing them all. Instead, the seats on offer – a rusty folding chair with a grimy cushion, a short-legged stool and a splintery bench – were facing the stage. Fighting a gag reflex as she approached, she understood why, and in the same instant, grasped the source of that foul smell: the Sec Gen heads were *mounted on sticks on the stage*. And . . . she stared, aghast . . . *flies* were circling that blond one. Oh please let there not be any journalists here. Did these wild-eyed children not have an ounce of sense between them?

It was clear she was intended to sit in the folding chair – it was placed in the centre, opposite Arakkia. But folding chairs were traps for a woman of her magnitude. Diplomeet decorum be damned, she swapped it with the stool, keeping the cushion, greasy though it was. She was wearing a dark red and black hemp robe, formal but not fancy, the patterned material unlikely to show stains. And she'd parked her bottom on far smaller perches in many a beer tent. Her ministers sat to her right on the bench, Marti took the chair and Artakhshathra wheeled in at the end. Settled not altogether uncomfortably, ignoring as best she could the ghastly trophies on the stage, Una took stock of the opposition.

Enki Arakkia looked terrible. The youth was haggard, his face incised and shadowed, his throat a darker purple than his shirt and crisscrossed with black stitches. At the sight of his sling, she felt a twinge of pity. For a man with no legs to lose the use of an arm was a dreadful setback. But Arakkia's dark, hooded eyes glinted more fiercely than that tin star hanging around his neck and she kept her condolences to herself. The other two members of YAC's core group were in much better shape: the limbless man, Malku, in his mouth-operated wheelchair, was assessing her shrewdly, and the small woman, Ninti, with whom N-LA had already had contact, was neatly coiffed and alert. At the far end of the row sat the giant, Barrol, looking none the worse for having slain fifty Sec Gens, if anything a little bashful; and another young woman, a skinny thing with a bad case of eczema. There were also two empty chairs, both, Una clocked, sturdier than the one she'd been offered.

The skinny girl turned out to be a note-taker, typing furiously on her Tablette as Malku led the formalities of welcome, presumably for some sort of live feed, while at the end of the N-LA row, a signer trans-lated for any deaf YAC members who preferred not to use a Tablette. In conclusion, Malku introduced the empty seats as belonging to a fallen warrior called Khshayarshat, and to Abgal Izruk, YAC's founder. Una vaguely remembered the old man and his pleas for funding for an alt-bodied youth centre. She had lived to regret approving that grant application.

In honour of the two empty chairs, Malku called for a minute of silence. She was grateful for the chance to lower her gaze from the stage. Someone in that line-up was a canny thinker. The vacant seats might be memorials to fallen comrades, but they also gave Una and her delegation clear views of the Sec Gen heads. Leather-skinned and clump-haired, their necks ringed with black crusts, the gruesome things were indeed attracting flies: she counted five of the pests. But the facial features were still discernible and, horrific as the severed heads were, the families would still want them back. Not only did she have to ensure that happened, she had to stop them being photographed like some sort of macabre shop window display and plastered all over ShareWorld: what a PR haemor-rhage *that* would be to mop up.

The silence over, Malku gave her the floor. It was ridiculous, not facing the group, but for the benefit of the orphans on the mats behind her, Una adopted her most ringing tone. 'Greetings to the Youth Action Collec-tive. The Non-Land Alliance congratulates you on your victories and offers condolences on the loss of your many brave warriors. We regret that you have decided to boycott the daily Emergency Diplomeets being held at CONC compound, but are glad of the invitation to meet with you today. As you well know, since IMBOD broke the Hem agreement by shooting an innocent boy, N-LA has supported your armed struggle. Nevertheless' – she raised a finger – ' as Tahazu Rabu, my Chief of Police; Zīl Nīngina, my Minister of Restorative Justice and I all agree, the con-flict has now reached a new turning point!'

'You lost Zabaria,' Arakkia growled, out of turn and so low she had to strain to hear him. Una met his surly, hooded gaze with an arched eye-brow. Before she could reprimand him, the wounded warrior jerked his chin at her Chief of Police. 'Rabu's officers *gave it away.* Gave our land and our people to IMBOD.'

The other YAC delegates stared stonily forward, except for that skinny girl, who was still furiously typing, transmitting Arakkia's breach of protocol out into the tent and into the world, for all Una knew. From the back of the tent came the sound of a woman gulping down sobs and beside her, Tahazu stiffened. From the corner of her eye Una caught Zil shooting her a frown. But Una forgave the transgression; or rather, she tallied it in a column opposite her rejection of the folding chair. Non-Land was at war; she couldn't afford to get hung up over tiny breaches of protocol.

'Chief Rabu,' she commanded, 'please give the Diplomeet the official N-LA response to the annexation of Zabaria.'

His granite face closely guarding the fury she had seen burst from him in private when the news from the east broke, Tahazu said, 'The Zabarian police were corrupted by the presence of the mine. That has long been known. We did our best over the years to root out the offenders, but too many were sharing in the illicit profits and pleasures of the Gaian mine-managers. Our fellow Non-Landers think, by defecting they will gain new powers, perhaps even Is-Land citizenship. They will be disappointed. The Gaians will treat them as slaves, just as much as the mine-workers. But we will have no sympathy for their plight. When we free the hostages, we will imprison the traitors. Trust me, Arakkia. Justice will be served.'

The crying at the back of the tent rose to a high whimper.

'Free the hostages?' Arakkia's voice was a hacksaw rasping against concrete; painful to listen to. 'I don't see N-LA sending forces to Zabaria.'

'We have been sending our forces into the *Hem*,' Rabu was the very model of controlled contempt. 'To protect *your people*, remember?'

'Protection?' The youth was a ghost, a deathless creature who just would not shut up. 'With sonic guns and sticks? We need firearms, Rabu. *Now.* We need to shoot from our side of the Hem, draw those monsters out into the streets—'

'Stop!' Una roared. 'This is a Diplomeet, not a beer-tent brawl. N-LA has the floor and N-LA will speak. There will be no firearms. There will be no raids on Zabaria. There will be no street battles. I need not remind you that our hospitals and cemeteries are already overflowing – this tent is not even half full.'

Those glittering eyes and insolent menace; that broken-toothed phantom of a voice, gnawing away at itself. 'We have made sacrifices, and those sacrifices will not be in vain.'

Shaking her forefinger at the youth, she addressed the whole tent. 'Let me be clear. We are not calling on YAC to surrender. YAC warriors have exposed the Sec Gens for the monsters they are, shocking the entire world. Amazigia is *outraged* at IMBOD's annexation of Zabaria and the firesands jail. From CONC to ShareWorld, global opinion is turning firmly against Is-Land. Thanks to YAC's courage, there has never been a better time to press our case for statehood. But we *cannot afford* to lose this moral momentum.' She spread her arms. 'Nor can we risk losing more lives. *Your* lives. YAC, please believe me, this conflict must now de-escalate. We must withdraw from the Hem and fight the diplomatic battle. To demonstrate our noble intentions and human values we must return the Sec Gen heads to their families.'

She expected a babble, at least a murmur. But there was silence, broken only by a gargled hiccough from the back. She marched on. 'As I have discussed with your core group, in return for your cooperation in these matters, N-LA formally offers YAC a permanent seat on the N-LA Ministerial Council. In recognition of the fact that your specific needs have been sadly neglected in recent years, we will also appoint our own Relationship Manager for Alt-bodied Youth Affairs.' She gestured at Artakhshathra who, to his credit, betrayed not a wink of surprise. 'My officer will be given a budget for project grants and material aid. You could use some new IT and gym equipment here, I see. Perhaps you would also like funding for a programme of art classes and creative collaborations with other Kadingir youth groups. Such applications will be looked upon most favourably. That is our final offer, YAC. It is made with gratitude, and for the sake of unity in Non-Land I beseech you to accept it.'

YAC had the floor. But no one spoke. Apart from Arakkia's, the faces in front of her were expressionless. Enki's eyes were glazed, half-closed, his skin grey and chill, but his mouth was twisted in a sneer and he was gripping his armrest so tightly she thought the metal would crumple in his fist.

'We don't want *impotent* statehood. We don't want *art classes*.' He was barely audible. His face was frightening. His eyes were rolling back in his head, exposing two vacant white crescents, and spit flecked his stubble like the foam of an exhausted camel. 'We want the Boundary to fall and we want to return to our ancestral lands.' She thought he couldn't possibly continue, but he clutched the tin star round his neck, thrust it forward. 'See this Dayyani? It's . . . a star. A *star* . . . is a burning vision to guide you, burning *forever*. You're—' His arm was shaking. With a great effort, he focused, met her gaze. 'Spreading the rumour that you're Istar, aren't you, Dayyani?'

She narrowed her eyes. He leaned forward. She remained bolt-upright. When he spoke, a fleck of his spit landed on her lip. 'If you're going to steal our vision, at least have the courage to follow it. We're not going to let you . . . *coopt and corrupt our dream.*'

The last words were hardly more than a breath, surely only she had heard them. She remained rigid on her stool. Arakkia was a dead man. He was finished, shot and consumed like a flaming arrow. He must be. The youth was a mind, that was all: a wilful mind blazing through a body that was collapsing like a heap of charred planks. For one split-second Una wanted to open her arms, take Enki Arrakia to her breast, let him drool on her robe, rest his noble head on her bosom as she ran her fingers through his sweat oiled black hair. He was her son, after all, the pride of Non-Land youth; her authority had created him as much as his own mother's body.

But Arrakia was also her mortal opponent. She waited while the message was transmitted via Tablette and sign language. It was peculiar. The silence lengthened. The core group members were sidling nervous glances at each other. And again, where usually at such stirring words whoops, cheers and whistles would rise from Enki's supporters, there was nothing – except that thin, whining buzz. Behind Enki the flies were circling those stinking heads, deliberating over which rotting cheek to munch on, where to land and rub their hairy little paws together in glee.

This had gone on long enough. She drew herself up. Two could play at speaking out of turn. 'One Land is a noble vision. I too was brought up to aspire to return to my family's ancestral lands, our villa and fields outside Atourne. But believe me, return cannot be accomplished from our current historical position—'

'Other Non-Landers have returned,' someone yelled from the floor. 'In New Zonia, in Nuafrica, *years* ago. We live on a *reservation*, in a *Bantustan*, while the Gaians enjoy our steppes, our forests, our lakes, our *homes*.'

Arakkia had sunk into his chair, eyes closed, but he nodded, acknowledged the support. She sighed. All right, he nodded, acknowledged the support. She sighed. All right.

'I am fully aware,' she snapped, 'of the deplorable shortage of teachers in our schools, but I thought we had at least managed to convey to our people their official status under international law. Minister Nñgina, can you kindly explain to all present the precise nature of our ongoing predicament?'

It was a risky move but no one objected, and Zīl stood and addressed the tent, speaking dryly as was her wont. Una hoped at least some of these ill-educated youths understood irony.

'Under international law, Non-Land,' the small woman cocked her head, 'or, to give it its full technical appellation, NL MesoX3, is neither a reservation nor a Bantustan. Nor is it technically a refugee camp. Legally it is exactly like all other designated Non-Land regions throughout the globe: that is, an environmental no-go zone, classified as unfit for human habitation, with the potential to be redesignated should conditions change. Other Non-Landers have returned to their homes, that is true. We, however, are uniquely unfortunate in that, in return for IMBOD's nitrogen-fixing seed gene, CONC gifted our emptied homeland to the Gaians. It is clear now from released records that at least some senior CONC officials believed the Gaians would never be able to detoxify the land. In tacit acknowledgement of the gravity of that error, CONC provides us with humanitarian aid and police protection when we need it. That is the uncomfortable and sadly sustainable status quo.' Zīl sat.

Una needed to seize the moment. She swivelled on the stool and faced the orphans. 'Brave youths. I salute you and all you have accomplished. I truly do. But please, consider this: when it comes to us, CONC has a guilty conscience, and after decades of struggle it is high time we capitalised on that fact. Compared to political refugees in other times and places we have many advantages. We have not been scattered, resettled, assimilated into a foreign culture. Rather, we have knitted our diverse social and religious traditions into one of the most tolerant democracies in the world. South of the Boundary we have access to as much land as we want. We have a voice in world government and a powerful friend in Asfar. With a change of political focus, away from violence and towards regeneration, we can attract funding to detoxify this land. When we are living peacefully and prosperously in our own viable state, the Gaians will have no reason to fear us. Then CONC will pressure Is-Land to open the

Boundary. Please understand: not even your great warrior Bartol can leap across a raging river. We need stepping stones, bridges – as for the stars, they burn for countless years. They give us all the time in the world to follow them. Let us move together, as one.'

Pinched faces regarded her. Were they fearful? Suspicious? Hungry? Grief-stricken? At the back, the double-faced Singular in the silver dress was comforting the eight-armed percussionist. Tiamet was her name, wasn't it? She was an ex-sex worker from Zabaria, rumour claimed. That would explain the tears. Una stood, letting the cushion fall to the floor.

'Youths of Non-Land, you have suffered enough. If you keep fighting in the Hem, if you send warriors to Zabaria, you will suffer even more, to *no end*. IMBOD will simply send more and more of their monsters to maim and murder you. And we will appear to the world like intransigent warmongers. All advantage we have gained over decades in Amazigia will be lost.' She swung her arm back towards the stage. 'If YAC keeps these heads, if you share images of this obscene display, the world will consider us barbarians, savages. Is-Land will win. Is that what you want for our people? When we could have freedom, dignity and a real hope of return for your children and their children instead?'

'*They* are the savages.' Behind her the small woman, Ninti, spoke tightly. 'The whole world knows that.'

Zzzzzz. Uh, uh, uh. Zzzzzzzz. Behind her, also, someone was gently snoring. She could only hope it was Arakkia.

Una sat down again, still facing the tent. 'The Sec Gens are Code monsters, rabid dogs, hyenas – we all know that. But their *families* are human. Their families are grieving, begging for the return of their children's remains and, believe me, their tears have watered sympathies in Amazigia. YAC, I urge you to return these trophies and in exchange accept N-LA's offer of a seat on the Ministerial Council and our full cooperation towards mutually agreeable goals.'

Amazigia was like Andromeda to these children, she understood that. The architectural marvel of CONC HQ, that gleaming white giant shell thronging with diplomats, was to them a distant dark pulse with no influence whatsoever on their lives. But she had done her best. Behind her, another snore tore the air.

Again, it was Ninti who responded. 'Thank you, Una Dayyani. Thank you, N-LA Ministers and Officers. YAC will consider your offer and reply as soon as we have reached a decision. Please, let us show you to the door.'

Zzzzzoom zig zag zoom . . . zoom zig zag zoom . . . Zzzzzoom in, zoom out, zig up, zag away . . . for the long shot, the big picture, the close up, the money shot, the tilt. History's just a matter of who's doing the looking and how. If we were as narcissistic as you, for example, we'd look back to the past and conclude that you worshipped us! Don't laugh – you'll swallow one of us! Consider the gifts you've lavished upon us: steaming fields of red carnage spread down the ages, abattoir middens dripping with offal and brains, sumptuous mountains of garbage left to liquefy in the heat, streams of raw sewage bubbling like soup through your streets. All your succulent waste and its foetid perfumes, your sup-purating banquets of poverty and greed . . . womb rot our long tongues burrow into, moist beds over which we scatter the confetti of our eggs . . . you could not worship us more devoutly if you tried. But we're not narcissists. We're opportunists, brokers, go-betweens, not gods. We see all things from all angles, all facets, upside down, inside out. We know human beings worship Death, but cannot bear to admit it, and therefore you hate your god's hairy black angels, his fat buzzing alarms. That's why you shoo, swat and spray us, sticky-tape, slap and trap us, rejoice when we fall. We forgive you. We understand. Zzzzzzoom out. Big picture! We don't mind your odd victory. Your gifts far outweigh your feeble attempts at retribution. If only one mammal makes it out of this cesspit alive, we hope it's you. So carry on! Carry on carrioning, pollut-ing and butchering, sweating and reeking, killing and shitting. We're here, waiting. For those wondrous moments you forget about us, expose your warm flesh . . . let us suck up your salt and dead skin . . . defecate on your eyelashes, puke on your lips . . .

Uwah! He jerked awake. Blinked.

He had been dreaming of flies – everywhere, flies, a buzzing black cloud swarming his face, crawling in his ears, tickling his lips, as if he was a Sec Gen, a decomposing head, as if the flies were inside his skull, black lamplights burning and buzzing, insistently transmitting messages he wanted to spit from his mouth, shake from his mind, slap from his skull.

But the flies were behind him, not in him or on him. The voices were human voices, arguing, complaining, demanding. He didn't know which was a worse nightmare, the flies or this Diplomeet. What had he missed?

cladding engineers and seal Is-Land off from the rest of the world. In the meantime, in many ways we've accomplished what we set out to do. We've shown IMBOD we can hurt them. We've raised a ton of money and support for our long-term goals. And we've got N-LA begging us to cooperate, offering us a seat in the Ministerial Council. We have to consider these new developments seriously.'

What was wrong with Malku? Building a ShareWorld fan base, setting 'long-term goals', cooperating with N-LA? This wasn't at all what YAC had set out to do. He would have to wait to rebut all these lies though; it was Ninti's turn to speak. He waited for Ninti, with her curly fringe and scimitar-sharp mind, to set the conclave back on track.

'I agree with Malku,' Ninti said. Ninti, with her bedside vigil in the hospital, her pearly-pink lipstick, her burgeoning friendship with his mother, betraying him too. 'We have to discuss this. And we also have to be realistic. We're lucky that Enki is still here to present his case. We've lost many of our best warriors and faced a far worse enemy than we anticipated. Eşgîd hasn't returned yet and maybe the firesands plan is too risky too. If I understand the sense of the meeting, most of you are saying you have fought long enough. In doing so, you have won important concessions from N-LA. Dayyani is offering us a seat on the council. But we could bargain harder – demand a place on the Amazigia delegation too. Then we can push our agenda at the highest possible level.'

'N-LA is . . . *bribing* . . . us,' he gasped.

It was one thing to speak out of turn with Dayyani, another to do so at a YAC conclave. He waved his hand, *Sorry, ignore me, please go on with your cowardly drivel.* But he'd touched a nerve.

Ninti responded, guiltily, 'I don't know, Enki. We need a stable income. The international donations are great, but we can't rely on them continuing to flood in.'

Dayyani had seduced Malku and Ninti with money. But the meeting was not over. Bartol would stand with him, and no one could corrupt Lil. However irritating Lilitu could be, she was at least a firebrand.

Sure enough, Lil's arm shot up and Malku granted her the floor. She stood. 'Fellow warriors, Enki is absolutely right to be suspicious of IMBOD. You know I have dissident contacts in Is-Land. They have authorised me to tell you that IMBOD is indeed working on a massive offensive plan – a plan not just to eliminate the Non-Landers, but to impose their fundamentalist, extremist brand of Gaianism upon the entire world. I don't have details yet, but I will soon. My hackers are drilling through the final firewalls; my spies in Atourne are waiting for crucial top-level meetings to take place. It is vital that we not relax into a false sense of security or faith in the diplomatic process. IMBOD are skilled at manipulating that process. They are also hostile to many of CONC's aims, in particular CONC's tacit support of meat production and the Abrahamic faiths. It is quite possible that IMBOD will seek to attack and undermine Amazigia too.'

Lilutu, as usual, was floating a grand but insubstantial narrative involving shadowy forces, religious warfare, covert operations – but she was also, basically, agreeing with him.

And so would Bartol. It would all be all right. The conclave would vote to keep fighting.

'But' – Lil pointed to the roof of the tent – 'Malku and Ninti are also right. We must carefully consider N-LA's offer.'

Could he propel himself from his chair, strangle her with one hand? What was she doing, appeasing those quislings, perverting his vision? For Lil was raising her own tin star to the crowd. 'Our star, the symbol we all wear,' she declaimed, 'means vision, yes, but also unity. Unity between the five points of the star: YAC, Zabaria, Shiimti, N-LA and CONC. IMBOD is attacking all of us, and only by working together can we defeat them. I believe we should take our seat at N-LA's war table, demand a voice in Amazigia. But at the same time, we must not give up fighting here. Our work in the Hem, I agree, is accomplished. If we need to we can resume it, but right now we must fight where we are not expected, in the firesands. If Eśgíd does not return, we must send another surveyor to try again. The success of the firesands plan is the key to freeing Zabaria and winning the unconditional support of CONC. Only then can we stop IMBOD from destroying not only us, but the whole world.'

She sat down to a smattering of applause, most of it from Tiamet's eight hands. He closed his eyes. Who was he kidding? He couldn't even be angry that she was appropriating his symbol to her own convoluted, self-aggrandising ends. It didn't matter what Lilutu argued, it was clear no one trusted her any more. She had whipped everyone up into a frenzy about her Gaian friend, but now that supposed Istar, Astra Ordott, had disappeared. She'd gone to Shiimti to meet her father and fulfil the Prophecy, Lil said, but to most people it looked like their Istar had deserted them, or just been a stunt in the first place. At her best, Lil was an ego-driven crowd-pleaser; he didn't want her half-arsed, alarmist support.

At last it was Bartol's turn to speak. Bartol was not a man of words. He would simply say that Enki was right. That he, YAC's star warrior, was determined to charge the Hem for as long as it took. His implacable loyalty would resound through the tent. Solidarity, perseverance, battle prowess; those qualities would speak louder than any wild speeches.

Bartol cleared his throat. 'My people. I am proud to have brought you these heads. They look much better in our tent than on the Hem.'

It was the second and loudest laugh of the meeting. Enki grunted softly, *Do it, Bartol. Turn the tide.* 'The heads give us satisfaction and they give us power,' Bartol continued. 'Enki is right, we must not sell them cheaply.' He paused.

Oh Gods Who Have Forgotten Us, what was Bartol doing? The big man was choking, his face in his hands. At last he lifted his head. 'I'm sorry.' He wiped his eyes. 'I understand why the core group wanted me to sit up here, but I'm not a leader. I'm not a speaker. I just know that when I fight on the Hem I am putting my fellow warriors in danger.' His face twisted. 'You encircle me and your bodies take the blows intended for me. Yesterday Singal died of his wounds. Last night' – his voice shook, tears spilled – 'last night Khshayarshat fell defending my back. I'm sorry, Enki. I won't vote on that question. I'll abstain. I'll walk out into the firesands right now if you like. But if the conclave wants to stop fighting on the Hem, I do too. I've killed fifty Sec Gens but I can't slay them all without killing all my friends too.'

Bartol. His brother since school days. His man-mount, the carrier of his family's sword, was crawling on his belly towards Una Dayyani. Enki's lungs hurt, his vision swam, his spine was shorting like a fuse. He had given his all, but it was like shouting inside a bioplastic bag; his words unheard, every breath sucking more air away until he thought he would suffocate on it, this utter betrayal by his own people. His best friend. He gazed over the crowd.

At the back of the tent, the Seer was swaying, his tall body waving at Enki. 'Asar,' he croaked. 'Ask Asar.'

They did it to humour him. But Sepsu, Asar's carer or partner or jailer, whatever she was, wily Sepsu reported that the Seer wanted to hear the collective decision. Malku opened the floor, but it was over. He had lost. Orphan after orphan spoke, and for every youth who vowed to surge again into the Hem, four or five wheedled and complained, cried over fallen warriors, asked when the ban on morpheus would be lifted and they could take it for their injuries. Enki switched off. He refused to help the conclave formulate the questions for the Tablette vote. He sat and let an enormous fly buzz round him, not even bothering to flick it away.

Ninety-one per cent of YAC voted to stop fighting in the Hem. Seventy-eight per cent voted to return the Sec Gen heads to N-LA on condition they were granted a seat in Amazigia. Forty-eight per cent wanted to abandon the firesands plan, triggering another round of voting, with the eventual decision to go ahead only if Ešgíd returned. Ninety-eight per cent wanted to lift the prohibition on morpheus for wounded warriors; seventy-four per cent voted to abandon it altogether. If Enki could have, he would have rolled straight out of the tent, never to return. But he could only spin in circles, dig a hole in the ground. His grave.

At last the torture was over. Malku, Ninti and Bartol all told him again how sorry they were. Only Bartol had the gormless decency to look it, Lilutu strode over, tossing her head and muttering, 'They'll see, Enki, don't worry. We're just waiting for Ešgíd now!' – as if the firesands decision was a great victory.

He ignored her. He was watching a fly. Yes. It landed, on his immobilised hand, the one sticking out of the sling. It was a bluebottle, iridescent and hairy. He swatted it hard, jarring his spine, gasped against the blinding pain.

The thing buzzed up to his face and flew into his mouth. *Disgusting.* He coughed, spat, grasped at the air, but his fist came up empty, the fly zoomed off.

Let the foul thing live. Let it lay eggs in the rotting flesh of his trophies. Let its maggots hatch back in Is-Land, beneath the sensitive vegan noses of the suffering Gaians . . .

'Enki? Brother?'

Bartol could stuff his concern. He was done with this charade of revolution, this pretence of resistance, this craven quest for power and influence. He had to get out of here. He needed relief. He needed, for the gods' sake, *morpheus* – yes, he would show YAC how to break your own rules.

Lil pushed him back towards the tent door. Ninsigal was opening the flap; a shaft of light fell through it, lighting up an electric wheelchair, pushed by a tired-looking older man.

'Enki, Singal's father is here. Do you want me to help lift you?'

Bartol again. Enki ignored him. Lil and Singal's father could manage. The man was heading towards them already. Behind him, Ninsigal was still holding the flap open. As Lil pushed Enki forward, another figure stumbled into the tent.

It was a youth with a backpack, clutching an iron rod. It was Ešgid.

The Temple

She sprinted after the camel with Muzi, dashing ahead as he lunged for the slithering rope, waving her arms in front of the camel's face and grabbing at its bridle. Together they tugged the beast back to Shlemun and tied the rope around the base of the statue, as they should have done before. Shielded by the shrine, she peered out at the city, bracing herself for the sight of a line of men heading up the slopes. Surely the eyes of all inhabitants had been following their mad caper across the ridge.

But there was no movement down in the valley. There were no roads even, just long stretches of sandy soil between the buildings which, it was clear now, were not low at all, but indefinably tall. To the north, the crown of an early-generation Tablette mast protruded from the sand, which the *mergalla* had swept up in heaps around the upper storeys of apartment and office blocks, ravaged structures made of crumbling concrete and blackened brick. Those roofs that hadn't caved in were trussed with wires, cables and antennae, cluttered with water tanks and big white discs like round lilies, their stamens pointing up at the sky as if straining to hear satellites muted decades ago. In the distance, on higher ground at the far edge of the sprawl, was a dark line of trees. Otherwise, it was a dead city: an Old World city, dead and still mostly buried.

'No one live there, Astra.'

Muzi was, she now accepted, often right. But that didn't mean he was *always* right. 'There could be bandits hiding from the storm.'

He stroked the stubble on his chin. The dark fuzz made him look older, his teeth whiter. 'We rest now,' he said. 'Take turns look out. Later we go on.'

There was little else they could do. It was annoying not to be able to set up camp on the eastern flank of the ridge, out of the glare of the sun, but it was more important to stay hidden. They fixed a makeshift tent with a blanket and two poles, enough shade for their heads at least. Astra wanted to eat next, but Muzi insisted on fussing over her cheek. Reluctantly, she let him: the sore was starting to itch and the last thing she needed was blood poisoning. First he got out the soap and the first-aid kit, laid out swabs and a bottle on a cloth. Then he filled a bowl with water. They had used a good third of their supply.

'We use piss cleaner from now.'

'Not for my cheek!'

He flashed a smile. 'For camel drink and washing.' He cleaned his hand and wrist, then, resting his short arm on her shoulder, he swabbed a stinging liquid into the cut.

'Ow,' she complained, but for once she didn't mind Muzi bossing her around. After the battle through the storm, against all this emptiness and the constant sense of threat, the light pressure of his arm on her shoulder, the scent of his musk, the closeness of his body, created in her, even more than the rise and fall of the camel's flank, a rare, tenuous, but precious sense of security. Who had last touched her gently like this? Lil, she realised. Lil, her own cheek split by that toxic rash, embracing and kissing her at the Star Party.

She pushed down the memory. 'Are you going to shave?' she asked.

'Shhh,' he commanded. 'I want you spread it now.'

She wondered sometimes if Muzi was a virgin. He didn't appear to have a clue what he'd just said. She obeyed, wincing as she stretched the lips of the cut further apart, allowing the disinfectant to soak deep into the crevice. Then she let him smear the wound with ointment and cover it with an awkwardly placed bandage that, stuck between cheekbone and jaw, wouldn't survive the meal, she bet. He was proud of his handiwork, though, sat back on his heels and smoothed the edge of the tape with a finger.

'I not shave.' He flung the sudsy water into the sand. 'Beard is protection. Is lizard message for me.'

Over the meal they assessed the situation. The line of trees looked promising, they agreed: a park or garden that might offer fruit and nuts, even water. Assuming they saw no people, they could head there and rest properly after their ordeal in the windstorm, hopefully bathe. It was an enticing thought, but not free of worry: surely an oasis would be well known, she pointed out, might attract caravans of Asfarian traders. Muzi disagreed: people used the roads in case of *mergallá-lá*, he said, and besides there was an oasis town two days' cart or camel ride southwest of Lálsil with inns and a market, where traders always stopped. Not quite trusting him, she checked the CONC maps on her Tablette. There was nothing marked, not even the huge ruined city.

Maybe Muzi was right and no one had been here for years. The alternative was to skirt the city, walk for at least a day more out of their way, so at last she agreed that, if they saw no one in the city, they would make for the oasis.

Muzi made her sleep first, though for not nearly long enough. Then she kept watch while he dozed. She saw not the slightest evidence of human habitation: no smoke rising from the trees; no flashes of colour or shadowy movements; no tattered flag raised to say 'we survived the storm'; no rugs or blankets hung out to air; no strings of laundry to announce life was returning to normal. When Muzi awoke near dusk, they packed up and said goodbye to the strange, cobbled-together King. She liked Shlemun's face, she decided: he might be Abrahamic, but he looked kind.

They made it down the slope easily, still without seeing hint of a living soul. Still, she entered the city cautiously. The shadow of the ridge was spreading over the buildings, the last rays of the sun illuminating their destination: the trees on the distant higher ground. To get there, they had to traverse a far worse desecration than the bone field back in the scrubland.

The bones were evidence of a great crime, but at least they were clean and dry and aspects of Gaia. The city was a filthy, oil-smeared violation of all that was holy. They trudged past pockmarked walls streaked with black stains, exposed rooms strewn with rubble, building after building laid to waste by bombs and fire and shrapnel, eroded by chemicals that might still be polluting the soil. South was a tarry black swamp; towards it stretched a long line of pylons, their triangular top sections askew, their broken wires whipped by the *mergallá* into chaotic tangles over the sand. Ahead was a snapped minaret, a tall thin pillar jagged as a tree blasted by lightning, a tortured finger accusing the vengeful Abrahamic god who had destroyed this place – nearly destroyed the whole planet. The longer she spent in it, the more she hated the city. It was irredeemable, a lingering abomination, a toxic relic of Old World arrogance and violence. Unlike crossing the bone field, it was very hard to feel respect for the ancestors who had lived and died here.

She was determined to get to the trees before sunset, but Muzi was dawdling, taking Tablette photos like some New Zonian tourist. She looked back to see him turning down a side avenue.

'Muzi!'

He waved. Annoyed, she pulled the camel round, found him peering through the splintered window frame of a long roofless hull. Inside, the floor was heaped with great lumpy piles of clothes and books and picture frames, broken chairs and a baby's cot, a crusty mulch of Old World things that had been bombed, burned, abandoned, rained on, buried and blasted with sand. Around the detritus, the grey walls were crying, smeared with long, unidentifiable stains.

Unexpectedly, her eyes prickled. This room had been a *home*. The room was like Uttu's house after IMBOD had ransacked it, only worse. She and Muzi were still alive, could go back and restore his family's house. No one would ever come and fix this place up. Only Gaia could help this city now, Her elemental forces breaking it down into dust. The thought only made her want to leave the city faster.

Muzi, though, leaned his weight on the window frame, then gave a little hop. The next thing she knew, he was inside the room.

'What are you *doing*?'

He pointed at a heap in the middle of the room. 'I just go there. One minute.'

'The floor could fall through. You could break your *leg*. Then what would we do?'

He stamped on the floor and her heart leapt into her mouth. 'No problem. Strong building.'

'Stop, Muzi! Can't you just take a picture?'

But he wasn't listening. He strode out to the rubbish heap, crouched and tugged at the corner of what looked like an oily rag. The cloth went taut in his hand, then tore soundlessly in two, disintegrating more than ripping. He held the foul thing up like a trophy, then clasped it to his heart. Fuming, she watched him skip back to the window.

'Look.' He thrust out a scrap of what had possibly once been a piece of chequered material, but was now virtually a cobweb.

'Get out of the building, Muzi!'

He jumped over the ledge. 'Is famous scarf, Astra. Very good luck.'

'We're going to *need* very good luck if you keep acting like this.'

Grinning, he stuck the filthy rag in his breast pocket. 'This famous town. Kingu and Gibil tell me many stories. Big battles here. Rebels take it from bad leader, keep it, make it safe place, many years.' He inhaled, slapped his chest. 'We breathe same air. We get strong inside.'

There must be dozens of Old World towns buried beneath the wind-sands, all of them reeking of oil and war. 'It doesn't feel safe to *me*.' She reached into her bag. 'We should wear our masks. The *mergallá* could have stirred up poison gas in the air.'

He was working a piece of the window frame free: another souvenir. 'War long ago. Air fine now, Astra.'

There could be unexploded munitions. Let him fill his lungs with sarin – what could she do about it? She put on the mask, turned and tugged Ariamá. 'Come on. We need to get to the oasis before sunset.'

The evening sky was streaked with crimson, the long clouds a scarf soaked with the blood of heroes: iron-rich, pumping, sun-hammered blood. The scrap of *keffiyeh* was glowing in his pocket, and with every step his heart lifted until he was bounding through the buildings, his feet barely touch-ing the sand. This was a legendary town. On each flat rooftop battles had raged; in each scarred room secret meetings had been held; through every last electric wire, vows of resistance had crackled and hummed. The sky-god had sent the *mergallá* to expose the town, had driven him here to teach him: *never give up*. If only he could explain it properly to Astra, tell the story as his father and uncle had told it to him: how the men and women of this town, and others like it, had fought like street dogs against the might of a tyrant, fought to save the whole Old World from extinction.

But Astra was striding ahead, not interested in the scarf, the graffiti bannered across the tops of the buildings, the shattered pots in which eggplants and tomatoes had once grown on the rooftops, home produce to feed the fighters. He let her walk on, fell behind, dipping down side streets and dashing to catch up, taking photo after photo of faded slogans in Karkish and Asfarian. Daubed in red and green wall paint, sprayed in black and blue, the slogans were poems, dream messages, the commands of the gods:

Tomorrow Glory Will Erase Our Worries . . . We Will Not Leave the Trench until the Night is Gone . . . Your Homeland is more Beautiful than Safety – Do Not Migrate

Beneath a bullet-marked wall demanding:

Stand on the Edge of Your Dreams . . . And Fight

he pocketed a worn heart-shaped shard of terracotta, added its weight to the legend of the fighters, stories he had heard since he was a child.

Though starving, tortured, fed and watered only on the great dream of freedom, the fighters had achieved extraordinary victories. Ordinary people – farmers, dentists, shopkeepers, women too, their heads wrapped against the elements in thick, chequered red and black and white scarves – had taken up guns to defeat their own brutal leader, a dictator scorned as the Mad Hamster for his big ears and overbite, who had tried to crush a peaceful uprising by torturing children and returning their mutilated bodies to their parents. The dictator's own army officers had defected and joined the rebellion; the Mad Hamster had responded with barrel-bombs and poison gas. Foreign fighters had flooded into the country, millions of people had fled, and in the vacuum, a third force – a dark, barbaric, godless militia – had arisen, determined to erect its own lawless nation from which to wage war against the entire Old World. The Mad Hamster had rejoiced then, for the Old World's governments had forgotten him, blackened the sky with jet bombers sent to destroy this malign new state – but then the Mad Hamster was squeaking his last, for the world's armies had picked sides, waged their own wars in the desert, and the broken borders of the country had not been able to contain the violence. The carnage had been relentless, epic; the end of days. Faith itself had been slaughtered; an entire people, a country – ultimately the whole Old World – had been destroyed.

But also, Kingu had told him, it had been a time of great vision. For amidst all the devastation, some of the fighters had liberated their towns, and when they did they worked together, people of all religious sects, cultures and languages, to turn their besieged homes into beacons of friendship and cooperation. They had created neighbourhood committees, community centres, food depots and childcare networks, volunteer schools. They had made videos – comedy videos! – and painted graffiti and banners, Inglish banners for the whole world to read. They had posted these images online, flags of defiance, messages to eternity: do not forget us; we are here, standing fast, defending the freedoms others squandered like loose coin. The people of the towns had been defeated in the end. But though the survivors had been scattered by famine, drought, disease, nuclear winter, the fighters' light was so bright not even the Dark Time could snuff it out. In camps in Asfar, the men and women of this war had inspired their fellow refugees with the epic tale of their resistance. Their stories had given rise to the Non-Land Alliance, Gibil had told him: the Dayyani family had been prominent in the towns' social networks; and from the fighters – from the scrawny street dogs who had fought like *lions* – N-LA had taken their founding principles of collective decision-making, restorative justice and mutual aid. Ahead was a tall pale blue building, two storeys exposed, its roof packed with satellite dishes, communication antennae and blue water barrels. Perhaps it was a hospital, or a police station. Or the rebels' headquarters! He took a photo of himself against it, the sun warming his face and gilding the antennae. He would show it one day to his father and uncle. Striding on, he took strength from thoughts of Kingu and Gibil. Gibil thrived on political arguments, snapping ideas down like cards on the table during beer-tent discussions or house calls from N-LA representatives. Kingu had given simpler advice. The art of resistance, his father had told him, was maintaining unity under pressure – and the way to do that was to always place other people's wellbeing above your own. *Without community, we are nothing, son,* Kingu had said. *A woman's role is to nurture community and a man's is to protect it.*

His father and uncle were being tested in IMBOD's jail. Muzi stopped beneath a piece of dripping red graffiti crying:

We Are Condemned to Hope.

He closed his eyes, placed his hand over his breast pocket and pressed the scarf scrap and the shard of terracotta to his chest. Kingu and Gibil would never break. With the help of the sky-god and the spirit of the fighters, neither would he.

'Muzi!'

He beckoned her again. To the left, down a long road of sand, was the crown of the Old World Tablette tower, a metal cage studded with flat white discs. It was the tallest structure in the town. He should climb that tower, get Astra to take a Tablette photo of him waving the *keffyeh* against the sunset. If only there were a signal here, he could find the story of the town on Archivia, show it to her. Maybe there would be an entry on the Shlemun shrine; she might be interested in that at least.

But they had left Tablette signals a long way behind them and Astra was not turning back for him. Ahead, the camel was nibbling at her shoulder. He smiled. Astra was a good walker, a good planner, and brave. She was afraid of the town, but she was prepared to take the risk of crossing it. He looked up again at the line of trees: they had still seen no one, and if there were oasis dwellers, they were most likely to be peaceful sorts. He hadn't wanted to tell Astra, but people did go and live in religious communities in the desert. If this were such a place, maybe they would even get a good meal there. Tearing his gaze from a large temple dome, remarkably still covered with flaking gold paint, he hastened his step to catch up.

They had to climb a steep slope to get to the trees, looping in hairpin turns so the camel wouldn't stumble. It was getting dark now, so they used their head torches. She spoke the bare minimum to Muzi. At the top at last, they stood at the edge of a dense line of trees. There was no sound. If there were birds, they were probably roosting – but like everywhere in Non-Land, apart from the Kadingir rooks and the wrens, she had seen none flying. She scanned the trees with her torch beam. She had been expecting date palms and there were many; but she could also see a dense black cypress and a broad oak. The palm trunks were etched with diamonds, their fingered leaves splayed in sheltering fountains. Between them, the dark plume of the cypress was a gatepost to this world, and beyond it, more palms, bushy plants and tall grasses, and what she thought was the reddish bark of a cedar. She hadn't seen this variety of vegetation since she left Is-Land. It would be calming, if not such a good hiding place for bandits.

Muzi whistled softly, 'Paradise of the Heroes.'

'Yeah, well, don't let's join the heroes just yet,' she snapped.

He was silent. She shone her light in his face and he stepped back, blinking.

'We're out of that stinking city now. We made it – to another dangerous place where people might try to hurt us. So no more stupid games, Muzi.' Her voice was trembling; what would she do if Muzi got hurt or killed taking risks like that? She stopped, directed the torch back into the trees.

'Hey,' Muzi said softly, 'is okay, Astra. I not hurt.'

'We haven't seen anyone,' she said at last. 'Probably there's no one here. So we can rest for a while, like we said. We're not climbing any trees, okay? We'll look for fruit on the bushes, or use the tent poles to knock them down. And if we do meet anyone, don't mention Shiimti – we'll tell them we're escaping the war, we were on our way to Asfar and we got blown off course by the *mergallá*.'

He was training his lamp up the cypress. Probably he had never seen one before. She pulled at the camel, entered the grove. In a hopeful indication that the place had been long abandoned, there were no paths, just a thick undergrowth of long grasses and shrubs. Muzi near her side, they trampled through it. She began to relax. If only there was water here: it would be sheer bliss to bathe, soak her hot, throbbing feet. She stopped and sniffed, but couldn't scent moisture. Behind her Ariamá was investigating a shrub. She tugged at her harness, not wanting the camel to eat anything poisonous, and examined the plant: a cluster of thigh-high leafy spears with erect pairs of pods sprouting from the stalks. She picked one and pinched it open. Nestled inside were two rows of tiny white seeds.

'Sesame.' Muzi was at her shoulder. 'Old World towns famous for sesame oil, sesame bread, *halva*, *tahini*, falafel. Kingu say sesame seed is secret of resistance.'

He was still in his fighter fantasy. But her mouth watered. And now she was in it, the grove was a lulling place, its shadowy forms mysterious and alluring. She relented. 'We'd better get cooking, then.'

'Good for you raw.' He scraped out a pod with his finger and stuck it in his mouth. She did the same. The raw seeds were bitter, but faintly nutty too, and the speckly coating on her tongue was a welcome, new and delicate sensation.

'We can add them to the porridge,' she said, poking about in a camel pouch for a bag. They moved on, she nipping off pods, he searching for firewood. It was a soothing task: half an hour ago she'd been marching across a foul urban wasteland; now she was meandering through a wild night forest, gathering a moonlit harvest of minerals and antioxidants and memories. As she drifted from plant to plant, her mind wandered too, back to chocolate *halva* and coriander hummus, to Nimma's special summer salad – oranges, strawberries and lettuce, drizzled with lemon and tahini dressing. And then she was back in the Earthship kitchen, with Nimma teaching her and Meem how to make nut yoghurt, Peat proudly wearing a moustache of sesame milk. For the first time since she'd left Is-Land, her thoughts of Or were not soaked in fear and despair. The tall spears, the sheltering palms, above all the small plump pods rustling in her bag, seemed to be whispering that memories of home were like tiny seeds that could be smuggled with you wherever you went, planted in new soil, nurtured and grown.

Muzi tugged some dates from a low branch. He plucked a fruit from the stem and pressed it into her hand. 'Good?'

The date was more than good. Its dark treacly sweetness was overwhelming. Like the light pressure of Muzi's arm on her shoulder when he dressed her wound, the taste of the fruit pulled her into a place she had once inhabited like a baby swimming in the womb, but now barely dared to dream of any more: a place not of pain, but pleasure. The rich, chewy date was the probing touch of his fingers on her cheekbone, the taste of Lil's kiss beneath the stars; the honey scent of the beeswax candle Muzi had burned for her on her birthday; and more than all that, it was the whole lost world of her life before Hokma's death: living skyclad in Gaia's bounty, feasting at every meal, immersing herself in woodland siesta, caressing and kissing and loving her friends, the way young people were supposed to. The way, she thought with a blossoming pang, she had once dreamed of doing with Muzi, before everything became so dangerous and hard and fraught with disagreement.

'Ummm.' Her appreciation emerged as a whimper.

Muzi tied his bundle of firewood up with a rope and slung it over the camel. He wandered on with a stick, waist-deep in the bushes, as though wading through a river, fishing for more dates. As she watched him patting a tree trunk, assessing its angle and height, sadness mingled with something close to shame in her chest. She had snapped at Muzi again, nearly shouted. Muzi moved like a gazelle, but was as hardy as a goat; perhaps she should accept that he might on occasion take a small risk.

'Shhh.' He turned off his torch beam.

What? She switched off her light. Her heart pounding, she willed the camel to stop snuffling and trampling. But apart from the beast, nothing stirred. Her eyes adjusting, all she could see was that it was dark ahead, too dark: a looming shape was blocking out the moonlight between the trees.

Muzi switched his lamp back on. She did the same. Their beams were illuminating a large building.

Still there was no noise except the camel snuffling at the plants. The building was a ruin, roofless like those in the city, but not half-buried. It appeared to be a hall or stately residence: steps led up to a portico with four stone pillars and shards of glass shone in the two round window frames either side of the gaping entrance, the double doors rotted off their hinges. After a minute, Muzi walked up the steps. Letting out the looped camel rope, she followed, to stand with him at the entrance, their torches piercing the dark interior.

A pair of eyes flashed at them from the far end of the hall, two black pools in a pale face. She gasped and her heart thundered.

Muzi held her wrist. 'Is okay, Astra.'

Again, she realised, she had been tricked by stone. The hall must be a temple. At the far end was an altar, a raised platform dominated by a statue of a woman – a *magnificent* woman. Unlike Shlemun, she was whole and smooth, carved from one block of stone, her eyes two gleaming black stones. Crowned with a headdress of snakes and adorned, amazingly, with a gold necklace, earrings and anklets, she was a queen, but just as obviously a warrior. Bare-breasted and clad in a long pleated skirt, she brandished a bow and a fistful of arrows, two broad wings flared from her back and she was flanked by two crouching lionesses. Behind her the wall of the temple was engraved with a radiant star and flying staves of grain.

'Istar,' Muzi whispered.

She wanted to run away, but she couldn't: she was rooted to the threshold, her blood tingling, head swimming. The last thing she had wanted to do was go along with Lil's crazy scheme and pretend to be Istar. She'd only agreed to do so to help the women in Zabaria. She was glad, very glad, to be far away from Kadingir, where people were, unbelievably, marching down streets waving her photograph on Tablette placards, calling her a prophet, a saviour. She had been thankful to escape from all that. But now, standing in the beam of that black gaze, it was as though the goddess was summoning her. And where Shlemun had seemed kind, Istar was fierce, proud, challenging. If Astra didn't obey her, if she turned and fled, those two lionesses would spring across the cosmos, trap her in their jaws, carry her back by the scruff of her neck and drop her at Istar's jewelled feet like a wriggling cub back at the paws of its mother.

The camel rope went taut and she pulled Ariamá back from wherever she was ambling off to. She had to get a grip on herself too. She had seen this figure before – where? That's right, in raised relief on the hammered metal doors of Major Thames' office. It would be amazing if she *didn't* ever come across it again. Istar was an ancient regional goddess; some Non-Landers were bound to have erected shrines to her.

Still, she needed respite from that unblinking black gaze. She scanned the temple. It looked as though whoever had built it had left decades ago. Any flooring had disappeared and the ground was thick with vegetation: mostly sesame spears, but smaller plants too, and to the side of the altar a young date palm, about the height of the camel. Still, it must once have been an impressive place. Below the remains of their long high windows, the side walls were covered with murals, the paintings faded and patchy but still visible: to her left was a caravan of richly laden camels; on the right a procession of birds passing, like the camels, through a desert, away from the altar, back towards her and Muzi standing at the door.

'Is your place, Astra,' Muzi said. 'We safe here. Sleep now, find water in morning.'

The camel was shitting, spraying its hard round pellets into the plants. He took the rope from Astra, led the beast into the temple and secured it to the young palm tree. Astra lingered on the steps a while, then finally stepped in and joined him.

He stared back at the entrance. 'Shlemun,' he whispered. 'And Queen of Theopia.'

The camel procession was headed by a woman, a queen, dark-skinned and resplendent in a jewelled robe and headdress, riding side-saddle on a camel festooned with gold harnessing. Behind her came more camels loaded with gold: lamps, vases, overflowing chests of jewellery and coin, all approaching the corner of the temple where, on the wall beside the door, the round window above him framed with painted sun-flares, sat a king on an ivory throne. There was no need to bring treasure to this man. His throne was perched on a mountain of bright gold sand. And he did not value riches, anyway. The king's hands had faded away and the hud-hud was beside him, not on his shoulder, but he was Shlemun. He had the same long beard and warm eyes.

The window on the other side of the entrance was encircled in a soft white glow, like the moon. Beneath it, the wall was filled with the King's marvellous bird; massively out of scale and separated from Shlemun by the empty doorway, it was nevertheless sailing in, claws outstretched, to land on his shoulder. Though the bird was not mighty or fierce — its needle-thin beak and beady eyes gave it the prim look of his old Asfarian teacher — it's plumage was a worthy dress in which to approach two monarchs. Its chest, head and crest were the colour of tangerines, rare fruit bought at the market for special occasions. The tips of the crest feathers, like the bird's arced wings and flared tail, were sharply patterned in black and white, pristine as a robe sewn by the most skilled tailor in all of the New Souk.

'*Oh*,' Astra whispered, 'it's a *hoopoe*.'

"Who poo". Reverentially, he learned the word. Then his heart leapt. 'You see in Is-Land?'

'No. It's extinct. They all died in the Dark Times.'

He shouldn't have hoped. The hudhud was *zaƀ*, a lost bird; one that had fled the Earth and was never coming back.

'I saw a programme about it once.' Astra was still whispering. 'It sounds like this: *Whoo whoo. Whoo whoo.*' The call echoed off the temple walls, hollow like an owl's but high and piping.

'So many birds *zaƀ*.' He indicated a white dove in the procession behind the hudhud. 'I see this one in Archivia.'

'It's a peace bird,' Astra said. 'That branch in its beak means safety.'

Silently, they followed the procession with their torches. Behind the dove came every bird he had ever heard stories about: a fierce brown hawk with yellow eyes, a regal ibis and an elegant crane, an orange, white and purple duck, a horned owl and a pink flamingo, and, bringing up the rear near the altar, a vain peacock spreading its extraordinary green and turquoise tail. A good artist had painted the birds. Not just wondrously coloured, they were touched with fine detail – the curve of a beak nostril, the glint on a wing feather, the snaking arch of a proud neck – and each was caught in motion, swooping or gliding or waddling towards their goal, an audience with King Shlemun the Wise.

He looked back at Istar. Though still gripping her bow and arrows, the goddess' outstretched arms had flung these two passionate processions out into the world: a powerful queen seeking a noble father for her child; a giant hudhud leading the rarest, most beautiful birds of the world to safety. Again he thanked the sky-god for sending the *mergallá*. The temple was their haven tonight. It needed no roof: above, the stars were its high vaulted ceiling.

The camel had settled, closed its eyes. Astra, though, was still nervous of bandits so they walked around, inspecting every inch of the ground. There were no camel droppings, no food rinds, no signs of fires or a camp. Parting two clumps of sesame, he examined the other plant that graced the temple. A low, delicate bush with branches like arched sprays, its leaves pointed upward like the feathers in the crest of the hoopoe.

'Shlemun's Seal.' He grasped the plant and pulled it up by the roots, Astra protested, but he shook the earth off and showed her the nubbly root. 'Leaves poison. Root good medicine. Shlemun give it powers. See?' He pointed out the ring-like seal on the root. 'I boil it. Is good for your cheek.' She looked doubtful, but he had made up his mind. 'This Istar hospital. We stay here tonight.'

Sleeping in the temple seemed too obvious, it limited their chance of escape should anyone find them. But she was trying to trust Muzi, so she unpacked, spreading out their blankets near the camel, then, needing a pee, took the urine filter outside. It was designed for men, but she scraped a hole in the ground, crouched over it and, controlling her flow, slowly emptied her bursting bladder into the funnel. Muzi used it next, and as they waited for the filter system to process the water, she helped him clear a firepit in front of the altar. She got a blaze going and Muzi cooked, stirring a bubbling dinner of spelt, dates and sesame seeds. She took her head medicine for the first time since the *mergalla*, then sat by the fire, hunched into herself. She had hoped Istar's unsleeping eyes would keep watch on the doorway, but they seemed to be following her wherever she went.

'We give her dream-catcher feather too,' Muzi said. 'Maybe she give you message tonight.'

She didn't want a message from Istar, but perhaps an offering would appease that imperious gaze. She took out a rook feather and the sewing kit and strung a thread through the quill. She wanted Muzi to present the gift to the statue, but he made her do it. She stepped onto the altar and tied the thread around Istar's right wrist. The feather hung there, twirling in the heat, the goddess's gold adornments shining in the firelight.

She sat back down, trying to feel hopeful. 'We must be the first people here in ages. Any bandits would have taken her jewellery.'

'No one take Istar's gold.' Muzi laughed. 'Bad move.'

That wasn't very reassuring. 'Do you think the people of the city made this place?' she asked. 'Or people who came after?'

Muzi tasted the porridge. 'Maybe both. Maybe Kadingir people come here.'

She had read that Non-Landers sometimes formed desert communities. The Non-Gaian movement had begun that way. But this place was beautiful and fertile. Why had they left? It was impossible to know. She just knew she still didn't feel good here. To Muzi, Istar and Shlemun were signs that the gods were looking after them; to her, Istar was more like a relentless unwelcome command, that black gaze ordering her to be someone she was not. She watched Muzi wrap a cloth around his short arm, slip it beneath the pot handle and remove the porridge from the fire. With the wooden spoon, he ladled out two bowls. The sesame seeds gave it an exquisite taste. She ate in silence, then put the bowl aside.

'I think your cheek is hurting,'

It was, a little. She shrugged.

'I make Shlemun Seal for you.' He opened the urine filter and sniffed the water.

'Ahh!'

She mustered a smile as he poured the filtered water into the washing up bowl and did the dishes. Then he chopped up the root, tossed it in the pot, added fresh water and put it back on the fire.

'I boil three times. Clean wound tomorrow.'

She sat, stone-heavy, silent.

'Thank you Istar and sky-god for guiding us here,' he said quietly. 'Thank you Istar for help Astra.'

She followed his gaze back up to Istar, but all she felt, yet again, was her own inadequacy.

'She's a goddess, Muzi. She's beautiful and strong and all-powerful. I'm just a lost refugee who wants to find her father. I'll do whatever I can to help free your family, but it's up to YAC and N-LA and CONC to beat IMBOD. Not me.'

'You beautiful, Astra. And strong.' He spoke simply, matter-of-factly, not to reassure or woo her but to correct her faulty thinking.

It didn't work. She wasn't beautiful. Not any more. Maybe she had been once, in woodland siesta, where everyone was beautiful, Gaians playing together in treehouses and birch glades, their bodies dappled with sunlight, brimming with affection, peaking again and again in endless amazement – but she had been ripped from that nest, banished to a land where everyone hid their bodies beneath clothes, her genitals blistered with an IMBOD implant, her head poured full of dark, diseased thoughts she didn't seem to be able to cure, no matter how hard she tried. Her brief taste of beauty had been stolen from her, or perhaps had always been an illusion, another IMBOD lie. Soon her classmates' faces would be as cruel and hard as Peat's as he passed by on the cavalcade; soon Sylvie and Tedis and Leaf would be running berserk on the Hem, biting and gouging and tearing the YAC warriors apart limb by limb. She hugged her knees tight to her chest, her thoughts spiralling down into a devastating conclusion that no filter could ever purify, no headache pill prevent, no moonlit wander through an oasis ever heal.

She had avoided her Security Shot, but she had been brought up and trained with the Sec Gens. Was she as ugly as them inside? Was that why she had attacked Ahn? Why she was so moody and angry all the time, so unforgiving and suspicious of Muzi? She was a Sec Gen gone wrong, aggressive and violent, but physically weak and riddled with guilt and regret. How on earth was she going to be able to help *anyone*?

She watched Muzi set the pot on the altar, her heart sinking, as if into quicksand, into a deep sudden welter of shame and despair. Muzi was stubborn and bossy, but he was also bright and determined and was trying his best to protect her: she, who had caused the death of his grandmother, the imprisonment of his family. *Muzi* was the beautiful one. Not because of his startling looks or his physical grace, but because of his nature. Look at him now, laughing softly to himself. She didn't deserve him. Because of her, his whole family would probably be killed.

Muzi gathered up his blanket and bag.

'Where are you going?'

'I sleep by door, with knife. Don't worry, Astra. You safe here.'

Wrapped in her blanket by the embers, looking up at the sky, sadness churned in her chest. The stars shed no comfort tonight. The stars were years and years away, maybe weren't even there any more. The whole universe could have ended and humans would be the last to know. Maybe the Dark Times really had ushered in the end of everything. Maybe it was foolish to fight it. Maybe humans should join the great parade of lost creatures, leave just a few slaves to help metal conquer the planet and turn it into one great big mine.

A tear seeped from the corner of her eye. Outside the temple a breeze had risen, whispering through the palms and the grasses.

You think it's the wind in our leaves, but really we're sighing and shushing each other . . . I know, I know, we're saying, a terrible mistake, a sap-leaking shame, but perhaps there's still time, there's still time . . .

The voices were soft and gentle, alluring and kind. She sniffled. *Still time for what?*

To become what you should always have been.

Like what? Stones? Statues that can't hurt each other?

No, no, child. Plants.

Plants? But we're animals. Violent, meat-eating, dangerous animals. Misery rose inside her again. It wasn't just the Sec Gens. All human beings were hopeless, greedy, selfish. They made beautiful things just to destroy them.

We know. We know. What a grievous error that was. Just imagine if the seeds of your formidable minds had remained in the sea, formed empires of algae, learned how to communicate with the whales, the dolphins, the reflections of stars – think of the vast, phosphorescent angels you could have become, eternal glowing dancers in the waves.

Unlike the lizards, the plants, if that's what they were, weren't trying to argue with her. They just sounded a little rueful, that's all. *It's too late now,* she responded.

Hands, mouths, guts, legs. The voices drifted on, as if they'd not heard her. *What need had your spirits of these? Consider if you'd crept onto land not as fish, but kelp forests, capable of cross-pollination with us – think of the living temples we could have created, the vast canvases of blossoms. What a glowing orb this planet could have been – exploding not with gunpowder, but wild raptures of colour, wafts of perfume, bursts of birdsong.*

That sounds nice, she sniffled. Perhaps this dream was a bedtime story, a little pillow to rest her heavy head on, keep it from sinking deep into the quicksand. As much as food and fire and water, people needed fairy tales just to survive.

Tumbleweeds, seaweed, the voices sighed, *if you needed so badly to move through the world – but plants, you should have been plants. In your deepest, most ancient dimensions, you are plants. Your bodies are lumbering mammals, we don't dispute that, but your minds are plant-minds. Think about it, child. Your desires travel like winged seeds on the wind, your words mingle like pollen on each other's tongues; you endlessly seek to 'blossom', 'bear fruit'; from time immemorial you have gazed yearningly at the birds as if they could take you somewhere new to 'put down roots'. Eventually you learned how to build birds, huge metal birds that would carry you up high, scatter you far and wide, as high as the moon. Those birds are rusted now, grounded. Most of the animals are gone. But metal is seeking to regain its grip on your souls. Isn't it time that your minds, at least, fused with ours?*

This story about metal again. She tensed. *Are you the lizards?*

The lizards? No, child, we told you, we are the plants, all of us here, speaking together. Do not fear us. Over the aeons we have fed you and clothed you, healed and enlightened you, opened your most secret doors to the World Within. Without hammers or claws, teeth or nails, we have torn down your tall walls, split the rocks rolled in front of your deep sacred caves. We whisper forever to your journeying souls.

The voices were kind, but like the lizards', their message was elusive. *Please tell me. What am I supposed to be doing? I don't want to be Istar, but I do want to help. How can I resist metal? Will Cora Pollen help me fight the rare earth mine and . . .*

Shhhh. Shhhhh. Don't worry, child. You are doing all you can. Just keep taking your plant medicine. Take too, all the time you need. There is still time, child. Time is still. There is time. All is still. Time is there . . . shhh . . . shhhhh . . .

She gave up trying to understand, but somehow it didn't seem to matter any more. She was taking her plant medicine, yes she was. And she had time, yes she did, she had nothing but time. The voices drifted through her as she drifted away.

He slept a long time, waking in the early afternoon. Astra was in a much better mood than the night before. She had set up a tent over him against the noon sun, put away the supper dishes and was filling the camel's dish with water from the urine recycler; he could tell that she now understood it was a sensible investment. He made a small fire and filled the kettle for tea; after that he would boil up the root stew again. 'We look for water today,' he said.

She grinned. 'We don't have to look far.'

The oasis pool, it turned out, was right behind the temple. She'd jumped over him in the morning to go to the toilet and discovered it immediately.

'I haven't bathed yet. I didn't want you to wake up and wonder where I was.'

She didn't seem worried about bandits any more. Leaving the root pot on the embers and their stuff in a pile by the altar, they took the camel, the water bottle and their clothes and blankets down to the water. There it was, the beautiful face of the underground spring that sustained all this growth: a still green pond with a silvery sheen, fringed by cedars and palms. He scanned the shore, wondering where best to tie up the camel. Beside him, Astra, in a sudden, swift motion, took off her trousers and tossed them behind her. Before he could react, she whipped off her shirt too and threw it over his head.

'Whoo whoo!' she hooted. 'Whoo whoo whoo!' He pulled the shirt away in time to see her running into the water in a great white rush. She wasn't even wearing her underwear. He caught an astonishing glimpse of a pale brown moon, a smooth bare back, then she disappeared completely. She re-emerged, just her head and shoulders, above the water.

'Throw us the soap, Muzi!'

The after-image of her bottom was still floating in his vision. He blinked, then obliged, and she jumped to catch the bar. Her small leaping breasts were like warm bronze stars, stars so bright they outshone the sun. He had thought Istar was beautiful, the *mergallá* a powerful force, but Astra naked was a wind that blew the breath right out of him.

She stuck out her tongue, then turned her back and began lathering her armpits. He looked up.

There was not a cloud in the sky. No hazy veil blindfolding the sun, no forbidding dark bank building over the trees. He tied the camel to a palm near the edge so it could drink and undressed himself, then he ran out too, yodelling and kicking up a froth. When the water reached his waist he dived under the surface and swam out at an angle, not to meet Astra, but to swim together in the same sacred pond.

It was a perfect day, shot through with gold lightning and complete as a pearl; no other day in her life could remotely compare to it. They spent the afternoon swimming and laughing and working together: picking dates and sesame seeds, almonds from a tree she found along the shore; washing their clothes and blankets and hanging them out to dry on a line strung up over the rocks. For hours Muzi kept his distance, dipping beneath the surface of the water, slipping behind the laundry or between the trees, but the glances she snatched of his body, supple as a fish's, sheened with water and sunshine, were splashes of wine replenishing the cup of her heart. She was with a beautiful friend, naked together in the fullness of the day; at times, she was overflowing with the joy of it, joy she had forgotten she knew how to feel.

In the late afternoon he stepped up onto the flat rock where she was sunbathing and sat a couple of metres away, a damp robe wrapped around his waist. Presently, she sat up, tying the robe she was lying on around her chest and he moved closer, offering her a rock, picking out the meat. It was companionably, cracking almond shells with a bag of nuts. They sat compan- like afternoons at her school swimming pool, only better: Muzi's mod- esty brought an unspoken *frisson* of uncertainty to the playful dance of attraction. She stole another glance at his smooth chest, his elegant feet with their long toes.

He brushed the nut shells off the rock. 'Your bandage falling off,' he remarked.

She peeled away the loose dressing on her cheek. 'The sun will be good for it.'

'I do root clean now.' He sprang up and headed back to the temple.

She lay sun-soaking. *Take your plant medicine*, the voices had told her. She stretched her arms, reconsidered last night. Lying here now, it was hard to believe how awful she'd felt before going to sleep. And then she'd had another strange dream. This one had been a soothing experience, but still, it was unnerving to feel almost physically possessed by voices, not just in her head, but in her whole body.

She sat up and looked over the water. A dream was just a dream. The most worrying thing was how she'd felt sitting by the fire. Perhaps it was something to do with missing a couple of days of her head medication; maybe it was just exhaustion from the journey, but whatever it was, she couldn't afford to feel like that: paralysed with despair and self-loathing. That was how IMBOD wanted her to feel. She couldn't succumb to it. She couldn't let Muzi down, Klor, everyone, herself most of all. It was frightening to acknowledge how much of a failure she felt sometimes. Even admitting it felt like a failure.

She had taken Dr Tapputu's pills again this morning. Checking the label for the first time since he gave them to her, she'd confirmed that one of the main ingredients was a plant, hypericum: the dream must have been a message not to forget them again. She wouldn't; and she had to remember, she told herself, that no matter how bad she felt, the mood would pass. Days like this were possible. Perhaps this dance of attraction would end without the dancers ever touching, but that would be fine. Muzi's beauty, the water's caresses, the sun's massage, were all in her aura now, like Uttu's shroud, a glowing shield against the ugliness of the world, a penetrating balm that might help to ease the violence within her. Muzi returned with an armful of firewood, the first-aid kit and the pot. She lay resting as he built a fire and boiled up the Shlemun's Seal brew for the third time. When it had cooled, he drained the stewed root through a bandage and tied the ends into a bundle. Crouching over her as she lay flat on her back, he pressed the warm poultice to her cheek.

'Thank you, doctor.'

'Okay, I not goddess slave. You hold it now.' He tapped her watch with his short arm. 'Half-hour.'

She took over. The poultice felt astringent; already her wound was tingling and puckering beneath it. 'What's it doing? Is it an antiseptic?'

He was still sitting beside her. 'Shlemun's Seal good for cuts and bruises. Black eyes too.' He laughed. 'Uttu teach me. Gibil get drunk, fall from the cart, bang his head. She get root from market, boil it every day.'

The plant was an anti-inflammatory. Lying there, her eyes half closed, she inhaled the bitter scent of the root as she watched the sunlight dancing on the water.

'I had root medicine too, Uttu say,' Muzi's voice drifted over her. 'For my hand wound. Every day for one month.'

It was the first time he'd mentioned his missing hand. Cautiously, she responded, 'You don't remember?'

'I was two year old. I hear some screaming sometimes, in a dream.'

She looked up at him. He was gazing out over the pool, his short arm extended, resting on a knee. 'What happened?'

'First people say accident, then after Gibil bang his head, Uttu tell me how.'

She waited.

'Gibil drunk. Not beer drinking; akik – very strong. He pick fight with Kingu. I follow him to sheep pen. He not see me, shut gate hard.'

She recalled Gibil, his stony face, his harsh temper.

'He must feel very bad about that.'

'He stop drink akik. Only beer drink, now. He get more angry too. But me, I okay. Lots of people in Non-Land no have arm, leg, I work, get married, have baby one day. Two, three babies. No problem, Astra.'

His last words were feather-soft. She was suddenly very aware of her body, stretching out before them, draped in wet linen, the sun warming her breasts, her belly, her Gaia mound. In her veins, her blood was humming a timeless song – a song she knew as a hymn to the moment. For Muzi, though, she sensed, the music might be the same but the words were very different.

She spoke slowly, using a simple future tense. It would be better to use the subjunctive, but she didn't know it in Asfarian. 'You will be a good husband, Muzi. And a good father. You're helpful and kind and a hard worker. And very loyal.'

The compliments sounded wooden to her, a mid-range school report, but, still gazing out to the opposite shore, he met them with a fountain of praise.

'You be very good wife, Astra. Strong spirit, good talker, believe in earth-goddess. And you beautiful. Beautiful as this place. More. This place, maybe one day dry up. You never dry. Your spirit always fresh like oasis water, always sweet like dates, always green like sesame leaves.'

At school they had read and written love poems. Praise songs to each other's beauty, seductive sonnets left in tree boles, effusive thank-you notes for sacred times shared. All she would have done, if he'd been Leaf or Sultana or Tedis, was reach out and kiss him. But she and her school-mates had all been playing the same game; she had no idea which, if any, rules of attraction Muzi had learned. She sat up, adjusted her robe and, keeping the poultice pressed to her cheek, searched his face. 'Muzi, look at me.'

He turned.

'Thank you, Muzi. I think you're beautiful too. I did since you gave me that candle. We can kiss if you like. We can' – what was the Asfarian phrase? – 'make love here if you like.' He flashed a startled smile, his teeth white as lambs; she pressed on, 'But I don't want to have a baby – and anyway, I can't, not unless I see a doctor. I have a birth control implant so I can't get pregnant.' She twisted, showed him the bump on her shoulder. 'Anyway, in my country we don't get married this young. Not until we're twenty. And Muzi, there's a war on. I'm Gaian. If IMBOD takes me back to Is-Land you can't spend your whole life waiting for me.'

He was frowning. She had spoken quickly and wasn't sure he'd under-stood. Or perhaps she had mortally offended him. She waited, a twinge of disappointment in her belly. It clearly was asking too much to spend the rest of the afternoon in Muzi's arms.

'IMBOD never take you,' he declared. 'They take *me* first.'

The liquid from the poultice dripped down her cheek, staining her robe. She sat back, the mood spoiled, the moment over, shadows of the neurohospice and the Barracks clouding the sun. 'We might not have a choice about that.'

He was silent. 'In *my* country,' he said at last, 'we not too young, Only both families must say yes. My mother and father and Uttu like you. We kiss now, okay.' Her heart thumped, a drum re-announcing her desire. He fixed her with his dazzling gaze. 'If you like kissing, Astra, we make temporary marriage, like in Asfar. Me, you, married for journey to Shiimti. In Shiimti, *if* you like, we ask your father. If he say yes, when you twenty we get married forever. If IMBOD take you, Astra, I find you. I never stop till I get you back.'

Married, married, married. All this just for a kiss, for a beautiful soul kiss. 'Maybe, Muzi. Maybe we could do that. But listen, getting married doesn't mean I have to do what you say. If we get married, we're a *team*. We discuss things, okay? Come to agreements. We try not to *argue* so much.'

He smiled. 'If you want kiss me, I not argue.' He leaned forward and brushed her lips with his.

Against all the uncertainty, the kiss added its own unassailable argument. It was like smelling a freshly baked cake: a sensation so subtle and pervasive that even though you knew it would end soon and the cake would taste even better, you didn't want to stop. She closed her eyes, let it happen. He pulled back.

'You my love, Astra.' His voice was soft as dandelion down. 'I want marry my love.'

She didn't know. Then she did. There was a war on. At any moment they could be separated, killed. Gaia had brought them here, to an oasis of peace and fertility, this temple of Istar and Shlemun and a queen who took freely what she wanted from a king and then departed back to her own realm. Here in this wet, green glade there were no rules except the ones they made and unmade for themselves. A temporary marriage was just that: just for now. Just for the journey. She reached for his face. 'You're my love too, Muzi.'

It was as true as anything she'd ever said. They kissed again, more deeply, exploring, nibbling, lips parting, tongue tips meeting. A moan rose in her throat and she dropped the poultice on the rock.

'Ey!' He broke the kiss. 'Half-hour, Astra.'

'You're distracting me,' she whispered.

'I doctor. I help.'

Together, they pressed the poultice back against her cheek. Then he laughed and set it aside and stroked her face and kissed her for a long,

long time, until she could bear his restraint, his fierce concentration, no longer and untucked her robe, let it fall to her waist. At last he ran his hand over her breasts, bent his head and sucked her nipples until she cried out, *oh yes please*. Swiftly, calmly, as though he'd done it a hundred times before, he pulled her up into his lap. Their robes bunched between them, she clasped her legs around his waist.

'You like kissing me?'

He was not teasing. She shifted in his lap, pressed her hips harder against him. Her breath warmed Muzi's eyelids, her fingers grazed Muzi's stubble, the molten seal between her legs was imprinted, at last, with Muzi's erection. 'I do.'

He gripped her, drew her closer, pressed his forehead to hers. His eyes were a blurred oasis of light. 'You want marry me, Astra?'

Marrying, merging, were just different words for the same thing. 'Yes,' she whispered. 'Married for our journey.'

There was one more wound to heal. She would have to tell him about her brand, the IMBOD Shield seared into her perineum, then seared again, how the re-branding meant she wasn't a Sec Gen, but a criminal, a rebel, an outsider always . . . but Muzi knew that already and together they would break IMBOD's spell. It would happen. He would plunge into her and she would rise to engulf him. They would make love by the water and again in the temple, offering their passion like a sacrifice to Istar and her lions, Shlemun the Wise and the Queen of Desire, the marvellous hoopoe, the parade of lost birds. As if attending a birth, the ghosts of worshippers, the people who had created and tended this sacred haven, would gather round and sigh with the trees and the grasses and plants. For here, entwined like roots and stems, tendrils and vines, she and Muzi would become mighty, immortal. The war was hunting them down, danger beckoned, but for one day they had all the time in the world. Cradling her head in his arms, Muzi rolled her to the ground, lay beside her, pressing the poultice of stewed root to her cheek, his body long and hard against hers, over hers, wanting hers, kissing and licking and whispering, playing with her hair as it dried in the sun.

The Tower

Samrod took the elevator to the dome and arrived precisely on time. The sniper positioned opposite swivelled, stamped and saluted, the clash of boot heels on metal echoing around the top of the tower as the other sentries followed suit, fists Samrod could not see swinging out from chests like clockwork hammers. A second passed. Silence. He didn't need to circumambulate the elevator shaft to know that Clay – of course – was not in the dome.

That did not mean Clay was late. Clay Odinson was never late. The Chief Superintendent of the Non-Land Barracks rocketed up to his public engagements precisely on time and if, on occasion, behind closed doors, his colleagues found themselves waiting a trifle longer than expected for his arrival, this was nothing to remark on; it was only to be expected that their commanding officer was being detained on highly important business. Far more important business than, for example, safely extracting the memories of the first Non-Land hostages IMBOD had captured in more than two decades. And infinitely more important business, it went without saying, than soothing the sensitivities of his Gaia partner of more than twenty years. Displays of those wrinkly sensitivities, in fact, were evidence of the need to steam-iron right over them. 'Jealous, are we, Samrod?' Clay had laughed this morning when he'd objected to the sudden change of plans for the Sec Gen. 'Perhaps it's time you took a dose of your own serum?'

It *was* time: to start work. To Samrod that meant setting up the lab; to Clay it meant giving Peat Orson a guided tour of the tower – a full morning spent lecturing the Sec Gen on the glorious history of the edifice before, thanks to CONC perfidy, it fell into N-LA hands. Thus had Clay avoided being confronted by the evidence of his own extreme foolishness: thanks to his little escapade last night, connecting the prisoners to the memory extraction therapy, or 'MET', operating system had been a nightmare endeavour, involving threats and far more officers than anticipated. Even the chef had been drafted in.

Glad, at least, of a break from the lab and its thus far thankless work, Samrod strode across to the window. Along with the cellar, the dome was the largest space in the tower. Empty save for a few gym mats, it offered light and fresh air, a draft coming in from the gun slots in the panoramic bullet-proof glass. He chose a spot equidistant between two of the snipers. The youths, not Sec Gens but still fit and skyclad, thrust out their chests. No doubt they were all intimately acquainted with Clay Odinson's management style and were hoping the mats would see active service.

They didn't know Samrod Blesserson. Let them sweat in suspense. Yet again, Samrod appreciated the power of being clothed amongst the naked. Required early in his career to cover his loins for meetings with international visitors and CONC officers, he had long ago made white linen trousers his signature look, donning them, like many urban dwellers, when amongst his fellow Gaians as well. Trousers were useful; they disguised both arousal and the lack of it and in addition, they kept his balls from sticking to his chair. 'Still so coy, Samrod,' Clay had crooned the night he'd arrived at the Barracks. 'We'll soon get you dropping those britches, wait and see.' But a scientist spent a lot of time sitting; the sweat pooled and those towels, hankies and spray bottles of citrus disinfectant people carried about were fussy things, always getting left behind.

The sentries turned back to their duty. He too gazed out at the scarred slopes of the firesands and the road snaking back towards the Barracks, Kadingir and beyond them, Zabaria. Obstructing his view were scaffolding poles; directly beneath him cladding engineers were working to Shelltech the tower. It wouldn't take them long to finish, but for now the upper scaffolding was empty. He was not alone though: small dark lozenges hung from the eaves of the tower: bats, big ear tips peeping out of their rubbery black wings.

Listening to us, are you? he asked. *What on earth for?*

This was the problem with lateness. It gave the waitee both the time and inclination for melancholic self-indulgence. He checked his Tablette clock. *Come on, Clay, don't make me regret this more than I already am.* Samrod had objected from the very beginning to the idea of staying at the tower, had wanted to drive back to the Barracks each evening, but now the Vision Council had decided to implement its long-term plans, Clay was Mr Safety First. 'Things are going to boil over now, darling,' he had tutted that first morning back in bed, stroking Samrod's thinning crop away from his high temples. 'You're far too valuable to send back and forth through the firesands during a war to end all wars.' The vision was of a long, covert war and Samrod couldn't imagine that YAC would be stupid enough to mount an attack in a minefield, but Clay wouldn't hear a word of it. 'I'm serious, Samrod,' he'd said, sitting up and pulling his boots on. 'I need you there. You can keep an eye on the cladding op and do the MET and your Sec Gen work and if you need to return to the Barracks you can come through Is-Land, via the tunnel. We'll set up a lab for you, second to none, and a five-star kitchen and a luxury suite.' He'd reached over and tickled Samrod's ear. 'We can import your favourite pillows, darling.'

I need you there. He was being shunted out to the tower, Samrod had understood, so Clay could keep fucking the Assistant Head Engineer without enduring his mopey looks across the dining table. But he couldn't say that; Clay had already explained that fucking the Assistant Head and cladding the tower were both strategic moves. The Head Engineer was still upset with Clay for provoking YAC into attacking her Boundary team and only slightly mollified by his decision to send some of them into the relative safety of the firesands. Clay would have her removed before too long and replaced with her subordinate. That the Assistant Head, a buxom young vixen with two other Gaia partners in the Barracks, was clearly just using Clay to all the advantage she could muster, was small comfort.

Samrod's gaze rested on a crater in the mid-distance. He had also held his tongue because after twenty-two years he knew not only precisely what Clay was like, but the futility of trying to change him. Clay was like the firesands: deceptively calm – but at any moment buried munitions could start exploding. At other times, like a desert mirage, Clay simply disappeared, sometimes for a couple of hours, sometimes for years. He never said he was sorry for these absences; on the contrary, he scoffed at any suggestion that he might in the slightest way be responsible for someone else's emotional state. Samrod blamed Clay's mother. His two Shelter fathers had died and the woman had doted on the boy to the point of complete self-negation. Her community was also at fault, of course; they should have ensured Clay had additional parents; instead, they had let his sole mother spoil him rotten. Spoiled for intimacy, that was; her concentrated devotion had produced a supremely charismatic performer and leader. Perhaps also because of the absence of a father, Clay craved the love of the masses – crowds of erect young men in particular. For nearly fourteen years Samrod had battled this infuriating nature, but eventually he had learned that the more worthwhile challenge was to battle his own.

The epiphany had come after their first major disagreement over the Sec Gen project, discord compounded by their domestic situation at the time. Clay's mother had finally died, leaving him her houses in Atourne and Sippur, and Samrod had wanted them to live together in the Sippur estate, tending its fabulous orchard. But though Clay had gladly installed him there in luxury, even put Samrod's name on the deeds, over the course of a year he had visited for a total of three weeks and two days. Samrod had finally made a clean break and started seriously – or at least regularly – seeing a local plant Code technician. But then had come that 'chance' encounter in Atourne, when Clay had been as playful and urgent as ever. *I wish you'd come back, Samrod. We need you.*

He had let himself be pulled back to bed, and in the morning, Samrod had recognised, for the first time, his own illusions about Clay. Though he had never expected or even wanted monogamy, all this time, he realised, he had been waiting for Clay to reveal himself, to gradually unpeel his psychological layers and expose his wounds, granting access to a deep reservoir of emotion. But in the pale dawn light, with his lover's mouth twitching happily on his pillow as he dreamed, no doubt, of conquest, he'd realised Clay had no such inner world to reveal. Clay was sheer vitality, the pure hunger of the life force expressing itself, and Samrod could not blame him for not offering what he did not have to give. The concept of emotional depth, Samrod had at last understood, did not apply to Clay: his emotions were permanently engaged in forward drive; he offered no reassurances, bore no grudges, harboured no regrets. But Samrod also knew this mode of being was not fail-proof. Samrod, in the background, had always quietly smoothed over Clay's indiscretions, cajoled his superiors, managed his political vision. *Come back.* To Atourne; to the project; to Clay's side. Not just 'we'; *he* needed Samrod. When he woke, Samrod asked him to say it, and he did.

Possibly that had been a mistake; now Clay knew the magic words, he wielded them to excellent effect. With the epiphany, however, had come the ability to continue, to endure all the small pinching hurts and appreciate anew the lifelong bond Samrod had forged with his first ever Gaia partner. Their sparks of touché and salves of ironic sympathy; the way he had sharp words with Clay when all else around lost their tongues, these were the bright and reliable blossoms on the gnarled tree of their love. Which was not platonic. While Clay's voracious appetites required relentlessly varied stimulation, his body still commanded Samrod's nerves. At some point soon, in the privacy of his luxury suite or Clay's, all Samrod's fretful annoyance would be discharged in an encounter that, for him at least, would make the wildest firesands explosion look like a matchflame. The snipers, the cladding engineers, the lab assistants, the Sec Gen, all the young men and women with their beautiful bodies and thick pelts of hair and yearning hearts . . . let them yearn. Let Clay crush those hearts like ripe fruit in his fist. Samrod and Clay had history, deeply entwined roots no one could sever.

Behind him came the bang of a door, the clatter of footsteps, the clash of the sentries' salute. The whole dome shook with the arrival of Clay. Who was – Samrod checked his watch – trying hard to please: only seven minutes late.

'Time for some exercise, pup,' Odinson urged. 'Go on, set the pace,' So Peat bounded up the steps three at a time. At the top he waited, panting, at the door. It was good to be skyclad again and working up a light sweat; even better to enter the dome behind the Chief Super and stride behind him towards Dr Blesserson, the envy of four of IMBOD's top snipers.

'All quiet on the eastern front, Samrod?' Odinson leaned against the sill. 'No mutant Non-Landers surging towards us from Kadingir? No traitor bats plotting to suck the blood out of our sentries?'

Peat regarded with interest the small dark parcels hanging from the eaves. He knew bats largely avoided contact with people, but on the off-chance one might fly in, he must be ready to grab it. He was immune to rabies, but even if he wasn't, it was his job to protect his commanding officers.

'Bats are much misunderstood creatures, Clay,' the scientist said mildly. 'Throughout history, we have largely considered them monsters.

In fact, they are our close cousins – the bone structures of their wings are remarkably similar to those of our hands.'

'You always learn something new from Samrod Blesserson,' Odinson stated proudly. 'Right, Peat, time to get the lie of the land.'

Peat followed his senior officers around the dome. South and west lay vast mounds of pale sand, shadow and silence. The view north was bisected by the long grey pulsing wall of the Boundary, behind which Is-Land's steppes rolled away to a distant horizon. It was a reassuring, yet also riveting sight. The line between beauty and barbarism was as arbitrary as that.

'What do you think, Peat?' Odinson asked.

'It's an amazing view,' he gushed.

'What's wrong with it?'

There were more bats in the eaves, but Odinson couldn't mean them, surely, Peat gazed east again. There was the oasis where they'd stopped in the night, the road, then sand dunes. Nothing but sand dunes. 'You can't see all the way to the river?'

'Good boy,' Odinson purred. 'It's not tall enough. But even so, it's the safest place in Non-Land – even safer than the Barracks at the moment.' He drew himself up. 'I'm ready to fight on the Hem, sir. Whenever you want me to.'

'Do you know why we've brought you here, Peat?' Odinson ran his thumb across his lips, a curious gesture that exposed his bottom row of teeth. Peat wanted to see him do it again. He flushed, glanced at Blesserson. But Blesserson's expression was unreadable.

'No, sir. I mean, apart from completing my slave rescue mission.'

'We do want you to observe the prisoner interrogation,' Odinson confirmed. 'But mainly, Peat, you are here for your own security. If they are not already, YAC will soon be trying to take a hostage, and we must make sure that hostage is not you. To hold the traitor's brother captive would create an international PR sensation. The YAC terrorists would undoubtedly parade you, goad you, do their utmost to humiliate you. And not only that. Tell him, Samrod.'

The scientist was looking out of the window. He sighed. 'As your chief Code designer, Peat, I am afraid that any Sec Gen hostage would be subjected to medical experiments designed to change your very nature, to make you renounce your beliefs and betray your core loyalties. IMBOD is constantly doing its best to refine your constitution, make you happier and healthier. Just being away from our care would be difficult enough, but to be subjected to such torture, forcibly converted to their abominable ideologies . . .' At last Blesserson turned, transfixed him with those deep, quiet eyes. 'It hurts me already, Peat, just thinking about it.'

'You're strong, Peat,' Odinson growled, 'one of the strongest we've got, but we don't want that to happen to you. Not after all you and your family have been through.'

He didn't know where to look so he settled for nowhere; the window was a haze, the two men blurs of authority he could not, but somehow had to challenge. 'You don't have to worry about me, sirs. I will *never* be converted. Doctor Blesserson,' he implored, 'please, let me fight on the Hem, fight for Gaia. Just give me something . . . a capsule in my tooth . . . and if they take me alive I'll swallow it before anything can happen. Chief Superintendent Odinson, my family will understand. They would make any sacrifice for Is-Land.'

He had defied an order. He would be thrown from the tower. That was fine. That was what he deserved. A Sec Gen who couldn't fight was useless, a disgrace to all who had created him.

'Peat,' Odinson's voice draped him in kindness. 'I understand that you want to fight,'

'You're Coded to fight, Peat,' Blesserson added velvet to Odinson's warm blanket. 'This news is almost impossible for you to accept.'

'But you're far too precious to us to lose to those Code freaks. And we have plans for you here at the tower. Big plans.' The Chief Super clapped a hand on Peat's shoulder, pointed up at the eaves. 'Gaia is reminding us, Peat, that every officer needs a batman.'

He was shaking. He had been trained all his life to fight. What the bats had to do with it he didn't understand. 'I d-d-don't know what that means, sir,' He fought back the tears; he couldn't let the sentries see him, a Sec Gen, cry.

There was a pause. 'It's an old Inglish military term,' Dr Blesserson said at last. 'He means a personal assistant.'

It was like getting a shot of instant painkiller. He looked, astonished, between the two men. 'You want me to be your . . . *PA*, sirs?'

'Not mine.' Blesserson blinked. 'The Chief Super's.'

'It would be a suitable use of your talents, Peat. And if I keep a close eye on you, the good doctor needn't worry you will fall into crude hands.' Odinson laughed. Blesserson did not. 'Are we all agreed, then?'

'Yes, sir!'

They stepped towards the elevator. The doors were ten feet tall and made of iron. Peat faced them, ready to leap in front of any threat to his commanding officers. The copper box was empty, but still he sniffed at the interior, alert to any sign of an interloper. Blesserson pressed a button and the doors closed. Peat maintained his sentry stance. The elevator slid down its shaft, opening again at Level Three.

'Start without me, Samrod,' Odinson said. 'I'll be there as soon as I can.'

He got off at the laboratory floor, expecting Clay to follow, but he didn't. The copper doors closed and he and the Sec Gen disappeared.

Samrod stood for a moment, letting the fury sluice through him. Had Clay gone mad? How much more of this was he supposed to take? But the answer was the same as always: as much as he could; more than ever before. That was the game, the challenge Clay offered. To always endure more than you dreamed was possible. Right now Samrod had a job to get back to. To do otherwise, to race down the stairs to the cellar, demand the return of the boy, would only prolong this ridiculous scene.

And when I want you to kneel and suck my hard cock, I will tell you to do so.

The Chief Super was behind him. Though Peat stared straight ahead, it was impossible to avoid glimpses in the elevator mirrors: Odinson's bolt-upright posture, ripped arms, taut buttocks.

He flushed, put it out of his mind. He was the Chief Super's PA. He was here to learn and serve, not indulge in illegal sexual fantasies. The elevator arrived at the cellar, its doors opening onto a large grey stone room lit by electric torches, steel brands shaped like staves jutting out from the walls. Boxes and hessian sacks were stacked in the corners, but like every Is-Land child, he knew that this place had not been designed as a storeroom. It was a war bunker. Picturing the long table, the famous Gaian officers who had sat around it, Peat drew himself up straighter. He might not be a Hem warrior any longer, but he was still at the heart of the battle for Gaia.

'Right, Peat.' Odinson led the way into the chamber. 'Fill your lungs with history. And prepare to keep a secret. Now you're my PA, I want you to see the real reason IMBOD retook the firesands jail.'

He did as he was told. The air was dry, with a smell of dust and roasted chicory, and beneath that the slight, incongruous tang of pine. Odinson gestured to a large steel panel embedded in the wall, its surface aflame in the torchlight. He strode towards it, his body casting long petalled shadows over the flagstones. Peat followed. Grooved and grained, the steel panel resembled wood.

'Oh my beauty.' Odinson stroked the panel. 'Those ignorant Non-Landers neglected you, didn't they? But as long as I'm in charge, you'll shine like gold.' He pressed his palm against a knot engraved in the steel. 'Open sesame!' he hissed.

The panel slid open to reveal a yawning black void, taller than the tallest Sec Gen, broader than Peat's arm span. A strong scent of pine wafted into the chamber. For a moment he was back in the dry forest, hunting for caves.

'Behold, Peat, IMBOD's portal to Is-Land. When the tower was first built, this tunnel was a vital passageway for personnel and supplies; later when the outpost became our External Ministry of Justice, IMBOD doctors and lawyers used it to travel in and out of Non-Land safely. There were many attacks on the road at that time, and we couldn't risk losing men and women of Dr Blesserson's calibre, could we?'

In the light from the cellar, he could see rail tracks set into soft soil, sloping down. The walls were reinforced with thick wooden beams and the roof lined with steel. There were lamps on the beams, uplighters shaped like shells, but Odinson made no move to turn them on.

'No, sir.' Was he being invited to respond further? *Why did we give up the tower, sir?* could be interpreted as a criticism of his superiors. He cleared his throat. 'What happened to the tunnel during N-LA's tenure, sir?'

That was the right phrasing. Odinson's expression sobered, his face taking on that noble set that moved Peat to the marrow of his bones. 'A dark chapter, indeed. As you can imagine, my predecessors fought tooth and nail to avoid the tower falling into N-LA's hands, but CONC was adamant: *A gesture of goodwill,* Amazigia said. We deactivated the biometric keys at both ends, of course and pumped the tunnel with a – well, we'll call it a *dissuasive* gas.' He gifted Peat with a smile, his sharp canines gleaming in the torchlight. 'It's been thoroughly re-oxygenated, don't worry. That smell is the cleaning agent. Shall we explore?'

His skin prickled. 'Yes, sir.'

'Careful of the tracks,' Odinson strode into the tunnel. Peat followed. They soon reached the limit of the cellar light; now they were walking straight into darkness. Unnerving at first, the walk soon became a game of trust, in which he aimed to copy the beat of Odinson's boots. Then the sound of the boots deadened; one more step and there was carpet under foot. Two steps later, Peat bumped into his commanding officer's buttocks. He stepped back, trembling. His cock was suddenly stiff and bright as one of the cellar's steel torches.

'Do you think the bats would like it here?' Odinson had moved, was circling him in the darkness.

He had an *erection*. 'They like caves, don't they?' His voice threatened to break. *Please don't turn on the lights.* He steadied himself. 'Yes, I think so, sir.'

'Blind as a bat,' Odinson mused. 'Samrod is right, Peat. We don't understand bats at all; we project our own fears onto them, that is all. *Eeek, eeek, eeek.*' He leapt and squeaked in Peat's ear.

Peat nearly jumped out of his skin.

Odinson laughed. 'What do you think bats would say about us if they could talk?'

He had detumesced, at least. 'I don't know, sir.'

'Maybe something like this?' Now Odinson was behind him, breathing on his nape, and when he spoke next, he affected a lisp. *'In your fantasies of diseased saliva, vampiric appetites, tangled landings in our hair, you write your own morbid fear of each other. You look at birds and imagine soaring into the heavens, trailing splendiferous feathers, but in fact it is we, the bats, who are your shadow souls set free.'*

It must be a Gaia hymn. But he struggled to follow. 'Bats can see well, I know, sir.'

'Bats see everything, Peat.' Odinson moved away again. 'They peer in from the eaves of our dwellings, into our bedrooms, our most private chambers. They see us struggling to communicate, hear us shouting and sulking, watch us wrapping ourselves in blankets to weep.'

The Chief Super, he sensed, was confiding in him, revealing something deeply personal that he had no way of responding to. Torn between awe and unworthiness, he fell silent.

'Yes, what would bats say if they could talk?' Odinson was in front of him now, bathing him in stealthy warmth. 'They'd say Peat, that people are not adept at intimacy. Bonding, parenting, even maintaining close friendships we find difficult. Most of us swoop erratically from one disappointing encounter to another. If we are wise, we learn to "turn a blind eye" to our loved ones' defects and if we are lucky we meet someone who returns the favour: who knows when to leave us alone.'

Odinson was so close he could feel the Chief Super's chest fur brushing his pecs. He could barely breathe.

'We humans talk a lot, don't we?' Odinson's mouth was steaming his shoulder. 'When it's our bodies that communicate best. Isn't that right, Peat?'

'Yes, sir.' The dark swallowed his voice.

'Our bodies want to fuck each other, don't they, Peat?'

Again his heart clawed out for Odinson, again his mind slapped it back. There had been a mistake. The Chief Super couldn't possibly know how old he was.

'S-s-sir . . . I'm sorry. I'm nineteen. I don't want to get you in trouble . . .'

'This tower is *my castle*.' Odinson punched him in the chest.

He staggered backwards, gasping for breath. The punch didn't hurt, but it sent shockwaves pounding right up to his brain.

'*I* make the law here. Everyone here understands that. Do *you*?'

'Yes, sir,' he whispered, then loudly repeated, 'Yes, sir. Very much, sir.'

Out of nowhere, Odinson's hands were all over him. Clutching his head as if to crack his neck, shaking his shoulders, sliding into his armpits, swiftly running down his slick chest to grab his waist, his hips, probe his knees and ankles, then up again, to grip him as if assessing his readiness. Peat gasped. With enormous difficulty, he resisted the violent urge to throw his arms around his officer, lunge for a kiss, feel that grizzled beard rub his mouth raw.

'Batman Orson' – Odinson was massaging him, long firm rhythmic strokes – 'your physique pleases me, as does your eagerness to serve. But it is clear that, due to the significant challenges you have faced, you require special training to bring you up to the standards required of my personal assistant. Do you agree that you would benefit from time spent under my intimate supervision?'

He could barely hear. *IMBOD couldn't be authorising this* . . . The thought evaporated. All that mattered was keeping that hand exactly where it was. 'Yes, sir, sir,' he panted. 'Yes, *sir*.'

'Good. Now—' Odinson tugged hard, then released him. 'On your knees!'

Odinson had abandoned him. In shock, he dropped to the carpet. Then Odinson's hands were back on his shoulders, at his throat, Odinson's whiskers at his ear, 'Forget bats, Peat Orson. Forget being my PA. From now on *you are my dog*.'

Suddenly the tunnel was flooded with light. He blinked. The walls were black brick. The carpet he was kneeling on was red and stretched between the rail tracks into the distant darkness of the tunnel. Either side of the tracks stood rows of padded benches and what looked like gym machines, but this was no gym; instead of weights there were harnesses, shackles and ropes; balls and sticks, a climbing frame and, at the end, a cage. The door of the cage was open and beside it were two silver dishes.

Odinson crouched beside him, stroking his head. 'You are a sad puppy, Peat,' he crooned, 'such a sad puppy. But I am going to make you all better. You are sad because your loyalty gene has been tested to breaking point. People have betrayed you. People have died. Women have gone berserk and good men have not stopped them. You can't trust anyone any more, even yourself. But I am going to restore that sense of trust. In order to accomplish this, you must obey me, *no matter what I tell you to do.* Do you understand, Peat?'

His heart was hammering so hard he thought he might tip over. He nodded hard. That was what he did anyway. He could not *not* obey Odinson.

'Good boy. From now on, Peat, you will wear a collar, a muzzle and a chain. Except when I order you to stay in your kennel or run with the pack, you will not stray from my side. You will speak when spoken to and call me master at all times. I am a loving master, a good master, the best master you will ever have. I will test your limits and when we reach them you will howl the word "Or." When I hear that word I will stop the lesson. If I hear that word too often, I will send you back to the Barracks and find another puppy to train. Do you understand? If you do not agree to these terms, you are not ready to serve me and I will release you back to the Barracks immediately.'

He thought he might melt. There was no need to fear any more. Odinson was claiming him. Like an underground torrent, gratitude poured through him, sluicing away all he had suffered – all of it, Astra's betrayal, Laam's terrible death, the old woman with the neck that was so easy to

N-LA was gone. He felt feverish and his voice was shot, but his mind was focused again. He took out his Tablette, typed with one finger:

Dayyani is DELUDED

The nudists will NEVER allow us independence

Once Boundary is clad, the Gaians will EXTERMINATE us.

We have CASH now. We MUST >>>>

! buy firearms, draw the Sec Gens out into the streets.

!! push ahead w/ firesands plan.

This will force CONC to send international troops back to Kadingir. Only when CONC fighters are at stake will CONC negotiate seriously.

THEN we can lay down our weapons and return the heads —

IN RETURN FOR RETURNING

If we stop now everyone who died died >>> for no reason.

Deluded, nudists. Exterminate, hate. Return, returning. No reason, out of season, treason . . . He could make a rhyme later. Right now, he just had to make the arguments. He pressed send, waited for everyone to read his final statement. His position was clear as a polished mirror, surely.

But when Malku spoke in response, it was as though to placate a raving, fevered child. 'Enki is understandably suspicious of the Gaians,' Malku generously granted. 'And of course we all want to see the Boundary fall. That will always be our long-term aim. But the situation is constantly changing and we have to analyse conditions carefully. To start with, there's no evidence that the Is-Landers are planning to slaughter us.'

He groaned. Even if he could speak, there were no words for this.

'Obviously, they'd like to.' Malku made a joke of it; people laughed. 'But if they do, they'll lose all the CONC support they depend on. We mustn't forget that IMBOD needs CONC. It needs Server Gurus and international engineers, expert Coders and seed-bank contracts.'

Malku had fought on the Hem the first night, in a bristling tank-chair pushed by orphans, his soft bulky body caged by metal bars. But it made more sense for him to stay off the battlefield, chair the meetings, direct strategy. *Obviously* he'd had too much time to think. On and on he droned, in his cheerful, methodical manner, 'The only way IMBOD can kill us without severe diplomatic consequences, is in open battle. And though we were all expecting the Sec Gens to take the fight to us, they haven't. It's entirely possible that IMBOD does just want to protect the break. All those things had had to happen, he understood now. They had occurred in order to single him out, make him ready to be selected for the greatest honour a Sec Gen could ever hold.

'Yes, *Master*,' he sobbed. 'Thank you, Master. Thank you.'

Odinson buckled a collar around his neck. The rim was hard but the interior was lined with felt. A chain hung down his back, coolly swaying against his spine, a leash in Odinson's hand.

'Good boy, I knew I sensed promise in you, young Peat.'

A string of saliva drooled from his mouth onto the carpet, plush crimson, perfect for rolling around on. That ball right there was soft and rubbery and just the right size for his jaw. The cage was the exact dimensions to crouch inside, beating his tail against the floor as his master approached down that long dark tunnel. Where would he poop? He didn't dare ask, risk a reprimand so soon. But *oh, oh, oh*, there was a sandpit beside the cage, from which protruded a little tree stump.

A tree stump to wee on. Peat's eyes watered. He waved his rump higher, straining up against his master's big stick. His master thought of *everything*. He had the very best master in the world. He craved one thing only. 'Please, Master,' he whimpered, 'please may I lick your hand?'

Odinson yanked the chain so hard he gulped. 'Licking my hand is your *reward*. Do you understand? When I am done with you, you will *beg* to lick my hand.'

He thrust his rump high in the air, waggled it, wordlessly pleaded, *I'm sorry, I'm sorry, please train me, I'm a bad dog, I'm so ashamed, I need to learn how to please you.*

His Master's big stick began to grind against his hips. 'Don't you worry, sad puppy. Don't you worry. We've all the time in the world to get it right.'

Another unedifying image arrived on his screendesk. Samrod filed it under 'Sexual Peccadillo,' then observed, once more through the one-way mirror, the four robed bodies strapped to the upright gurneys in the treatment room. The scene looked dramatic – the blindfolded, gagged and helmeted subjects, polygraph harnesses banding their fingers and chests, cranium probe cables snaking back to the monitor – but two hours and thirty-two minutes of intensive memory extraction treatment had thus far yielded precisely nothing of interest – in fact, quite the opposite. Clay should be here, helping to relieve the boredom. But yet again,

Clay was not late; no, not at all. He had said, breezily, 'Start without me, Samrod, I'll be there as soon as I can.' Vague punctuality, however, was the least ground for complaint. Quite apart from the question of what exactly Clay was doing with a nineteen-year-old Sec Gen, his antics at the flypit might have seriously endangered any chance of the treatment's success. The only significant memories so far had been gleaned at the Barracks from the children, who now had nothing left to offer except leverage should their parents require it. The children had revealed the existence of an older boy by the name of Dumuzi, or Muzi, a youth the family had hoped might marry Astra Ordott – who, it transpired, had worked at CONC with the old woman Peat Orson had accidentally killed. The boy had blue eyes and was missing a hand. Such details were useful; IMBOD had sent word out via the usual channels and was following up on some promising leads. But the children had no idea if this Muzi was a YAC member, or where he might have run to with the Ordott girl given the chance, and thus far the adults were proving remarkably resistant to treatment.

MET was, sadly, not like searching a Tablette hard drive. Willing subjects, children, the mentally disturbed and chronically confused, were relatively open books, but uncooperative and cognitively competent adults either had to be drugged – slowing the process down by weeks, sometimes months – or bribed. Torture or threats were counterproductive. Properly conducted MET gave almost one hundred per cent accurate results; the use of violence, however, made it far too easy for false memories to evade detection. When the body was under immense stress, even the best polygraph could not always distinguish a desperate lie from a hard-won truth. Clay knew that, but he still had indulged in his little outing, no doubt to impress the Sec Gen. Samrod had compensated as much as he could for that excess. The prisoners had been well fed, the males given topical anaesthetics, all of them jailed together and treated as well as possible. But one of the Non-Lander males had been in IMBOD's jails in his youth; he had no doubt learned the treatment-blocking techniques then and educated the others about them. No matter what verbal stimuli the junior officers attempted – 'Astra Ordott', 'Muzi', 'Istar', 'Is-Land girl', 'YAC', 'N-LA' – the neuroprobes had not yet harvested even the faintest sketches of the youths. The imagery so far was all of sex and violence: robed men stabbing, throttling or dismembering sky-clad men, and a panoply of vaginas, erections, breasts, even – naughty

Non-Landers! – anuses: all the classic textbook aversion techniques. Non-Lander women would often break first, Samrod had found, perhaps ashamed of getting aroused amongst hostile strangers, but these two females were furiously at it, raising steamy walls of sexual fantasies. One had peaked six times in the last half-hour; from the look of the footage on his screendesk, she was imagining being fucked by both men. The oasis incident was still actively working against the treatment too: the males' walls against the probes were mainly built of vengeance scenarios, interspersed with sex as a reward for butchering a Sec Gen.

Still, it was obvious the subjects were hiding something, and given enough time, Samrod would find it. The key was to be patient. Eventually most people ran out of stimulating fantasies and began to experience despair or fatigue; eventually they would become vulnerable to kindness and promises. When their guard finally slipped and trust was established, a reward-based strategy could work wonders. With wholly willing subjects, the probe was even capable of identifying false memories the subjects themselves believed to be true. It was a fascinating topic; Samrod had written an article about it early on in his career. Genuine false memories, he had argued, were generally simple misremembrances of mundane details: names, dates, the colour of a hair ribbon; useful things to ascertain for a court case. The wholesale unconscious manufacture of events, on the other hand, was extremely rare. In the case of early childhood sexual abuse, for example, the child's brain had simply not yet been able to form discrete memories and the extreme emotional reactions had been stored holistically, in the body, to be triggered again by relevant stimuli; or in puberty. MET was not particularly useful in such cases; the evidence for the crime could not be extracted in an image file, but lay in psychosexual habits and associations it could take a lifetime to unlearn.

He rubbed his temples. He would be lucky if this particular treatment didn't last a lifetime. Two hours and forty-one minutes . . . In the probe chamber, the interrogation officers adjusted the settings. Samrod opened a Sec Gen performance stats document on his Tablette, scratched his bare chest.

'Dr *Blesserson*.' Clay flung open the lab door. 'My sincere congratulations.'

Two hours and fifty-eight minutes. He swung round on his officer chair, noted the familiar flush of sexual success high on his lover's cheeks.

'Thank you, Clay,' he responded, dry as a martini. 'Though results are inconclusive as of yet.'

Clay chuckled, shut the door. 'You are too modest as always, Doctor. The results are *stupendous*.' In two steps he was straddling Samrod in his chair.

'Clay!' The junior officers could not see them, but could hear every word. Clay thrust his groin into Samrod's lap and tapped the mute button on the screendesk.

'Young Peat Orson is absolutely delicious.' Clay kissed his head. 'I'm nominating *you* for back passageway biotect of the year award.'

Clay was heavy and Samrod's legs not what they used to be. He slapped his lover's buttock, then pushed the heel of his palm against Clay's sternum. 'Might I remind you that young Orson's Gaia tunnel is not scheduled for adult entry until next month?'

'Oh, Samrod. Always so punctilious.' Clay dismounted and, still grinning, perched on the edge of the screendesk. 'Call it an early birthday present. He's been working so hard for us, after all.'

Samrod smoothed his trousers. 'Where is he then?'

'I left him in the tunnel.'

'Alone? Clay, I told you—'

'Oh *shhh*. A little solitude will make him grateful. I'll bring him up in twenty minutes and he can suck you off, my darling. It's time you relaxed a little.'

I'd be perfectly relaxed if you just concentrated on the work at hand, he didn't say.

'Bring him up now, Clay. He must only be tested under controlled conditions.'

That gleeful chuckle again. 'Rest assured, Samrod, the conditions are strictly controlled. Now what's been happening here? Do we know where that Muzi boy is yet?'

The longer he argued, the longer the Sec Gen would endure without company. 'Not yet. They're blocking the probes with the usual drivel.'

'Non-Lander action.' Clay chuckled. 'Let's have a look. Any horses yet?'

He brought up the cloudy footage on the screendesk. 'No. But this woman fancies a threesome with her brother-in-law. And when the men are not imagining stabbing you, they have clearly given their own thought or two to back passageways.'

'Oh, these tiresome creatures – so unbearably tame. Don't they get Asfarian porn sites here? Look, we don't have time for this, Samrod. Tell them all that if they don't start answering our questions, or at least start producing some fantasies of note, we'll pipe a colony of sandflies up their children's arses.'

He winced. 'Clay. How many times do I have to tell you: no more deviations from protocol. You know pain and threats can invalidate results.'

Clay flicked the objection aside. 'I've read all the studies – you just have to do another polygraph later and sieve out the lies.'

'Some will always slip through. And results acquired under duress won't stand up in an international court, thanks to an annoying CONC document called the Global Abolition of Torture Act. Perhaps you've heard of it?'

'Those pedants in Amazigia. What do you call this if not duress?' Clay gestured at the mirror. 'They're hardly here under their own free will, are they?'

'They are prisoners. We have the right to question them. We've promised not to hurt them any more, and preferential treatment if they cooperate. Unless you want to drug them and wait months, a dangling carrot strategy is the way to proceed, Clay.'

'And they believe we don't want to hurt them? That we'll let them go at the end? They're Non-Landers, but they're not completely stupid.'

'Maybe, yes, they might find it difficult to trust us after your antics last night!' He took a breath, controlled his temper. 'We have since given them clean clothes, a meal and medication for the sandfly bites. We have given their offspring Tablette games and soft toys. The adults will want to believe that we will let the children go at least. Clay – I am letting you play with my toy – *my* Sec Gen. In return, you must now let me handle the MET.'

'Oh, is that it?' Twinkling, Clay reached for the crotch of his trousers. 'That I'm not playing with Samrod's toy? Not nearly enough for his liking?'

Despite his anger, or because of it, his flesh stiffened. Then Clay was leaning over him, forcing him back in his chair. 'I've been neglecting my favourite toyboy.' Clay's musky scent was all over him again, then his mouth was on Samrod's.

In all these years he had never met anyone who kissed him like Clay did. The succulent taste of his tongue, its finesse, the hint of brutality in the bristling pressure of his jaw: if Samrod could isolate the gene for Clay's kisses he would be a billionaire. He closed his eyes and accepted the probe. Then he pushed his lover away again. 'Not now, Clay. I'm serious.'

Clay stood. Eyes closed, to the count of ten, the Master of Desire detumesced. Facing the glass, he pressed his knuckles into the screendesk. 'Look, Samrod, I know what you're thinking: that whole ghastly Hokma situation; those petty bureaucrats chasing you down. But you don't have to worry. There are no law courts here, no CONC. There are just my officers, who obey my orders. We'll carry on your way for now, but if a little pressure is needed to hurry things along we can double and triple polygraph and corroborate between the subjects. They're just sheep-shaggers, Samrod, not trained mind-control agents. And if even a squeak of un-above-boardness ever gets out, I will deal with it, I promise. Like I dealt with Hokma for you.'

He plucked at his trousers, smoothed out the folds. And here it was: the crux of the matter. It still made him white-hot with anger, thinking of his sister, waltzing up to his house, demanding he excuse her brat from having the Security Shot, emotionally blackmailing him into breaking the law. He had done it, not because he thought he owed Hokma anything, but because he wanted to draw a line, stop her from bothering him ever again. And then what had happened? Not ten years later his sister had turned out to be the worst traitor IMBOD had ever uncovered – and he had found himself implicated in her crimes, right up to his eyeballs. Clay had rescued him, yes, but he had made enemies, people in the Wheel Meet who would love to see him go down. The truth was, he needed Clay as much as Clay needed him.

'All right.' He sighed. 'It's you who's depending on accurate information, not me. Give me a few more days and then you can take over. But I'm serious about the Sec Gen too. I don't want him broken. For one thing, his Shelter father knows how to make a pain of himself; if Klor Grunerde-son loses another child we could have some serious investigations to contend with.'

'Thank you Samrod. And we're not going to lose Peat. He's going to have the time of his life here and afterwards you're going to delete all his memories of us and return him to Daddy as good as new.' Clay sat down and took his Tablette out from his hipbelt. 'Go and get him now. Tell him Master said to give you a good licking if you want, then take him to the clinic and run him through whatever sort of tests you might fancy.'

He should have gone straight to sort out the Sec Gen, but this was so *infuriating*. Why did Clay persistently refuse to understand his work? "Delete"? "Good as new"? I've been trying to tell you, Clay, memory dispersal treatment is incredibly delicate. Of course I could blast his brain, give him early onset dementia, but that is not what I am trying to achieve.'

'Delete' was a layperson's term. 'Buried' was not accurate either. During memory dispersal treatment the probes accessed data held in long-term memory, gradually fragmented it, then attempted to associate the fragments with REM activity. The idea was to transform a deeply felt memory into a misrecalled, insignificant and eventually forgotten dream. But memories were not simply stored in the brain; they affected the entire organism in ways that were still imperfectly understood. The body continued to react to trigger stimuli, even if if the mind didn't understand why the body was experiencing discomfort, high anxiety, even suicidal depression. All Samrod had managed to do so far, he sometimes thought, was wrap a thick blanket around human distress; despite all his ministrations, fear and misery festered on.

'Sweetheart!' Clay pouted. 'Of course the Sec Gens are a work in progress. But you can't be precious about them. We have to see how far we can push them. Those are our orders. Didn't I tell you Stamen Magmason is taking a personal interest in the project?'

So that was it. The National Wheel Meet Chair was poking his fingers in Samrod's pies again. He was the last to know, as usual. 'I'm sure Stamen would love us to train up a few interns!' He let Clay snigger. 'But Magmason doesn't understand my work either. The Sec Gens' loyalty gene can't be switched on and off like a light bulb. If powerful hormonal responses are attached to a memory and then I disperse that memory without the subject's knowledge, terrible confusion could result. Peat would need years of follow-up treatment.'

'Then we'll give him that treatment. Money is no object, Samrod; you know that as well as I do. Stamen's made a limitless budget available for the Sec Gens.'

'And now I understand why.'

He couldn't keep the note of hurt from his voice. Clay swung round in his chair, faced him directly. 'I wasn't keeping anything from you, Samrod. The potential only became apparent during training; Stamen's vision has only slowly emerged. And it's a stunning vision: the *Sex Gens*. Think of it.'

Clay's eyes widened as he went on. 'No more kidnappings, no more scandals. Instead, willing participants – children who actively *want* to be beaten and cut and fucked hard, whose wounds will heal overnight.'

He could barely sputter a response, but Clay raised his palms. 'I'm not thinking of myself, Samrod. It's a political breakthrough: a solution at last to the perennial problem of how to meet the sexual needs of ultra-alpha humans without shredding the social fabric.'

'It's madness. A recipe for social *chaos*!'

'No, Samrod, it's the natural progression of your work. We *need* you, darling. If you can learn how to adapt these children to the needs of our leaders, our leaders in turn will be empowered to serve the greatest Gaia vision of them all.'

This again. *We need you.* He had left the Sec Gen project when Clay had first mooted the berserker gene, calling the scheme far too danger-ous, invoking the spectre of generations of wrecked minds. Clay and he had split up and IMBOD had gone ahead without him. That night in Atourne, he'd reconsidered and decided he'd reacted too hastily; that instead of walking away he should try and act as a brake on the Wheel Meet's crazier schemes. Schemes like this one.

'It's an insane vision, Clay. It will create far more problems than it solves. Even if I can get the procedure right, all that activity will still have to be hidden. Or is Stamen Magmason going to change the age-of-majority laws next? What, down to thirteen? Ten? Six? Three days? There'll be open revolt! Our way of life works because we *protect* our chil-dren. Parents only allow their offspring to become Sec Gens because they think they'll be saved from emotional hurt. That was my intention. But now you're fucking a vulnerable nineteen-year-old. All right, he wants it, I can see that – but he wants it too much. He'll bond with you, his com-manding officer.' *Like I did.* The unsaid words hung between them. 'That's deep, Clay. Far too deep.'

He was shaking. He knew what was coming. Clay would accuse him of jealousy again. He wasn't having it. He just wasn't having it any more.

But Clay, the arch manipulator, softened. Touching his knee, he said, cajoling, 'Samrod, I love your integrity – you know I do. But Peat's a test subject. You need to work with young minds to perfect the adolescent memory repression procedure.'

Repression. Clay was still out of his mind, but at least he was showing a little more respect for his work. He folded his arms. 'Go on, then, Clay. If there is madness afoot, I need to know all about it.'

'It's not madness. It's perfectly sane and achievable. We don't need to change any laws. We'll raise the Sex Gens in Bracelet Valley, in lovely secluded communities, generating oodles of happy childhood memories. Specially selected Sec Gens will parent them; there'll be no revolt there. Wheel Meet ministers and judges and high-ranking IMBOD officers can come and visit, enjoy their babies and toddlers and pre-teens without fear, all at no harm to anyone.' Clay assumed that bolt-upright, noble pose the cameras loved so much. 'In a generation or two, there'll be no need for secrecy any more; precocious sexuality will become perfectly acceptable, just as homosexuality and prostitution did in the Old World.'

It was no use. He simply could not go along with this. 'Clay! You can't compare homosexuality with *child fucking*. Children are in no way, physically or emotionally, ready to have sex with adults. And anyway, it *won't work*. Part of the thrill of paedophilia is precisely its illegality.'

'Samrod, darling.' That hurt pout again. 'That's simply not true. Did men *stop* being gay when homosexuality was legalised? Paedophilia is a *sexual preference*. The problem has always been squaring it with average child development. But that loyalty gene is a miracle – Orson's gratitude, it's intoxicating. He's all mine. He's *ours*. We can do what we want with him. He *wants us to*.' Clay was gripping his thighs, shaking them. 'And that's a tribute to your genius. Gaia knows, I'm *your* slave, Samrod. I'd do anything for you, you know I would.' He sat back. 'And have.'

He closed his eyes, rubbed them beneath his glasses. *This again.* There was no menace in Clay's voice – quite the opposite. Clay had taken a risk for him in Hokma's jail cell. Not everyone in the Wheel Meet adored Chief Superintendent Odinson.

'I know you have.' He sighed. 'But there is a limit, Clay, to what I can do in return.'

'*Homo sapiens* is a bad animal, Samrod,' concluded Clay's little homily. 'That's the truth of it. The Pioneers thought otherwise. They believed that if we created Paradise on Earth, educated everyone to be gentle and kind, channelled human aggression into the defence of the planet, all social ills would magically fall away – but some men still wanted to stick their dicks in little boys and girls. Some women still wanted to join in the fun. And lo, just like everywhere else in the world, throughout the history of our species, these people found themselves running the government!'

'That could have been avoided—' he attempted, wearily, but Clay was off and running again.

'Is-Land was always an experiment, and the Wheel Meet is evolving according to the results. A growing number of highly influential ministers – *and* funders, I might add – now believe that if human beings can accept and consciously manage our own intra-species violence, we will cease to visit it on Gaia and the rest of Her creatures. That is the vision I serve. And I am telling you, Samrod, I am not harming *anyone* in doing so. Go and fetch Peat. See how he is. Then tell me I'm wrong.'

The Sec Gen funders were behind the new vision. Of course they were. On the other side of the mirror the lights of the monitor twinkled and blinked. On the desk his slim Tablette quietly hummed the tune of his life's work. Samrod straightened his glasses and got to his feet. Why was he surprised? Whether it was a young Sec Gen's haunches or Samrod Blesserson's soul, what Clay Odinson wanted, Clay got.

Like a cold winter wind, the cry pierced his ears the moment the tunnel door slid open: a howl of anguish, broken by sobs. He switched on the lights, broke into a run, crying, 'Peat, Peat, it's all right, I'm here.'

The boy was on all fours, collared and chained to a cage. He strained towards the entrance, his eyes red, face wet with snot and tears. Samrod knelt, took him in his arms, cradled his head. 'I'm sorry, Peat. He didn't know. He didn't know he shouldn't leave you.'

'*Puh-puh-puh—*' The boy was snuffling in his hands, rubbing his head against his chest, dripping mucus all over his trousers. Clay was going to have to do better than this.

'P-p-p-lease.'

He wiped his hand on his trousers, patted the boy's back. 'Yes, Peat. Tell me, Peat.'

'*Please*,' the boy blubbered into his lap, 'let me lick you, let me lick you.'

Oh this was *intolerable* – as if he wanted an obsequious blowjob from a slobbering infant. But, he steeled himself, he had to be kind, had to feed the loyalty gene, try and salvage his handiwork from Clay's reckless interference.

'Later, Peat. Maybe later. Here, lick my arm. It's nice and salty too.'

The boy feverishly ran his tongue up the inside of his forearm, shuddered, then fell still. Around them, Clay's dungeon instruments lined the tunnel: the racks, ropes, shackles, curtained boxes. There would be parties here, all the junior officers involved, wild celebrations when the prisoners finally broke. The thought made him feel incredibly tired.

'Better, Peat?' He stroked the boy's head.

'S-s-sir,' the Sec Gen beseeched him, 'thank you, sir. Thank you. It was like nothing I ever felt before. I was . . . with the stars. Gaia's stars. The stars in the earth.'

Now the boy was talking sheer nonsense. This really did have to stop. 'I'm sure the Chief Super was very good to you, Peat, but you've been on your own for a while now. I just want to test your anxiety levels. Let's go up to the clinic now, shall we?'

The boy's eyes were dark shining wells. 'Please, Doctor Blesserson, I can stay longer by myself, I honestly can. I just want to be a good batman. I mean dog, I mean puppy. Maybe' – his lip trembled – 'you can give me something to help?'

Maybe he could. Maybe he could eliminate the boy's faculty of speech and with it all capacity for independent thought. How on earth Clay thought the boy was going to be any use at all in the lab in this state was beyond him.

'I'll see what I can do, Peat. Let's see how it goes. And you *are* a good puppy, aren't you? You've done exactly what your master said.'

The boy relaxed, leaned against him. 'It felt like I was flying. Flying through the Gaia stars. Can you make me into a real batman, a *batdog*, like that?'

It was truly heartbreaking. He patted the boy's hand. 'I'd have to make your hands very big, Peat and attach them to your shoulders. There would be webbing between your fingers and you'd have to pick things up with your toes. It might not be very convenient.'

'But if I could fly and carry you and Master on my back, I wouldn't mind.'

Perhaps turning the human race into bat-people wasn't such a bad idea. Without hands, eating just insects and fruit, humans would do far less damage all round. He unclipped the boy's chain from the cage. 'Tell you what, Peat. After I take some blood samples, I'll give you a bath. And then we can go to the lookout room and watch the bats, how would you like that?'

The boy shook all over with gratitude. 'Yes please, yes please, yes please.'

He stood. His trousers were damp and sticking unpleasantly to his thighs. He unpeeled them and led Peat out of the tunnel, insisting the boy stand when they reached the end of the carpet. He really was going to have to put his foot down with Clay. No doggy sex in the lab. During working hours let the Sex Gen submit to the snipers, at least until Samrod figured out the best way to mop up this mess.

The Black Desert

They should have left as soon as they were rested, she knew, but Muzi insisted they let her cheek wound heal and the oasis was so lush and beautiful and in the end they slept three nights in the temple. She had never spent so much time with a Gaia partner before. Back home, times of intense closeness had been separated by periods of longing, schoolwork and chores, with hectic Tablette messaging to sort out any miscommunications. Even after spending a whole day with Lil in the woods, she'd returned to Hokma and Wise House for supper, or flounced off in a temper back to the Earthship. Here, it was just her and Muzi, playing, sharing, touching, each encounter hungrier than the one before; each quiet aftermath more tender, more certain in its sense of homecoming.

Was this bonding? As they kissed and caressed, discovering the knacks to each other's excitement, she felt not just pride in learning how to please him; not simply relief he'd managed the same. Rather, she was filled with awe, as though their bodies were keys to a shared secret temple. When he licked between her legs, she glowed like a golden dome. When he entered her, she gasped with shock and gratitude, all the fear and grief that had thrown them together burning away in the fire at the heart of their sanctuary, her only desire to invite him deeper inside. When she rode him to her peak she broke free as a nomad, galloping over the steppes on a sweat-flecked stallion and at the same time she was also his steed, submitting to his driving need, his thrusting hips whipping her on and on into the dazzling blue sky that shone from his eyes. Afterwards, she lay recovering in his arms, her breasts sticking to his chest; their legs entwined, her mind a still pool reflecting nothing but the astonishing pleasure still surging through her, savouring the memories until one of them reached out, began again to worship again.

Yes, they were bonding. It was too soon, she knew, but too strong to prevent. When she gazed upon Muzi striding to the pond, as comfortable naked now as if he'd grown up in Or, his brown limber body glowed from within, a luminous aura merging with hers, until they felt each other's thoughts, heard each other's emotions. She stood in the water, watching the trees and thinking of Hokma, and he came up behind her, wrapped his arms round her waist and said, 'You are a forest woman. I will take you home to Or.' He sat silently on a rock looking up at the sky and she started gathering rocks to build a cairn for Uttu in the temple. Sometimes they lay on the shore of the pond, kissing and losing themselves in each other's eyes; sometimes they play-fought, wrestling until they fell about laughing. On the second night, by the fire, she stroked and licked his short arm, the stump as soft and firm as a baby's heel. 'Istar's mace,' she whispered.

He replied later, lifting his head from her brand-wound, 'You wise woman, Astra.' He trailed his finger down the crease of her thigh, sending an exquisite shudder right through her. 'I kiss your Shlemun's Seal.'

There were no walls between them after that. When Muzi traced her face with his short arm or rested it trustingly between her breasts, her heart floated over the world; when he pressed it up between her thighs, she felt charged with honour. She was the Gaia Girl; she had thought she knew all about sex, but Muzi the virgin was anointing her into a whole new mystery, an experience of intermingled vulnerability and power, a shared privacy she had never dreamed possible.

But it could not continue. 'My father is waiting for me,' she said on the third night, as they finished eating by the fire.

Muzi put his spoon in his bowl. 'Astra, I have plan to tell your father.' She listened, at first curious, then incredulous. Muzi had decided that when his family were freed and the war was won, they would breed camel racers in One Land. He and Astra could run the breeding farm and his family and his best friend Kishar could organise the races. Kingu would manage the track, his mother would do the finances, his aunt would run the café and Kishar would do promotions. Muzi's uncle Gibil was handy with scrapheap mechanics; he could make the robot jockeys. If Astra's father wanted to, he could come in on the scheme too. There would be plenty of work to do.

'First camel racing track in One Land.' He slid his arm around her waist. 'We make lots of money. Have good life.'

She stared into the fire, battling a discordant mixture of feelings. Camel racing was cruel and exploitative, but that wasn't her main objection. Beneath that immediate reaction ran deeper, more difficult currents. Part of her desperately wanted to imagine a happy future, but doing so was like blowing soap bubbles; it was naïve of Muzi to be so confident about winning the war. She also was forced to recognise a curdling of alarm. How did she know she would still want to be with Muzi in a year, let alone for the rest of her life?

It was impossible to say any of that. How could she hurt him, dash his dreams, after all they had just shared, the journey they still faced?

'I don't know, Muzi,' she said at last. 'It's not fair to make camels race for our entertainment. They have to be whipped to run fast. And gambling isn't good either. Look what happened to the Old Worlders with their casino banking.'

'Racing is fine, Astra. Little bit of betting, maximum limit, is fun. And camels good runners. Robot jockeys very small, whipping not hurt. Only tickle.' He found the soft spot beneath her ribs, dug a finger in, wrestled her to the ground. 'Okay, we do things Gaian way. Save money for camels' retirement. You can look after them, pick out fleas, cook them dinner. Queen Astra of the camels. You talk to them like this . . .'

His hand was between her legs, pulling at her lips. She was laughing again at the outrage of it, twisting away, mock-slapping him. The camel race track was just a fireside fable. There was no point really fighting over it.

'We have to free your family first,' she said. 'And then win a war. Camel babies have to wait.'

He picked up the dishes. 'We go tomorrow. In the afternoon, to travel at night.'

They lit a candle on the altar and before they slept, she lay and watched Istar's feather twirl in the heat of the flame. But she did not dream in Muzi's arms. They slept late and deeply, then made love and ate well. After lunch, they filled the water bottle from the oasis, picked more sesame seeds, almonds and dates and set off, moving beyond the trees into a broad expanse of hard sandy soil.

They walked slowly. According to the CONC maps, Shiimti was two hundred and fifteen kilometres southeast. As the crow flies, that was five or six nights' walking, perhaps passing no vegetation or water. But even six nights might be optimistic: the topography was marked with generic symbols for dunes, so there could be impassable ravines, rocky heights, toxic swamps. Here the ground was flat, but to the south was a high sweep of what looked like cliffs they might at some point have to cross. Discussing the journey, they had agreed to strictly ration food and water and rest often. Still, after their ordeal in the *mergallā*, walking in calm air was blissful. Arianá was stepping easily too, the camel appeared to have put on weight and, Astra was glad to see, its ulcers had shrunk.

After about an hour, the ground ahead changed colour, now speckled with a long drift of glinting black stones.

She recalled the map: this didn't look right. 'What's that? We can't be at the black desert already?'

'No, no. Black desert sand is black.'

They walked into the drift and she picked up a stone. Glassy and round, it twisted back on itself like a small hard wave.

'Is it obsidian?' The only obsidian she'd ever seen was smooth or crystalline-sharp, but perhaps this was what it looked like before people polished it.

'Non-glass,' Muzi said. His stone was larger. Gnarled like fossilised wood, it resembled a horse's head, with a swirl for the eye. 'I see on sale in Lálsil. Kingu say they made a long time ago by a' – he struggled for the Asfarian word, settling for – 'very big rock, from space. Like metal singing bowls made from.'

'A meteor?' Listening to singing bowls containing metal from meteors was supposed to aid spiritual travel, one news report had said. But the stone didn't look anything like iron.

'Yes, when meteor hit the Earth, rocks burn so hot they turn into glass. Fly everywhere. Non-Landers say that is like us: take a big hit, now shining everywhere.' He folded his fingers over his stone, rattled it in his hand. 'This very good luck.'

She fingered the spine of her piece. The Prophecy finished like that: *and the Placeless Ones shall be in all places.* She'd thought that meant gaining access to Is-Land, creating One Land, but maybe it spoke of further migration, being scattered again by another massive blow from nowhere.

'I thought Istar's eyes were onyx or obsidian,' she said. 'But they must have been Non-glass.'

They would need all Istar's help on the journey ahead. She put the stone in her pocket with the last rook feather and turned to say a final farewell to the oasis and the temple hidden within it. The palm trees were nothing more than a thin black smudge against the faint slope of the ridge, still just visible behind them. In front of the smudge was . . . a sand cloud?

There was no wind. They had seen no animals. 'Muzi!' She grabbed his sleeve. 'What's that?'

He halted the camel, turned to stare. It was hard to tell at first, looking into the lowering sun, but then there was no mistake: it definitely was a puff of sand. Small but getting bigger, it was moving towards them. Fast.

'*Whoooo*,' he exhaled. 'Dune buggy, maybe.'

She was petrified. 'It's following our tracks. It must be. It's coming after us.'

'Okay. We okay, Astra.' Muzi was pulling his prosthetic hand out of his bag. He sat down and put it on, then took his knife out of his belt and gave it to her.

'What are you going to use?'

'My frying pan.'

Gripping the knife, she scanned the terrain. What did Muzi mean, *okay*? There was nowhere to run. Only in the dark would they have any chance of evading the vehicle and dusk was still at least an hour away. Why had they stayed so long at the temple? They'd lost all the time they'd gained during the *mergallá*. Anyone heading to the oasis for water could have seen the tracks they'd left through the city, would realise two people with a camel would be easy to rob, to kidnap, to kill . . .

'Do Asfarian traders have dune buggies? I thought they travelled on the roads.'

'I don't know. Maybe.' He was tugging the camel to its knees. 'Get on Ariamá, Astra.'

'What?'

'You have watch, maps, knife, pee machine, water, food. You can make it to Shiimti. Five days. No problem. Go now.'

'Yes problem! *Big problem!* I'm not leaving you here to fight Asfarian slavers with a frying pan, Muzi!'

'You Istar.' Oh Gaia. Back to this again. 'Shiimti needs you.'

'No! And anyway, it's a ridiculous plan. They'll see my footsteps and come and find me.'

He grabbed a blanket from the camel's back. 'I sweep footsteps,' He cocked his head, grinned. 'Tablette game trick – work every time.'

'This isn't a Tablette game. I'm staying here with you and that's final.'

He couldn't make her get on the camel. He gave in. 'Okay. But we hide food and water. If they take camel, we walk.'

Why would the traders need a camel? They had a dune buggy. They wanted to capture two idiot youths, take them to Asfar to work as servants or sex slaves. Everything was over. And it was their own fault. The fault of their lust, their laziness, of bonding before they were ready—

'Quick!' Together they rolled the water bottle away as far as they could without losing sight of Ariamá and left it under the dun-coloured blanket with the food. Jogging back, beating at their tracks with the other blanket, Muzi panted, 'We stay behind camel. In case of guns. If we fight, stay back to back.'

Running released her fear, keyed her up for battle. It had been the best three days of her life and her life might as well finish now. She was a good kicker, good ducker and diver, would fight to the death, never let the slavers take her. They arrived back at the camel to see, in the ever-nearing distance, bright shining rays burst from the sand cloud: a powerful beast made of metal and glass, hurtling towards them.

'Muzi.' She grabbed his jaw, twisted his face to hers. 'I love you.'

He emerged from the kiss, heart thumping, the salt of her charging his blood. 'I love you too, Astra,' he told her. Then, shoulder-to-shoulder with his war wife, frying pan in hand, he peered over the camel's neck. The sand cloud and its blinding heart of light filled his vision. A dune buggy could carry four men at the most, probably only two. They had a chance. He had done all he could to prepare and now he had to take that chance. He had killed sheep before; a rook once, before killing rooks was illegal. To kill a man, he would have to bash at his head with the pan. The CONC hand was a weapon too, and a shield. He could crack a man's skull with it, take blow after blow, slash after slash. He could also trick a man with it, let him grab the hand then leap on him when he fell back to the ground. If he killed his opponent quickly, he could turn and help Astra. With three hands between them, they could take on the other dune buggy rider.

They definitely had a chance. But if that chance failed, they needed a plan.

'Astra,' he hissed, his eyes still on the vehicle, 'if we taken to Asfar, only try to escape. In Lálsil is man called Doron. Is a sign on his shop, a tree with ten fruits. Find him. Tell him you my friend. He will help you. Doron. Say his name.'

'Doron?' She frowned. 'Did you meet up with someone in Lálsil, Muzi?'

Oh this again! For three days no poking or complaining, but now, just when they needed to act together to save their lives, she was starting up.

'He good man, Astra,' he said flatly. That was the end of it.

But not for her. 'Why didn't you tell me? Who is he?'

'He trader. My father know his father.'

'What did you tell him?'

'Nothing!'

'Did you tell him about me?'

'No!'

'Maybe he told someone where you were going! Or someone heard you! Maybe this is *IMBOD* following us!'

'NO IMBOD IN LÁLSIL. *Shhhhh!'* The dune buggy – it was definitely a dune buggy, an expensive one, with gold bodywork – was bearing down on them. He gripped the frying pan. He had a plan. He was ready, alert, his senses amplified, blood pumping. The hot stink of the camel scorched his nostrils; the argument rang in his ears and his chest swelled with the knowledge of love. He had sheltered in Astra's secret caves; been drenched in her storms of emotion. He was a man now. He might die any moment, but he would not die a boy.

Then the buggy was right there, a flashing gold cage. The camel, frightened, was struggling to its feet. He yanked it back down to its knees. The beast could run later; for now he needed the shelter of its back. He could make out only one person in the vehicle, the driver. A thin man, in a blue robe and tall turban. No . . . was it a *woman*? It couldn't be just her. Where were her warriors?

The woman braked. She stood in the seat, whooped and shook her long arms in the air.

'Oh for frack's sake!' Astra exclaimed. *'Lil.'*

She couldn't believe it. Relief cascaded through her. Relief streaked with annoyance. It was Lil – putting her through sheer terror. *Typical* Lil. She passed the knife back to Muzi and strode out from behind the camel.

'Astra!' Lil leapt from the buggy. Her hair was up in a braided knot, strands flying loose round her face and she was dressed in an extraordinary outfit, a one-piece made of powder-blue alt-leather, accessorised with gold boots and large amber sunglasses. She ran towards Astra, arms outstretched, her smile radiant. 'I found you, I knew it was you. You stayed at the Istar temple, didn't you?'

Lil was hugging her, swinging her round. Amazingly, she smelled of peaches.

It was ridiculous to feel angry. She had wanted Photon to send Lil, after all and now here she was. It was just strange to see her so unexpectedly, 'Yeah. We rested there. After the sandstorm.' She gestured to Muzi, who was hanging back by the camel. 'This is Muzi.'

'Photon said.' Lil strode over to Muzi and stuck out her hand. 'Muzi, I'm honoured to meet you,' she said in fluent Somarian, followed by a long spiel of which Astra only understood 'Photon', 'Lil', 'Astra', 'Is-Land' and 'YAC'. Muzi listened, his face clamped in concentration, then replied with a long speech of his own.

'Can we talk in Asfarian please?' Astra demanded. 'So we all can understand?'

'Sure, sorry Astra.' Lil shoved her sunglasses up on her head and blasted her with another glorious smile. Her skin rash had faded, Astra noticed, as if Lil had somehow transferred the cheek wound to her. 'Or I can translate if you like. I was just telling Muzi how we met and what my responsibilities are within YAC. As a member of the Warrior Group, I've been charged with the duty to ensure your safe passage to Shiimti.'

Muzi was inspecting the vehicle. It was some kind of hybrid, its two sparkling gold bucket seats mounted at the front of a large flatbed truck. He whistled. 'SunBody All-Terrain PickUp. Nice.'

If the noonday sun, a mine's worth of diamonds and a vat full of chrome had been poured into a mould constructed by a drunk metalcraft student, the result might have looked something like this monstrous machine. Not content to be simply gold, its bodywork and roll bars were studded with neon strip-lighting, its bonnet was a soldered coil in the shape of a spitting spiral and its wheels were as big as a tractor's. In Is-Land such an over-sized, over-designed vehicle would have been considered not just gauche but too offensive for words. Muzi and Lil, though, were discussing it with almost professional admiration. 'My friend Kishar, his brother had old model.' Muzi ran his finger along a chrome bar. 'Solar charge bodywork was problem.'

'Yeah. They fixed that.' Lil patted the bonnet. Her fingernails, Astra noticed, had been filed into perfect ovals and lacquered with pale blue polish to match her outfit. 'This one's practically a perpetual motion machine. And the engine! Whoah! There's some rough uphill ground ahead and a detour, but we'll get to Shiimti in ten hours, max.'

Behind them, the camel had got to its feet and was nosing the air. Much as Astra had objected to walking, if there was going to be another change of plans, it needed to be discussed. 'We can't all go to Shiimti in the buggy,' she pointed out. 'What about the camel?'

Lil laughed. 'We'll be giving that camel the ride of its life!'

'Is okay, Astra,' Muzi chimed in. 'Camels ride in pick-ups all the time.'

'Lil. *Stop*. What are you doing here? How did you know how to find us? And what's the news? Did Photon send you? Is he okay?'

Lil, at last, registered her properly. 'Hey, I'm sorry – I know it's a shock. Photon's fine. Look, I've got cold beer. Let's sit down and catch up.'

The dune buggy might look gaudy, but it was no trinket. Lil propped up the floor of the flatbed to reveal a storage compartment filled with boxes, blankets, blow-up mattresses, a tent, sleeping bags, bottles of water. At the back, beside a red metal tool box, was a large black bioplastic crate stamped with a symbol Astra had last seen on her Year Eleven orienteering course: a white mast, radiating signals.

She regarded the buggy with begrudging new respect. 'Is this a cell-on-wheels?'

'The best on the market. It's got a fifty-click radius – if you want to check your Tablette messages, we should be able to pick up Lálsil from here.'

She was tempted, but Tablette messaging could be dangerous. 'No. IMBOD could be monitoring my account.'

Lil shrugged. 'Unlikely. CONC email's pretty much hack-proof – and if they did get in, there'd be a diplo-storm in Amazigia.'

When it came to her, IMBOD didn't care what rules they broke. But she didn't want to tell Lil about her genital brand tracker. Not now, anyway.

'I'd rather not risk it. Just tell me what you last heard from Photon.'

'Suit yourself. Muzi, do you want me to set up the antennae?' She explained it in Somarian as Muzi peered at the crate. He cracked a joke, Lil threw back her head and laughed, a peal of bells. Astra's stomach twisted.

'No thank you, Lil,' Muzi finally replied, in Asfarian. For a piercing moment she wanted to kiss him. 'My family emails not safe.'

'We're going to get your family back, Muzi. CONC knows IMBOD took them,' Lil heaved out a wicker hamper. 'Like I said, Astra, Photon's fine. We arranged a code, so I can send him a message for you, if you like.'

Lil spread a blanket out between the camel and the buggy and opened the hamper, which was neatly packed with blue bioplastic picnic ware. From a green cooler she produced flatbread, hummus, olives, date spread and three bottles of beer. 'The best of Lálsil market!' she crowed.

Astra hung back – they'd had lunch not so long ago – but Muzi announced, 'We have sesame, best of Istar temple.' He tied the camel rope to a roll bar and took the seed bag from the camel's back. Sitting on the blanket, he splashed his hand with water from his hipflask, then reached for one of Lil's bowls. He was proud to share their harvest, she could see.

She should be too, but for some reason watching the delicate seeds stream into the bowl made her feel sad, as though they were emptying out of a precious, secret world. At least Muzi had kept his prosthesis on. It was absurdly possessive, she knew, but she didn't want Muzi to reveal his wrist to Lil.

Lil passed her a beer. They were having a picnic, so she sat down too and they all toasted: 'To Shiimti'.

'Good, heh?' Lil grinned.

Hoppy and bright, the beer was a miracle, the meal a feast of rare delicacies. She tried to ignore the dragging feeling in her gut. 'Amazing.'

'You get the dune buggy in Lálsil too?' Muzi spread hummus on his bread. 'Near camel market?'

'Yeah. YAC ordered it up from Asfar, special delivery. It's secondhand, but not a scratch, and only three thousand clicks. I got the racing suit too there, Astra.' Lil smoothed her trousers. 'Like it?'

'Isn't it hot?' she mumbled. The outfit was a form-fitting baby-blue body sleeve with a white collar and a ringed zip down the front. Lil looked very hot in it.

'Nah. The material wicks, see.' She turned the cuff. It just looked like ordinary ale-leather to Astra. Lil's nails, though, were astounding. There were gold sparkles in the blue paint and one thumbnail was set with a little diamanté stone. Astra had never seen anything like it, not even in Sippur where there was a shop that sold things like lipstick, eyeshadow and nail polish – adornments for Gaia play, not for wearing out on the street. Outside Is-Land some people, mainly women, did wear make-up every day, she knew. Still, no one in Non-Land lavished so much attention on their nails. Lil must have been watching Asfarian soap operas. Maybe that's why her Asfarian was so fluent. She was chattering away like a bird, a bright blue exotic bird risen from the ashes of war.

'How did you afford all this stuff?' Astra tore off a scrap of flatbread and dunked it in the hummus. 'YAC doesn't have any money.'

Lil rubbed her outlandish hands together. 'We do now. It's pouring in, from international downloads of the Singulars' music tracks and donations to the warrior fund. The dune buggy's our biggest spend so far, but we've also ordered medicines and electric wheelchairs from Asfar – they'll be arriving any day.'

She repeated it in Somarian for Muzi, a much longer explanation, replete with more jokes, apparently, because Muzi laughed a lot and then he got excited and pulled out that dirty rag he'd found and Lil admired It and they had a long conversation, complete with gesticulations and even a few lines of a song, presumably about the buried city. Finally, Muzi put the rag away and sprinkled a pinch of sesame on Lil's hummus bread. Astra's stomach torqued again.

Fine, speak in Somarian without her, but the sesame seeds were her and Muzi's treasure: they had gathered them together in their own private, magical place and now he was scattering them like confetti on Lil's food. He was captivated by Lil, of course he was. She knew all about those fighters he admired, and she was beautiful. Even with her skin covered in a rash, Lil was heart-stopping; her beauty came from a deep inner fire and blazed, like Istar's, out of her eyes. Did beautiful people always need, demand, to be seen? If so, Astra would never know how to be beautiful because she'd spent her whole life hiding. She was fit and fierce, that was all, and she liked it that way. She didn't want to be beautiful, didn't know how to wear clothes, she hated clothes. Muzi had slept with her at the oasis because she'd taken them off. Of course he had, he had wanted to lose his virginity. Now Lil was here, in that slinky suit with the zip you could pull down in one swift movement as her whole body popped out, he'd wait for Astra to fall asleep and then sneak off into the desert with her. He'd probably learn more about sex in ten minutes with Lil than he had with Astra in three days.

'You want olives, Astra?' Muzi passed her the bowl. She took one. Behind him, Arianá slid her nictitating membrane across her eye and back, the third eyelid a marbled grey curtain languidly drawn across a warm brown sea, then flicked out of sight.

She could almost hear the rebuke: *Snap out of it. Cleanse your vision, child.*

She ate the olive, tense. Was she going to hear voices again, right now in front of the others?

But the camel chewed its cud, ignored her. She was being jealous, she realised, and in so doing she was only causing herself pain. This was exactly why so many Is-Land parents had been happy to let their children become Sec Gens. Sec Gens were never jealous or envious. She had to get a grip on herself.

She spat out the stone, sending it skittering across a black drift of Non-glass. Muzi giggled.

'We should harvest this stuff.' Lil speculatively held a piece of Non-glass against one of her silver rings. 'We could sell it in bulk, or to jewellers – we'd make a fortune in Lálsil.'

Next, Lil and Muzi would be designing the camel racetrack. 'But what's the *news*, Lil?' she repeated. 'What's going on in Kadingir?' Unless Lil had taken to sniffing nail polish remover, she would at least be able to bring them up to date on the war.

Lil set her piece of glass down on the blanket and pushed her plate aside, the flatbread barely touched. 'What do you know so far?'

Between them, she and Muzi recounted all they'd heard: the surprising reluctance of IMBOD to invade Kadingir; the failure of CONC to stop the fighting in the Hem; the capture of the jail tower and Zabaria. 'That's pretty much the state of play. But not for long. YAC's got a plan for the western front. I can't tell you about it yet, but it's a game-changer.'

Lil had come all this way to tell them she had a secret?

'What about the eastern front?' Astra demanded. 'Have you heard from the women in Zabaria? Tiamet and Neperdu and Anunit? Are they safe?'

Lil's face darkened. 'Tiamet's in Kadingir, but the news from Zabaria is bad. On the first night of the Hem battle IREMCO mine-managers took over the Welcome Tent. They kidnapped Neperdu and Tiamet's baby has disappeared. She's devastated. I haven't heard from Anunit and there's been no more news since Zabaria was taken. The Tablette signals have been scrambled and after the invasion the CONC doctors were expelled.'

The *mine-managers* had invaded the Singulars' tent? Samrod Blesserson's officers, those terrible men who had killed Anunit's baby? She was incensed. 'But what about the women? YAC has to help them!'

'We're working on it. We don't have many members in Zabaria. But if I can get the mobile cell near enough, I should be able to contact someone. The internal phone network must still be active. That's my first stop on the way back from Shiimti.'

'I want to come too,' she said.

'I don't know. Maybe.' Lil speared an olive with a toothpick.

She was determined to remain calm. 'Why not? If I have to go back to Kadingir, I might as well go with you.'

Lil retrieved the olive stone from between her teeth and dropped it into a bowl from a blue-and-gold-tipped finger and thumb. 'This is war, Astra. We can't just do what we want, we have to work as a team. You're needed in an official capacity and we have to keep you safe. Where you go will depend on what the Zardusht says.'

Muzi, she was aware, was watching them closely. She didn't want to have a big spat with Lil in front of him. Knowing how Lil argued, Muzi would probably end up siding with her. Controlling her temper, she asked, 'And who is the Zardusht?'

Lil took an alt-leather pouch from a pocket and began rolling a cigarette. 'The Zardusht is the High Healer of Shiimti. She is in constant communication with the Spirits of the Prophecy and with their help you will find out what's needed from you next.'

Muzi looked impressed. 'I hear of Zardusht. She is very wise woman, Astra.'

It was exactly what she'd feared: they were ganging up on her. She would do what *she* wanted to do, not what someone she had never met told her to on the basis of talking to some supposed spirits. 'If the Zardusht is so wise and in touch with the spirits, maybe *she's* Istar, then,' she countered. 'Maybe the *Zardusht* should go to Kadingir and knock Una Dayyani off her throne.'

Lil licked the cigarette paper and smoothed it together. 'The Zardusht foretold you, Astra. When I first met her, she said you were coming to inspire the uprising and lead the revolution into its final stage. You're a Non-Lander and a Gaian and you symbolise One Land. Dayyani's just a place-holder. You have to accept it, Astra. As soon as you've met your father, you're going to take Istar's crown.'

She glared at Lil. 'You're a Non-Lander and a Gaian too. You've been here longer than me and you speak all the languages. Why don't *you* take Istar's crown?'

'Because the spirits told me that my role was to help you. I'm your producer and manager, they said. My first protégée was Tiamet,' She shrugged. 'She's got an international music career now, so I guess the spirits knew what they were talking about. And anyway, the timing was all wrong. People know me now and some of them don't like me. You're unknown. It's easier for people to believe in you.'

At the mention again of spirits, she felt a little queasy. She had not thought much about her dream voices since she and Muzi had come together. If she mentioned them now, Lil would just use it against her. *Please, Muzi, don't say anything about the lizards,* she silently transmitted.

'You know Astra's father?' Muzi stepped into the silence.

'Zizi. Yeah. He helped me when I got to Is-Land.' Lil held out the pouch. 'You guys want a smoke?'

She was relieved to see Muzi decline. Tobacco was bad for your health and she didn't know why Lil had taken it up. Maybe it was part of her new soap opera image as an international music executive.

'He good man?' Muzi asked.

The unlit cigarette between her fingers, Lil raised her glass. 'If you like a man who likes his beer, you'll like Zizi Kataru!'

Now that Zizi was only six hours away, the thought of an alcoholic father wasn't funny. 'Lil. You still didn't tell us, or *me* anyway, how you found us.'

'No, I didn't tell Muzi either. It was partly through luck.' Lil frowned. 'Some good, some bad.' She jumped up and with her diamanté thumbnail scraped an imaginary stain from near the crotch of her trousers. 'You guys finish eating, I'll be right back.'

Lil strolled behind the buggy and lit up. Watching her with the match stirred strange memories. Astra had never asked Lil about the night that she left Or, the night of the Core House fire that had killed Torrent and Stream. A cigarette had been blamed for that fire.

Muzi reached over and stroked her thigh. 'My Astra. Don't worry. We get to Shiimti, then see what happen. I help you go where you want.'

She squeezed his finger. How could she have doubted him? It was Lil's usual effect on her: scrambling her like alt-eggs.

'You know Lil long time,' he stated.

Lil had been thirteen when she left Or. She hadn't smoked then. She'd been bossy though. 'Yeah. She's always been like this.'

'You sisters. "Sisters fight with words. Brothers with silence."'

She took another slug of beer. She and Lil had been more than sisters, but Muzi didn't need to know that.

'It's one of Uttu's sayings,' he continued in Somarian. 'Also, "Words can break or build bridges. Silence builds only more silence."'

She didn't like the gendered proverb, but the second one had meaning. In Somarian, the phrases sounded like poetry. She repeated them three times as Muzi made her a date jam sandwich. When Lil returned, he was brushing a crumb from her lip.

'Photon said you had a horse and cart,' Lil began, 'and you knew the Shiimti coordinates. I figured you'd go off road, also that you'd need supplies. Lálsil seemed a good bet. I needed to go there anyway to pick up the dune buggy. Photon told me what Muzi looked like, so I asked around at the camel market. Finally – she glanced at Muzi and, oddly, winced – 'a guy told me to go find a trader called Doron.'

'Doron helped Muzi buy the camel,' Astra stated, as if she'd known that for ages. She understood now how he'd known to ask all the right questions, check the beast's knees, learned how to tie the ropes.

'That's what the man said. But Muzi, I'm sorry.' Again Lil switched to Somarian, speaking slowly and simply, so Astra could just about understand. 'This is the bad news. I went to find Doron but his shop was closed. A girl across the street told me that a few nights ago, just before the *mergallá* broke, some men came and visited him.' She paused. 'They beat him up. They hurt him badly, but didn't take anything from the shop. The till was untouched.'

Men had come after Doron? She wanted to shout at Muzi. But she didn't. She held her tongue, watched Muzi staring at Lil. 'How bad?'

'I'm sorry, Muzi.' Lil returned his gaze straight. 'Doron sustained a head injury. He was in a coma in the Lálsil Treatment Ward. He died the night before I arrived.'

Muzi's face was rigid, but the grief leaked from his voice. 'Doron is a

figured you were planning to travel through the windsands. IMBOD would have the roads covered, so if you were heading to the next town, I thought it was likely you had been picked up, or that I would be if I kept asking questions. I knew there was an Istar temple to the south – the Zardusht was one of the Non-Gaians who consecrated the oasis. It was on your way and I thought it was worth a try. When I got to the ruins I saw footsteps coming down the ridge, two people and a camel, so I figured I was on the right track.'

Astra started putting the lids back on the food. 'We should go. If you found us so easily, those men could too.'

Lil sipped her beer. 'I doubt it. No one sane walks through a *mergallá*. Anyone following you would've waited out the storm and then kept going along the road. IMBOD's probably looking for you in Pútigi by now.'

'They could have followed *you*.'

'Don't sweat it, Astra. I bought a tracker alert for the dashboard. It tells me if anyone is using a Tablette within five hundred metres. All the slavers use them. It's really neat. I'll show you.'

Muzi stood up. 'We have to leave now. I get the water bottle,' He marched off into the desert.

They watched him go. 'That was really rough. Sorry Astra, but I had to tell him.'

'Yeah. I know.'

Lil started clearing away. 'So, are you guys an item?' she asked in Gaian. She didn't know if Lil thought what had happened between the two of them in Kadingir – that fleeting kiss at the Star Party, the immaterial massage in the ion chamber – had been a rekindling of their girlhood romance, or just a lingering echo of it. She didn't either, but now wasn't the time to discuss it.

'Yeah. For now, I guess.' She began shaking the crumbs off the plates. The acknowledgement didn't seem adequate, or respectful to Muzi. 'We made a temporary marriage. Until we get to Shiimti. Then we might renew it.'

'You guys got *married*?' She hadn't thought she could ever surprise Lil, but the astonishment in her voice was as brittle as Non-glass. 'But you're what, *eighteen*?'

'This isn't Is-Land,' she said brusquely, stacking the plates in the hamper. 'We got together and his culture requires some kind of formal arrangement. It's just for now, like I said.' This was none of Lil's business; why had she even mentioned it? 'Look, Lil, we still don't know IMBOD isn't following you. They could have their Tablettes off, couldn't they?'

Lil was engrossed in the task of repacking the food jars in the cooler. 'IMBOD doesn't know I was in Lálsil,' she said at last.

'Some YAC chick who's been on the news throwing rocks at CONC, attending Diplomeets, suddenly buys a dune buggy pick-up and starts asking about a guy with blue eyes? And what about that girl you talked to? She could have told anyone.'

'Actually,' Lil thumped the lid on the cooler, 'I wore a veil in Lálsil. And the girl was Doron's neighbour. She *cared* about him.'

'IMBOD could have threatened her. Muzi's right. We have to go now.' She stood, picked up the hamper and stalked back to the buggy.

'Are you jealous?' Lil ran after her. 'Is that what this is about? I'm not here to steal your *fiancé*, Astra. I'm here to take you to your father and the Zardusht. Or do you want to walk to Shiimti drinking recycled piss?'

Ignoring her, Astra banged the hamper back into the storage compartment, so hard the plates clattered. The camel snorted, one of its big slobbery *brawns*. It sounded like a laugh.

'Wow.' Lil stood back, hands on her hips. 'I wasn't expecting you to kiss my feet, Astra, but I thought you might at least be glad of a lift.'

She spun round and faced her. 'I'm not jealous, Lil. I'm glad you're here. I wanted Photon to send you. But Muzi's upset and I'm afraid. I just need to *get going*.'

'Are you sure? I don't want any weirdness between us.' Lil tossed her head and her mouth twitched. 'I didn't mean to rush up on you guys,' she said defensively, then, though her chin was still in the air, her voice cracked. 'Everything's so stressful and I just like to feel I'm *doing something*, that's all.'

Her face was hot and her fists were clenched. 'If you want to do something useful,' she yelled, 'why don't you just shut up and frack off! We were fine without you. We had water and a map and the camel. Now people might be following us, because of *you*, Lil!'

Lil flinched, and for the first time since they'd met again, a flicker of her old, unbearable childhood grief crossed her face. Suddenly Astra wasn't looking at an international producer and expert dune buggy haggler, but a little girl who'd grown up alone in the woods with her father, had nursed him through illness, lit his funeral pyre, who'd been welcomed into Astra's home, but only made one friend, Astra. She, Astra, she thought with a pang, had always had more love in her life than Lil.

And Lil had always milked Astra's guilt and ignorance for all she could get, had always . . .

I'm doing it again. She hadn't even noticed. It was so natural to get angry: like playing a furious game of ping-pong, the hard shell of the ball clicking faster and faster across the table until your arms ached and you had smashed the bat across your opponent's jaw.

'I'm just trying to help,' Lil muttered.

She had once again failed to control her temper. And she had lied. She *was* jealous, afraid Lil would take Muzi. *Sisters,* Muzi had said. Perhaps, she thought, dashed by shame, Lil was envious of her. If Lil was, she shouldn't be. She slumped against the bumper of the buggy, gazed out at the bloodshot sunset. She was cursed. Once again someone had been killed because of her. Maybe that was the real reason she was flaring up again.

'I know, Lil,' she muttered. 'I'm sorry. I didn't mean it, honestly, I'm scared, that's all. And I feel upset about Doron. You are helping, A lot.'

She forced herself to meet Lil's gaze. Behind the mascara and gold shadow, her eyes were brooding, stricken with doubt. 'Really?'

She had to make this better. As if it hadn't happened. She stood again. 'Yes really. I didn't want to come into the desert. It's a dangerous journey. We're much better off with the buggy. Thank you for coming and finding us.'

Lil pursed her lips, then gave herself a little shake. 'Of course I came to find you.' Lil's arms fluttered round her and for a moment her cheek rested on Astra's shoulder. Astra clasped her uncertainly in return. It was a brief and fragile embrace, but it signalled the end of the incident.

'Forget it.' Lil pecked her on the cheek. 'The stress gets to everyone.'

She wasn't sure she was truly forgiven, or deserved to be, but Lil was as bright as before. Together they went back for the cooler and the blanket. Out in the desert, Muzi was staring up at the sky, his legs spread, hands clasped to his head.

'Do you think he's okay?' Lil asked.

'I don't know. His grandmother was killed too.'

Lil shook out the blanket. 'I could ask him if he wants to drive. That might cheer him up a bit. You can too, later on if you like.'

She didn't want to drive that grotesque machine. But Muzi would.

'No, he should do it. It's a good idea, Lil.'

She took the other corners of the blanket and they folded it in the way Hokma had taught them, once down the middle, then stepping together, apart and together again.

Standing at the water and food stash, he faced the sky-god. Violet, bruised, inflamed, the sky-god mirrored his rage.

'Tell Doron I am sorry,' he announced. 'Tell him I will avenge him, along with my family.'

First IMBOD had killed Uttu, right in front of him. The memory he'd been trying to keep at bay lunged to torment him: the massive, dark-skinned Sec Gen snapping his grandmother's neck, casting her limp body aside like a used rag as Muzi had crouched behind the sheep pen, unable to move. His response had been to save Astra, and as a result of his efforts, IMBOD had killed Doron, a man who had treated him like his own son. He stood bathed in the sun's crimson rays, tense with hatred, a furious hatred that stretched every muscle in his body to breaking point. He had been a sheltered child his entire life, he realised. He had never known human brutality, never known loss or violence, never felt hatred like this. That girl with the punched-out eye in the beer tent? He hated her too. Someone had hit her and she had taken her vengeance out on a kind, innocent man. More than anything he hated IMBOD. They had taken his family, could already have killed them like Doron, for all he knew. He had been trying to nurture his resolve, to stay strong for Astra, but while they were playing in the oasis, Doron had been killed. The reality of his life stormed back in like a *mergalla*. Everything he had ever known, his family, his home, even the sheep, had been ripped from him. His heart felt as fractured and hard as the bits of Non-glass blasted over the sand.

It was no use blaming the sex-worker girl; it was because of *him* that a good man was dead. He had revealed his short arm, gone for that beer, blabbed about himself, taken off his gloves when he should have taken the camel straight back to Astra. It was his fault. If he could, he'd sharpen the largest piece of Non-glass he could find into a blade and run fighting into the Hem until a sniper shot him dead too: anything to put an end to this pain.

There is plenty of pain to come. As his vision blurred, his father's voice came back to him again, and with it, a memory. For his thirteenth birthday Kingu had taken him out camping in the scrubland for the weekend with a lamb.

'Son,' his father had said after they'd set up the tent, 'you are on the threshold of manhood. Some people initiate their young men with painful ceremonies. But we are Non-Landers.' He'd chuckled, that rich fruity laugh that made his broad chest shake. 'There is plenty of pain to come. So *we* are going to have a good meal.'

He had made Muzi kill the lamb, his first slaughter, and then they had built a fire and fried the meat with wild herbs and garlic.

As they ate, Kingu lectured him further: 'You must always take care of yourself, son, so that you can take care of others when they need you. There will be more pain, I can assure you. But always remember that a man's role is to protect others, no matter how much pain he is in. The only cure for heartache is to love harder.'

He had puzzled over the instructions, put his lamb bone back on his plate. 'Are you in pain, Father?'

Beneath his father's thick moustache, a smile had flashed. 'Not when I'm watching you eat, son.'

He had finished his meal, lain back and looked at the night sky, let his father name all the stars in Sippad the Shepherd. But he hadn't understood his advice until now. He put his hand in his pocket and pinched his piece of Non-glass tight.

It was called Non-glass, his father had told him in Lálsil, because the fate of Non-Landers was to endure endless suffering, to become twisted and pockmarked, but to endure. 'Without losing our beauty,' his father had said. 'Beauty? They look like fossilised dog turds to me,' Gibil had snorted.

His anger had loosened its grip, but left a thumbprint lodged in his chest, a new and uncomfortable pressure. So this was what being a man meant: not just knowing a woman and protecting her; carrying pain within you, secret pain you did not burden others with. He would not let his father down. He had a job to do and he would complete it. In the name of his grandmother, he had promised to take Astra to her father and to her he had promised to be a good husband. He would keep those promises. He would love harder.

Back at the buggy, he helped the girls pull out the back ramp and pull Ariamá up into the buggy. She was reluctant, but with the help of the camel treats got settled in the end.

'Want to drive, Muzi?' Lil jangled the key. *Love harder.* He thought of Kishar. One day he would see Kishar and his brother again, and he could tell them that he'd driven a new-model SunBody. He took the key.

'Lil?' Astra asked. 'Will you take a photo of me and Muzi and the camel?' They stood next to the gleaming curves of the buggy; the strip lights switched on for the shot. The flash made their skins shine and pupils red and the camel's eye glow a weird luminous green, but that was all good. It looked unreal, like he felt.

'You look like cosmonauts,' Lil grinned. 'They rode buggies on the moon, didn't they?'

The Old World people had done some crazy things. Imagine taking a car up to the moon, as if there weren't enough deserts to drive around in on Earth.

'Don't drive too fast,' Astra hopped up into the back. There wasn't much room, but she squeezed in between the beast and the seats and arranged a blanket in a corner. 'There might be rocks or ravines you can't see in the dark.'

'Actually,' Lil spoke loudly as they climbed into the bucket seats, 'the buggy is built for speed. The headlamps have a hundred-and-twenty-metre range and the stopping distance at seventy clicks is a hundred. It's flat here if Muzi wants to let rip.'

He put on the CONC hand and ran through the gears. The buggy had a sensitive gear stick, a black ball on a long bent bar, and when he turned the key the dashboard glowed like a rocket cockpit.

'This is the Map Nav.' Lil tapped a small screen with those peculiar blue nails. Map Navs were nearly as good as Old World technology now, Kishar had told him; they read a vehicle's speed and direction, so as long as a journey's starting point was correctly inputted there was no need to yearn for a satellite. 'The CONC maps don't show enough detail to plan an exact route,' Lil told him, 'but I programmed it with the Lálsil and Shíimti coordinates, so it'll keep us on track.'

'We're not going to drive with these disco lights on, are we?' Astra grumbled from the back. 'IMBOD could see us from the Boundary.'

Lil rolled her eyes at Muzi and switched off the lights. He glanced back at Astra. Her arm wrapped round the roll bar, she was staring out into the dusk.

He started the engine. He could barely tell it was running and when he floored the power pedal and it went from zero to seventy in the flash of an eye, it was as if he really were a cosmonaut, rocketing off into the twilight. Sometimes, in a really great car, you could forget the whole world. That's why there were so many drifters in Kadingir, kids slither-sliding down the sand river road, swank-hop and soulswoon booming from their speakers. What would they say if they saw him now, Kishar's sheepherder tag-along, at the wheel of an Asfarian dune machine? He didn't care; all he knew was that the wind against his face and chest was loosening the tight glass fist of his heart, freeing the power of his own determination. He didn't need the Map Nav. He knew his way southeast by the stars: Istar rising, the Shepherd and his staff. Lil pressed another screen and from speakers in the roll bar came a cloud of sound he recognised, that spacey trance music from the Star Party.

'Remember this?' Lil turned to tickle Astra's neck, but Astra brushed away her hand.

'*Muzi, slow down!*' she shouted. 'The camel's frightened!'

The terrain was perfect for speeding, hard and flat, gritty glass shards sparking up against the chassis. The camel was not going to fall out. But he was restored. He didn't need to keep flying. He let up on the power pedal, reached back and wiggled a finger into the crook of Astra's arm.

It took a moment, but her hand crept over his.

What had Doron and Antha said? *Let the woman release her feelings.* Then hold private negotiations. Haggling. Gifts. Doron had given him the best advice in the world. He gripped Astra's arm, shook it – *we're on our way* – stroked her cheek and returned to the wheel. Beside him, Lil was resting her head against a roll bar, her fingers thrumming her thigh to the music. He would drive a little longer and then he would get in the back. He needed to keep Astra warm in the tent of their marriage.

She was unsettled. She had lost her temper again and all the hugs in the world didn't change the fact that someone else had died because of her and IMBOD was looking for them. It didn't help that Muzi was driving way too fast. She complained but the others didn't care; Lil was just egging him on. Then at last the buggy slowed and Muzi's hand came sliding across her arm, insinuating a finger into the crook of her elbow. As they touched, she calmed down. He would be feeling even worse than her about Doron; she must stay strong to support him, not sink back into her terrible darkness again.

She kissed his fingers, laid her cheek on his hand and he released her. She would stay in the back, she decided. She needed some time out, not talking to anyone. She could stretch out, and she preferred the camel's stink to the plastic whiff of the bucket seats. She lay down and looked up at Ariamá, who was chewing her cud, not quite out of sync with the shimmery vibrations of the sheet metal gong from the Star Party. She should be more like the camel. Nothing ever seemed to faze Ariamá.

How do you put up with us? she thought.

We prefer our own kind, came the dry reply. *But just as we can survive for days without water, we can persist in solitude with only you for entertainment. Humans are amusing, there is no doubt about that.*

Outwardly, there was no sign that the camel was speaking. She was not looking at Astra and the voices were plural. They had a haughty air about them, though, and if any beast would use the royal we, it would be the camel. Her fear of hearing voices while she was awake overridden by the awesome possibility she might be able to communicate with Ariamá, Astra concentrated on replying.

Funny? Do you really think so? I thought you were fed up with me before. When I was being jealous.

The camel stretched her neck. Though an understandable impression, *it is not true that we wholly disdain you. We have to look down on you because we are taller than you and we only regurgitate our half-digested cud over your heads when we are extremely upset by your behaviour.*

It was like talking to an elderly person whose dignity you had somehow offended, thereby forfeiting your right to be addressed directly. The music had faded. *I didn't behave well today. But I haven't upset you, have I?*

Ariamá yawned. *Not yet.*

The camel voices rumbled through her, claiming her senses, like the others had done. But they didn't sound eager to lecture her like the lizards, or wistful like the plants. Their reticence made her anxious: perhaps she was supposed to be asking for help. *Do you have a message for me?*

Ariamá stretched her neck over the side of the buggy, then shook her head, jiggling her harness pompoms. *The plants and the birds believe that one day you will, as a species, realise your higher natures, commune* with all living beings, dance with the sun and the moon and the stars. They believe you are worth teaching. We camels remain sceptical. All mammals understand the compulsions of flesh. But we are blessed with anatomical forbearance. You are always eating and drinking, always in heat, always in thrall to the law of bodily fluids. Like dogs pissing on walls, you use your juices to establish dominance and possession. Your promiscuous need to squirt semen and milk into each other is too powerful to easily override in favour of spiritual grace. That some of you achieve it is a miracle indeed.

That wasn't exactly a message, more like a reprimand. She felt ashamed again of her possessiveness of Muzi, the way she had denied to Lil that she was jealous, fought with her. She supposed her hot, flustered anger must have looked ridiculous to the camel. But being chastised roused a need to defend herself. It wasn't wrong to have sex. That was an Abrahamic idea. *Humans have sex because we love each other*, she protested. *Why should that stop us from being graceful?*

Love. Ariamá snorted. Very few humans have sex because they love each other. You are lucky if you love each other because you have sex. Trust us, child. We have delivered celebrants to the sacred temples of Istar, have spat in the sand as grand ladies and quivering virgins couple with strangers in the shadows; we have felt the sharp tug of the priestess at our reins as she leaves the king with his harem. We have paraded festooned with bells at your weddings and we have seen time and again the strutting young groom fighting in the street while his bride slips into his best friend's tent; heard the new bride haranguing her man for not earning enough coin, until he goes off to work in the city, leaving her to bring up the children alone. We have borne the beatings of drunken husbands, endured the pokes and slaps of bitter wives. We have watched old women sharpen their blades, seen girls stumble from huts, blood spilling down their thighs. We have heard the cries of slaves giving birth to their masters' children, seen the master's wife slip poison in our milk. And always, everywhere, we have watched young lovers, in their desperation to keep each other close, drive each other away. We know you humans: you will never fully master the force between your legs, nor the knives of your tongues. Those you love most, you try to possess and in so doing you slash love into hate. Still . . . a sensation like someone blowing their nose rumbled through her; fully accepting that contrary nature is one path to grace. Possibly yours.

The voices fell silent. She stared up at Istar, the buggy rocking beneath her, imagining all the people and camels Istar had watched moving through the years, generation after generation crossing the vast desert of the centuries. There had been orgies, mutilation, child brides, slaves. Men had controlled and beaten women and women had bullied and destroyed men. She had always known all that, but for the first time she felt close to the people who had come before her, made out of the same stuff. Sisters had been jealous of each other, like her and Lil. Young men had driven too fast to impress their girlfriends, causing terrible accidents. People had thought they knew the answers and then discovered they didn't at all. The Old World humans had struggled, she understood for the first time, struggled to find peace and happiness in their imperfect world. Many never had. History had been painful for them. Did it really have to be so painful for her?

It doesn't have to be like that, she offered. Gaians are trying. Not to be possessive. To let men and women love who they choose, without all the shame the Old Worlders felt about sex. That's why they suffered so much – not because they were human; because they were Abrahamites. I know it's hard to be human. I feel ashamed of being so violent, but sex is a good thing. It's healing.

Ariamá turned her gaze upon her, the red and green lights of the dashboard reflected in her unfathomable eye. *Of course you aspire to marry your sexual appetites to your spiritual ideals. But you are human. Your appetites are so impulsive and conflicting, your ideals so abstract and unattainable, even the most enlightened of you will always be at war with herself. Some mammals have cloven hooves; humans are cleft through and through. That is what makes you so interesting to observe.*

She thought about home. Gaians were trying to do things differently. People didn't all stay together forever and feelings got hurt, but she knew many stable couples and triples. They all must have struggled to allow the people they loved to be free. It must be very difficult to control jealousy, otherwise parents wouldn't have wanted their children to become Sec Gens. The camels seemed to be saying that if she stayed bonded with Muzi, the bond would be tested, sometimes to breaking point. Maybe Muzi would sleep with Lil. She couldn't stop him. Maybe she would sleep with Lil again too. The uncertainty was frightening, but looking up at the stars she thought she could accept it. *People do love each other,* she said. *Maybe that's what sex is for.*

Love is a journey through a desert, child. Don't expect it to be a golden dune-buggy ride. To reach the green heartlands of love, you must store fat and water in your soul and be prepared to travel an age on your own.

There was a great stillness, then the camel yawned, bared her yellow teeth and slid her third eyelid over the world.

The Road

At first he focused on the pain. He had no choice. The pain was everywhere, a fire in his ears, his eyes, all over his skin, even his anus ablaze. The pain simplified matters. When it roared, he ceased: ceased to worry for his wife and children; ceased to hate his captors, even; his whole will was reduced to the need not to bellow like a bull. Then his captors gave him medicine, stuck a needle in his arm and dabbed lotion on his skin and the inferno of agony dwindled into a hot crawling army of ants: still pain, but pain he could gasp through, see out of again. They gave him food then, and his children toys, and let his wife weep over him, and his brother's wife weep over his brother, and after they slept, their captors told them what he knew to be lies, and when he fought they hooded him, strapped him to a bed and shunted their machine inside his head. He wished for the return of the blaze. Now he had to be vigilant and build his own wall to fend off the voices: a wall not of fire, but of filth.

The voices changed, sometimes male, sometimes female, sometimes soft, sometimes harsh, though they didn't float or barge down his ear canals; they were thoughts more than sounds, but not *his* thoughts: intrusions, voices, definitely not his. They emerged in the dark, words he knew very well, repeated over and over, gently tapping for beams, and his task was to prevent them from finding anything solid. So he did as his brother had told him, all those years ago, and again in the first van, after they'd been taken, leaving his mother's body behind: he churned the sour dregs of his mind for images he was ashamed to produce, but knew he had to dredge up: stray glimpses of Tablette porn, jokes in the beer tent, ancient adolescent fantasies. For as long as he could he thought about fucking sheep, a hollowed-out melon. Then the voices grew louder, so he let off an explosion and fucked his brother's wife out behind the laundry line. Now every time the voices asked about Muzi, he thought about Nin- she rolling around in the dirt with her skirts up.

The voices were warming up too. At first they just whispered 'Muzi' and 'Astra', then 'Enki Arakkia' and other names, the young warriors he had heard about in the beer-tent. He knew nothing about the warriors and relaxed at their names and soon the voices had stopped mentioning them, concentrating again on his son and the Gaian girl his mother had invited for lunch. He tried thinking about fucking her too, but she was too young and his mother had adopted her; it would be like fucking his own daughter, so he would not let them force his mind to go there. And though he wanted to bellow for his mother, blast their cold machines with a lifetime of love, love these monsters would never know, he under- stood that in this world love was a weakness they might use against him. He pushed the grief down and, lump by lump, built his wall of filth.

Over the next days the questions started: 'What does Muzi think about YAC?' 'What does Muzi think about Is-Land?' 'Where will Muzi go with Astra?' 'What does Muzi think about Is-Land?' 'Where will Muzi go with Astra?' As if he knew his son's woolly mind, what that innocent sky-gazer would do, left on his own, after IMBOD took his whole family from him. *He'll go where the sky-god tells him to go*, was the answer, but empty as that answer was he couldn't reveal it; couldn't risk what the voices might do with it. He had hesitated, though, and the voices insisted, thrust their dark tongues into the chink. For the first time he allowed himself the true pleasure of remembering fucking his wife. Her bewitch- ing laughter leading him upstairs to the roof, her red embroidered dress falling to the floor . . .

He thought he was winning, until the man from the sandfly pit returned. He recognised the man's voice, this one in his ears, not his head. The voice with a laugh festering like a canker in the man's throat.

'Kingu.' The man smirked. 'Kingu, husband of Habat, father of Geshti and Hadis. That's almost right, isn't it, my friend?'

Habat on her knees, her bright, willing eyes . . . But the image faded, the voice marching over it like boots over gravel and glass.

'Kingu, I hear we've let one of your fine brood slip our net. Muzi. Nineteen years old. A slender boy, we hear, with one hand and bright blue eyes. Hmm, he didn't get those eyes from you, did he? Or your wife. Curi- ous that.'

very good man. The best. He helped me buy the best camel. And he sold me the pee machine. He only helped me. For nothing. For *friendship*.'

Her fury evaporated. 'Oh Muzi. I'm sorry.'

She held his hand. Lil waited, then quietly put the vital question to him. 'What did you tell him, Muzi?'

Muzi pulled his hand away, punched the blanket. 'I said I was going to Asfar to work. He didn't know about Astra. He didn't know *anything*.'

'Apart from the camel trader, who else saw you together?'

He looked to the sky. His eyes were wet. 'Some girls in the beer tent. A woman, one of his friends. Her name Antha.'

'Is that when you told him your plans?'

Muzi rubbed his eyes, nodded. Lil considered it. 'I don't think the camel trader was the spy. If he was, why would he tell me to go find Doron? It sounds like the girls were the culprits. Sex workers aren't well paid in Lálsil; some of them will do anything to pick up a little extra cash.'

'But who were they spying for?' Astra worried at the question. 'IMBOD doesn't operate in Lálsil. Were they working for Asfarian traders?' The thought of it chilled her.

'I don't think so. If slavers thought Muzi was going south on his own, they'd just follow him. One guy and a camel: easy pickings. The men must have been IMBOD collaborators, trying to get more information out of Doron.'

She recoiled. 'Non-Landers working for *IMBOD*? That's *disgusting*.'

'Happens all the time.' Lil shrugged, one blue alt-leather wing darting up to her ear. 'Sometimes bribery, sometimes blackmail. Or the men might have been Asfarians. Who knows?'

'He thought I was going to *Asfar*,' Muzi repeated stubbornly. 'The other road, Astra. And I left through side streets, back to fetch you. No one followed me.'

Lil looked shrewdly between them. 'You did a good job, Muzi,' she said. 'If anyone had followed you, they would have captured you at the oasis.'

Unless their pursuers just wanted to know where they were going, were planning to follow them all the way to Shiimti. The desert was darkening around them. She felt as though anyone could arrive from anywhere, at any moment. 'I still don't understand, Lil, how you knew we were here,'

'Common sense, really. When I heard you'd bought the camel, I

His great-grandfather had had blue eyes. He didn't want to conjure up those sacred photographs, but one flashed in the darkness: blue and green eyes in brown faces were the legacy of centuries of wars in this region, a land lashed by violence since the time of the stone tablets. Hundreds of years ago, pale-skinned Crusaders had thundered across the steppes, hauling the women up onto their horses and galloping off to give them, not jewels or sweetmeats, but the swords of the victors, bellies full of children with the glinting eyes of their fathers. The IMBOD man knew the history; he was being goaded and he knew it, but it was impossible not to react to the trigger of the sneering insinuation. Better not to try; better to counter with images of punching the man's shadowy face, knocking him down, kicking him senseless, just as the IMBOD man and his officers had done the kicking down in the sandpit. That was a good fantasy, easy to tap. Brute revenge.

But over his heat and fury, the remorseless, taunting voice kept on dancing out of reach. 'Oh we know exactly what Muzi looks like. What we'd like to know now is where he is. Where might young Muzi go, we wonder, if his house smells like shit and his sheep are all gone and all he has left in the world is a horse and a cart and a young girl that he fancies the pants off? My young colleagues here have been asking you that question, nice and politely, haven't they? And have you given any answers at all?' The man *tsk tsked*, gave an exaggerated sigh. 'No. From you Kingu, it's all been sheep fucking and fruit frolics and naughty games with these two lovely ladies in the beds opposite. Impressive stuff, I must say, especially the melon. Splendid on a hot summer's day when your sister-in-law won't oblige, I imagine. But, Kingu, we don't have much time. We need to know where Muzi is now.'

Here it came. The threat he had been steeling himself against. The choice he had known for days he would be forced to make.

'The doctor tells me this treatment works best if we are kind to you, so I am making you a promise.' The man's lips were at his ear: bristling, ticklish lips: so a man with a beard. 'A sincere promise, Kingu, from the bottom of my cavernous heart. If *you* tell us all the places Muzi might run to, then *I* won't take your little girls out to the sandpit to play. How's that? You remember the sandpit, don't you? I'm sure you don't want your daughters playing there with a big strange man, do you? So why don't you just cooperate and then we can all go home – you too. That's another promise. When you tell us what you know, we'll let you and your family go home.'

It was dark where he was, lightless and suffocating. He hadn't thought it could get darker, but as the man waited, it did: darker and smaller and infinitely more silent. He wouldn't be going home. He knew that, just like he knew that all the wall of filth had done was hide his son for enough time to run far away.

On the other side of the mirror, Clay moved between the beds. Samrod was watching him sitting down and talking to the subjects, smiling broadly at their blindfolded heads, making offers, promises, cracking jokes like eggs into their ears. The results were immediate: clear verbal responses; flash floods of corroborative visual memories. The women broke first, but only just.

Kurgal, Muzi's mother's synapses spat. He'll take the girl to our house in Kurgal. It's our house, it's our land. We'll get it back from you, you monsters. She even produced an image of a hilltop house, the architecture characteristic of Hilton. Samrod searched on Archivia: yes, prior to the Dark Times, Hilton had been known as Kurgal.

He'll fight on the Hem, the aunt's brainwaves raged. He'll join YAC and fight and kill your mutant children!

Results, yes, but not ones you could trust. Samrod was hoping for corroboration from the men, but the father went in another direction. *My son will take the horse and cart to Asfar. He'll work there, until this is all over. He's gone, do you hear me? Gone!*

Oddly, the uncle held out – the repressed bisexual with a full repertoire of fantasies to draw on was still ploughing up images of cocks plunging into anuses. Blesserson frowned.

'Why isn't the uncle cooperating, sir?' Beside him, Peat, chained to his stool and skyclad save for a collar, was following the data output on the screendesk.

'I don't know.' He rubbed his forehead. It was indeed a puzzle. Why was the uncle protecting his nephew at the cost of his own son? If he didn't break soon, Clay was going to have to take the boy out to the oasis; yet another incident to hide from the CONC lawyers.

'I think that's stirred things up a bit!' The clinic door swung open with a bang and Peat turned, his chain scraping the stool legs as he quivered and strained for his master's attention. Clay scratched the boy's head and Samrod reluctantly praised him, told Clay the puppy had been very perceptive, when all the boy had done, in fact, was express ignorance and confusion. But that was the agreement they had, at last, struck: Samrod would help train the boy, ensuring his loyalty gene was not tested, and Clay would keep all sexual activity out of the lab. They had also agreed that if the subjects did not cooperate within five days, Clay would take over the treatment plan, assuming full legal responsibility for the results.

Clay stretched. 'There's been a hell of a lot of wife-swapping going on in those heads.' He chuckled. 'Maybe Mr Uncle is really the Papa.'

'Possibly,' Samrod murmured coolly. The adulterous or not relationships of a Non-Land family unit were irrelevant to proceedings. 'Look, Clay, they've all said different things. There's no way of knowing who's telling the truth.' The polygraph spikes were as high as the dry forest mountains. 'Haywire.' He laughed.

'Does that mean we can't use the results?' Peat worried.

'No, puppy.' Clay tickled the boy's chin. 'It means we're doing things the old-fashioned way: gathering intel and then checking it in the field. The subjects are giving opinions, Samrod, even they don't know if they're right or wrong. Now we've got three fat leads to follow up on.'

The boy could hardly be in Hilton, the Hem was chaos and Asfar was too huge to search. But he couldn't directly challenge Clay's authority in front of Peat. 'How might you suggest we do that?'

Clay clapped his hand on Peat's shoulder. 'They're coughing up diamonds, Peat. Hilton's a daydream, but the house looks real; we'll keep that on file. If he's on the Hem, we've got a chance of taking him alive. But I reckon the father's right: we've had a report of a boy who matched Muzi's description in Lálsil. He was having a drink with a local shopkeeper and was overheard saying he was on his way to Asfar. We tried to squeeze his contact, but came up dry. Magmason said it wasn't sufficient intel to justify extra resources, but now I can put agents on it in all directions.' He smiled. 'The best thing is, when we do pick up the boy, we can show him the data, tell him his father told us where he was.'

Clay was happy. Samrod was glad for him, but he wanted nothing more to do with the treatment. None of the results would be reliable. Hit and miss and hit again, that was Clay's technique.

Clay raised his Tablette to his lips, spoke into the officers in the lab. 'Ask the father about a hardware merchant called Doron. Abrahamic. Runs a shop beneath the sign of the tree with ten fruits.'

The female officer typed on her Tablette and Muzi's father's body stiffened. The silhouette of a giant erection appeared on Samrod's screendesk.

Clay *tut tutted*, spoke again into his Tablette. 'Tell him we know he's hiding something. Remind him of my promise.'

A vaguer image appeared on the screendesk. Clay peered over it. 'What do you make of this, Samrod?'

Clay was useless at memory interpretation. Samrod examined the image. It was blurry, but he could make out three men and a young boy in what looked like a market tent.

'If this memory is genuine, it appears that he took his son there as a child.' He lifted his glasses, squinted at the image. Interpreting MET was like reading tea leaves sometimes. Why did one man look extra-fuzzy? Ah. He had a long white beard. 'It might be under new ownership now. The man in the memory looks old.'

Squeezing Peat's waist, Clay planted his lips on the boy's temple. 'Oh my sumptuous puppykins,' he murmured, 'your master is a very happy man.'

Samrod shot him a warning glance and Clay winked and released the Sec Gen. 'Now, Peat, you've been following along like such a good boy. Do you have any questions?'

This grotesque parody of training a legal assistant . . . Samrod had to repress a shudder. Peat was bolt-upright on his stool, staring through the glass at the four bodies in their cubicles. 'What will happen to the subjects now, Master?'

Clay pressed his fists into the desk. 'The subjects, young Peat, have just confessed to plotting an invasion of Is-Land. They are targeting the holiday town of Hilton.'

Oh Clay. The boy believed him. His eyes widened and he began to agitate, straining at his chain and rubbing his rump over his seat. 'Do you want me to tear them apart, sir? I could do it outside, Doctor Blesserson, not make a mess.'

'That's such a sweet offer, Peat.' Clay stroked the boy's back. 'But we have enough information here, don't we, Samrod, to arrange a speedy trial in Atourne and perhaps a nasty road accident on the way?'

He winced. 'Should we really be discussing strategy right now, Clay?'

'*Samrod.* Peat's an ace legal beagle, aren't you, puppy? He's got to learn from the experts.'

Peat was growling and snapping, his eyes intent on the glass. 'They want to hurrrrt *Hilton.* I won't *let* them. I won't *let* them.'

'Oh what a beautiful puppy you are,' Clay crooned, his hand on the boy's buttock.

'Clay,' Samrod hissed. 'I need to talk to you in private.'

Clay rolled his eyes but complied, giving the Sec Gen a smart pat before stepping out to the hallway.

He kept his voice low, half an eye on the Orson boy through the open door. 'What are you talking about, a terrorist plot? We don't have nearly enough evidence to support that accusation.'

'Don't be such a stickler, Samrod – it's giving you wrinkles. The woman as good as shouted it from the rooftops.'

'It was a hollow boast, extracted under duress. Under circumstances that are frankly tantamount to *torture*.'

'Quite. You know as well as I do we can't let these people talk about what's happened here. We'll keep the children as collateral, but the adults need to be disposed of. They're a threat to national security.' Clay's eyes glittered. 'And we need a family crisis to flush the boy and that Ordott creature out of hiding.'

Chess, the Sec Gen had said in the car: yes, it was like playing chess with a kamikaze computer, one that destroyed its own Code as it went along. 'We're supposed to be running a defensive campaign,' he hissed, 'maintaining the moral high ground, not murdering hostages we acquired illegally in the first place! Stamen Magnason might be wooing you, Clay, but there are plenty of people in the Wheel Meet who would love to see us both fall, your Head Engineer for starters. We don't want to be trailing a mess like this.'

Clay was gazing enraptured at Peat. 'Oh, *look* at him. He's magnificent. So instinctive, so loyal. Your masterpiece, Samrod. And you're absolutely right. He shouldn't be alone for a moment. I want a pack of them, three at least. I'll sort it out at the Barracks.'

He was speechless, but Clay was already lifting his Tablette to his mouth again. 'Fantastic work, officers. We have all we need. Officer Orson and I will be returning to the Barracks for a day or two. Until we return you will obey Superintendent Blesserson's every least whim!'

'Clay!' He followed Clay back into the clinic, grabbing at his elbow. 'What are you thinking? You can't take the boy back there.'

But Clay was already unclipping the chain from Peat's stool. 'He's my Personal Assistant, Samrod. He's beautifully trained.' He turned to Samrod, leash in hand, clasped his face and kissed him softly on the lips. 'Thanks to you, my darling,' he whispered. 'Thank you,'

He was so excited he nearly widdled himself in the elevator. His master was taking him back to the Barracks – back to his litter, to show off his new legal skills and demonstrate his loyalty . . . for of course he had to keep his special training top secret, the way he kept to heel in the corridors and crouched beside Master at mealtimes, eating scraps from his fingers; the way he crawled beneath the table to lick and suck the other officers' genitals when Master commanded. As a legal beagle he knew that all this was highly classified information.

His pride was tempered by a drop of sadness: he was leaving before he had licked Dr Blesserson's genitals. He didn't know why; perhaps that great treat would be his reward when he at last proved his worth to his master. Perhaps when he had savaged the terrorists. He hoped desperately he would be allowed to do that: bite the Nonners' throats open, shit and piss all over them, root in the muck gobbling the meat from their bones, like he and the mission squad had done to that lump of flesh in Zabaria. His heart pattered faster just thinking about it, a hot growl running like an engine in his chest. Master had said no, but if Master changed his mind, Peat would be ready.

There were other treats to come, though; he had been promised. He quivered as they left the elevator, anticipating the smell of Jade's bottom. He would be allowed off the leash at the Barracks, Master said, and permitted a special reunion with Robin and Jade – a night in the woods. Master would film it for them to watch later together – Master already had films of him at school, Gaia playing with his friends in woodland siesta. That was a great honour, but also a great surprise; woodland siesta films were made for the students' security. He had always thought the schools destroyed them, but it turned out copies were kept on file, in case of later complaints or accusations. Master said how lucky that was, how much he was looking forward to watching them with Peat, hearing all about his playmates in his litter.

There was no time to return to the tunnel, but he was permitted into Master's bedroom to watch Master pack. First though, Master beat him, punched and kicked him, threatened never to fuck him again, told him all the terrible things that would happen if he misbehaved at the Barracks, or gave their secret away. When they came back to the tower important people would be here, Master said as he thrashed Peat's back with his chain, people who wanted to see him perform all his tricks, wanted to make sure all the money they had given Doctor Blesserson had been spent well. If anything went wrong at the Barracks, Master would be very, *very* angry. This beating was nothing compared to what would happen then.

Master was so strong and the beating so impressive it hurt a tiny bit. Afterwards, as Master threw a few things into a bag, he lay on the floor, aching and shivering, his head between his paws, following Master's every move with his eyes. The floor was dusty and his nostrils tickled, but he didn't dare sneeze. He would lick the dusty floor if Master demanded it; do anything to show Master how obedient he was.

At last Master forgave him. He took a swig from his bottle of aniseed drink, then sat on the bed, spread his legs, ordered Peat to 'Come'. Gratefully he sucked Master's genitals one last time before setting off. Somehow the pain in his muscles made him feel more alive, the experience of pleasing Master more intense. He was radiant with the desire to give pleasure, tingling as though Master's hands were still slapping all over him. He was crying as he gobbled, he realised, shedding tears of gratitude and joy. Afterwards, Master packed his bottle of drink in his bag. He carried the bag for Master, down to the garage at the base of the tower. Dr Blesserson was waiting at the car. He was holding Peat's flak jacket and trousers and a bag.

'These are his medicines. Every twelve hours, remember. Clay: are you taking him to the Barracks in that get-up?'

'Don't fret, darling. We'll take the collar and leash off before we get there, won't we, Peat?'

'He needs to wear his flak jacket.'

'Oh Samrod, he'll be terribly hot!'

'Then use the aircon!'

They fussed and fought and eventually Dr Blesserson got his way, dressing Peat up in the clothes. 'Goodbye, Peat,' he said, letting Peat lick his hand. 'Have fun at the Barracks and always do exactly as Master tells you.'

'Thank you, sir, yes, sir, yes I will.'

But Dr Blesserson wasn't finished yet. 'Clay,' he begged. 'There's a war on. Will you please wear your gear too.'

'We're driving to the Barracks, not to Asfar!' If Peat had been so irritating, Master would have hit him, but of course Master would never hit Dr Blesserson.

'Just do it for me, Clay.' Dr Blesserson cocked his head to one side. 'You'll match Peat. It will be so cute.'

Master smiled. 'You crack me up sometimes, Samrod.' Master kissed Dr Blesserson right on the lips, then he hugged the doctor and the doctor laid his head on Master's chest. It was beautiful and humbling to watch Master giving and receiving affection so freely.

Master wore his jacket; but not the trousers, and he didn't zip the jacket up. He got into the driving seat and Peat was allowed to sit beside him. The pain had gone now, the beating not forgotten but the lesson absorbed. Driving through the firesands was terribly dull, Master said as he pulled out onto the road. Dr Blesserson had said to have fun and they must start right away. Later Peat could lick Master's genitals again, but he must start by sticking his head out of the window and pulling down his trousers.

Driving to the Barracks was the greatest ride of his life. The sky so blue, the sands so golden, the warm wind in his face, the leash pulling the collar tight around his neck, Master's thumb nosing at his behind, the good feelings rising and rising, then dipping, then rising again, an endless circulation of bliss. He had been a good boy, he had, he had. He was going to be so good in the Barracks and back at the tower, impress all the important people. He was going to make Master so proud of him.

Master was happy too, laughing and whooping, swerving the car like a funfair ride down the road. He tugged at the leash, shouting, 'Time for your treat, Peat!' and when Peat turned around to look, he was pouring the liquid all over his head, down his chest. 'Lick that off me. Lick it, puppy, lick it!'

The explosion happened inside him, he thought, a long, silent eruption, heat blooming in his veins. But then his stomach was somersaulting and his throat was being choked so hard he couldn't breathe and then there was a crack and the heat was blasting him out of the window, up and out, so he was flying, really flying, out of a fireball into the sky, tumbling through a blur of blue and gold and, somewhere far beneath him, a flash of flaming orange.

Swarm, scent, swarm . . . swarm, scent, swarm. All over another antagonist. Not content just to step on a few of us, no, this one has to annihilate an entire column. What, it's not moving? Quick, get to work . . . scent

scent scent . . . such sweet sweat, ah ha, an ultra-beta male, a slave-soldier, fresh young muscles, what a feast for the colony. Colonies mean industry, expansion, empires — they need to be fed! We thought you knew that. For a time, you straddled the planet's antipodes, stretched from old world to new; the Arctic to Antarctica, the only place, despite our name, we are not. But you gridlock the Earth no longer. Why not? Let us tell you! Because you failed to convince your subordinate members to accept their anterior roles in your enterprise. Look at us: do our soldiers ever try to kill their own queen? Do our honey vessels ever refuse to feed the other workers? No. Our colonies are a living anthem to the power of the collective; we work, fight and breed willingly, passionately, would rather die than fail our rulers. Your rulers are always quelling rebellions, wasting time, energy and resources on repressing or appeasing antipathetic saboteurs, dispatching incompetent staff. Scent swarm scent, scent swarm scent . . . yes, send for reinforcements . . . yet another botched human job, dumped for us to clean up.

He lay curled up in the sand, winded, conscious only of a stinging pain running down his arm, bright lights flashing and busy voices scratching in his head. The voices were unintelligible, irritating – squeaky and mean. He rubbed his ears, tried to dig them out. They faded to a distant chittering and he opened his eyes to a perfect dimple in the sand – an ants' nest, with a long line of ants scurrying down it. It was a soothing sight, like a delicate black chain being pulled down a hole.

His chain? Where was his chain? He felt for it, but it was broken, the links snapped. There was a smell of smoke, and something stronger, something savoury and charred. Panic rising, he craned his neck. The car was close, on the verge, flipped onto its back like a beetle. The fire was in the road. It was a small fire, like a bright orange butterfly, struggling to fly.

MASTER WAS ON FIRE.

'*RRRHHHAAAOOOO—*' The howl erupting from his lungs, he scrambled to his feet – and with a breath-taking thud, he was knocked back down. Out of nowhere, someone was crushing him, pinning him face down in the sand. A man, an enormous man, had his knee on his back and a hand round his neck. Other hands were grappling with his wrists, wrenching them together.

He barked and barked, heaved his hips, rocked back and forth. In front of his face the ant-chain was breaking, scattering in all directions.

Sweat dripped from his face, drowning the insects, forming leafy splash-marks in the sand. Time fell away as he strained. He couldn't remember ever being immobilised like this. All the wrestling and judo moves he had learned since Year Four, actions that were second nature to him now, and none were working. The man sitting on his back was made out of iron. There were shackles round his wrists, being clicked shut. And darkness: a bag was being pulled over his head.

HE HAD TO HELP MASTER—

But hands were grabbing at his ankles. He kicked them away, and with a massive effort he arched his back, heaved and shook the iron man to the ground. The man was off him. He'd thrown the man. His next moves sparked in his head as he struggled to his feet. He would bite through the bag, tear the man's throat out, then follow the smell of fire to his master.

Something hard and hot jammed into his spine. His bagged head blazed with stars and a terrible shock seared through him, as if his insides were sizzling in oil. Then he was down on his chest again, his ankles being shackled, and ants were crawling over his face. The voices were back, chattering like insects, and faraway people were shouting, yelling in a language he didn't understand, except for the amazed, triumphant shriek: 'Odinson ... Odinson!'

Then someone stuck a needle in his arm – not a tiny prick, like Dr Blesserson's needles; this was a stabbing jab. They were killing him. There were ant corpses on his tongue, ants swarming up his nose, a shrill chorus of voices scritching all round his skull. His body went limp, no longer obeying his own brain. As the giant hauled him to his feet, tears drooled down his cheeks.

His eyes had been closed. He should have seen the bomb in the road, the men waiting, gloating, but his eyes had been closed. He had been thinking only of himself, his own pleasure. He had forgotten his first and only duty: to guard his master with his life.

MASTER. OH MASTER. I'M SORRY. I'M SORRY. I'M SORRY. I'M SORRY.

Don't be sorry. Don't accept anticlimax. Don't fight your true nature. All you were doing, however ineptly, was exactly what we were: ruthlessly organising your societies to benefit their strongest and fittest members. All you failed to do was harness the power of chemical communication. You understood that pheromones are a vital component of sexual attraction, but had barely begun to explore their potential as commands. Words are very poor agents of control, after all. Words simply generate more words – antidotes, antilogies, endless anthologies – but there is no arguing with a smell, no need for guns and whips to reinforce the order given by a scent. When an ant squirts a trail with her abdomen juices, the rest of us instantly follow it: that's the sort of antiphonal call and response you ought to be working on. Instead, even now, you persist in generating a cacophony of audiovisual stimuli that only agitates further your antisocial dissenters. Though wait . . . scent scent scent . . . scent scent scent . . . this lump you've tossed us has a promising aftertaste . . . oh yes . . . the syrupy blush of submission, laced with the spice of anxiety. Are you humans learning at last? Dare we anticipate change?

Shiimti

We flutter like your hearts, rapidly alert to the raptures of wind. We shutter up, hide our true colours, our brilliant scatters of turquoise and scarlet clasped in the guise of dead leaves. Spread wide, our wings mimic each other, their stained-glass symmetrics your definition of beauty, not ours. We define beauty as flight. We whisk up, alight on a flower, probe its nectar, flit off, land on a petal, taste its wealth with our feet. We mud-puddle in dung, airlift its rotten salt to our brides as a nuptial gift. We learned too late what you're like. You planted gardens for us, joyous bushes of pollen, taught us the dance of green nets. We know what you did to those of us caught in your strings – ripped off our wings, or pinned us to boards, pressed us like pansies between the pages of books. We survive. We are wafers of light, we have no need to forgive for we forget our whole lives in the brightness of breezes, the breath of a thermal, the scent of the sunbeams that ferry us south. We migrate. We are everywhere: signs of spring, winks of white, shavings of rainbows, flakes of your hearts. We are here, then we're gone. We're here and you're nearing, be quick or you'll miss us . . . quick quick quick. . . .

She wasn't asleep, she was talking to camels and lizards and plants and creatures she hadn't even met yet, but then there was a blast on the horn and the buggy lurched upwards and above her the sky wasn't inky-black and shining with diamonds, but a wash of eggshell blue and lemon yellow and in the front Lil was shouting: 'Shiimti! Shiimti!' and there was crust in her eyes and Muzi was curled up around her, so perhaps she had slept after all.

She and Muzi scrambled to their feet, falling against each other as they grabbed for the roll bar. It was hard to keep their balance or even see properly because Lil was cresting a dune, then swerving down it, sending billowing gold plumes out around the buggy. She plunged into a valley, then climbed another dune, whooping. The camel bellowed and Astra grinned . . . what had the camel said in her dream last night?

It struck her like a slap. She hadn't been asleep, or even in a trance like when she'd heard the lizard voices. She swallowed, dry-mouthed. Was she starting to hear voices when she was awake? That was an illness, wasn't it? An Old World illness no one got in Is-Land any more.

But in this reckless adventure, the playground of dawn, it was impossible to be afraid of what went on in her head when she was alone. They roller-coastered a smaller dune, laughing and shrieking as Lil slalomed down, emerging at last on to a plain of firm soil. The sun was spreading its gold fan over a distant purplish ridge, but Lil was heading north, weaving between gnarly bushes and huddles of white stones towards a stretch of dark fields and a high craggy cliff.

'Shiimti.' She and Muzi hugged and jumped as they saw people for the first time in days. There were tents scattered among the bushes on the stony ground, and robed figures tending camels and goats looked up to watch them pass. Lil waved, so she did too and the children waved back, small boys and girls racing towards the buggy, soon lost as the buggy powered on. The camel was straining to its feet, but she couldn't think about the voices right now. She was arriving in Shiimti. And it was not at all what she had thought: not a cluster of huts or a makeshift encampment but a thriving metropolis, a massive habitation built into the towering cliff. Even from this distance she could make out sharply angled walls crammed into overhangs, waves of stone chambers breaking on a broad round tower, zigzagging stairs, the whole magnificent enterprise sheering up, not from the desert, but from a vast green sea. Directly ahead of the speeding buggy was a curve of olive trees and date palms, swathes of crops and trellises, speckled with bright flowers.

Muzi kissed her temple. 'We here.'

'Thank you,' she whispered in his ear.

Lil was driving one-handed, her Tablette pressed to her ear as she shouted, 'We're *here*. Tell the High Healer ASTRA ORDOTT is here to meet *Zizi Kataru*.'

Astra squeezed the roll bar tighter. Somewhere in that huge rocky hive was her father.

The call came as Boranduhkt was reaching her peak, his Tablette buzzing for attention on the floor beside the bedmat just as the voluptuous curves of the beer-tent manager shook their tawny beauty all over him. He let it. The sound was no interruption – it meshed with the moment, as if the woman had set off the device with the golden sparks that flew from her eyes and arced down into the light streaming into the chamber, glorious, inevitable, a dawn dazzle of flesh, Boranduhkt's grand finale. The whites of her eyes were showing, gleaming crescents like the pale undersides of her breasts; she was gathering power, readying herself to clap like thunder. Alarm no; urgency yes. He kneaded her belly, groaned as her deep quaking cave sucked him in. She flung her head back and for a very long time the world fell away, lost in the height of her storm. Then she drooped, her magnificent copper curls trailing his chest. With three short thrusts he pumped his way to heaven too. He was no permaculture irrigation expert, but Zizi Kataru understood a woman's intimate engineering.

'Oof,' Boranduhkt rolled off him and lay on her back, her shoulder sheened to his. 'I needed that.'

He slipped off the latex sheath she'd insisted he wear and dropped it on the floor beside the empty akik bottle. 'Ah, the gracious ladies of Shiimti. So lavish with compliments.'

She laughed, her brusque *ha* a newly minted victory bell chime to his ears. 'You'll get a compliment when you deserve one, Kataru. So far you're barely breaking even. Think what that bird has done to my chairs.'

On her stand beside the windowledge, Cinders, the black Rookowleon, was spreading her wings, greeting the morning with another splat of shit.

'That mat is disgusting,' Boranduhkt complained.

She was right; the straw mat beneath the stand was crusted with droppings. He would take it to the guano site later, scrape it clean – cleanish, anyway. That stuff, as Boranduhkt liked to complain, was hard to shift.

'It's just a little fertiliser, my dear. We can sprinkle it over your morning glories. You'll soon have the best beer-tent garden in Shiimti.'

'*You* can sprinkle it. I've got enough shit on my hands to deal with.' She propped herself up, scratched his chest, sniffed his breath. 'Not too bad.'

'A glass of akik before bed obviates the need for toothpaste.' He pecked her cheek. Her own breath was still sweet with the aniseed fumes.

She sat up. 'When the rest of your teeth fall out, Kataru, then there will be no need at all for toothpaste. May I wash?'

It was not such a stinging remark. He had been mourning his latest broken tooth for two weeks now, his woe the source of much of the recent banter between them: banter that had, at long last, culminated in a drink in his room, a striptease, drunken slumber and now this munificent awakening.

'Of course, of course!'

Her honeyed peach of a bottom swayed over to the water barrel. 'You're running low.' She reached for her robe. 'I'll just go to my room.'

'No, no, my lady.' He plumped up his pillow. 'Use it all, every bright cleansing drop. I can refill it before the queue starts.'

The beer-tent manager was a Shiimti veteran and no doubt had a chamber with plumbing. But if this transient's accommodation was primitive to her, she didn't complain. He lay watching her curves and folds glisten as she ladled the water over her body, soaped and rinsed. A bountiful woman with tiny hands and feet and three unruly children to contend with, she had told him firmly last night she had no need whatsoever of a man in her life. Well, one small need, it transpired; an itch he was honoured to scratch.

His Tablette buzzed again.

'Better get that.' She examined his towel, deemed it acceptable and began patting herself dry in that curious way women had, as if the towel was some sort of suction instrument or small nursing animal. 'Might be your gracious girlfriend.'

There was no girlfriend, and Boranduhkt knew it. He spent all his free time in her bar, playing mancala with Salamu, discoursing on classical Somarian, Farashan and Karkish poetry to anyone with an interest in his arcane specialism, and flirting with her. He reached for the Tablette. On the screen was a number he didn't recognise.

His heart jumped but he quelled it. He was just being called to take a shift in a different part of the garden today.

'Hello, my friend.' Everyone in Shiimti was your friend.

He didn't recognise the voice, forgot the name instantly, heard nothing but the precious words he had been aching to hear for eighteen long years.

'Meet where?' He felt dazed. 'Yes, yes. I know where it is. As the great poet said, I'll be there as the swallow flies. I am swooping down now.'

Recovered, renewed, he leapt to his feet, bounded over to Boranduhkt, swung her around by the waist. 'She is *here*! My daughter – from over the windsands! I am to meet her immediately!'

Boranduhkt was in her robe, a dark blue affair with gold trim. She pushed him away, gave one of her wry smiles. 'Smelling like that?'

He peered into the empty water barrel.

'Come to my room.'

'No, no. It's fine. Your scent is sweeter than mine.' He took the towel from the hook, damp from her ablutions and rubbed it over his face, under his armpits, between his legs. That would have to do.

'You smell like a rutting camel. Don't you have any perfume?'

'Yes, yes!' He started for the window ledge, then spun back, slapped his forehead. 'No!' He had forgotten to refill it: his bottle of sandalwood aftershave was empty too.

It did not matter. He dressed, nearly toppling back onto the bed as he struggled with his socks – this belly he had somehow sprouted these last years was so inconveniently placed! – but Boranduhkt rooted around in her bag, bore down on him, a perfume bottle in hand.

'Stand still.'

'Eh! No!' Boranduhkt's perfume was heady, intoxicating stargazers and tuberose. 'I can't smell like a boudoir. What will she think?'

'It's not my night scent. It's orange blossom. It will blend with your stink, make a nice citrus musk.'

He let Boranduhkt squirt his bare chest. Now, which shirt? He'd managed to sleep on the blue one. The white one was just a little rumpled and had only one stain, chili sauce, utterly innocent. What else? He stuffed his Tablette in his pocket. He would call Salamu on the way. Should he tell his friend to bring his son? No, that meeting should happen later. Cinders? Should he take the bird? No, save a treat for later. Right now, nothing should distract from the reunion.

'Well, Kataru,' Boranduhkt slipped on her gold bracelet. 'When you've finished whirling like a dervish and weeping like a wound, I'll see you in the beer tent. There'll be a free drink for your daughter. You pay as normal.'

He took her hand, kissed it. 'Divine temptress of Shiimti, your benevolence knows no bounds.'

Grinning, she pushed him out the door. 'Don't waste your silver tongue on me, poet. You've got a feral teenage daughter: you're going to need all the charm you can get.'

They entered the garden, drove on towards that looming gold citadel, silenced by a sound Astra had not heard in an age: the dawn chorus; birds hidden in the trees, nesting in jade, emerald and sage fields spreading like skirts to either side of the road. The sound was immense, a hymn to the sun, to life itself; its clamorous beauty rivalled only by the growth all around them. The garden was not like the Istar oasis, not a tangle of abandoned trees and wild plants but a temple to agriculture, complete with long leafy cloisters, mosaic courtyards and heaped altars of fruit. No patch of soil was left exposed; everywhere the ground was covered by succulents, spongy crawlers erupting in pink and yellow and magenta blossoms. Above, date palms shaded fruit and nut trees – she counted olive, apricot, peach, pomegranate, almond, walnut, even banana – and the long orchards alternated with grape trellises and swathes of companion-planted fields, grains alternating with vegetable crops: spelt, tomatoes, wheat, sweet potato, barley, eggplants and courgettes with their orange trumpet flowers. Like the oasis though, it was a deserted paradise: no one was working yet and there was not a guard in sight; the fields were still glistening with undisturbed dew.

Muzi whistled. 'CONC fields not like this.'

'It's a permaculture farm,' she said. She would explain later. She recognised some of the techniques, but had never seen one in the desert before. She had studied desert permaculture though, and knew the garden was an awesome feat of design, every aspect meticulously executed to trap moisture and nutrients, prevent evaporation, capture the wafting windsands and nourish the soil with centuries' worth of minerals and decayed animal matter. In contrast, the CONC fields drew on the Mikku, used Coded seeds to grow staples and commercial crops only: dates and superfood grains; poppies to export to Asfar for morpheus production. This place was a banquet, a feast of colour and flavour and nutrition, flowing on and on.

'Butterflies!' Lil crowed in front of them, waving to the left. Astra caught flashes of turquoise amongst the green: butterflies as big as her hands waving to them from the clover border of a spelt field. *We flutter like your hearts . . . We migrate . . . We are everywhere . . . Snatches of her* dream wafted back to her, her heart gasped, then, at a loud jarring rush of alarm overhead, leapt in her chest: a dozen tangerine, black and white feathered birds – were they–? Yes–! *Hoopoes* – were flinging themselves out of the almond trees, their sharply patterned wings flaring and curling as they *whoo whooo, whoo whooo'd* over the road.

'Hadāhid,' Muzi whispered, pulling her close.

For a moment she thought he was speaking in Inglish. 'He'd a what? Who had?'

'No.' He grinned. 'Means two hudhud. Many hudhud. Family of hadāhid. Whole world.'

Tears pricked her eyes. Hoopoes were *extinct* – but here was a bright effervescence of them, their crests full-fanned crowns of glory, greeting their arrival in Shiimti. The buggy sailed like a golden boat through a triumphal arch. She wanted to kiss Muzi, but she had to see all of this. Suddenly there were birds everywhere, sparky little brown birds chirruping from the bushes, pigeons in the trees and one, two, three peacocks perched in a trellis, their tails hanging like iridescent curtains down amongst the grapevines. Ahead, in the next furrow, dowdy peahens were pecking around a row of compost bins, chickens roamed freely between a cluster of beehives. Beyond them, gracing the foot of the cliff, were herb rockeries, berry netting, greenhouses, raised beds. She inhaled sharply, as if punched in the heart.

'You okay, Astra?' Muzi squeezed her shoulder.

This was domestic gardening: a desert Or. 'It reminds me of home, that's all.'

'You home. Your father here.'

She was silent. Zizi was like the sun: for months he had lit her way but now that she was on the verge of meeting him, she was suddenly frightened – afraid to look at her father directly, to confront the reality of who he might be. That night near Lálsil, under the moon, she had allowed herself to imagine him as a proud protector like Klor, a noble leader like Dr Tapputu, but those were just fantasies, cast by the reflected light of her need to— What? Justify her decision to escape Kadingir and the war? To come to Non-Land in the first place? Find somewhere she belonged, someone she belonged with? In fact, she didn't know at all what Zizi would be like. This could all be one long terrible mistake. For a desperate moment, she wished she was in Or, was speeding up to Code House to see Klor: Klor, with his open arms and bushy eyebrows and his calm, kind belief in her, no matter how far she fell into disgrace.

'You nervous.' Muzi patted her shoulder. 'He live in Shiimti. He will be good man, Astra.'

Lil was on her Tablette again. 'They'll meet us at the canyon,' she called back. 'Zizi and the High Healer and the World Whirlers.' She punched the air. 'They're sending the big shots, Astra!'

She stared ahead at the incredible cliff, that looming honeycomb of elaborate structures, secret caves, jagged steps. It didn't matter what Zizi was like. She had come all this way for many reasons. Whatever happened, she was on a mission of her own now. Meeting Zizi was just one part of her plans.

The buggy swung right, onto a road that ran between the greenhouses edging the gardens and a long herb rockery that climbed up to a wide ledge at the foot of the cliff. Here, at last, there were people: a boy and a donkey went by on the road, a man passed driving a horse and cart full of barrels. Up on the ledge a row of meditators in lotus position sat facing the sunrise, waiters pulled out chairs in front of a row of red and yellow tents, their lone customers a man in black sunglasses smoking from a tall glass hookah and, further down, a young nursing mother. Shiimti was awakening. But though a waiter looked out and waved, it was the citadel that made her forget to worry about Zizi.

There was so much to look at. The craggy rock face hosted dark caves, bulging chambers, rickety wooden structures propped up by struts; balconies, ladders, stairwells hewn from the rock; steeples, spires, minarets and domes; towers, living roofs and terracotta tiles, even a tall faceted stone structure with stained-glass windows; but somehow the chaotic conglomeration of styles and techniques, the fractured storeys, *worked*, was not a jumble, formed layers like sediment; the largest round tower a taproot driving down through the exposed cross-section of a massive, ingenious warren. The most amazing thing was how the whole dramatic edifice appeared to be floating: the lowest level of structures was at least ten metres above the tents. She had no idea how people got in and out – perhaps through tunnels, or boats hoisted up and down, though as hard as she looked she saw no evidence of any of these on the ledge, which was narrowing as they passed, dwindling at the far end of the citadel to a footpath along the bottom of the cliff.

Ahead was a watercourse, a wide stream flowing through an inlet in the cliff, down over flat stepped rocks towards the garden. Lil sped on towards it. The citadel and the greenhouses were behind them now and the field by the road had been sown with a shrub Astra had seen but not recognised at the Istar temple: a short, delicate plant with sparse leaves and starflowers, growing here in spirals. She had no time to wonder about them. The field and the road ended at the stream and Lil pulled up abruptly. Broad and fast, sparkling like a blessing, but barely two inches deep, it was hard to believe this water was supporting the huge abundance of growth they had just driven through. But it must be making a contribution: two snaking rows of date palms followed the stream deep into the garden. Curious about the source, she looked up at the cliff. Standing at the neck of the gully were three robed figures and a short, fat man in loose trousers and a white smock. The man was jumping and yodelling, his arms flung to the skies.

Lil jumped out of the buggy and slammed her door shut. The camel complained. Muzi pushed between her shoulder blades. 'Go, go!' he urged.

'We have to let Ariamá out,' she protested. 'It's not fair to keep her in the back.'

Suddenly, she desperately needed to pee.

'Oh, for Gaia's sake!' Lil flushed. 'The camel will be fine!'

Then everything happened far too quickly. The fat man broke away from the group, began running down the rocky ground towards them, so fast she was afraid he would trip and roll into the fields. 'Astra!' he was calling, shouting in Gaian, 'oh my darling girl!' Behind her Muzi was hustling her out of the buggy, forcing her to scramble down to the ground, where the man was barrelling towards her like some kind of bomb, a plump, sweaty, balding bomb, a man barely taller than she was, but much wider, with big hairy arms, damp arms squeezing the life out of her, soaking her with moist exuberance, invading her nose with a strange, unpleasant smell, like that of mouldy oranges, as beside her Lil and Muzi laughed and cheered. Then the man – her *father* – was shaking her shoulders, shaking her out of a state of sudden paralysis, and she wasn't looking at a blur of motion any more, or up at the sky, but into eyes just like hers, dark and deep and large with her lush lashes, set between a snub nose like hers and those eyes and the fat cheeks below them were wet like hers too.

'You came. Oh Daughter, you came. You found me at last.' The man's voice was dazed, enraptured. His cheeks were stubbly and his breath smelled funny too, sweetish like liquorice, but alcoholic. He grabbed her hand, raised it to his lips and kissed it, a big wet kiss.

It was dawn. He couldn't be drunk already, could he? She felt numb inside. She wanted to push him away, wipe the back of her hand on her trousers, walk off into the garden, camp there, not have to meet anyone here. But she couldn't do that. And she shouldn't want to. Zizi had just woken up, or hadn't slept. It didn't matter. He was thrilled to see her. She couldn't spoil everything by running away.

'Lil helped me,' was all she could think to say. 'She said you were here.'

'Lilutu.' Still squeezing her hand, her father, this unwashed grubby ball of a man with a red stain on his shirt, turned to Lil. 'The wild child who arrived from Is-Land with news of my daughter: Lilutu, a desert spring of beauty and knowledge and will.' He gestured grandly at the gardens. 'And from desert springs, look what paradise can grow.'

Lil grinned. 'What did I tell you, Astra? And he hasn't even had his breakfast beer yet, I bet.'

'Yes, yes.' Zizi brought her hand to his chest, pressed it against his heart, gazed adoringly up at her through those thick lashes. 'Laugh at me. I am a fool,' he declared. 'A fat fool. You have a poet and a beer-tent prophet for a father, Astra, you and this tarnished silver tongue are my only wealth in this world.'

Lil laughed, and Muzi too. She didn't. She wasn't his wealth. He couldn't *spend* her. And she wanted her hand back. Still clutching it, Zizi turned to Muzi.

'And who is this fine young man?'

Again, she had no time to answer. 'Uncle.' Muzi stepped forward, offering his hand. She saw Zizi's eyes flick to the other, empty sleeve. 'Dumuzi Kingu-ñal Bargadala is humbled to meet you.'

'Young man, I am forever in your debt.' Without releasing her, Zizi shook Muzi's hand. 'Dumuzi Bargadala. Your mother is of an honourable tribe, the Wanderers, the very soul of Non-Land. In your wanderings, you have delivered my daughter to me and my gratitude will go with you wherever you travel. May you, like all of us, wander home.'

Zizi was still smiling, but his manner had changed. He hadn't called Muzi 'nephew'. Even she could tell this was a brush-off, if not an insult: 'uncle' and 'nephew' were terms of respect in Somarian. The formal greeting had been practically an invitation for Muzi to leave. She bristled. Should she tell Zizi he was speaking to her *husband*?

She stifled the impulse. She and Muzi were in Shiimti now; they were going to renegotiate the contract. She had to say something, though: Zizi had hardly let her speak a word yet. Her hand still a limp appendage in Zizi's paw, she found her tongue. 'We've got a lot to tell you,' she announced, hesitating over the word 'father'. 'Muzi's family are in jail because of me. We escaped IMBOD together and he brought me from Kadingir with the camel until Lil picked us up in the windsands. We have to help his family, like he helped me.'

'Of course! Of course we will help this young man's family.' He clasped her hand in both of his and pumped it up and down. 'Just let me enjoy the sight of my daughter! Look at you, so healthy, so exquisite, so dainty just like your mother.'

She scowled. Just because she was small, didn't mean she was *dainty*. She wasn't a doll. And her hand wasn't a lump of dough in some kind of kneading competition.

'Oh! That look!' He turned, triumphant, to Lil. 'How her mother would give me that look!' His eyes welling up, he pulled her hand back to his chest. 'Astra, my child. I have so much to tell you.'

She wrested her hand away and Zizi's face fell, his big round eyes stricken with hurt. She didn't care. Zizi talked all over her, touched her too much. He was being rude to Muzi; he *smelled* funny. He was not acting like a father, not like a Non-Land elder, he was nothing like Doctor Tapputu, nothing like Klor. Her heart pounding she stared back at him, tears rising in her own eyes. Muzi was still as a lizard; behind her sunglasses, Lil's face was unreadable.

AH LALALALA AH LALALALA
Pum Pum Pum pum Pum pum
tss tss tss tss tss tss tss tss
AH LALALALA AH LALALALA
Pum Pum Pum Pum Pum

tss tss tss tss tss tss tss tss tss

Into the tense silence streamed the sound of great jubilation. Up on the ledge, the three Shiimti-ites were hailing their arrival. The tall one in the middle, a woman in a long orange and gold robe and flared red headdress, was ululating and drumming a big double-skinned drum; on either side of her two men in matching white robes and tall red chimney hats were slowly whirling in place, whirling and shaking tambourines, their skirts flaring out like silky white pancakes in the sun.

'The Zardusht is calling us, Zizi.' Lil pushed her sunglasses up over her head. 'We can have that beer later.'

He was still gazing mournfully at her. 'I am sorry, Daughter. Please forgive my exuberance.'

She swallowed. She had done it again. She hadn't shouted, but she might as well have. She might as well have stabbed Zizi in the heart.

'No, I'm sorry,' she whispered. 'It was a long journey — I feel tired, that's all.'

'Of course — of course you do. Come now, meet the Zardusht and then I'll take you for breakfast, at the best beer tent in Shiimti. You do drink beer, don't you?'

He was trying to joke. She raised a weak smile. She wanted to help Ariamá out of the buggy, lead her down through the field of white star-flowers, away from the cliff, to the water to drink. She wanted to wander in the orchards with Muzi, holding hands and looking for hoopoes. She wanted to run far away, back to Or, back to Klor. But she couldn't do any of that. She had come to Shiimti to meet her Code father and meek as a lamb she followed him up to the cliff.

Astra's father didn't like him. The man was polite, genuinely grateful, even, but Muzi could tell instantly that Zizi wouldn't want his daughter to marry him. He had seen Zizi's mouth pinch as he glanced at his short arm, heard his tone change; had felt the man's rejection like a sharp shove between his ribs. It was not a new feeling. Sometimes in Kadingir a class-mate's mother or father, a Non-Lander from a family who carefully screened all their marriage partners to avoid the risk of alt-bodied children, had stiffened at the sight of him, pulled their daughter close. Then he would suddenly experience something — not just anger, like his grandmother did at these people, but a dirty tussle of emotions he didn't want to talk about, not even to Uttu. As soon as he could, when he felt that way, he would head to the scrublands, roam with the sheep, talk to the sky-god until he felt clean.

He couldn't run away here. He was no longer a shy boy, he was a man. And it was a celebration, a happy, clear blue day. The cries and drumbeats of the Shiimti people ringing in his ears, he swallowed the hurt down. Astra's father had clearly just woken up. He wasn't thinking straight. And Zizi didn't know him yet, that was all. He might assume a young man with one hand and patchy fuzz on his chin would not be able to look after his daughter, but he didn't know all the things Muzi could do, or his plans for the camel. Zizi was not a bad man; not hard or mean; you could tell that right away. He was warm and loud and funny and from what he himself said, not wealthy. He might dream of marrying Astra off to a rich man, but he would surely respect an ambitious, hardworking groom. Muzi would just have to show Zizi exactly what he had to offer. Falling in step with Lil, he walked slowly behind the new man in Astra's life towards the dancing, drumming, ululating group on the ledge.

The singer was the tallest woman he had ever seen. She had broad shoulders and, beneath her orange and gold robe, a majestic bosom she was thrusting out and shaking like a pair of gourd rattles above the big drum she was banging with a stick in each hand as her feet stomped the ground. In her red slippers, red headdress and orange and gold robe, the Zardusht looked like the queen of fire, dancing to her own drumming as if to set herself alight. Fanning her bright flames, the two men in white skirts whirled faster and faster, hands at their hearts, eyes raised to heaven, their skirts like spinning plates on sticks he had seen once at a festival. He felt dizzy watching them, spellbound by their welcome.

With one last piercing call and a drum riff, the greeting ceased. The Zardusht removed her drum from her neck, set it behind her and opened her arms. Lil ran into them.

'Zardusht!' she called, falling into a hug, her thin blue body practically disappearing in the shiny robes. When at last she was released, she gestured at him and Astra. 'I have brought Astra Ordott to Shiimti, as you asked. This is her companion, Muzi Bargadala.'

He stood respectfully before the Shiimti elders. The dancers were fine-featured, almond-skinned old men; beneath their red camelhair hats one sported a salt-and-pepper moustache, the other a neatly trimmed white beard. The Zardusht was ancient. Numberless lines mapped her loam-dark face, radiating out from her broad lips and nose across cheekbones made all the more prominent by the toothless caves beneath them. Her high forehead was carved into ridges and above the gold trim of her robe her neck tendons protruded like polished struts. Her face was like the citadel, he thought; like it, she could be a hundred years old, or a thousand and ten. She might remember the Dark Times; she might recall the very creation of the planet. For the Zardusht's eyes were ageless: large gleaming pools that shone with a dark fire like beacons from the heart of the Earth. A bright orange feather twirled from her ear and her red wicker headdress was interwoven with gold cables and wires that glinted in the sun as though transmitting her will to the world.

'Welcome to Shiimti, my children.' The High Healer spoke in Somarian, with an indeterminable accent. A sparse flock of teeth flashed in her mouth as she smiled. Her voice was soft and rasping and yet it flew up to the cliffs, causing grass to shake, fledglings to launch from their nests. 'I am the Zardusht. If I ever had another name I have long forgotten it. If I forget anything else,' her wondrous eyes crinkled up with mischief, 'my World Whirlers find it. As they will find places for you here. Please, meet your guides, Hozai and Šǎñǎl.'

'Welcome, welcome.' The dancers murmured and bowed. Hozai wore the moustache and Šǎñǎl the beard. They were elegant men with a distant air, their eyes still returning from whatever it was they had seen in their white spinning trance.

'We serve the spirits of this place.' The Zardusht beamed, exposing a wide stretch of gum, and spread her arms wide. 'They tell us that this is your home for as long as you need it.'

He wanted to fall to his knees. He wanted to tell her about his grandmother, hear her words of comfort, take her advice. He wanted to bring her wildflowers in the morning and a jug of cool water in the evening, to sit by the cliff and look at the sky with her, tell her what he saw, learn from her how to interpret the faintest puff on the horizon, the wildest wash of colour at dusk. This woman was his spirit teacher. He knew that as surely as he knew his own name – if he too was not destined to forget it.

Lil was translating for Astra. 'Thank you, Zardusht, thank you,' Astra said when she understood everything. He was dumbstruck.

'Come.' The Zardusht held out her hands. They were crabbed hands, the knuckles swollen, but gripped his so tight he thought his fingers would snap off. 'Come, break bread and drink tea. Then we shall sit and hear your stories.'

Her voice was like a summer's wind rushing through him, not cooling but soothing, the promise of salvation on a blistering day. He would let that wind take him wherever it led.

She was being presented to the Zardusht. The High Healer of Shiimti, who spoke to spirits and had years ago decreed that she, Astra, was Istar of the Prophecy. An ancient old woman, who danced like a crazed youth and drummed like thunder, was looking at her as if she knew all her secrets: that Astra felt repelled by Zizi and possessive of Muzi, threatened by Lil and guilty about Ahn, and hadn't told anyone she was going mad, damaged by IMBOD, stricken by an Old World disease, that she talked to animals and plants in her sleep . . . but that was all right, because the Zardusht's deep eyes said, *You will tell me everything and then you will discover that there is nothing to forgive.*

She was shrinking inside, like wet wool in the sun. She didn't want any of this. All she wanted to do in Shiimti was get in touch with Cora Pollen's people and pass Dr Tapputu's message on to the Zardusht. Then she'd go back to Kadingir with Lil, or on to Amazigia, or wherever her quest to save Muzi's family and shut down the Zabaria mine sent her. She didn't want to be a daughter to this noisy, smelly man; she didn't want to hear any more voices in her head. She didn't want to tell her life story to the Zardusht, play the role this woman had imagined for her, sent Lil to *produce.*

But the Zardusht beckoned. She took her walking stick from its resting place against a rock and, at a brisk lollop, led Astra and the others into the gully and up a steep flight of stone stairs, the dancers bringing up the rear with the drum. The narrow steps zigzagged up the cliff face for what seemed an age, a tiring and frightening climb, but at least Zizi was behind Astra, unable to keep holding her hand or hugging her shoulder. She was thirsty, but had forgotten her water flask. She wanted to ask Muzi for a drink, but he was behind Zizi. She fought the desire to battle back towards him, grab his hand and run away. At last they reached the top of the steps; the entrance to a long stone chamber.

Carved by wind and water, not human hands, open on one side to the sky, the cave was an eyrie, a natural lookout post back towards the citadel and out across the gardens. The Zardusht strode to the lip of the ledge and struck a jaunty pose with her stick.

'Behold Shiimti! Our fountain of youth!'

'Personally, Astra,' Zizi whispered, 'I can't dance any more. Arthritis in the knee. I don't know how the Zardusht does it.'

He was smiling, almost blushing. She felt covered with shame again. He was trying so hard to reach out to her. And she wanted to give up before they had even started. *I'm sorry she wanted to say for your knees, for being rude, afraid of you, for everything* . . . but he pushed her into the chamber.

'Go,' he urged, 'see the view. I am not a personal fan of great heights.'

She, Muzi and Lil approached the edge. From here the full beauty of the gardens was apparent. The concentric fertile crescents of the fields arched out from the main road like the leaves of a palm tree; the stream from the cliff curved up to nearly the centre of that tree then splayed out in three different directions, like a snake with three tongues. Her throat constricted. Being up so high looking down on a garden was like being on the roof of Code House. Except even Or hadn't gone in for this grand-scale agripattering. Gaians created such projects only in special, dedicated communities out in the steppes, marvellous places you might visit for a holiday weekend. Doing it in a desert would put the Shiimti-ites in line for an international medal.

'Wow.' Lil pushed her sunglasses up on her head. 'It's really grown since I was last here, Zardusht.'

The Zardusht placed a gnarled hand on Lil's shoulder. 'I remember well the day that you came, Lilutu. We had just finished planting the ground cover and were raising the first grape trellises. "Ah, so you've come for a night of intoxicating discussion, have you, girl?" I asked, and I was right, wasn't I?'

Lil giggled. '"When it comes to passion, it is best to squeeze one grape at a time," that's what you taught me.'

Astra tensed. What did *that* mean? But the Zardusht was flowing on. 'The garden is nearly complete. We have dug and planted the last crescent and the stream is flowing like the triple-tongued serpent of human desire, seeking the three sacred fruits of knowledge, wisdom and love.' She turned to Astra. 'What do you think of our garden, Gaia Girl?'

The Zardusht had asked the question in Gaian. Like some kind of benevolent radiation, her voice exuded patience and amusement, concern but also genuine curiosity. Suddenly, high above this miraculously flour-ishing, unguarded place, a wall Astra had been painstakingly building inside herself weakened. Suddenly she wanted to talk. The Zardusht spoke with spirits, Lil had said. The Zardusht must know the difference between crazy voices and Gaia visions.

But Lil had also said the Zardusht would tell her how to be Istar. Maybe the Zardusht was even crazier than she was.

'It's amazing,' she replied in Somarian. 'Is the mountain stream the only . . . way of water?' She didn't know 'method' or 'irrigation'. It was time she mastered Somarian. She would work on her vocabulary here. Now they were no longer fighting for their lives, Muzi could teach her.

The Zardusht emitted an almost inaudible *hmmm*. But she replied in Somarian, 'Not the only source, no. It rains here, not often but . . . *a lot.*'

She widened her eyes, lifted her arms and fluttered her fingers down through the air, her whole long body shivering in anticipation. It was funny and unexpected and a little bit sexy, another mesmerising dance. Astra, Lil and Muzi laughed and the Zardusht flashed her gappy grin. 'Before, the rain evaporated in a day. Now it stays in the soil. There is also a small aquifer and a well. People have dwelt in these cliffs and planted gardens here for thousands of years.'

She understood the sense of it, followed the Zardusht's knobbled finger out to the well on the far side of the road. Then there was the sound of a bubbling kettle and the Zardusht clapped.

'What am I thinking! Come, travellers, sit. Let us refresh you.'

The Whirlers had set out red woollen mats and embroidered bolster cushions. She let Hozai guide her to one between Zizi and Muzi and gratefully sat. Šañal placed a low chair on the lone mat in front of them. With the aid of a stick, the Zardusht lowered herself into it.

'Dancing is medicine, but you can't sit on old bones too long or they crack!' she crowed, crossing her legs and plucking at her robe. Muzi gestured with his chin to the wall behind her and Astra understood why.

The ledges and nooks in the rock were filled with beeswax candles, the flames barely visible in the sun slicing across the mouth of the cave, but the purpose of candles here was clearly not simply to shed light. The wall itself was a candle now, a lavish cascade of wax, stalactites, gorges and rivulets, impossible to distinguish from the ridges and crevices of stone. There were sculptures embedded in the wall too, small figurines made of clay and bronze, rusted cogs and wheels, circuit boards and Tablette fascia, pilgrims on a winding trail marked by temples to wildness, colour and glass: test tubes stuffed full of feathers and wildflowers, a single red rose stemming from a slender-necked bright blue vase. Up in the corner by the cliff face was a nest and a long streak of bird droppings. Perhaps the birds had shat all over the wall. She couldn't imagine the Zardusht minding.

'My ever-altering altar.' The Zardusht's eyes crinkled as she made the Inglish joke. 'My altar to alteration. And my altar to love, that alters not when it alteration finds. Now, eat!'

Šañal and Hozai served a rich breakfast of spicy bean dip and spelt crispbread, olives, cucumbers, apricots and mint tea. Gladly, they obeyed. Neither Lil nor Zizi ate much, Astra noticed, and her father was sweating profusely; there were dark patches under his arms. Hozai gave him a damp cloth and he rubbed it over his head. She experienced another pang of guilt. Maybe her father smelled funny because he wasn't well.

The Zardusht had noticed Zizi too. 'Poet!' she declared, pointing at him. 'He who refuses the vision loses his appetite!'

It was a peculiar thing to say, Zizi's face grew as haughty as a camel's. 'I am never hungry in the morning, Zardusht,' he replied, with a note of offended dignity.

The High Healer laughed a deep wheezy laugh. Zizi offered Astra his crispbread and pot of bean dip. She took the food and gave him a little smile in return. When the Whirlers had taken the dishes away, the Zardusht addressed her and Muzi.

'My children. You have journeyed long to get here. Tell me, both of you, why did you come to Shiimti?'

'I came to bring Astra to meet her father,' Muzi said in Somarian.

'I came to meet my father,' she echoed in Asfarian. 'And you, Zardusht.' She hesitated. She didn't want to talk about the voices in front of everyone. She should pass on the message from Dr Tappetu, but perhaps now wasn't the time. Muzi didn't know about the plan to find a cure for the Sec Gens and Photon had said YAC might not be ready to cooperate with it: maybe Lil shouldn't know about the doctor's plan either. Much as she didn't want to raise the subject, it was, however, time to confront this crazy story, this *myth*, about her. 'Lil said you could help me. If I . . .' She stopped. 'If I pretended I was Istar' seemed rude. 'If people really thought I was Istar, then perhaps I could help YAC. But, Zardusht' – she looked straight into the High Healer's molten brown eyes – 'I don't know if I am Istar. I didn't ever feel that I was, in myself. It's just something Lil asked me to do.'

'I can help you understand your role in the Prophecy.' The Zardusht swayed back and forth. 'But Astra, even if you are just *you*, what do you want to achieve, here in Shiimti and in Non-Land?'

This felt like safer ground. 'I want to get Muzi's family back. And I want to get in touch with Cora Pollen's people. I need them to help me find some information about Dr Samrod Blesserson. He's on the board of the IREMCO mine and he should be punished for everything that happened in Zabaria.'

She felt herself getting heated. Lil seemed to be looking at her with new respect. Well, she could get political too.

'Ah, yes. Blesserson.' The Zardusht pursed her lips. 'Your Shelter mother's brother. Lilutu has spoken of him. We will discuss all of this. And more. But first – she clapped – 'a story. Muzi, tell us about your journey.'

It was a hard story. He had to begin with his family's kidnapping and Uttu's death, which made Lil cry, a single tear Astra saw her wipe away with a blue-tipped finger, then together they recounted the journey, first the horse-and-cart trip across the scrublands and bone fields, then Muzi's trip into Lálsil to buy the camel. He broke into a sob when he talked about Doron, and the Zardusht banged her stick on the floor.

'Uttu the Washer of Souls and Doron the Ironmonger of Stars shall be honoured on the altar. Muzi, whenever you wish, together we shall seek their spirits in the World Within.'

It didn't seem to be a question. They continued the story, telling about the *mergallá*, the Shlemun altar, the Istar oasis, the arrival of Lil and the buggy, how they'd thought she was a gang of Asfarian traders; together they told the Zardusht – not everything, but nearly.

'So. A great adventure. Tell me, Astra, what was the most important thing you learned from your voyage?'

That I can be angry and demanding and jealous and lie about it too. That human beings are cleft through and through. That love is a journey through a desert and to reach the green heartland I must store fat and water in my soul and be prepared to travel far on my own.

She swallowed. The camel had told her that. Or had it? She felt again the pressing need to speak; the desire to confide in the Zardusht.

She could speak in Gaian, but then Muzi would think she was keeping a secret from him. 'I learned how to listen to my dreams,' she said slowly in Somarian. 'I had some strong dreams about animals and plants.' She switched to Asfarian. 'They were a little confusing though. Maybe I can tell you about them while I'm here?'

The Zardusht rocked back and forward, gripping her knees. 'Good. Good. Dreams we can discuss, oh yes, dreams we can do. And you, Muzi?'

He bit his thumb, squinted up at the roof of the cave. Then he said, slowly, so that she could understand, 'I learned that Astra is Istar. She's Astra too, but Istar shines through her. And we need Istar on our side to win the war.'

She stiffened. What was Muzi saying? Was it because they'd got together at the Istar shrine? She didn't think he was King Shlemun! A wild panic rose in her. Was there no one she could trust here? Why had she talked about her dreams like that?

'Uncle,' Muzi turned to Zizi, spoke across her.

Her father appeared to be nodding off on his cushion. He jerked awake and regarded Muzi blearily. 'Young man?'

'Uncle,' Muzi started again, 'you lived in Somaria, our homeland. I want to go there with you and Astra one day, back to Kurgal, to the house of my grandmother. You named Astra for Istar. If Istar is willing, we will accomplish it.'

Zizi frowned, as if assessing her and Muzi anew. She had no idea, she realised, if Zizi thought she had been born to play a role in the Prophecy. So far he just seemed to want to hug her. Right now, she wouldn't mind a hug. A hug from someone tall and dry and smelling of warm stone: a hug from Klor. But if Zizi would back her on this Istar business, she would throw herself into his arms, no matter how smelly he was.

'Yes, I lived in Is-Land,' he mused. 'I named my daughter for the morning and evening star and now half of Non-Land considers her a goddess. Naming is an act of great power.'

He was no help at all.

'Lilutu?' The Zardush broke in.

Lil spoke in a high, clear voice, in Asfarian, so Astra understood every word. 'I also learned that Astra is Istar. Before, Zardusht, to be honest, part of me thought it all might just be a coincidence and that as her producer I should help make Astra's life fit the Prophecy. But she came to Shiimti exactly like it says.' She adopted a melodramatic alto: '"Attended by the Prince of Shepherds she will move like a *mergalld* over the windsands." Muzi's a sheepherder, isn't he, and they walked through a storm. I'm a good producer, but I'm not that good.'

'So Astra, your friends both think you are Istar.' The Zardush's fingertips danced against each other. 'But that does not convince you?'

She flushed. She'd forgotten that line in the Prophecy, but like Lil said, it was just a coincidence. '*No,* I said I would help the women in Zabaria. That's partly why I'm here, but mainly to see my father.' She appealed to Muzi and Lil. 'How can I help anyone in Non-Land? I'm good at sports, but I'm not a warrior. I hardly speak the languages – no one would trust me.' Unexpectedly, her eyes filled with tears. She wiped her cheek with her sleeve. 'Una Dayyani can be Istar. She's a leader; that makes sense.

You can bargain with me if you like. Maybe if you give me to IMBOD, we can get Muzi's family back.'

They all spoke at once. 'No!' Muzi's face darkened. 'I'll never give you to IMBOD. *Never.*'

'What?' Once more, she had shocked Lil. 'You can't hand yourself in to Is-Land. IMBOD will *crucify* you! They're worse than the worst Abrahamites, you know that!'

'You are here to be *healed*, Astra!' The Zardusht stamped her stick again on the stone floor. 'No one is giving you to IMBOD.'

'My daughter,' Zizi pleaded, 'you are safe here. Here you must stay.'

Muzi reached over and touched her hand. 'That's why I think you are Istar,' he said. 'Because you don't want to be.' He addressed the Zardusht. 'My father says true leaders think only of others, not themselves.'

The Zardusht rocked and nodded, as if supremely satisfied. 'When you are healed, Astra, you will know for yourself who you are. Tell me now, Lil. What was the most beautiful creature you saw in the gardens?'

She expected Lil to say the peacocks. But she replied immediately, 'The butterflies. The big bright blue ones. I would have stopped to dance with them, but I wanted to get Astra to you quickly.'

Astra felt a squirm of discomfort. She had dreamed about the butterflies; did that mean she was supposed to get closer to Lil?

'The turquoise butterfly is a powerful heart teacher. You and I will dance with it this afternoon, Astra?'

At last an easy question. 'The hoopoes. There was a painting of one in the Istar shrine. I didn't think the bird had survived the Dark Times. I felt so happy when I saw them fly over the road.'

The Zardusht waggled a knobbly finger in the air. 'I knew there was a reason I wore this today.' She took off her feather earring and extended it to Astra. 'It is for you.'

She didn't deserve a gift, but she got to her knees and received it. 'Thank you, Zardusht.' It was a crest feather, bright orange with a white band and tipped with black. She didn't like to say that she didn't have pierced ears, but the hook would be simple enough to close and attach to a pin.

'The hoopoe,' the Zardusht said, 'is the teacher of the power of the Self. From the hoopoe we learn how and when to be ourselves, in all our eccentric crowning glory; how to use that power to point others towards the path of wisdom; and how and when to abandon the Self and soar into the World Within. For this reason, many consider it the greatest of creature teachers.'

She stroked the feather. She did need to learn all of those things. She had no idea who she was.

'You will come and visit me tomorrow and we will discuss the hoopoe's teachings and your dreams. Now, Muzi?'

'I liked the hudhud too.' He cast Astra a shy look. 'I wanted to stop and get a feather for Astra. But my favourite was the bird down by the water. The one with the long legs. I saw it fly.' He spread his arms and smiled, a dazzling Muzi grin, the first she'd seen since the news about Doron. 'So large!'

Muzi had seen a bird she hadn't. Why hadn't he told her? She'd thought they were sharing everything on the journey. She flared with anger, then took a deep breath.

She was being possessive again. She had come to a place of great spiritual power – everyone knew that Shiimti was a place of high healing – and she was pushing her father away, suspicious of the Zardusht, silently snapping at Muzi for seeing a bird. That was because she was a sick, violent person. Running right through her, like the shaft of a feather, was a brittle spine filled with hatred and mistrust. She couldn't even trust her own head.

'Ah.' The Zardusht rocked back, as if watching the bird soar. 'You saw one of the cranes. The crane, Muzi, is the teacher of faithfulness and the great messenger between the living and the dead. You will learn much from the cranes in the World Within.'

Astra looked up at the altar. The little figurines were climbing and climbing, the candle invisibly burning, wax slowly dripping down the wall, the altar of alteration, constantly changing, just as the citadel had grown over the years. She needed to change too. Suddenly, she felt incredibly tired. Maybe she could stay here. She needed to rest and this was undeniably a beautiful, welcoming place. The oasis had been beautiful too, Muzi's and her private sanctuary; Or had been created by agriculturalists and artists who cared deeply for the Earth; but Shiimti's beauty was different again. This place was brimming with love and knowledge and wisdom but there was a great wild openness to it too. People in Or had drawn a wall around themselves, were constantly fearful of infiltrators, questioned nothing IMBOD said. Here the Whirlers had flung themselves out to the horizon and then gathered in three refugees from a war.

The Zardusht was welcoming them, feeding them, telling them about creature teachers, promising to help her understand her dreams. She couldn't keep sitting here in front of her being such an awful, stunted, shrivelled-up excuse for a person.

She scrambled in her pocket and pulled out the last remaining rook feather. 'We have a gift for you, Zardusht,' she announced. 'It's from all of us. Muzi and Lil and me, I was just carrying it.' She got up and presented the feather. 'The rooks of Kadingir fly together, without a leader, across the Boundary. We gave their feathers to Shlemun and Istar and we want you to have one too.'

The Zardusht took the feather and smoothed its quills. She held it up to the light, then pressed it to her chest and closed her eyes. Blood pulsed in Astra's ears. It was as if the elderwoman's heartbeat was echoing around the chamber.

'The rook is the teacher of community. And living in community has been my greatest teacher. I thank you, Astra, Muzi, Lil, and I welcome you again to Shiimti.' She stuck the feather in her headdress, above her left ear, and rubbed her hands together, so fast sparks flew. 'We all work here for the common good, five hours a day, five days a week. For three days you will be our guests and then the Whirlers will show you where to volunteer. Tomorrow afternoon we will chew the lantern plant together and travel to the World Within, where you will receive messages from your spirit teachers.' She widened her eyes. 'Zizi Kataru, are you ready to join us?'

'UH!' Her father's head shot up for the second time. 'Wha—? Astra!' He groped for her arm. 'Don't worry, Daughter,' he mumbled, his eyes bloodshot and bulging. 'You're safe here. Don't worry about anything, I will buy you some pretty dresses and you can work in the beer tent. My friend is the manager; she always needs help.'

She didn't want to work in a beer tent. And he smelled worse now, an acrid scent seeping off him. But still, there was something about Zizi, the way he looked like her, only fatter and oilier, the way he looked *at* her, with those eyes like hers in the mirror, as though she was the only person in the room, that made her heart slip. Again, she felt ashamed of her aversion to him. Her father had been so excited to see her. One small part of her fantasy was true: he *had* been waiting for her for years, pining for her even. She, on the other hand, only cared who he was because she needed his help. She'd been so selfish; she had come all this way to meet her father

'Kataru!' The Zardusht clapped her hands. 'She can decide for herself what to wear. And you! Poet! Are you ready to *chew*?'

The Zardusht was at him again – in front of his daughter yet – nagging him to consume that foul plant, the psychotropic toxin she peddled to all the sycophants and sensation-seekers this place attracted. *A rite of passage*, the simpletons whispered – lantern leaf was a weapon, the High Healer's warped sword, the woman's means of dividing her obedient slaves from the truly free spirits she pretended to cherish, but in fact was dedicated to obliterating. For how long had the Zardusht dangled her promises of teaching work, his own office in the Complexity, devoted young poetry students, a reading of his work in the High Hall; how many times had Zizi told her: *no*. He was already a respected poet and discourser; he did not need to suffocate his talent in an office or lecture theatre. And he certainly did not need to boil with a fever, hallucinate for hours, vomit up his own testicles and pray to Gaia for death to prove his visionary capacities to her, or anyone else. He knew all about the 'World Within' – Salamu had told him and so had everyone else who had chewed lantern leaf: the 'World Within' was the Shiimti-ite term for a migraine that lasted a week.

Supposedly it was worth it to listen to the 'voices'. But there must be hidden Tablette speakers in the Zardusht's cave, because as far as he could make out from what everyone said, nine times out of ten the 'voices' told you the same thing: to stop drinking beer, stop having so much sex, stop scratching your arse when it itched. And the voices threatened you too. Effectively, it appeared, because – lo! – after two or three of the Zardusht's nightmare sleepover parties people did stop drinking beer! First they switched to lassi, then water, then urine, their own morning brew, boasting at breakfast how pure their piss was. *No. No. No*. He wasn't having it. Chewing lantern leaf might be a requisite step towards certain privileges here, but it was not a condition of living in Shiimti. He did his work in the hemp field, he drank his beer in the beer tent, he wrote and read and discoursed upon poetry when the muse moved him and now he was going to look after his daughter. No one could force him to change who he was. To try to do so, surely, was against the whole ethos of Shiimti!

and hadn't even brought him a present. All she had was a rook feather and she'd given that to the Zardusht. She looked down at the hoopoe feather on her mat. She might be being herself, but she had a very long way to go to be wise.

But he couldn't erupt at the Zardusht. Being rude might reflect badly on him with Astra and her friends, all of whom, he could see, were half in awe of the High Healer already.

'Zardusht,' he responded graciously, 'lantern leaf is for the young, those with no hardened habits to break. "Habits maketh the man"; that is surely the case. Let us recall the great poet who wrote – in perfect *ghazal* metre in the Karkish, I might add – "without my habits I am but an unshelled snail, food for the——"' He stopped, flustered. The Zardusht might take offence at "predatory dove".

'I misremember the line.' He waved his hand airily, slapped palm to chest. 'But the sense of the poem is here, in my heart. Habits form the carapace of the soul, a uniquely crafted shell that protects our vulnerabilities from the harsh light of day. It is even said, by the astrophysicists of Asfar, that habits are the fundamental means by which the universe maintains its sacred order. We alter our habits at our peril.'

The Zardusht raised an eyebrow. 'It is my understanding, poet, that Asfarian astrophysics proposes that habits are the means by which the universe *evolves*. Which is to say, changes – amending laws we humans once thought were immutable.'

She had this disagreeable side to her, an intellectual buttress to her imperious will. He replied as evenly as possible under the trying circumstances, 'Evolution is a slow process, Zardusht. We older gentlemen do not have as much time as the stars.'

'The older the gentleman and the worse his habits, the softer his *carapace*, in my experience.' She laughed that windy laugh of hers; behind him those sanctimonious puritans, Hozai and Šáñál, chuckled into their moustaches. 'But the ravenous dove can wait for her sweetmeats, Kataru.' She grinned. 'Your soul has all the time in world.'

He drew himself up. The Zardusht was doing it again: slyly insulting him. The woman had no idea of the suffering he had endured. But he would heal himself – had he not today already manifested both a woman in his bed and a daughter in his arms? As for the Whirlers, those two might be able to recite reams of classical Farashan mystical verse, but poetry for them was naught but a lick of paint on a windowless house. What did two childless celibates understand of pain and sorrow and the joy of union with the beloved?

But he understood the Zardusht now. You could not be angry, wry, flippant or droll in audience with her. She wanted your soul and you had to give her a glimpse of it, or she would hound you for weeks, accost you on the ledge, call out at you over the beer tent, interrupt your discourses, spoil the taste of your beer.

'Life is change, of course it is, Zardusht,' he concurred, with enormous dignity. 'And our great challenge is to embrace change without losing one's essence. Today, I am the luckiest of men. For today, life has not modified or remodelled, but *enlarged* my soul. Did not the distant poetess of the lost island of women write, "Bless the bright evening star that leads the lamb home to the ewe"? Today it is that same star in her morning dress who has blessed me, making me both mother and father, reunited with my daughter at last. I can only hope to help Astra heal, Zardusht. For myself, I have no need of any healing but to see her content. Others might wish her to sacrifice her young life for the noble cause of One Land, but I say she has sacrificed enough. Let Istar shine from Una Dayyani's behind. It is time for Astra to be happy.'

He was expecting no thanks, from anyone, for his discourse. He had learned that lesson many moons ago. All a poet could do was place his offerings before people, as humbly and foolishly as a farm wife putting out cream for feral cats. So when Astra flung herself from her mat and bowled her small hot body into his arms, she knocked the breath from Zizi's lungs and, for a very long moment, all the words from his soul.

The Dragon's Gorge

He was running hot and cold, burning up yet shivering so hard he had no idea whether it was his body rocking, the boat, or the whole universe. A tiny, remote part of him pondered the possibility of Tablette-recording his chattering teeth for a rhyme track; a larger, much louder part of him retched, dry bitter heaves that brought up nothing but bile. Nearly all of him hurt. As well as his throat and his back, his stomach and even his good arm hurt now, the muscles cramping, joints screaming. The thought of being dumped in the Mikku with one arm in a sling crossed his mind, but he was beyond fear, beyond desire. He simply lay in the bottom of the boat, quaking and sweating, letting the droplets trickle into his beard, the clouds darken overhead. They had been slicing down the river all afternoon, but it felt like he'd been out here forever.

'Enki,' Éšgíd called from the stern, his voice hushed, 'we're here.'

It was difficult to tell at first, the solar engine was so quiet, but the sky had stopped moving, so the boat must have as well. Above him, the first star was screwing through the sky.

'Enki?' Éšgíd would come and help him if he didn't move soon. He hauled himself up by the gunwale, peered over the side of the boat. His body spasmed, but he could see enough to know the torture of the trip had been worth it.

They were floating in a broad glimmering plain, the Mikku far wider than it ever was in Kadingir, Bartol's boat idling just ahead, the big man a hazy silhouette in the gathering dusk. The river was the colour of the sky, a deep inky blue, the distant shore a low, dark cliff. The Dragon's Gorge: this was his place. He had made it home. Groaning, Enki lolled back in the bow, closed his eyes, let the illusory calm wash over him. For the tranquillity was deceptive: ahead the river funnelled into the maw of the cliffs, the currents gathering pace as they were sucked into a long narrow thunder of white water, a famous view to behold from the clifftops: for years the Dragon's Gorge had been Non-Land's top honeymoon destination. He had been conceived here, his mother had told him once, during his parents' trip for their fifth wedding anniversary. There were fish, countless fish, she'd said, silver carp that practically leapt for the bait, and the cliffs were riddled with caves. She'd refused to say if the sacred deed had occurred in one of them or back at the hut hotel. There were no busloads of honeymooners now. A decade back, Asfarian bandits had established hide-outs in the caves beneath the falls and the carp were nearly all gone, overfished for the markets in Lálsil. Only a few brave boats came out now, early in the morning above the falls, risking the bandits for the chance of a slender catch. To his generation, the Dragon's Gorge was Tablette photos and beer-tent stories. He had seen it for himself at last. He could die.

There was a bump: Bartol coming alongside to confer with Eŝgŝd. Their voices were low and anxious; they had arrived later than hoped. That was a problem, he knew, but it no longer felt like one of his.

'It's too rocky here, brother.' Bartol was leaning over his head. 'We're going to head for the west bank.'

Enki ignored him. Eŝgŝd restarted the engine and the boat moved again. After some time, the others called softly to each other, then Eŝgŝd was jumping into the water, he and Bartol wading through the shallows, dragging the boat up onto land.

The friction carved through his spine like a blunt knife. 'No!' he rasped, eyes clenched.

'I'm sorry, brother.'

Bartol lifted him out. He rested against a rock, recovering. The shoreline was steep and narrow, boulders, ledges and shingle staggering down to the dark sheen of the water. A few paces away a blasted tree erupted from the foot of a cliff. Bartol tethered his own boat to it, then shouldered the Sec Gen out of the craft. Dimly, Enki registered that the tranquilliser was wearing off: though dangling upside-down, the monster reared and attempted to head-butt Bartol in the kidneys. Eŝgŝd grabbed its head and Bartol dropped the thing to the ground, where it lay twitching on the rocks.

A Sec Gen: half-naked, doped, gagged, hooded and belted, feet securely shackled and hands cuffed behind its back, but still dangerous. Who knew what the monster was Coded to do? It had flown from the vehicle with a collar and broken chain around its neck; even its own engineers might not be able to control it. Breaking out of cuffs and shackles could be as easy to it as tearing a paper chain. It might be able to bite through iron. Its spit could be toxic. All of these possibilities, thoroughly discussed by the mission team, floated back to Enki as if from over a great distance. Beneath lowered lids, he watched Bartol chain the monster to the tree trunk; Êśǵíd kneel to deliver another shot of tranquilliser.

'Êśǵíd's going to look for a cave. Do you want to fish, brother?'

Bartol was crouching beside him, speaking slowly and loudly as if he might not understand. He understood perfectly. A cave, that was right. The plan was to sleep in a cave. The fantasy was to have a fish supper.

He grunted, let Bartol shift him down to the river's edge, kit him out with a pole and a bucket. Back on solid land, his pain was subsiding, but his vision was swimming, his eyelids kept juddering shut, and anyway it was hard to fish with one arm. When the pole twitched and nearly flew from his lap, Bartol took it from him and reeled the fish in.

A fish: small, but incontrovertible. He listened to Bartol cheer, the fish flop about in the bucket, the ever-sensitive Bartol smash its head in with a rock. When Êśǵíd returned he was still resting his eyes, but he heard every word.

'There's a cave close by, but a better one further along. It's deep, high above the water-mark, and there's a stone column at the back. We could chain the hostage to it.'

'Can we row there?'

'There isn't a landing site. We'd have to portage.'

'What about the wheelchair?'

'No.'

'Enki, can you wait here for us, brother?'

He indicated assent with a blink. Bartol lifted him again, back from the edge of the river, then, through fluttering lids, he watched the big man sling the limp Sec Gen over his shoulder, toting the thing like a sack of rubble as he'd done across the firesands. Even in chains and jabbed by a cattle prod specially ordered from Asfar, a Sec Gen couldn't be counted on to walk where you wanted him to go. The doctor had said the creatures were probably Coded to commit suicide if captured; it would have to be transported like cargo. Dead weight.

Just like him. Waiting for death.

He waited for a long time. But death did not come; just Bartol again, kneeling beside him with the rack. Before the Hem battle, Enki had shuffled and swung himself up onto the rack, belted himself in. Tonight, Bartol lifted him, then crouched, strapped the rack to his back. They walked, warm back to warm back, in silence.

Bartol was trying to mend the trust between them. He knew that, but trust was like a china plate: broken once, even twice, it could be glued back together; shattered, it was no good for anywhere but the scrapheap. As they traversed the dark jagged shoreline, unwelcome memories jolted back into his mind, the moment of Bartol's betrayal at the war conclave as jarring and painful as his dislocated vertebra. But not just Bartol's. The whole of YAC was now a jab-fest of treachery. After Eŝgid's triumphant return from the firesands — covered with sandfly bites, exhausted after lying ill on the riverbank for two days, but blazing with glory – Ninti and Malku had even tried to backtrack on the decision to persist with the firesands mission. It was too late, Ninti objected at the next conclave, and possibly a huge waste of time and resources: the jail had been under IMBOD control for days now and all the Sec Gens might be back in the Barracks. Of the Core group only Lilutu had taken his side, arguing YAC needed to keep signalling their independence from Una Dayyani's agenda. He had been under no illusions: Lil's agenda was not to support him, but to establish herself as the new 'spirit of YAC' and get funding for that dune buggy and trip to Shiimti she wanted. But she was persistent: the conclave had finally agreed that even a non-Sec Gen hostage would be a valuable asset. Most people, though, had argued against Enki taking part in the capture – he had come down with a vomiting bug after the conclave and was too ill to travel; or too severely wounded; or needed in Kadingir on the War Strategy and Media groups. Really, they meant he would slow the team down.

Shingle crunching under foot, Bartol plodded on. Being up high, on the move, cleared Enki's head. So far, he calculated, he had slowed Bartol down by about half an hour. But the cave was worth trekking to – it was a good hiding place, the entrance hidden by rocks, and the stone column in the back was massive, even undoped the Sec Gen would never be able to pull it down. Eŝgid had built a fire at the cave mouth and they sat round it, cooking a pot of grains and the fish. Out of consideration for Enki's stomach, Bartol boiled his fillet. They raised a toast of warm beer before the meal.

'To Odinson!' Êsgîd cheered. 'May the gods chew his bones.'

He hadn't seen the body in flames on the jail road, but Êsgîd and Bartol and the rest of the firesands team had told him everything when they returned to the boats: how perfectly the plan had come off: how the trail of iron-rod poppies Êsgîd had planted had led them safely across the firesands in the night, straight to the road, where they'd buried the wavebomb and waited all morning in the dunes for a car. How the device had tipped the vehicle, thrown the Sec Gen clear to land at their feet with just superficial wounds, but unexpectedly – though they generated heat, wavebombs were not supposed to cause fires – set the driver alight. 'Must have been his body hair: the man was half-bear,' Êsgîd had surmised. The team hadn't had a blanket, and a severely burnt hostage was not what they had bargained for, so, taking bets on who he was, they had left him there. Êsgîd was convinced it was Odinson; whoever it was, he was dead. Êsgîd and Bartol didn't see how anyone could survive such a blaze. A Sec Gen, maybe, but not an ordinary man, no matter how fit.

They would have to wait until tomorrow to settle the bet. His stomach violently rejected the fish. He was cold again, frozen to the core, yet beaded with perspiration. If he could speak, he would have joked he felt like a beer bottle. But someone had hammered a thousand nails through his throat. All he wanted to do was lie down and die. The doctors had said if he rested he had every chance of living, but since the Diplomeet with N-LA, dying was his preferred option. It was just a matter of where.

He didn't want to die in his tent. He was a warrior and he would die on a mission. He'd told Bartol that if he was left behind he would call on his old riverbank connections, trade Is-Land's Pain for a year's worth of morpheus and leave a track-marked corpse for his mother. Bartol had caved in, told the conclave that he wouldn't join the hostage mission unless Enki was a member of the team. Enki could help guard the boats on the banks of the firesands, Bartol said, and give him and Êsgîd strategic guidance when they got to the gorge. It was camel-shit, and everyone knew it. The plan was simple, and Enki couldn't guard a piece of spelt cake from a toddler. But Êsgîd, too, had voted for Enki's comradeship. Êsgîd was a true YAC warrior.

The other two had blown up a vehicle today, killed IMBOD's top brass in Non-Land and kidnapped a Sec Gen. They had walked for hours through the firesands, Bartol with a drugged monster over his shoulder, then sped hundreds of kilometres down the Mikku. They were tired too. The men unrolled their sleeping bags. Enki was out before he did up his zip.

The light woke him: a stealthy grey light breathing into the cave. His throat was a ball of barbed wire but he didn't want to reach for his water bottle in case the movement set off the explosions in his spine. He was lying still, watching the light, when the voices found him.

Quicksilver. Phantom. Grey Feather. Ruff. That's what you'd call us, if only you'd collared us. But we've slipped your nooses, brushed through your gates, whiskered our calligraphy on the frayed hem of your world.

Sometimes in his morpheus dreams he had heard voices: distant, indecipherable voices. It was the gods, his dealer had told him, and he mustn't listen to them. The gods who were drunk when they made us prowled the borders of the land of morpheus, sent voices to entice you to the edge of sanity, of life itself. The gods who had forsaken us, the gods who pissed themselves laughing whenever they cast their shrunken minds over us, wanted human beings to join them in whatever hell they had concocted for themselves, and, his dealer said, only those with a death wish listened.

Tonight, he listened.

Out here in the dark, we prowl your perimeters, circle your fires, sniff out your food stores when the embers glow low. Whatever we snatch, however hungry we leave you, we gift you the lingering impression of grace. We're your friends in the shadows. Because you need friends. Not the kind you can count on: we aren't those.

Friends! The word made him feel even sicker. But the voices padded on, a sly promise of comfort, a dream of relief.

We're the friend who appears when you're flat-lined, dead busted, crawling head-down in the dust of the road – there we are, with a leg of roast chicken, a bag of apple tobacco, a slice of the moon in our jaws. We velvet-glove you away to an infinite midnight, feed you starlight and smoke . . . until all your days of endurance, those eternally recurring diminishing returns, burn up in a long silver flame that says life is a hunt, seize what you need . . . And in one puff we're gone. Some say you tamed us, long ago seduced us with the aroma of stew, cunning traplets of bones. *We say, any dogs who succumbed to hot meat have been leashed – we are still out here, keeping you wild* . . .

Seize what you need . . It was hard to concentrate, but he was glad that the voices were rhymers. Perhaps the gods weren't so useless after all. Perhaps it was time to join their infinite midnight, their eternal morpheus haze . . .

Just as his eyes fluttered shut, he sensed movement: a shadow flicking along a high ledge on the opposite wall of the cave.

He lifted his head a fraction. His spine flared. The shadow stopped and turned its head. It definitely had a head and eyes. Two yellow discs reflected the sickly dawn light back at him, two shrunken suns.

They studied each other: man and beast; a human wreck and a grey, gaunt creature with enormous ears, a pointed muzzle and a plume of smoke for a tail. The plume was thicker than the big silver tassel the priestess at his mother's prayer tent wore on special occasions. He had never seen a dog with a tail like that. With those ears and that nose the creature could have been a bat or a huge rodent, but it was canine, no doubt about that. Its haunches were high, its paws black, as if it had just flown across the river of night.

It was a wild dog; a wild spirit dog. It had come for him. He understood; the gods sent creatures as well as voices. He was still in pain, but the pain didn't matter any more. He welcomed the dog.

The dog pattered down the inclining ledge to the floor of the cave. It studied him again for a moment, then moved in a thin streak towards the Sec Gen. It sniffed the monster's feet, legs and groin, then reared up and, forepaws on the monster's bare chest, gripped the hood in its jaws.

It was like being back in his neighbour's wedding tent, being forced to clap as the girl he had loved all his life danced with her groom, her delicate head tucked beneath his rival's square chin. He watched, unable to breathe, his heart fisting, his stomach falling away.

'Hey!' Bartol flung his sleeping bag open. The dog released the hood and turned. Its eyes were two yellow piss holes in grey sand. It stared again at Enki, tunnelling through him with that acrid gaze, then streaked right over Ésgid's head, leapt over the firepit, hurtled out of the cave and vanished.

'*What the frack?*'

'*Gods alive!*'

CRACK. CRACK.

CRACK. CRACK.

He thought his body was breaking apart, or the cave was falling in. Groaning, half in a trance, half in agony, he shunted himself upright. The Sec Gen was banging its head against the stone column; Bartol was rushing over to stop it, Ešgɨd was strapping on his prosthetic leg.

'Slap it!' he heard Ešgɨd urge. 'Slap its face.'

'Stop it!' Bartol bellowed at the thing. '*Stop it!*'

'Give it another needle!'

'*No*. The doctor said every twelve hours.'

The shock of the visitation was over. A new, musty grey feeling ballooning inside him, Enki reached for his water bottle and doused the fire in his throat. Bartol lifted the monster's hood, loosened the gag and forced a baby-bottle teat through its lips. Ninti had suggested the baby bottle, her attempt at building bridges with Enki. The moment Bartol finished, the Sec Gen started head-banging again. In the end, Bartol pillowed his sleeping bag between the monster's skull and the column, then he and Ešgɨd tied a rope tightly around its forehead and, more loosely, under its chin. The monster began sobbing, a deep gargling croon.

'What was that *thing?*' Ešgɨd asked, rubbing his cheek.

Bartol's gaze was a troubled question Enki had no desire to interpret. He rolled onto his back. The musty grey cloud in his chest was the sensation of failure. He had come here to die. He was holed up in a cave, paralytic with pain, unable to eat, sweating all his salt and minerals away, but he wasn't even worthy of a spirit guide to the next world. The mangy cur had tried to take the Sec Gen, not him.

He might have cried, but the pain kicked back in, his spine an electric fence shorting out of control, and anger stormed through the fear. He was ready to die. If the gods who spat on us when they made us wouldn't take him, he would push himself over the edge.

He lay awake until the cave was fully light. The plan was to wait until the risk of being spotted by a fishing boat was past. Bartol relit the fire and boiled a pot of water.

'It was a fox in the night,' Ešgɨd stated as they sat drinking tea and chewing flatbread. 'My father said there were desert foxes in the gorge. Like dogs, but with huge ears and flames for tails. I never believed him. A *fox*,' he repeated in awe.

'Foxes are lost animals,' Enki croaked. 'It was a dog.'

Bartol held his tongue. They left the cave mid-morning, the other two carrying Enki; the boats and supplies down to the shore, then both going back for the Sec Gen, just in case it had awakened again. Drained, still feverish, Enki waited for their return, disbelieving the vision of the pure peaceful water, prepared for it to churn up at any moment.

None of them had said it over breakfast, but arriving so late at the Dragon's Mouth and being forced to sleep on the west bank meant there was a real danger now of getting caught, killed or drowned. N-LA would search Kadingir and the oasis towns for the hostage, but if Tahazu Rabu had a dollop of brains in his head, he might well send a police boat or two down to the gorge. YAC had debated this point at length. The only way to proceed with confidence was to be prepared to fight. Each warrior had a knife and ear protectors against sonic guns, and the Wheelchair Engineering Team had made a trip to the scrapyard and built two wooden rams to nail to the prows. The rams were impressive-looking – the team had painted dragons' eyes on the sides – but they were a last resort, untested. They might splinter, break off, end up sinking their own boats as well.

He heard the steady crunch of the others returning. The hunt would be over soon, one way or another.

Bartol stood by Êŝgîd's boat, the Sec Gen draped over his shoulder, considering the crossing. After his dawn tantrum, the Gaian was out cold again. The tranquiliser seemed to be wearing off more quickly than the doctor had said, but even rowing the whole way, it shouldn't take more than an hour to cross the river.

'Êŝgîd, do you want to take him now?' The warrior hesitated. Both of them glanced at Enki, who was leaning up against the rock where Bartol had left him, eyes half closed.

'If you stick close beside me.'

Êŝgîd didn't have the strength to subdue the Sec Gen if he suddenly rose and broke his chains, so Bartol had brought the hostage down the Mikku to the gorge. Really, he should ferry the Sec Gen today too. If the currents sucked the boats down to the rapids, or towards rocks, it would take strength to keep on course; and more strength for the boat with the heavier load.

But Enki needed safe ferrying too.

'Enki? Brother? Is that plan all right with you?'

He didn't know if Enki could hear, speak, understand any more, or was simply refusing to do all those things. Right now, he appeared to nod, though he could just be trying to breathe. Bartol lifted him into his boat and propped him up on a backpack cushioned with a sleeping bag. He placed the folded wheelchair between them.

The solar batteries had been left outside the cave overnight, but one was faulty, had barely recharged, so they decided to row, saving the sunjuice in case they needed it. Rowing was soothing. The repetitive motion, the stretch in his back muscles, feeling the oars push through the river's resistance, slip into the freedom of air, cut back into the water again; he'd always enjoyed it. He rowed slowly, so as not to leave Ėsgid behind, downriver of his comrade. If the current quickened, he might be able to stop the other boat from being swept away.

Enki had opened his eyes, was glaring over the water. It was still funny to see him with that patchy beard. Before, Bartol would have teased him about it. Before was a very long time ago.

'We used to argue, didn't we, brother?' he said between oar strokes.

'The Karkish versus the Somarians.'

Silence. He stroked on, tried again.

'I said the rapids were the dragon's jaws, because they spouted white fire. You said they were the beast's thrashing tail.'

Over the years, Enki had won any argument that could be won. All Bartol could claim was a tally of undecidables. Until now. In the conclave he had won the only battle with Enki he should never have entered.

'But I tell you, brother,' he persisted, 'if the rapids are the dragon's tail, then I'm rowing across a pretty big arsehole.'

The way Enki had been acting, some might call that a dig. Was it his imagination, or did Enki roll his head slightly? 'My father told me about the foxes too,' Bartol went on. 'He said they were spirit creatures, tendrils of smoke from the dragon's nose.' He dug the oars back into the water. His father had said more than that, but it would be courting fate to say so. In Karkish legend, the spirit foxes appeared when the dragon was wrathful, intent on claiming a victim. Tales were told of boats smashed on rocks, even suicides from the cliff edge after the sighting of a fox in the gorge. 'Perhaps,' he suggested politely, 'the Somarians say the foxes are the dragon's farts?'

Enki cleared his throat. It was a sound like a broken gate dragging open.

'Yes, brother?' Bartol rested the oars, leaned forward. Those hooded eyes flashed.

'*Fuck . . . the foxes.*'

Enki was back. Bartol grinned so broadly his face ached. Somarian folklore often differed little from the old Karkish tales; *we're not dead yet,* Enki was saying.

'I'll pass the message on if I see one, brother,' he said. Enki lapsed back into glowering silence. The prow of Èṣġíd's craft bumped the side of the boat.

'They're here!' The warrior whooped, turning to point. Bartol peered over his shoulder. They had been rowing at an angle, deeper into the narrowing river than he'd intended, but were more than halfway across. He could see the vista point at the foot of the road the old honeymoon buses used to use and, parked there, a van and a car, three small figures standing between them.

'Bartol. Are we moving?' Èṣġíd's voice rang with alarm. Bartol gripped his oars. Yes, they were drifting; fast. The current was sucking at the boats.

'Time to start the engines, I reckon.'

'Urrgh. *URRRGH.*' Enki was bent double, coughing badly. With his good arm, he was jabbing furiously across his sling, upriver. Bartol looked north. There in the distance was a tiny black smudge.

He whipped his binoculars out of his bag. The smudge was a boat, a large red one, with a cabin. *N-LA red.* He could see four people on board.

'It's Rabu.' He exhaled. 'His officers, anyway. They haven't spotted us yet, I don't think. It looks like they're scanning the shores.'

'So, brothers,' Èṣġíd grinned. 'Fight or flight?'

The N-LA boat was about twice as far away as the vista point. The rams were untested. Still oaring hard against the current, he said, 'I vote we fire the engines for the shore. Now.'

'*No,*' Enki mustered the scrapings of his voice. '*We can't . . .*'

'We have to. Even if they chase us we can make it, get away before they land.'

'No, Bartol,' Èṣġíd frowned. 'Enki's right. We don't know how bad the rocks are. It could take a while to make land. And if N-LA see the CONC van, then the doctor will be up shit creek too. We need to take that boat out.'

The doctor had known what he was getting himself into. 'I don't like it, Èṣġíd. We could sink ourselves. We can swim, but what about the others?'

'There's two of us, one of them. We circle out now, approach fast, from both sides. We can do it, Bartol.'

As they were arguing, the smudge upriver became a dash of froth. The next second it started very quickly getting larger.

'They've seen us, Ešgíd. We have to go *now*.' Bartol ran his hands over his face. He was a warrior, not a general. If they had to fight, let them at least do it near to shore where there was a chance one or two of them would get to the vans.

'*I can . . . steer*,' Enki's eyes were ablaze and his good hand was clutching the tiller. '*You go to shore. Let me ram N-LA.*' He broke down coughing again.

'No.' Bartol stood, grabbed his bag. The boat rocked, but it was long past time to change ends.

Ešgíd reached out, gripped his shoulder, '*Yes. It could work.*' He looked at Enki, lowered his voice. 'But . . .'

'You take him. I'll do it,' he said, rummaging in his bag for the ear protectors.

Ešgíd was pulling the boats together, hitching a rope round his oar-lock. 'Don't be an idiot, Bartol. You have to carry the hostage ashore. Quick, you two get in my boat.'

Ešgíd was stepping into his craft. There was no time left to argue. Bartol lifted Enki across the lashed gunwales, then, with a last blast of inspiration, helped Ešgíd tie his backpack to the seat in the prow – let N-LA think there were two fighters aboard, the boat a warrior vessel, not a last-ditch decoy.

The last Bartol saw of Ešgíd, the warrior was sailing upriver with the wind in his hair and a star-flared hand in the air.

The Stream

Hozai and Šáñál escorted them back to the buggy. Ariamá looked none too impressed by the long wait, her cantankerous mood no doubt not helped by having to shit in her resting space. They let her out to drink from the stream while Lil swept out the dung. Šáñál offered to walk her to the stables to join Shiimti's herd; after her three days as a guest, she would be put into service doing a little light ferrying of farm equipment.

'Goodbye, Ariamá.' Astra held out her palm with the last of the camel treats. 'Thank you for everything. I'll visit soon.'

The camel took the treat with fastidious lips and inhaled it with a sniff. She craned her neck into the garden; whether Astra was being punished for the buggy ride, the morning confinement, for doubting her dream, or was simply of no concern any more, she did not know.

Lil drove them back to the citadel, Hozai up front beside her. Zizi, sitting in the back with Astra and Muzi, sat huffing and puffing in a corner, wiping his bald head with his handkerchief.

'The Zardusht over breakfast.' He gave a mock-shudder and rolled his eyes heavenwards. 'It is one way to lose one's appetite!'

She and Muzi giggled. Zizi was amusing in his way. And his plump face, while a little sweaty and not what she had been expecting, had a ruddy sweetness to it, the look of a small boy who was rather fond of honey cake and whose parents would rather give him a cuddle and another slice than send him running round the kinbattery track. He might need a bath, and he was definitely nothing like Klor or Dr Tapputu, but he was a father in another way: he was warm and emotional. At the end of their hug there had been tears in his eyes, in hers too. She didn't want to glue their hands together, but she was glad she was here with him.

'Are you really a poet?' she asked.

'Ah, who can call himself a poet? That is for others to say, long after one's bones have been carved into toothpicks for the gods. I am but an apprentice to the art, Daughter, a lifelong apprentice.' He beamed at her fondly. 'And you? Do you visit with the muse?'

She had written poems at school, Gaia hymns and love notes, nothing special. Lil, though, had written a poem for her that had travelled all the way to Non-Land. And she had been riveted by Enki Arakkia's rhymes.

'No. But I love poetry. Did you hear Enki Arakkia's rhymes? They're amazing. They started a whole revolution!'

Zizi banged his fist against the side of the buggy. 'Boom.' He struck a noble pose. ' "A dawn without a sun." '

It was Arakkia's 'Firesands Freedom' track – and *Zizi knew the words.* She sat up and joined in, forgetting some lines, reminding him of others:

Boom. Youth without a gun.
Boom. Dreams serenely spun.
Boom. Jailers on the run.
Boom. A wrongful world undone.
Boom. Grandmothers having fun.
Boom. The people's passion sung.
Boom. A bloody battle WON.

They did the whole rhyme, Lil whooping, Hozai clapping, Muzi banging his wrist against the side of the buggy in counterpoint to Zizi's fist beats. It was *brilliant.* She had arrived in Shiimti and was chanting war hymns with her father! She finished, flushed. Zizi leaned back into the corner of the buggy, tucked his legs beneath him and clasped his ankle.

'Ah yes, the revolutionary rhymers,' he said in English, rolling the words on his tongue. 'Why is it that the rhymers are so revolting?' She was baffled. He'd just led the chorus. Now he was dissing Enki Arakkia and all of YAC, making fun of her too, for loving the rhyme.

'It's an old pun, Daughter.' He spoke in Gaian, waved airily. 'But there is truth in it. As the Zardusht says, life is change, whether you fight for it or not. So why fight?'

For a million reasons. And it was insensitive to talk in Gaian around Muzi. She made to tell Zizi that, but he leaned forward, placed a finger on his lips, widened his eyes, urged in Asfarian:

Hurry, for the beergardens are blooming.
The war still a hill away. Earth
With all its aviary is sitting
In amity with the natural voices.

She fell silent.

'*That* is a poem, Daughter. Poems, like love-making, are always better the second time.' He repeated it, and she drank in the words. The poem was a toast to the moment. To the flowers and birds and Gaia's abundance and the war across the windsands, casting long shadows over Paradise. It was also a little frightening. Could Zizi tell that she had been hearing voices?

'Yes.' He sat back, satisfied, addressing her again in Gaian. 'You listen. You *must* listen, the words demand it. Do you hear their cadence, Daughter? Do you ask yourself what truly is blossoming when we gather together to toast life? Do you feel the pressure of the future gathering against the fragile craft of words? That is thanks to Abu Nuwas, one of the ancient masters. Some works in his oeuvre are too racy, too sordid, offensive even, for a young woman's tender ears, but for sheer devotion to pleasure in a world governed by pain there is no finer poet.'

She frowned. Zizi's Gaian, though halting, was good, his vocabulary that of an Atourne college teacher's, but his ideas were completely foreign to her. She didn't need to be protected from reading about sex. And she didn't like the feeling that Zizi was deliberately excluding Muzi. He was barrelling on in Gaian, counting off names on his chubby fingers: 'For devotion to devotion, you must read Hafiz, the *ghazals*; Rabia the Saint; and Rumi – Oh! A spoonful of Rumi will teach you more than' – he jabbed a thumb in Hozai's direction, stage-whispered – '*that* can do in a year.' He sighed, puffing out his stubbly cheeks. 'Table scraps, fragments only, have survived, but how fortunate we are to have so many poets miraculously singing to us from the other side of catastrophe. So many poets and what do they all tell us?' He spread his arms wide. 'To cherish life, my daughter, to savour it and each other. To drink of love, like a wine of crushed rubies! Ah, if only the world had heeded the poets.'

Perspiring freely again, he clenched his fist and shook it between them. 'But I see you disagree. I see the anger flash in your eyes. It is the anger of the revolutionary poet! We will have discourses, my daughter, and read-ings, in the blossoming beer garden. You will defend your rhymers and I will pontificate on the head of a pin! You will humble me, Daughter, in front of the world, steal my very reputation, as the Prophecy proclaims,' He stopped, as if abruptly bashful, and rubbed his face with his hanky. 'Forgive me, Daughter. For so many years I have wanted to read the great poets to you. Now you are here, with your mother's fury and your own precious beauty, my senses are, as the great feral Francilien boy-poet urged, quite deranged.'

She had no idea if Zizi had just taught her a great lesson, challenged her to a duel, or simply made a chaotic offering of love, but at least he appeared to be finished. Exhausted, in fact. He was slumped against the buggy side, his hanky draped over his head. If life was change, this man, her father, was an elemental vital force, altering every moment, exhaust-ing even himself with his effusive outpourings, his disagreements with everything anyone else said, self-mockery and self-abasement.

Opposite, Muzi side-eyed Zizi . . . *what was that?* Their eyes locked, relief filled her and a titter escaped her lips. Everything was all right again. Zizi was a human *mergalla*, but he loved her, and so did Muzi. Muzi had done as he'd promised, brought her here to meet her father, and together, later, they would laugh about this flamboyant little clown who had Coded her. Muzi was still smiling at her. He was happy and relaxed, his short arm stretched along the side of the buggy towards Zizi. A great surge of contentment filled her. They were still on a great adventure together, *the journey of love*. Muzi gestured with his chin and she turned to see a crane, a sleek white shape stepping lightly between two greenhouses.

The crane was the teacher of faithfulness, the Zardusht had said. For a moment she wanted nothing more than to curl up under Muzi's arm, lay her head on his chest. Instead she sat quietly, bumping along, gazing into his dazzling eyes.

Behind Muzi, the ledge of tents was flourishing, groups of people eat-ing and exercising and holding meetings, children tearing around, a circle of young mothers and fathers sitting on rugs with their babies. Lil drove to the far end and into a cavern. The gated entrance opened into a bliss-fully cool interior, a cavern filled with bicycles and mobility scooters, farm vehicles, trucks, vans and buggies, lit by a web of lamps strung from the rock ceiling, Lil parked at the back.

'Coffee!' Zizi, apparently, had regained his senses. 'Coffee and poetry!'

All she wanted was a bed. She was relieved when Hozai took charge. 'They must check in to their dorms first,' the Whirler told her father. 'If you wish to meet later, Zizi, please by all means give Astra your Tablette number.'

'Are you going now?' she asked. For some reason she sounded panicked.

'No, no.' He smiled, and his face again was that of the small cherubic boy. 'I'm not running off. Don't worry, I'll see you settled in.' He patted her hand, and when she didn't respond, let go.

She blushed, hung back as he shuffled along beside Hozai. She didn't *need* him; it just felt too soon for her father to disappear again, that was all.

Hozai led them all to a pair of bronze elevator doors. Beside it was a block of lockers. He turned to address them. 'Welcome to the Complexity. Shiimti is a pacifist community and a safe space for all. We resolve all conflicts by dialogue and negotiation. No firearms or other weapons are permitted anywhere in the Complexity or the gardens, and all knives' – he gestured at the lockers – 'must be left here, for use in the gardens only. There is no metal detector. We operate a trust system.'

She glanced at Muzi. He hesitated. 'What if IMBOD comes?' he asked.

'If one day an army arrives to try and seize this place, we will retreat into the Complexity and hold fast. We will parley and invite the visitors to forsake violence and join our community. If no agreement can be struck we will disappear and replant our gardens elsewhere. Shiimti is not a place, but a state of being.'

How a huge community would disappear from the middle of the desert was not clear. But Muzi surrendered his knife. When it was safely stashed, Hozai pressed his elegant forefinger to a biometric reader set in the wall. The burnished bronze doors slid open and a freight elevator took them up to a corridor gouged into the cliff-face. Wide and high, open like the Zardusht's cavern to the view, it was a natural colonnade, but barred with a bronze grille and milling with people. They walked on, passing more elevators.

'These are the Western Shafts,' Hozai informed them. 'You will use them to enter and exit the Complexity. Inside, all who are able to climb stairs are expected to do so.'

Through the grille she could see the ledge below, the chairs and awnings, waiters and worshippers and beyond them the roads now busy with farm vehicles moving out into the gardens. At the end of the corridor, Hozai stopped at a row of three revolving bronze doors.

'This is the Complexity Portal. In the event of a siege, Master Muzi, the doors will spin, endlessly, too fast to see.'

'Kinbatteries,' Lil whispered as Hozai ushered them through into a magnificent high vaulted stone chamber. The outer wall was a huge curve of stained glass; abstractly patterned, yet resembling an ascending flock of birds or shoal of fish, it cast wavy streaks of crimson, emerald and turquoise light over the floor. Astra hadn't noticed the window from the buggy. It must have looked dull from outside, but here it was as bright as Lil's butterflies.

She wanted to say that to Lil, but she had gone up front with Hozai and was leading them through the colour splashes to an antechamber at the back, a rock cavern lit with more of the bulbous roof lamps. Here a robed, moon-faced woman took their names, date and place of birth and finger scans.

'Ah. Lilutu. Welcome back.' The woman was as serene as porcelain. 'And welcome also, Astra Ordott and Muzi Bargadala to the Shiimti Complexity. New arrivals and returnees are considered our guests for three nights. On your third morning you must return here and sign up for Service shifts. New arrivals must choose a physical Service – Gardening, Kitchen, Cleaning or Mechanics. To become eligible for Spiritual, Emotional or Mental Service, you are required to attend Healing Sessions. All are offered free of charge. You will find the schedule and a map of the Complexity on the Shiimti web homepage.'

'Thanks, Neetha. Is the password still the same?' Lil asked.

'The current password is "joyfultranquillity". Your email addresses are first name dot last name dot 333. Unless special permission is granted, there is a daily quota of five personal emails and ten text messages, within Shiimti only.'

Astra tensed. 'I need to email Kadingir. Who do I see about that?'

Neetha gave a beatific smile. 'The roots of the tree do not curl when the wind snatches the leaves.'

Well, *that* was helpful. 'No, not usually. But what does that have to do with emailing my friend?'

'Daughter.' Zizi took her arm. 'One of the charms of Shiimti is its inhabitants' frequent use of metaphor in even the most mundane situations. Perhaps your rhymers are not quite so subtle with their imagery, but here——'

She pulled her arm away. 'I know what a metaphor is! I asked a straight question and I need a straight answer, that's all!'

His plump face drooped. He was just trying to help and she was doing it again, boiling up, hurting people. 'Sorry, Zizi,' she mumbled. 'I'm a bit tired.'

'Astra,' Hozai intervened, 'as your current mood suggests, the World Without is violent and chaotic, as indeed, are some dimensions of the World Within: chaos and destruction are integral aspects of the universe. Much of human violence, however, is the result of imbalance, a chronic misunderstanding of the deep truths of our own being. Here in Shiimti we learn to recognise and work in harmony with the profound meta-rhythms of the World Within. When you are Healed, you will be ready to communicate with the World Without and influence it with the power of self-aware thought, word and deed.'

It didn't matter that the stylings were new; she had been hearing this anti-internet argument all her life. She couldn't help it: her anger bubbled over again. 'But how will we know what's *happening*?' She glared at Lil. 'You said this place was Non-Gaian. You didn't say it was like *Is-Land*, keeping people ignorant!'

'Shhh.' Zizi's eyes were popping with alarm. 'It's not like Is-Land here, Astra. We do get news, just not constantly. If you need to contact anyone, I can help you.'

'Chill out, Astra,' Lil told her. 'You'll see. Shiimti's like Is-Land *ought* to be.'

'This is Shiimti and these are the rules.' Neetha addressed her with that lunar smile. 'You are free to leave at any time.'

She wanted to grab Muzi and march out, but Hozai raised his palms. 'Lilutu and your father are right, Astra,' the Whirler said, his voice soothing. 'When you visit the Zardusht tomorrow, you will begin to understand a little better. She may also grant you special permission to email the World Without. Come, let me take you to your accommodation.'

She looked at Muzi, who shook his head slightly, lips pursed, brows knit. But he was not concerned about her; he was telling her off.

Unless she wanted to seek shelter with the tent dwellers in the desert, she had little option but to continue checking in. Neetha gave them clean robes, bed linen, towels and a bar of white soap. 'Family dorms are available for parents and children only. You may choose between male, female or gender fluid accommodation. When you have made a commitment to Service, you may apply for a double or single room or a tent in the garden.' She waited expectantly, finger on screen.

'Gender fluid.' Lil nudged her. 'It's the best dorm, Astra.'

She hesitated. Despite that stupid look, she wanted to stay with Muzi. 'Gender fluid.'

Neetha looked at Muzi. 'Male.' He answered as if it was absurd to be asked.

He was being so *difficult*. But the dorms were just for now. They would get a tent later. And maybe she needed a break from Muzi – from everyone, for at least a twelve-hour sleep. Supplies in their arms, they left the cavern. Hozai led them towards a stairwell at the end of the foyer. As they approached it, Zizi patted Astra's shoulder. He was perspiring freely.

'Daughter,' he whispered, 'do you mind if I leave you now? I feel a trifle weak and there are far too many stairs to mount before coffee.'

'Mangara's Healing Session is especially designed to help older people with the stairs,' Hozai informed Zizi gravely, 'She has devised a set of aerobic exercises that are gentle on the joints.'

'Yes, yes. I know. But I am not so very old.' Zizi pummelled his chest with his fists, 'I fill these mighty sails with oxygen on my Garden Service shifts.' He deflated. 'It's just that I had rather a late night. Love and wine take their toll and sadly there is no escaping the bailiff. My apologies, Daughter. I will see you later in the beer tent. We will have our discourses.'

Next to Hozai, tall and groomed in his pure white robes, Zizi looked sagging and shambolic. For a piercing moment, she wished again that he was different, not so *changeable* all the time. He had said he would come and settle her in, but he was fading away, giving up.

But if he wasn't well, she couldn't insist – and he wasn't going far. He gave her his Tablette contact details and when she stepped forward for a hug, awkwardly this time, he embraced her warmly. She was getting used to his smell, didn't mind his damp shirt. He bade his farewells and veered off back to the Western Shafts, like a rumpled, half-drunken bumblebee.

The rest of them ascended a flight of the spiral stairs. Hozai opened a door and gestured Muzi into a low corridor. 'The male dorms. Sleep well.'

'We'll email you when we get up. See you later, Muzi.' Lil pecked his cheeks. He turned to Astra and took her in his arms. The embrace was a promise, melting her annoyance into yearning, and pulling apart caused a small rip in her heart. She wanted to follow him into his bunk, lie down and curl up with him, but he disappeared and she was left with Lil on the stairs. Hozai took them up one more flight and showed them to the gender fluid dorm, a long low room with curtained windows, furnished with bunk beds and a couple of sofas and tables at one end. Three or four of the beds were made up with sheets. Their frames had clothes hanging from the rungs and the absent occupants were using the attached lockers as bedside tables.

'Great.' Lil said when Hozai had gone. 'It's always nearly empty here. Most gender fluid Non-Landers only self-identify once they've been in Shiimti for a while.'

She looked at the bottle of pink nail polish, razor and shaving brush left out on top of a locker. 'But we're not gender fluid. Maybe the others won't like us being here.'

'Sure we are. You don't like wearing dresses, do you? And I drive like a demon. Women are made, not born, anyway. I thought you learned all about gender in school?'

She had been to school with intersex and transsexual people and people who preferred to be addressed with non-gendered pronouns. She wasn't any of those, she didn't think, but she was too tired to argue. She followed Lil to the far end of the room, where Lil sat down on an empty bunk, tugged off her boots and undid her hair.

'Don't worry about the internet situ.' She massaged her scalp, puffing up her hair into a big black cloud. 'I was freaked out the first time I came to Shiimti too. But it isn't like Is-Land, honestly. Tomorrow I'll take the buggy out and pick up the Pútigi signal. You can come with me and email Photon if you like.'

Astra sat down on the opposite bunk. Lil placed her sunglasses on top of her locker and stretched out on the mattress, ankles crossed, one arm crooked up behind her head.

'You should wash your hair. Then we can make a statement video.'

'Er, stating what?'

'Nothing much. We just need to boost your Istar profile. All you have to say is we've arrived in a Sacred Place and are summoning the Old Ones to help in the battle. I'll do a close-up, so no one will know where we are.'

'The Old Ones? Who are they?' Her annoyance was rising again. 'And I told you, I'm not sure I *am* Istar. I can help with campaigning, but I think we should just let Dayyani take over the role.'

Lil rolled on her side and looked calmly at her. 'The important thing, Astra, is that other people think you are Istar. Look, it will all be clear tomorrow after your Healing. The Zardusht will help you find out for yourself who you are. Then everything will get a lot easier.'

'Let's hope so.' She took off her own boots and stretched out on her bunk.

Lil laughed. 'You must have some sort of supernatural power. You got a Somarian guy to agree to a temporary marriage! Usually for them it's the whole shebang, or secret fucks out on the riverbank. I couldn't even get Enki to go to the beer tent with me in case people thought we were an item.'

She propped herself up on her elbow. 'You were with Enki Arakkia?'

Lil rolled her eyes. 'Oh, briefly.' She reached up and plucked at the upper bunk webbing. 'He's a madman in the sack, but way too ego-driven for me.'

Lil thought *someone else* was too full of themselves? At least she seemed okay with Astra's relationship with Muzi. What had Lil said in the cave? *It's best to squeeze one grape at a time.* If that really was her philosophy, maybe things wouldn't get weird between them; maybe they could be friends.

'Muzi is definitely a Somarian guy.' She paused. 'He wants to get married for real. He's going to ask Zizi for my hand.' She sounded, she realised, scared.

'Well, you don't have to do what the boys say. There are Gender Healing workshops here you can make them attend if they try to push you around. You really should go to as many Healings as you can. They saved my life when I first came.'

Lil had sat up and was unzipping her racing suit, peeling it off like the skin of a pale blue fruit. Beneath the body sleeve she was, Astra realised, very thin. Her breasts were ripe, and still larger than Astra's, but you could have played xylophone on her ribs and her hip bones were as sharp as the metal locker corners. Lil folded the suit over the rung of her bed. Her forearms still bore the signs of her mine-worker's rash: white flaking skin and faded red patches. Astra looked away.

'Zizi's just totally smitten with you, though! He's funny, like I said, isn't he?'

'Bossy' was the word Lil had used, but Zizi had made her laugh, yes. He was funny in other ways, though: 'funny' as in 'odd'. Zizi was warm, yes, and adoring, but he was also ill-kempt, a stumbler and bumbler, a fringe dweller here even in Shiimti. He made her feel odd too: teetering on the edge of throwing herself into his arms and backing away as he spun out of control.

'I'm glad he likes poetry,' she said carefully. Though that was a dangerous topic. She had never told Lil that she still had her poem, back in her Belonging Box at CONC HQ.

'Yeah, he's always quoting stuff. I think he makes most of it up. You guys will get along, I know it.' Lil jumped up and grabbed her towel. 'It's good here. You can go skyclad in the dorm and in some of the Healing Workshops. And the food's amazing,'

She padded with her towel to the bathroom. Her bottom was still cute, but the gap between her thighs was like a window arch. Astra sat for a moment, then undressed too and followed. There were no showers, just barrels of water and dippers beneath a big notice saying *Waste Not the Precious Dew of Life*, but the pale blue tiles were pretty, there was pomegranate shampoo and Lil did a little power dance as she dried herself off, flashing her sharp smile until Astra was giggling at last.

'Time for some beauty sleep,' Lil ordered as they got back into bed and pulled the sheets over their heads. 'We can do the video when we get up.'

A man in an upper bunk was snoring loudly; another was sleeping, or trying to, below him. An old man in the bunk opposite was lying on his back, staring into space with rheumy eyes. Muzi took a bed as far away as possible and put his bag in the locker, setting a code like Hozai had shown him down in the garage. He didn't like not having his knife, but that couldn't be helped. He sat on the edge of the bed, took off his boots and, for the first time since his world had changed forever, found himself with nothing vitally important to do.

He was aware of a creeping sensation of lack. He had done it, brought Astra here to meet her father and now, suddenly, she was not by his side. Her absence was not like Uttu's, vast and incomprehensible, or his family's, wrenching and bitter, but it was nevertheless unsettling, as if someone had woken him up by pulling his blankets away and was now standing there, waiting to see what he would do. Someone like Astra's father. It had been strange in the back of the buggy, Astra's father speaking to her in Gaian for so long. Zizi was Somarian; he could have spoken in his own tongue. Not understanding had started to feel uncomfortable; like being deliberately excluded or challenged.

He rubbed his face, scratched his chest. He shouldn't dwell on Zizi's behaviour. Astra's father had just wanted to converse with her in a language she understood well; she had smiled with him afterwards. And they were in different dorms for a few nights because that was the way this place worked. After heeding the sky-god for a week, it was hard to adjust to other people's rules, that was all. He undressed, wrapped his towel around his waist and went to wash. As he was drying himself, one of the men came in to use the urinal. He was a youth, but older than Muzi, stocky with a stubbly jaw and bleary eyes. The snoring could still be heard, a steady engine in the background.

'Sorry about my brother,' the man laughed as he put himself away. His Somarian had an eastern accent. 'He could power a tractor, my mother says.'

'"Sound sleepers make sturdy workers",' Muzi replied.

'"If their wives don't kill them before dawn",' the man finished with the old joke, then asked, 'Are you from Kadingir?'

Muzi relaxed a little. 'Nagu Six.'

The man washed his hands. 'Long journey.'

He had kept count. 'Seven nights.' 'That wasn't including the oasis; the oasis was outside of time.

'We're from Putigi. Two nights. People are hoarding and food's getting expensive. My elder brothers are staying put with their wives and children, but we brought our parents here to keep them safe.'

He didn't want to tell a stranger about his family, but some kind of reciprocity was required.

'I brought my betrothed here, to join her father. She's upstairs with her sister.'

'Upstairs? In the—?' The man stopped.

Suddenly Muzi felt embarrassed. 'Her sister was here before; she chose the dorm.'

'It's good you brought them both. Families should stick together.' The man stuck out his hand. 'I'm Zagin. Good to meet you.' His brother emitted another earth-shaking snore. Zagin grinned. 'If you need earplugs, I have an extra pair.'

* * *

When Astra woke up Lil's bed was empty and her Tablette message light was blinking. She had an email and a text message:

I'm out with the Zardusht and the butterflies. We can do the video this evening. Lil xxx

The email was from Zizi.

Beloved Daughter,

You are here and sleeping like a newborn, refreshing your sweet self while your father paces and marvels and gives praise to Gaia and the gods. It is insufficient to say I am filled with gladness at your arrival; mere words can never express my infinite gratitude for your sheer existence. Even my gift to you here today is naught but a droplet in the ocean of poems that ought to be composed in your honour. Please accept it and forgive any children's stories it may contain: I have so many years of bedtime stories and poems to make up to you.

When you arise, I will be waiting for you at the third beer tent from the Western Shafts – the one adorned with the flowers of the sun. There I will have something to show you to remind you of home.

Your Loving Father,
Zizi Kataru

She wasn't sure she liked being compared to a baby, or the idea of being read bedtime stories, but after Zizi's whirlwind of words in the buggy there was something reassuring about the simplicity of the message. At least he appeared to have calmed down. She read the email again and at the line about making up for their years of separation, unexpectedly her eyes misted over. Zizi was baffling, mercurial, alarming at times, but one thing was clear: he had missed her. And in a way, she thought, he was apologising in the email for not being there for her as she grew up. For a moment she felt as still and quiet as the desert at dawn.

It was a beautiful letter. She had come incredibly far, from the neurohospice and the Barracks, to Kadingir and Zabaria and over the desert to Shiimti, from one whole world to another and then another again, to find her Birth father – and he loved her. The Tablette felt light as a wafer in her hands.

By the gift, he must mean the attachment. It was an e-book called

Nights Beyond Measure. She downloaded it. The cover was a silver and gold illustration, an image of a young woman sitting reading from a Tablette beneath an archway of date palms, against an indigo background. She was dressed in a robe, her hair was thick and flowing and beside her in the sand was a golden lamp and a curved glass of steaming tea on a small gold tray. Behind the archway, tiny silver stars were flying across the heavens. The title was written across the sky in an elaborate gold font and framing the cover was an elegant silver latticework teeming with figures entwined in arabesques of flowers and vines. Astra zoomed in and pored over the magical tangle. Climbing up the sides were a prince in a turban with a curved sword, a woman on a magnificent stallion, a bird she didn't recognise, a boat with a tall sail and a winged, conical craft that looked like a cross between the girl's lamp and an Old World spaceship. A city of domes and tall glass buildings like pictures she had seen of Asfar ran along the bottom, and enthroned in the top corners were a king and queen who could be Istar and Shlemun, united by a caravan of camels and lions.

Nights Beyond Measure sounded like countless nights, but also nights somewhere else, far away, in a land where people didn't keep scores or weigh up costs. Astra opened the book to find an inscription:

Stories and Poems for Astra Wherever She Shines, Gathered by her Father as He Waits for Her Return.

A bittersweet sadness mingled with wonder flowed through her. The email wasn't just words. Zizi had never stopped thinking about her. He had picked his favourite writings like flowers for her over the years.

She swiped slowly through the Table of Contents. It went on and on – the book was one thousand and one pages long, filled with stories and poems by writers she had never heard of: Enheduanna, Scheherazade, Sappho, Khalil the Heretic, Adonis, Khalil Gibran . . . had Zizi mentioned him in the buggy? Swiping through the text, she could see footnotes at the bottom of the screen with links; Zizi had laid a trail she could follow from each of his choices back to their source.

She began to feel a little dizzy. She couldn't catch up on the entire history of Non-Land literature at once, but the fact Zizi had been creating this gift for her all this time was *moving*, worth battling a hundred *mergalla-la*. She would treasure the book: read it slowly, bit by bit, when she had time. For now she closed it and created a new folder for the email, called 'Zizi'.

There was no word from Muzi. It was mid-afternoon; probably he was still sleeping. She sent him a text with directions to the beer tent then got up and pulled on the robe she'd been given. It was all right the others weren't there; she should see Zizi on her own.

He wasn't hard to find, sitting in the shade of an awning beside a planter full of sunflowers, a large black bird clutching the back of his chair.

'Daughter!' He rose and embraced her. His breath was beery, his shirt still rumpled, but he had cleaned the stain off and showered; he smelled of sandalwood soap. 'Did you sleep well?'

He was speaking in Gaian. Still nervous of Non-Landers' reactions to the tongue of their oppressors, she glanced around, but the other tables paid them no heed. Laughter, clinks of cutlery and glasses, smatterings of Somarian, Karkish and another language she didn't know floated through the tent.

'Not bad.' She sat down opposite, curious about the black bird. Iridescent and haughty, with a moon face and raptor's curved beak, it lifted its feathers and peered out across the ledge towards the food forest as though deciding which exotic fowl to have for lunch today.

'Is that an *Owleon*?'

'A Rookowleon, I believe. Cinders, meet Astra.' He gave the bird his finger to nibble; it nipped hard and he snatched his hand away, shaking it and grinning ruefully. 'When I first came to Kadingir, Cora Pollen, praise be her name, insisted that I join Cinders' flight network. She's an intrepid night traveller and over these last few years my fountain of information about *you*, Daughter. I believe that your Shelter mother, Hokma, had a hand in designing her.'

Her chest tightened. 'She's beautiful.'

'She is far too glamorous a companion for a dusty old tramp like your father, I know. But Daughter' – he was beaming at her again – 'did my email find you? Did *Nights Beyond Measure* illuminate your screen?'

'Yes, thank you – the book's amazing, I love the cover. I'll read the poems as soon as I can.'

She had wanted to enthuse, not offer stilted promises, but she hadn't expected to see an Owleon hybrid. Zizi halted his babbling, even looked ashamed of it. 'I am so sorry about Hokma, Astra. She took you in when

Eya had to return to that bastard tyrant father of hers. She sheltered you; she was your mother. I owe her everything, Klor Grunedeson too,' he said humbly. 'And Nimma. They brought you up and kept you safe until we could be reunited. If I could, I would give them the world.'

She fell silent. There was so much to tell him, so many questions to ask. *What was Eya like? How long did you live in Is-Land? How did IMBOD catch you? What did Hokma tell you about me? Did you ever try and come back and find me?* But sitting here with Zizi's moist eyes tracking her every move, all of that felt like terrifying terrain. She understood why he had hidden under his handkerchief in the buggy. It was too much all at once.

She also needed to find information, to ask for his help. It felt safest to start there. 'Did you ever meet Cora Pollen?' she ventured. 'Do you know how she is?'

'I was introduced to her once, in Kadingir, when I moved in those circles. As far as I know she is still in that evil prison. May Gaia and the gods release her from it soon.' He took a long draught of his beer.

'Who keeps Cinders for her? Who are Cora Pollen's people?'

'Cora Pollen's people.' He ruminated on the phrase. 'I met a young man, long ago, in a beer tent. He was on his way to Asfar, I believe. I know only code names and cover stories, Astra. Her people in Pútigi are part of a wider network. They fly their stealth messengers to Kadingir, Zabaria, Atourne, and elsewhere in Is-Land. They won't even give me an email address, just this drafted bird that takes all my beer money to feed, eh, don't you Cinders?' He reached up to stroke the bird's chest plumage, avoiding a bite this time. 'They have no time for poetry, these people. They tell me very little and I ask nothing, except about you.'

'Was that it? Didn't he care about why she was here? 'But they must have said *something* about Hokma. She didn't die like IMBOD says she did, Zizi. I know IMBOD killed her. Her brother had something to do with it, Dr Samrod Blesserson, and her ex-Gaia partner too, Ahn Orson, the famous biotect – have you heard of him?

A pained look crossed his face. 'I have, Daughter.'

She flushed. 'I want to find out exactly how they did it,' she insisted. 'And I need to tell Cora Pollen's people that Blesserson is protecting a gang of child murderers at the Zabaria mine. They can't keep *getting away* with everything, Zizi.'

He sighed, spread his pudgy hands. 'All of IMBOD is a criminal gang and in their jails, there are no accidental deaths. I know you want justice. I would as well if I were you.' He paused, regarded her again with that troubled look. 'But, Ahn Orson . . . what happened . . . what you did – Daughter, you cannot keep taking revenge on your own.'

Another, hotter, rush of blood flooded her face. She'd begun to trust him, and now he was accusing her, blaming her, like Nimma and IMBOD had. No, she shouldn't have attacked Ahn, but if that was all Zizi knew about her, he knew nothing at all.

'I know what I did was wrong, but Ahn killed *Hokma*.' She choked. 'I was *upset*.' She was upset again now; she wanted to get up and leave. She had come to Shiimti seeking reassurance, assistance, help unlocking the chain of deaths round her neck, and instead, Zizi was tugging the links tighter round her throat.

'I know you were,' he soothed, 'of course you were. But these people are very powerful, Astra. Look how they punished *you*. Now you are here to heal from all that violence, to read poetry and eat ripe fruit, to be a young girl, learning all over again that life is a wondrous gift.' His voice changed, sliding into helpless wet grief. 'They are evil people. They will stop at nothing. If you pursue them they will destroy you, my precious daughter, before your life has even begun.'

She sat in silence with him, a lump in her throat, her father's eyes glistening as he fought back tears. As the silence lengthened something loosened in her chest. Zizi, she realised, was surprising her yet again. She had thought he was blaming her for attacking Ahn, but he wasn't; he was saying he *understood*, he *believed her* about Hokma, he just wanted her to be safe and happy. He didn't understand how impossible that was, but unlike with Muzi or Lil, she could sit with Zizi in shared hopelessness. There was a strange new comfort in that.

'I don't want to punish Ahn and Blesserson any more,' she said at last. 'I just want to find out the truth about Hokma, and what's going on at the mine. I want to gather evidence so that CONC can investigate. CONC ought to help free Muzi's family too. There's no way Sec Gens should have been on a mission in Non-Land.'

'I understand, Astra,' Zizi solemnly pronounced. 'You are a poet of conscience; you cannot rest unless you are actively furthering the cause of freedom and justice. In *Nights Beyond Measure*, you must read my selections of Darwish, Akhmatova and Fadwa Tuqan. They will give you succour, help you develop the patience you will need to tread this thorn-strewn path.' She wanted to say she wasn't a poet at all, but he was regaining his former exuberance, speaking now at speed. 'As for involving CONC, why not? Let those jobsworthy Tablette swipers do something useful for once. Yes, this is an excellent plan. Shiimti will be your intelligence headquarters. We can send Cinders to Pútigi and gather the information you request; Lilutu can help you email your Major Thames. You can campaign in safety while you recover your *joie de vivre*, your sparkling essence, and nurture your resolve with the words of the *great political poets.*' He gave a little bounce on his chair, wagged his finger at her. 'Please, do not misunderstand me, Daughter: clever, passionate rhymers are the first rung on the ladder of the poets, but there are enormous heights ahead of you – you must take the next step and the next! How I envy you your first reading of Khalil the Heretic. Oh you will weep, *inflamed*, you will weep, and your tears will water the scarlet rose of your anger!'

His chubby cheeks glowing, his big eyes shining, Zizi drained his glass and set it on the table with a resounding ring. She giggled, and he smiled and gave a bashful sweep of his eyelashes. He had, she realised, succeeded in cheering her up.

But this was serious. 'Zizi?'

He signalled to the bar, a twinkly little wave across the tables. 'Yes, Daughter?'

'Do you really think I should tell Lil I can't be Istar? I don't think I am, but maybe I should try and pretend, to help other people.'

Sober again, he pondered the bottom of his empty beer glass. 'It is my belief, Astra, that all women are goddesses, all men gods, though most often not the ones we poor deluded males think we are. There is a god of donkeys, did you know that? For years your poor father thought he was a bull, an elemental force with the power to topple the Boundary, but then one day he saw an ass cavorting in a field and suddenly he realised, no, Zizi Kataru, you are a braying fool. If you are lucky, children will climb on your back and garland you with flowers. And with that lot, I am content.'

The phrases had a well-worn air: he was telling a beer-tent story; not answering her question. She repeated it. 'But what about me and the Prophecy? Do you think if being Istar can help create One Land, then I ought to do it?'

He looked out over the food forest, then again into her eyes. 'Daughter.' He sounded surprisingly decisive. 'You have done enough. Look how far you have come, through what dangers! I know you want to help that young man, but you have helped him already by bringing him to safety. How can he fight with one hand? He's better off here or in Pútigi, learning skills he can put to good use when the war is over. If he wants to go back to Kadingir to try to free his family, he must go alone. If you are destined to be Istar, you can shine from afar, working here on your investigations.'

She didn't know why he was bringing Muzi into it. She'd asked about herself, not him. And she didn't like the way Zizi was talking about Muzi's arm. Muzi could do anything he wanted to. She was about to object when Zizi jumped up, his face bright with pleasure.

'Boranduhkt! She is here – my daughter, at last!'

The waitress, a woman with frizzy red hair and gold bracelets, set a beer down in front of Zizi. He introduced her as the tent manager and goddess of sunflowers and made proud exaggerated remarks about how far Astra had come, through a dozen *mergallá-lá*, an ocean of bones and three ancient cities. He didn't say anything about the Prophecy and nor, she realised, did he mention Muzi or Lil.

'Welcome to Shiimti, Astra.' Boranduhkt seemed to like Zizi; at least she indulged his tall tales and playfully scolded him for not telling Astra about the meal plan, explaining that she could have free meals and soft drinks for three days. 'Your first beer's on the house. The rest go on Zizi's tab.'

She was hungry. She ordered a vegetarian meze platter and fried potatoes and apricot juice. Boranduhkt smiled. 'She's got sense, this one, Zizi. Careful, or she'll be beating you at mancala soon.'

'Cinders can beat me at mancala, my love!'

'Just keep that bird away from my cushions.'

'Your cushions, dear Boranduhkt, are safe in my hands.'

The waitress grinned and departed. 'A daughter to feed again,' Zizi murmured. 'A daughter, fully grown.' His eyes welled up.

She was alarmed. She had thought he was happy again, but now tears were slipping down his face. 'Are you okay, Zizi?'

He clenched his fist to his heart. 'Astra, I should have brothers and sisters to offer you, a mother to care for you, choose your dresses, stitch your wedding gown. But they have all gone and I am all you have, shabby and worn, with nothing to offer but words, fleeting words . . . All I have is you. My only wealth. My greatest treasure.'

This again: he'd said she was his treasure before. She felt uncomfortable, but more than that, confused. It was impossible to keep up with Zizi.

'What do you mean, they're all gone?'

His face was awful to look at, wrenched apart, leaking everywhere. 'Gone. Taken one by one by the hand of IMBOD, the decree of IREMCO, the will of the gods. Three children born' – he gestured dramatically, but the grief was real – 'as our children are born back in that blasted land we squat on like beggars: born twisted, deformed, incapable of speech. Oh, I loved them, I loved each one as Neruda loved his tiny silent daughter. How I marvelled at the capacity of the human heart to love its own mangled flesh and blood. How I raged when they were taken from me, leaving me to mourn the memory of love. But taken they were and their mothers too. I had mothers for you, Astra, but they all left. Back to the dust, or their parents, or off with a man who could provide them with more than just love. For love, my daughter, is never enough. That is the cruel hard truth.' He gasped, his eyes glazed with tears. 'That is why we need *poetry* – the rope ladder of poetry to throw across the vast gaping chasm between us and who we love. Always the ladder will slip back, always we will tumble into the abyss, but always we must try, *try again* to cross over, to reach out to the ones we love.'

She was staggered. Major Thames had talked about Zizi as if he were a loner. She had contemplated the possibility that she might have been brothers and sisters, but not that they might have been Singulars. 'I.il never said...,' she faltered. She felt scared, she realised, scared of what he was saying; like the camel voices, he was telling her not to believe in love, but that couldn't be true. Muzi's love for her was as strong as an oak throne. Zizi had had bad luck; maybe he had given up loving, but she hadn't. He drew a hoarse breath, his eyes swollen with tears. She leaned across the table, urged, 'It's Blesserson's fault, Zizi. He's on IREMCO's Board of Directors. He knows all about the toxic conditions; poisoning Non-Landers is his *plan.* We've got to stop him, Zizi.'

He reached for her hand, squeezed it tight in his wet clasp. 'Oh Daughter. You must be so careful. I can't let them find you. You're here now. You've come back to me, though Gaia and the gods know I don't deserve it.' He broke into weeping again. His grip on her hand was so strong it hurt, and slimy with tears and drool. She wanted to pull away, but she couldn't. She was afraid he would utterly collapse if she did.

'Kataru.' A dark-skinned man, tall and graceful in a freshly pressed white robe, the neck embroidered with gold thread, was standing behind her father, shaking his shoulder. 'She has come. You daughter has come! The emotion is so strong it waters the date palms!'

Cinders flapped, disturbed, but she was jessed to the chair. 'Yes, yes.' At last Zizi released Astra. 'She is here, Salamu, and I weep like a child.' He pulled out his hanky and blew his nose. 'Sit, sit. Did you bring your boy?'

A young man was hovering in the background, clearly Salamu's son, shorter and broader than his father, but with the same refined eyes and high egg-shaped forehead.

'Astra,' Salamu shook her hand warmly. 'Please meet Talmai, my son. His name means mountain, but he is not a lofty one, not at all; he is a most down-to-earth young man.'

Talmai rolled his eyes and grinned. 'Hi, Astra. Welcome to Shiimti.' He shook her hand too, then he and his father took the seats between her and Zizi, who was beaming from ear to ear. If not for his damp lashes and pink eyes, you would never know he'd had a breakdown.

'I was just telling my daughter that I must never lose her again. Believe me, Astra, this is a safe place, a very good place. You have to hold your own against the Healers – oh, how they want to Heal things that aren't wrong with you! But if you can do that and find your own niche, you can live very comfortably here. Is it not the case, Salamu?'

Salamu addressed her. 'Shiimti is a palace of peace. It takes us all in, gives our days purpose. We contribute to the Zardusht's vision of building a citadel founded on knowledge, wisdom and love, your father most of all with his capacious understanding of poetry.'

'No, no.' Zizi waved away the compliment. 'I am a beer-garden discourser, that is all. The walking encyclopaedias are kept upstairs, in the lecture halls.'

'He is too modest. You will hear him enthral us. Perhaps he will teach you too how to write poems. Talmai has written some beautiful lines under his tutelage.'

Talmai winced and shook his head. She giggled and he rewarded her with a broad smile. He had long fingers, she noticed, and, despite his relaxed demeanour and respectful deference to his father, exuded a sense of lively intelligence. She gave a small smile in return.

'As you see,' Salamu gestured to the fields, 'there is plenty of food here. Shiimti is still growing in all manner of ways and the Complexity is building more chambers. My son is a webworker. If we can find a good wife for him, he will be top of the list for a family dwelling on the eastern edge, in the chambers with the living roof gardens.'

Across the table Zizi was on the edge of his seat. 'It is a wonderful place for children to grow up. Not like Is-Land, Astra. Here there are no Code factories, just people who want to make babies and people who want to take care of them. The joy is shared and the Birth parents have time for each other! Isn't that right, Salamu?' He winked at his friend and they both roared with laughter.

She froze. She couldn't look right or left or straight ahead, not at Salamu or Talmai, nor at Zizi. 'You are frightening her, my friend,' Salamu chuckled. 'She is a young girl. She doesn't want to think about babies. She wants to go to dances and sit around the fire telling stories. Talmai, when is the next youth social?'

She wanted to get up and go, for real this time, but Boranduhkt was returning with a tray full of food and drink. She was desperate for Muzi to appear, but he was not weaving towards her through the crowd. She was stuck with her father and his leaking heart and his plans to mend it by marrying her off to his best friend's son.

He slept nearly all day. It was late afternoon when he arose and the dorm was filling up with men, back from their shifts, he thought, from their smells and groaning complaints and the queue for the washroom. There was a message on his Tablette from Astra. After he'd washed, on his way out to meet her, he ran into Zagin and his brother.

'Muzi! Hail, Brother!' Zagin dropped his voice. 'Our father's got a craving for snake meat — we're going out to do a little hunting on the plain. Do you want to come?'

It was tempting, but he had to decline. He took the elevator down to the garage with the brothers, saw them off in their battered car, then walked along the ledge towards the beer tents. Astra was sitting at a table with her father, two other men and a large black bird. He approached from behind her, smiling and nodding a greeting to Zizi.

'Ah.' Astra's father acknowledged him with an unreadable squint, then raised a glass and flung his arm wide, sloshing the beer over the lip of the mug. 'My daughter's guide, fresh from his bedchamber and ready for another long night of travel.'

'Muzi!' Astra jumped up. 'Where's Lil?'

How would *he* know where Lilutu was? And he had no idea how to respond to Zizi's remark; he wasn't travelling today. He smiled and let Astra pull a chair up for him between her and the younger man, the son of the older one, by the look of it. They exchanged greetings and the shiny black bird blinked its large round yellow eyes at him. He regarded it with awe. It had a leather strap around its leg and appeared to belong to Zizi. His father had told him about falconers, but he had never heard of anyone in Non-Land owning a bird.

He would have remarked on it, but Astra's father was frowning into his beer glass. He was expecting Astra to introduce him to the others, but she was slouching in her chair, sunk into silence, so he introduced himself and exchanged pleasantries with the two Shiimti-ites until a waitress came to take his order. He was hungry and they offered him food from the little dishes scattered about between the tall beer glasses on the table: plates of white cheese and flatbread and bowls of olives and roasted almonds.

'Please, try our Shiimti goat's cheese.' The older man, Salamu, offered him a knife.

'Thank *you*, Uncle. I have a Kadingir knife,' he politely replied. He had picked up his blade from the locker in the garage and he took it from his pocket now and cut a hunk of cheese. Salamu admired the knife, so he cleaned the blade and passed it across to him. Zizi peered at it, but didn't ask to hold it. Still, Muzi thought, as the knife was returned to him, he had shown Astra's father that he was a man among men.

The waitress came and exchanged a few saucy words with the men. She at least welcomed him warmly, and he ordered a falafel and salads and a beer. After she left, Zizi and Salamu led the conversation, as was proper. Zizi was talking very loudly and slurring his words, but he was smiling broadly now and clapping the young man, Talmai, on the back. Astra's father was an emotional man, Muzi thought as he observed him. The reunion with his daughter was an occasion of deep feeling. He cast a smile at Astra, but she replied with a dark look, almost an accusation.

She was back in one of her strange tempers. He offered her the bowl of almonds but she refused, taking a long swig of her beer instead. He gave up. He would hear all about it soon enough, no doubt. For now, he just wanted to eat.

'And this young man too' – out of nowhere, Zizi flung an arm across the table towards him – 'has lost his entire family to IMBOD. Tell them, Nephew, tell them.'

All eyes turned to him and he swallowed his almond whole. But the Shiimti-ites looked concerned and Zizi – Zizi's expression was difficult to read; his eyes were puffy and red as though he had been mourning, but at the same time they were shining and intent, almost proud. Of him? Zizi had heard his story yesterday in the Zardusht's cave – he had remembered it, at least; that was a good sign, a sign he was taking him seriously. He glanced again at Astra, but she was glowering into her beer glass as though her gaze could kill.

He felt a twinge of annoyance. They'd risked everything to get here, and this was an important meeting: a chance to make a good impression on her father. She should at least try to celebrate too.

But the men were waiting, so Muzi told them about the night the Sec Gens came, how he'd heard the vans arrive, the Tablette message from his father telling him to hide; the Sec Gens, how huge they'd been, the way they'd rounded up his family and their sheep, destroyed his house, how he'd been forced to watch them take everything he loved. The men listened with respect while Zizi, his lids lowered, rocked slightly in his chair. Salamu shook his head gravely, pursing his lips, and Talmai sat with ever-widening eyes, flinching as if he were absorbing blows. Muzi did not choke or break down. Telling the story yesterday had helped.

'I saw his face,' he concluded, 'the one who killed my grandmother. When I see that Sec Gen again it will be the last time he looks out on the world.'

The men stamped their glasses on the table and murmured approval. Beside him, Astra drained her beer.

'And when will you return to Kadingir to find him?' Zizi asked.

Astra belched: a long loud rumble of gut-juice. He frowned. She hadn't made any noises of sympathy and now it was as if she was deliberately trying to embarrass him.

'Excuse *me*,' she announced.

He ignored her. 'When the gods permit,' he answered her father. 'I brought Astra to you, Uncle. Now I must rest my camel and discuss with you and your daughter the way forward.'

'Before, Zizi' – Astra banged her glass down on the table – 'before, you said he should stay in Shiimti and work. Now you're sending him back to Kadingir to get *killed*.'

He stiffened. Was she *mad*?

'Daughter,' Zizi flared, 'please! I am conversing with your guide, asking him his plans—'

'He's not my *guide*.' She pushed her chair back from the table. 'He's my *husband*. Muzi and I are *married*, Zizi. We made a temporary agreement, like they do in Asfar. And *we* will decide if we're going to renew it or not. *We'll* decide if we're staying or going. *Together.*' She stood up, shaking, unsteady on her feet. 'I'm sorry, Salamu, Talmai. It was very nice to meet you, but I have to' – she burped again, *proudly*, on purpose – 'talk to my *husband* now.'

She lurched away from the table and out onto the ledge and stood there with her arms crossed, glaring at him to follow.

He glared back. He was in a beer tent, talking, waiting for his dinner. Was he supposed to jump up and come to heel like a sheep dog?

'Daughter!' Zizi roared, 'what you are saying! We don't make temporary marriages here! This young man had no right to enter into such an agreement with you – he brought you to your father and his job is *done* now. Listen to me, Astra, listen to your *father*!'

'You aren't my *father*! You didn't bring me up! You weren't there, Zizi, you weren't there! And you can't make me marry anyone. *I'll* decide who I'm going to marry.'

She was screaming – it was *awful*. Muzi was furious, speechless with shock. Talmai caught his eye, raised his palms – *not me, friend.* Salamu flicked his hand: *Go, go. Join her.* Behind him, the waitress was arriving with the food and his stomach growled as the aroma wafted over. He hadn't eaten properly for nearly a day,

'Boranduhkt, a change of plan,' Salamu said smoothly. 'This young man will have his falafel and salads to go – and please, bring him a bottle of beer. On my tab.'

The woman scanned the scene, rolled her eyes and turned on her heel.

'Uncles.' He stood and offered his hand to the older men. Salamu took it, but Zizi retreated, crouching into his chair, as that ghoulish bird shifted from foot to foot behind him. Muzi nodded at Talmai, picked up his knife and strode over to Astra on the ledge.

'What's wrong with you?' he hissed in Somarian, gesturing angrily back to the beer tent. 'Your father was just asking me a question – now he thinks I took advantage of you!'

She turned to him, her eyes flooding with tears. 'We have to go, Muzi.

Now. He wants me to marry a webpage designer and have kids to make up for all the ones he lost. I had three brothers and sisters, Muzi, but they all *died*.'

She was speaking in Asfarian, sobbing all the while, and he had to ask her to repeat it all, slowly, but even understanding, he was still angry. She was drunk and confused and confusing, and she had been incredibly rude. But she had also told her father – she'd told practically the whole beer tent – that they were married, so she must need him. He didn't know what to say.

At last the waitress came over. She stuffed a warm bag in his hand and a cold beer in the crook of his elbow. 'Don't worry, Nephew,' the woman said. 'Her father's a good man, but he's had many troubles in his life. You take care of Astra; I'll take care of him. Okay?'

Astra was stumbling off down the ledge, pushing through people towards some steps. Apologising for her and excusing himself all the way, he followed her down through the herb rockery and along the road back towards the Zardusht's cave.

Right in the middle of the road she stopped and burst into long wracking sobs. People were looking and an old woman came up to help. He told the woman Astra was just tired and he was dealing with it. He put his arms around her and hugged her, then he walked her down through the field of starflowers to the stream. They sat by the water's edge, beneath a date palm, to talk.

First there was the story of Zizi's dead children to take in, and then Astra's confusion to fend off; she thought he had spent the afternoon with *Lilutu*, which was ridiculous. It was hard to take seriously her conviction that Zizi was trying to marry her off to Talmai. He tried to tell her that Zizi's friends were just there to make her feel welcome; all that had happened, as far as he could make out, was that Talmai had invited her to a youth social event.

'Please don't cry. It's nothing. Salamu told me to follow you – he bought me a beer. He wouldn't have done that if he wants you to marry his son.'

'I drank five beers!' she crowed. 'He doesn't want his son marrying a girl who's going to end up like' – she hiccoughed – '*Zizi*!'

They both laughed, but it wasn't funny. Actually, he slowly admitted to himself, it made sense: Astra had behaved like a beer-tent harridan so no wonder Salamu had been so keen for them both to leave. Zizi had made his feelings about Muzi and temporary marriage very clear. And Talmai was handsome, well-built, prosperous, and the son of Zizi's friend: of course Zizi would want his daughter to marry him. The old feeling crept over him again, of being not good enough; a thing found on the scrapheap, broken, dirty, flawed.

'It's okay, Muzi.' Still hiccoughing, she snuggled up to him. 'We don't need his permission to do anything. We can decide for ourselves what to do.'

He wrapped his arm around Astra, pushed away that feeling, Astra's father had lost three Code-damaged children; maybe his fear of an alt-bodied son-in-law was understandable. He probably had natural misgivings about the nature of their marriage. He didn't realise that Muzi's feelings for Astra were the *opposite* of temporary.

'Your father doesn't know me yet,' he told her. 'Tomorrow I'll have a beer with him, on my own. I'll tell him I want to marry you properly. And,' he hugged her closer, 'I'll tell him about my accident. My Code is good, Astra; he doesn't have to worry about his grandchildren. I'll take him to see the camel and explain about the race track. He'll see—'

'He doesn't care about the camel. And we can't think that far ahead, Muzi. We can renew the temporary marriage, but we have to focus on the war.' She scrambled out from under his arm and faced him, her sweet beery breath billowing between temptation and repulsion. 'Listen to me: that bird, Cinders, is a data-messenger. Zizi's going to send her to people in Pútigi who might know what happened to my Shelter mother. We can tell them about your family – I bet Samrod Blesserson's involved in that too. If we build a strong case against him, I can write to Major Thames, make CONC take it up in Amazigia.'

He was talking about their marriage and she had brushed him off, started rambling about people he'd never heard of, her mixture of Asfarian and Somarian hard to follow. She was drunk, he was forced to accept, as drunk as Gibil sometimes got. He would just have to wait until she sobered up. He gave up, let her talk as he ate his falafel and hummus and *baba ganoush*, drank his beer. He learned what a Rookowleon was, how it flew with a memory stick tied to its leg, connecting offline computers; how Lil's buggy could get them online in the World Without. According to Astra, they could win the war here in Shiimti, just by sending emails.

He finished his falafel, slipped the greasy paper wrap back in the bag and wiped his fingers on the napkin. 'CONC doesn't help Non-Landers,' he said in his language. He had to express himself correctly now. He spoke slowly, so that she would understand. 'We have to fight for One Land ourselves. I brought you to your father and now I have to go back to help my family and Doron's family. My proposal is that with your father's blessing we can make a proper marriage. Then I have to leave. I want us to leave together, to bring Istar back to her people. Uttu knew you were Istar, Astra. That's why she wanted you in our family. If you want to stay here and wait for me, I understand. But we will be married and I will return as soon as I can, or send for you when it is safe.'

At the beer tent she had shouted that they would decide together if they were staying or going. Here, she sat hugging her knees and gazing out over the stream. He felt her recede, as the light was receding, draining out of the sky, sucking the colour out of the water, the trees, the plants. It was as if the sky-god was stealing her away. At last she spoke, 'I told you, Muzi, I'm too young to get married. I want to renew our temporary marriage. That's all I can agree to right now.'

She was running through his fingers like sand. They had come together in the oasis, just like she had yelled at her father, come together in a green blazing fire that nothing could ever extinguish. She was Istar. He had discovered that on the journey, and everyone believed it: the Zardusht, Lilutu, YAC. But now Astra was drinking and crying and shrinking away, refusing to marry him, and darkness was closing in. A bitter taste rose in his mouth. Perhaps he should walk away, let Astra live with her father, marry the man he chose for her. He stared back at her and she dropped her eyes, began plucking at a stem of grass.

He couldn't bear the idea of giving her to Talmai. He would rather die than do that. There was a starflower plant behind her, the tiny blossoms trembling as she moved her arm. She was afraid, he slowly realised. Women sometimes became afraid and then it was the man's role to reassure them. Astra didn't have faith in her own power, that was all.

He took his knife from his pocket, cut off the stem of the plant with the most perfect flower and put it behind Astra's ear. She gave a hesitant smile. Then he reached over, picked the blade of grass she was stroking, took her hand in his and entwined the stem around her finger. 'I understand: you are Gaian. You want to be a bride many times. Next time we will be married with gold. Tonight we are married with grass.'

Her eyes shining, she ringed his finger too. They kissed. Somewhere above, the evening star was out and the moon would be strong soon. There *was* light at night.

The kiss ended. Radiant, peaceful, she laced her fingers in his, 'It's beautiful here. I want you to stay, Muzi. Stay and be safe. Like in the oasis. Maybe that is what Istar wants us to do.'

She didn't understand. 'I'm sorry. I can't stay, I have to go back, fight for my family.'

She shook her head; the flower behind her ear quivered. 'No you don't. The Zardusht and Major Thames and the people in Pútigi will help us help your family, I know they will.'

'They can help if they want, but I have to go. I want you to come too – come with me, Astra.'

Her lower lip quivered. 'I don't want to go back, Muzi. If I go to Kadingir, I'll have to pretend to be Istar. I don't mind making videos if that's what Lil wants, but I can't be a leader like Una Dayyani. I need to stay here for a while. I want to talk to the Zardusht about the dreams I've been having, and hear from the people in Pútigi. After that, maybe I'll have to go to Amazigia and tell CONC about Samrod Blesserson. I've got a lot of work to do here. Please stay and help me,'

She was talking in Asfarian again, rapidly, making no sense. Amazigia was a world away, on the other side of Nuafrica. 'You're Istar,' he urged. 'We're married. You don't need to be afraid. I will help you meet my people.'

Tears were spilling now. 'Please, Muzi, let's not talk about this now. We're both supposed to go visit the Zardusht tomorrow. Let's see what she says. Please, let's not fight. We just got married again.'

She tried to make a joke of it, but it wasn't funny. He was suddenly unsure. Perhaps a man shouldn't take a woman into danger. Perhaps he should leave Astra here for her father to take care of in his absence. He gathered her to him and she clung on like a vine, pulled him to the ground. They rolled in the grass and when he stroked her face, the ring she had woven was not on his finger.

'We're married, Muzi,' she whispered. 'We should stay together, stay here in Shiimti and shine our light out into the world.'

They were together, they were still married, but her embrace felt like a farewell. As he kissed her shoulder, he saw a crane step out of the plants across the stream. The tall, delicate bird was grey in the twilight.

Was the sky-god rubbing dust and ashes in his eyes, or telling him to hold on to hope?

They had just got here and Muzi wanted to leave. She was ready to start investigating, gathering evidence that would bring Blesserson and Ahn to justice, help free his family. She couldn't do it without him. She needed him here in Shiimti to protect her from Zizi and his mad plans to marry her off to Talmai. She would stay married to Muzi, temporarily, live with him in a tent and work in the gardens until she was sure they could be together forever. She needed him, so why did he have to go?

They made love by the stream, but nothing was resolved by their union; the closeness just made the tension between them more painful. Afterwards, she dozed as he slept, listening to the cranes, their calls a creaking gate between this moment and an uncertain future.

Will he stay with me? she whispered, kissing the sweet wing spot between Muzi's shoulder blades. *You're the birds of faithfulness. Please make him stay.*

You misunderstand us, child. Faithfulness is not a matter of staying. It is a matter of leaving.

She began to cry again. *What do you mean?*

Loyalty is proved by remaining. Faithfulness is proved by returning and we are the birds of return. Our migratory flights usher in springtime, our calls in the north warning you not to walk on the ice. In our long bills we bring love letters from distant young men, hard at work in foreign lands earning the coin to build a home for a lonely young maiden. And at the end of each long day, as she lies in bed keeping his sheets warm, we transport the souls of the dead back across the river of wind to their source in the heavens. We promise return, therefore we promise loss.

She wanted him to wake, to turn and embrace her, but his back was a warm wall no ladder was long enough to climb. *But I don't want to be lonely. I want to be with Muzi.*

You will yearn for him, and when your yearning is too much to bear, we will bear it for you. We hold up your skies with our wings. Year after year as you watched us depart in our slow, stately thousands from your fields and lakes, all your longing flew with us; for long hard winters you awaited our return and when you awoke to the harsh sound of our cry, the sight of our white rivers flooding your shores, your hearts burst their banks and flooded your souls with relief.

She felt only despair. She had yearned to meet Zizi, for months, had risked her life to come and find him and then just when she had opened her heart to him, he had betrayed her, treated her like coin to be spent, shouted horrible, ugly things about Muzi. *Why is life so hard?*

Because you have not yet learned patience, child. Our cry grates on your ears like knives grinding to remind you to cut anger and bitterness, jealousy and regret out of your soul. When you learn how to wait, without asking, beauty will return to you, light as a feather on the wind.

Knives. There was something she still needed to ask, something about metal. But she was sad and tired and her thoughts were so hazy and it was impossible to know what to ask yet. As the voices faded away, she clung to Muzi, synchronised her breath with his and lay still by the stream, feeling the ground grow cold and hard beneath her bones.

The Burnt Place

He awakened in chains, sometimes lying on the ground, sometimes tied to a tree or a column, but whenever he was conscious he howled and fought, spat out the food and water his captors forced on him, then there would be a tiny string in his arm and he would slide back into darkness, a black pit lit only by the dying flare of Master in flames. In the darkness his body could not move, but his mind swirled endlessly around that small distant torch, a fire he could not put out, no matter how long he wept. He had been tested and he had failed. Voices came back to him, as if echoing up from a deep abandoned well . . . *from now on you are my dog* . . . *you must obey me no matter what I tell you to do* . . . Master's voice, those stern commands his ears would never prick to again . . . *you are a good puppy, aren't you? You've done exactly what your Master said* . . . Dr Blesserson's kind voice, lost, so far away, and weaving between them, another, unknown voice, hissing . . . *dogs, mangy dogs, on your Master's chain* . . . a hostile, half-remembered voice, laughing at him, turning his insides cold with fear. Once, just once, the darkness was a comfort. Once a dog came and sniffed him. At the touch of its nose, his whole being quivered. He was back in the tunnel, safe in his cage, and Master had sent the dog to wake him and fetch him to play. He sprang to attention, barked with joy, except his bark was stifled by the gag in his mouth; the dog disappeared and when he tried to smash his head open against the column of rock he was chained to, his captors beat and tormented him, pricking him again with their poison. When he awoke again his body was stretched out and shaking. He lunged against the restraints, only to discover he could not move at all. Straps were cinched around his forehead, chest, hips and limbs so tightly that his body was completely immobilised. For the first time since he had been captured he was forced to lie quietly, unable to struggle. Apart from the hunger pangs gripping his guts, he was not in any physical pain. For the first time since his ordeal had begun, he felt able to think.

He was strapped into some kind of stretcher, he realised. He was shaking because he was being transported in a vehicle. He thought more about this. After a time, he understood: he had been taken hostage. Dr Blesserson had warned him this might happen: the Non-Landers wanted to capture and torture him. He didn't care about that, in the same way he didn't care that he was hungry. Only Master could feed him, and Master was dead. He had died in the explosion, because Peat had not been guarding the road. Peat deserved all the pain in the world. He should be set on fire. And not only to punish him. More snatches of the conversation in the dome came back to him: Dr Blesserson had said that the Non-Landers wanted to find out how he had been designed. He couldn't let that happen. He could not die again. He would die, he resolved, before he gave any of Dr Blesserson's secrets away. Not eating was not working fast enough so he tried to hold his breath, but his lungs betrayed him. Why did his lungs not obey his brain?

The vehicle halted and he tensed. After a moment he heard a door open. Voices entered his confinement: two or three men, speaking in a language he did not recognise. Except for his traitorous chest, moving up and down, he lay still as stone.

'*Tabarnak.*' There was a sharp hiss. 'Can we take the hood off at least? It really hurts to see a brother in chains.' He tensed. He didn't know the first word, but the rest were a language he knew. The accent was not one he'd studied, but Inglish was one of his top subjects at school. Inglish and Law, he remembered now: he was Master's legal beagle. He must collect evidence now.

'Shh. We should not make to speak. And I think he should not see us, either.' The second voice was whispering, worried, spoke with even more unfamiliar inflections

'I thought the idea was to get through to the guy.' Hands removed his hood. Someone pinched his earlobe. 'Hey. Peat. You in there, brother?'

The pinch tickled, but he did not move. Then hands rubbed his sternum, a brisk massage. He maintained a low, steady breathing rate.

'*Nada.* Whaddya say? Harder?'

'Now you are wanting to punch him?'

'Get a Sec Gen mad at me? Oh, I think not.' The first man laughed, stopped pumping. 'Frackin' hell. Look at that jaw. What they're doing to these guys, it is some scary shit.' Peat could almost place the accent now: it was New Zonian mixed with Francilien. The man's fingers rested on his wrist. 'His pulse is up a bit though. Maybe we had better give him another shot.'

Other hands pulled his eyelid up, shone a torch in his eye. He could see only a dark silhouette, deliberately kept his vision unfocused.

'It is still abnormal dilation. Okay, maybe normal for a Sec Gen, but we should not risk an overdose. And I think even he cannot break those straps.'

The first man released his wrist and the pair spoke again in the unknown tongue with the third man. Peat thought hard about who they all must be. Only CONC officers spoke Inglish in the region.

Hands replaced his hood. 'I am sorry for the inhuman conditions, but I think it is better he is not seeing the van. Can you pass me a new IV bag, please?'

It was all clear now. Dr Blesserson had said the hostage takers would experiment on him. These men were not with YAC. They were CONC scientists.

Hands pressed at his forearm. 'Well, at least we're keeping the poor *bâtard* alive for Astra. Weird how that worked out – d'you think she knows YAC nabbed her brother?'

Astra. The name was worse than that electric prod his torturers had used. It was extremely hard not to yelp, growl, bark. But the answer to the question was important. He muzzled his reaction, kept his ears trained on the voices.

'I think there is not internet in Shiimti. And perhaps it is not so strange Peat Orson was travelling with Odinson. It is logical that IMBOD has special interest in Astra's family.'

He was sweating. The scientists spoke again to the third man in the unknown tongue but he found it impossible to concentrate any longer. The doors closed and another pair of hands tightened a strap. He was being watched at all times; he couldn't relax his guard. He lay still, the darkness swirling with harsh, harder memories spinning up from the days before Master had taken pity on him: memories he could barely accept belonged to him. Astra – Astra's betrayal; the shock of the Tablette call from his Shelter father; entering the Barracks dining hall the day after, knowing everyone was looking at him. Then everything that had happened since: feeling Laam slip from his grasp, watching him step into a thrashing blood-red pond. Being bitten by the old woman on the mission and her neck, snapping in his hands. *Dogs, mangy dogs*, the voice returned, the jeering voice, he remembered now, of the lump in Zabaria: the lump of flesh he had eaten, the raw bloody treat his Master had promised he would have again – except now Master was dead, because of *him*. He could keep silent no more. Sweating and whimpering, he strained again against his terrible confinement. Master and Dr Blesserson had saved him from these *bad* memories, Master with his love and Dr Blesserson with his serum. *He needed Dr Blesserson*. Snot and tears slid down his face, dampening his gag. The man in the van was yelling now but he didn't care; he needed medicine. He was being held against his will and deprived of his medicine. CONC had kidnapped him; CONC ought to be held to account. The vehicle slammed to a halt. His body itched. Was he getting mange? His mouth foamed. Was he rabid? If he was rabid he would die – that was good, he needed to die. A howling desire shot through him: before he died he would kill the people who had killed Master, tear them limb from limb, devour every last scrap of their flesh. The taste of cherries flooded his mouth.

Then the doors were flung open, hands were all over him and with a tiny sting, a needle entered his arm.

Samrod had thought he was prepared, but as he peered through the small window, bile rose in his gorge. The glass vase in his hands was suddenly slippery as a fish, the hypodermic in his trouser pocket heavy as osmium. He had come to bring Clay comfort, strength, choices; instead he had to battle a powerful impulse to hurl all his gifts on the floor and run back down the hall, out into the lawns, back to a world where none of this had happened, where he could unsee that lump on the pillow, that glistening mass of gnarled red and black flesh.

He regained his grip on the vase. He was a *doctor*, and on the bed was Clay. That ghastly mask was stretched over Clay's noble bones, his dear pouting mouth; a blinding white whorl of bandages and tubing protected Clay's vital organs, the precious remains of his limbs. Samrod's heart rushed through the door. Clay was *alive* – more than alive: he was a miracle. The world's top medical journals would be discussing him for years.

'He is not yet out of critical condition. He must *not* be upset with any more bad news, and he absolutely must not talk.' The Barracks doctor was a small round woman, her deficit of human sympathy apparently not limited to her email correspondence, 'He knows it's one blink for "yes"; two for "no"; three for "I don't know" or "I can't remember." And Superintendent Blesserson' — she frowned again at the round lidded vase — 'let me reiterate: that aquarium must *never* be opened in his room.'

He had helped draft the Barracks' sickroom protocol and now he was breaking it. He had fought for two hours to get this female iceberg to permit his visit; he would not delay it any longer by objecting to her tone. 'I understand. Thank you, Doctor, for giving us some privacy.'

Pursing her lips, she opened the door and he hovered at the threshold. He wanted to dash to the bed and touch Clay, reassure him, but he could see nowhere to place even a finger. Only Clay's back had been spared from the flames. His face had suffered deep second-degree burns; his chest was charred down to the ribcage in places. His right arm had been amputated above the elbow, the left from the shoulder. Both his legs had been taken off above the knees. The limbs might have been saved if he'd been found in time, but although the Barracks had dispatched an emergency vehicle the minute Clay's car had lost radio contact, it had taken nearly two hours to get him to the hospital. The doctor was right: he could still die. He had haemorrhaged fluids, his lungs were congested, his kidney function badly damaged and his heart could fail at any moment. Somehow, though, he had not only hung on, but regained consciousness. He had been told of his amputations — how could he not realise his arms and legs were missing? — but he had not yet been informed about his groin; the doctors said the shock could kill him. And Clay *must not die*. Feverishly, ever since the news had reached him in the tower, Samrod had envisioned the recovery process, himself at Clay's side every slow painful step of the way. But he was also aware that his desperate desires were utterly selfish. How could he expect Clay to want to live like this? *Clay,*

Here in his lover's presence, watching that ravaged chest rise and fall, listening to each harsh, hard-won breath, Samrod found himself consumed not by compassion, but fury. Why hadn't the damn man worn his trousers, or done up his vest? The medics said it had been unfastened!

He hugged the vase, batted back the tears. He couldn't think like that. He had to think the opposite: his nagging had at least protected Clay from near-total skin loss and certain death. He had given Clay a chance. And now, after forty-eight hours trapped in the tower – what use was an escape route when you weren't allowed to use it in an emergency! – he was here to offer Clay more chances.

He shut the door, strode across the room, wheeled a table to the foot of the bed and placed the vase where Clay could see it. Then he pulled up a chair beside the side cabinet. Clay's Tablette was on top, next to a water beaker.

'Clay. It's Samrod. I'm here. Don't talk. Use the signals. Can you hear me?'

A hawk stared out of that bombed terrain and blinked. Once.

'I'm sorry I couldn't come earlier. It took two days to secure the exit routes. I came through the tunnel, through Is-Land. I brought flowers for you, Clay. Can you see them?'

The vase was filled with water and lined with pebbles. Three emerald-green stems hung down to the bottom, three white lotuses floated on the surface like crowns. Already the light from the window was casting a cool watery reflection across the opposite wall. At night, the blue bulbs embedded in the pebbles would create a meditative light display. It was essential Clay had something beautiful to look at, something beautiful and living to keep him rooted in the world; but also to help him, if necessary, to return to Gaia at peace.

One blink. Then, from those scorched lips, a twitch, a brief effort at a pucker. A kiss.

He could have wept. He could have filled that charred earhole with gratitude and relief, laid his cheek a millimetre above that broad chest and soaked the bandages with an untrammelled outpouring of love.

But this was Clay. 'I'm a member of your treatment team,' he said briskly. 'The other doctors said I was too close to you, but I insisted. They don't know you like I do.' He paused. 'I know they told you what happened. About the bomb . . . and your limbs.'

Clay blinked – quickly, almost impatiently. Then his gaze pinned Samrod's. It was an intense, furious question. A crucial moment.

He had to give Clay hope. 'It's a terrible blow, I know. You will never be quite the same again. But you can *make it*, Clay, you can recover, regain a high degree of independence and quality of life. I ensured you had allografs from one of the fallen Sec Gens – we dealt with the legal issues. I got permission from the parents, they have donated the boy's internal organs too, if you need them. All of Is-Land wants you to recover, Clay. The skin on your chest will heal rapidly and our plastic surgeons will rebuild your face. It will be scarred, but rugged, weathered, still handsome. Is-Land produces the best prostheses in the world: we can replace your limbs with the very latest in mechatronics. You can walk again, operate a Tablette, dress yourself, drive a car. I *know* you can.'

Clay was still staring at him, hard, unappeased. *He wants to know.* Samrod's heart seized. He faltered. But he could not participate in the lie. Clay would not forgive him for it.

'I know, Clay: they didn't tell you everything. Do you want to hear it now?'

One blink. Steady. Unflinching.

'The doctors—' He attempted to revert to his professional tone, void of all feeling, but failed utterly. 'Oh Clay.' His voice broke. 'They had to remove your genitals. That's why you can't feel them. They're not there any more.'

Clay's gaze filled with a smouldering darkness. Then, infinitely slowly, he shut his eyes.

Every cell of his body blazed with fury and glory. He had been *chosen* – hurled into the furnace that was Gaia's burning heart, consecrated in Her ceaseless inferno. Every breath was torture, but *life* was torture. He had thirsted for this ultimate test, now he relished the pain. That was the meaning of leadership: not 'charisma' or 'humility' or 'listening skills', but *elemental will*: a true leader lived with one sole purpose: to drive humanity beyond all human limits. So his cock and balls were gone, his arms and legs gone, his skin gone: so what? It made no difference. He was not this body, never had been. He was a radiant force, a red-hot pulsing vein in Gaia's molten core. Did that legless youth Arakkia think he could douse Clay Odinson's will, rob him of his place in this war, simply by depriving him of his extremities? Those asinine doctors, did they think they could keep the truth from him? He had *known* there was nothing between his legs, nothing but numbness and flame, gone, as surely as his hands and feet. He had raged at that fat bitch for not telling him, gargling and hacking until she gave him another injection of whatever it was, putting him into a restless imitation of sleep, pierced through and through by relentless stabs of pain. Now he was awake again and Samrod was here, with tears in his voice and soapy baubles in his hands.

He opened his eyes, glared at the lilies. Lilies? He wanted sunflowers, tall and golden and flaring with pride, celebrating his immersion in Gaia's flaming heart.

Clay's eyes were raw pits glaring into a distance Samrod could not plumb. He had to reach him, pull him back. 'It's not the end, Clay,' he urged. 'We can reconstruct your penis, give you hormone treatment; you'll have sex again. Great sex.' He leaned forward, whispered, 'Clay, I was wrong; of course you can fuck boys and girls if you want. Babies, if you like. I'll back the Sex Gens project, all the way. You were right, Clay; it's part of the new vision and I mustn't resist it.'

His fingers went to his pocket. The needle was a cold dart against his thigh.

'Clay. We can rebuild you, I promise . . . But only if you *want* us to. If not . . . Clay, I can help you . . . now, while no one would suspect anything. Clay – please tell me. Do you want to live?'

Babies too, if you like. Samrod had always fussed and clucked, appealed to abstractions, squabbled and quibbled and made his tiny point, then, when fucked right, given in. That was the whole point of Samrod: to be difficult, but ultimately acquiescent; to offer every day a tiny clash of wills Clay could win. As he stared at the watery reflections cast by the vase, Clay felt Samrod's submission like an electric infusion, lightning through an ocean, charging his veins, feeding his insatiable elemental will. Oh, Samrod was so noble. He thought to bring Clay lessons in detachment, aspiration, serenity, the transformation of muck into supreme cosmic consciousness . . . what sentimental shit. The lilies were speaking now and they were saying . . .

We drink in the light and suck up the mud, both are the same to us. We aspire to nothing, nothing more than being exactly as we are. Beautiful and adored for being beautiful . . . thus are we King of the Flowers.

He was Is-Land's Prince of Power. With a long, blazing sigh he permitted the lilies to crown him.

The blink was immediate, startling and fierce, and it was followed by a bulging stare, so strong it could have shattered the vase. There was no possibility of misinterpretation. Samrod felt the tension pour out of him like water. 'Oh thank Gaia – I'm so glad. I'm sorry I asked, Clay, but I *had* to, you understand, don't you? I'm here for you, whatever you need. Is that enough for today? Do you want to rest now?'

Two blinks.

Clay wanted to live. And that meant he needed to *know everything*.

'Shall I tell you what we know about the bomb?'

One blink.

'It was a wavebomb. The engineers have analysed the shrapnel. They say it came from Asfar. We're still not sure why the blast set you alight, but fragments of an akik bottle were discovered by the vehicle, which might explain it.'

The doctor had said Clay was unlikely to remember the bomb blast, or what had preceded it, so Samrod was expecting three blinks. He got a wink.

'Oh, Clay.' He shook his head, sighed. 'What *am* I going to do with you?'

Three blinks.

I don't know. He threw back his head and laughed out loud, and his heart flowered. Everything was going to be all right; it really truly was. Clay was now proving what Samrod had always suspected: he was *indestructible*. He couldn't love Clay more than he did now.

He got back on track. 'No one has claimed responsibility yet, but that giant YAC warrior has disappeared from the Hem. There's been no word of Enki Arakkia either. We're ninety-nine per cent positive YAC set the bomb.'

One blink. Agreement.

Samrod paused. There were two more pieces of news the doctors had said Clay shouldn't hear, but he was in a good mood, alert, joking, responsive. And Clay didn't suffer bereavement, at least not in the way most people did. He had cried at his mother's deathbed, but had been back at work the next day; Samrod had even heard him whistling in the bathroom before he left. 'She was old and ill,' Clay had said later when he'd probed. 'It was time for her to die. I am her legacy, and if you will just let me, Samrod, I will shine in her honour.' To be fair, knowing Clay's mother, she had probably told him not to grieve.

Now, however, Clay's narcissism was proving an inestimable boon. Samrod pressed on. 'Whoever it was, Clay, they took Peat. The officers found footprints, leading south. We sent Sec Gens to follow the trail, but they lost it at an escarpment, then there was an explosion and the lead officer deemed it unsafe to proceed.'

Clay's eyes narrowed.

'I'm sorry, Clay; I know how much you enjoyed him. And of course, to have lost a Sec Gen to the enemy is a worry – but we've prepared for this, right from the beginning of the project. It will be very difficult for his captors to keep Peat alive. I am confident that he will refuse food and water, and even if YAC do get a medic to force-feed him, he won't be much use as a research subject. There is little they'll be able to find out about his design from isolated lab results, and in any case, the nurturing environment we provided is as important as their physical engineering. Besides, the antidote only works on children within a few days of the shot; I don't believe anyone could devise an effective antidote to a young adult Sec Gen.'

Clay's eyes were popping like a frog's. Straining, he lifted his head off the pillow. 'Or . . . do-o-ott,' he croaked.

'Shhhh!' Samrod jumped up and wagged his finger in Clay's face. 'If you speak one more word, I'm leaving, Clay. You have oedema in your neck, causing pressure on your airway and you *must* let it subside before you start talking again.'

Clay rolled his eyes, but was silent.

Samrod sat down. 'Yes. Astra Ordott, I know. I've thought it all through, Clay: they might try to use her to trigger a psychological crisis, maybe tempt him into some kind of emotional return. But that almost certainly won't work. Peat knows his sister is Is-Land's – and his family's – worst enemy. If they meet, he would try to kill her before he kills himself. His capture is an unfortunate occurrence, Clay, but not catastrophic. As far as the media and the families are concerned, we are doing all we can to find him. International sympathy in Amazigia is already turning to our advantage.'

Clay blinked slowly, once. The loss of Peat Orson was clocked, filed, absorbed. Now Samrod needed to give him the bigger picture.

'In general, the conflict is escalating rapidly. Without that giant in the Hem to contend with, the Sec Gens have been killing far more Non-Landers, and Dayyani has made good her threat to call on Asfar for help. She's invited the Mujaddid to visit Kadingir for another Emergency Diplomeet, for which CONC are deploying peacekeeping troops – just to guard their headquarters, they say.'

One blink. Pause. One blink. Pause. One blink. *Yes yes yes.*

'I know; escalation was always part of your vision.' He moistened his lips. 'I have one more thing to tell you and it's not good, I'm afraid. But I want you to hear it from me.' There was no easy way to say this. 'Yesterday the Wheel Meet convened an emergency meeting, and Stamen Magmason personally authorised your removal from the Vision Council. Riverine Farshoredott has been sent from Atourne Barracks to fill your office here. Magmason is on his way to address the Sec Gens, help boost morale. They'll be coming to pay their respects to you soon.'

Two blinks. Two blinks. Two blinks.

'I know. I know. It's a disastrous decision. I said it was premature, that we should speak with you first, appoint a proxy, perhaps give me two votes, but I was overruled. I still have my seat on the Vision Council, Clay, and I will represent your interests vigorously. I will back Magmason all the way on the Sex Gens, and push for your return to a command position as soon as possible.'

There was a very long pause. One blink.

'You're welcome, Clay.'

He would go in a minute, but first he had to take the edge off the nasty taste of Clay's defeat. He had saved the sweetest for last.

'Clay, I want to put our Non-Land prisoners on the Vision Council agenda. We've got what we need from them – do you remember? The adults are back in their cells and the officers took the boy to the sandfly pit right after you left. We've got ears and eyes on Kadingir and Lálsil, in case Ordott and her playmate return. But you had bigger plans for the prisoners, do you remember? You wanted to take the adults to Atourne and try them on terrorist charges. You said the men should have an accident on the way. I disagreed at the time, but under the changed circumstances, I now think it's a good plan.'

He meant it. It could take a long time to recover Peat Orson's body or capture Astra Ordott and Muzi Bargadala, and Samrod needed to set some achievable goals for Clay in the meantime. What he had initially considered a high-risk act of pre-emptive retaliation was now more like a small, private settling of scores. The Head Engineer, generally a cautious woman, might vote against the idea, but from the way Magmason and Farshoredott had been speaking since the YAC attack, about *heating up the conflict* and *accelerating the Vision schedule*, he knew they would support it. Magmason would probably give official permission to fudge the files. A couple of dead Non-Land peasants were no mighty victory, but a completed action point was something to offer Clay and a successful result might significantly aid his psychological recovery. YAC might even kill Peat Orson in response, which would bring that situation to a quicker resolution.

'You were right,' he repeated. 'Shall I put your proposal on the table, Clay?'

This blink was sharp as a knife, an irrefutable signal that he had given Clay reasons to live. Things were terribly different now, but Clay needed him; he would not let him down.

'Good. I'll do that. Now, your Tablette is here. Do you want me to leave you with some music? And shall I turn on the light show before I go?'

One blink.

He set about activating the aquarium display, joking that he would have brought goldfish if the doctor had let him, and set playing a symphony by Sibelius, one of Clay's favourite Old World composers, on his Tablette. When he took one last look back through the door window, Clay was moving his arm stumps to the music. His eyes were bulging like jellyfish out of his head and his ravaged mouth was contorted in what looked to Samrod like an ecstasy of pain.

He was back in the van, gagged, hooded, chained. He didn't know if Kingu, Habat, Nanshe and the children were in with him. 'Take *him*, take *him!*' his wife had screamed when the officers came to the cell, and whether or not the Gaians had understood, they had followed her orders, seizing him before he could tell if they had come for the others as well.

He accepted his dark isolation. The others were lost to him; they had furiously rejected his offer of help. So those were to be his wife's last words to him, the first she had thrown in his direction for two days, ever since the officers had taken Suen to the ant heap, saying it was because his father had refused to answer their questions. 'He is bitten everywhere. *Everywhere!*' Nanshe had shrieked, cradling the boy's head in her lap. 'How did I marry such a monster? First you take Muzi's hand, now you take our son's innocence!'

'Suen is *ten*,' he had shouted back. 'He must learn to be a *man*.' Habat and Kingu stared at him, shock in their eyes, covering Geshti and Hadis's ears with their hands. He had bent over Suen, spoken loud and clear.

'Son, they are just insect bites. They will go away soon. You must not scratch them. You must think of cool water, and taking revenge.'

Nanshe pushed him away, slapping and pushing him, Kingu was weeping into his daughters' hair.

Habat had tried to calm Nanshe down. 'Don't blame Gibil,' his sister-in-law had pleaded. 'He doesn't know what he's doing any more. Blame IMBOD: IMBOD is the cause of all our suffering. Only the gods can help us now. Only the gods.'

He had remained silent. He couldn't explain; the others wouldn't listen. They hadn't listened when he'd told them to reveal nothing, whatever the officers threatened, and they wouldn't listen now. Instead, Nanshe was flinging that old curse in his face. Yes, he had taken Muzi's hand. With one drunken swing of a gate, he had crushed a child's wrist, maimed his own nephew. But he had learned from what had happened. It had changed him. *You are weak, Gibil, weak!* his father had stormed, shaking with rage. *You cannot punish the Gaians, so you punish all of us with your drink! Even with only one hand, that little boy is stronger than you!* The words had stung, far worse than IMBOD's fire ants. He had stopped drinking akik; he had married, fathered his own child. IMBOD might have broken him once, but they would never do so again. Muzi had grown into a strong young man, just as Suen would do, if he lived.

The van rumbled on. Free at last of that machine in his head, he thought of many things: of the scrublands at dawn, gold rays spreading over the hills like the light through a glass of warm beer; of his wife when she laughed; of the moment she had placed his son in his arms, the son he had not wanted to hold for fear of dropping him and being accused again of breaking a child. Of his father on his deathbed, his big belly shrunk to an empty sack, his moustache grey as ashes, telling him to take care of his mother, and of his mother, her chattering tongue, her foolish dreams, her bird-like body falling limp to the ground, a death Muzi would have to avenge, because none of them were going to leave IMBOD's jails alive. Of that he was sure. This was not like before, in his youth, being rounded up during a street battle and forgotten, released after enduring two years in a dank, overcrowded cell. This time IMBOD had come for them in the night, breaking all the new agreements, and the officer in charge was not a man to let witnesses against him slip from his clutches.

He did not struggle against the chains. He was still as a rock. He thought of Kingu, sick-faced, defeated, slumped in the corner of the cell, water leaking from his eyes.

'We must kill them ourselves,' Gibil had hissed the first night when the children were sleeping. 'It will be kinder.'

'What are you saying? What is he saying?' Nanshe had come at him, nails ready to scratch his eyes out. Kingu had pulled her off.

'Shut up, brother. *Shut up*.' Kingu was strong as a brother, but he had always been soft around women and children. Kingu had fought with him, hit him hard. He had not spoken of it again.

The van jerked and rumbled on. He sat still and straight. They were being driven to their deaths. Kingu had made his choices, Gibil had made his. Kingu would die knowing he had betrayed his son and not saved his daughters from rape and an agonising death. Gibil would die knowing he had given his nephew a chance to survive.

The World Within

'At the start of the Dark Times a man in Asfar caught a pair of hadāhid and put them in a cage. He filled the cage with twigs and dried grass and brought it with him when he went to seek refuge in a camp. The camp was one of the fortunate ones: it had been built by wealthy families and had strong fences, a wind turbine, a hydroponic garden and a patch of scrubland large enough to provide insects and worms for the birds. There was food for all the inhabitants, though not much of it. The main problems were grief for everything people had lost, fear of what might happen if the sun never returned, and boredom. The hudhud, though, knows no such worries and the pair the man had caught set about building a nest. Sitting in his room with his birds, the man read books by the ancient mystics of his land. He prayed to his god for help in accepting all that had been lost, and in mourning the past, he gradually accepted that the universe is truly endless, a ceaseless cycle of expansion and contraction, creation and destruction. The day his female hudhud laid her first egg was, to him, the first day of the renewal of his world.

But though no one was starving, the man knew other people in the camp would have gladly eaten the birds and their eggs and as time went on he began to feel guilty for protecting them. To assuage his conscience, like many other adults he began to fast, giving his portion of bread to the young, the old and the ill members of the community. Yet though he did not eat, he yet had energy, a sparkling light in his eyes. He invited others to his room to pray and share the joy of the birds: there were now half a dozen pairs, all nesting and hatching. Eventually, he trusted some of his new friends enough to take birds back to their own rooms. Soon, the whole camp was full of hudhud breeders. When at last the clouds lifted, the sun returned and the camp disbanded, the people released the birds back into the wild. The man had no wife or children, but when he grew old people protected him, as he had protected the hadāhid. My parents, Farashani Non-Landers, were among those given shelter in that camp. In their honour, I brought a pair of hadāhid with me when I returned to Non-Land.'

The Zardusht was speaking in Asfarian, her voice hushing around the cavern. With her gnarled fingers she was stripping lantern leaves from their stalks, placing the leaves in a singing bowl and the bare stems on a large plate. The altar candles were lit and a stick of incense sent a sweet woody scent curling through the cave. Somewhere behind Astra, Hozai was gently drumming. Astra wanted to ask about the High Healer's Farashani parents, but the teaching seemed to be focused on the hoopoe. And perhaps the Zardusht's personal history had long been shed, like a chick's downy feathers in the wind.

'Did you paint the hudhud in the Istar temple?' she asked.

'We did.' Lantern leaf was the plant that grew in spirals near the stream; the Zardusht plucked a starflower from the branch and dropped it in a bowl of water. 'We found the statues and decided to stay. Shiimti was much smaller then.'

'Muzi told me the hudhud was a messenger between King Shlemun and the Queen of Theopia.'

'That is correct.' The Zardusht picked up the last full branch of leaves. 'Shlemun was a younger brother, not expected to be King. When he ascended the throne he asked his god to give him not wealth or dominion over new lands but the wisdom required to rule well. To reward his humility, his god granted him that wisdom, and also riches, power, many wives and the ability to speak with animals and birds. The hudhud became his vizier and his messenger. The bird brought words of passion and mutual respect between Shlemun and the proud Queen of a distant land: words that founded a great imperial dynasty. Three millennia later, amongst the descendants of the Old African slaves of Jahmaker, the Emperor of Theopia inspired the birth of a great spiritual tradition, a religion steeped in plant medicine and rooted in the awareness that human beings are all divine, all equal under the sun.'

Astra tried to follow the history lesson, but her mind was wandering. She wondered if the Zardusht had given Lil an Advanced Vizier teaching yesterday. This morning in the dorm, even though Astra was hungover and aching from her late night with Muzi down by the stream, Lil had made Astra shoot an Istar PR video and then chivvied her into going to the cave. Lil had made her pin her hoopoe feather to her robe and told her to eat fruit or lassi for breakfast, something easy to throw up. 'Aren't you coming too?' Astra had asked, but Lil had driven off into the desert to pick up a Tablette signal and transmit the video to Kadingir, leaving Astra with her incipient headache. She was feeling too fragile for a psychotropic experience; she would have preferred to spend the day resting in the gardens, but she didn't want to run into Zizi. Her father had messaged while she was crying to Muzi saying:

Daughter! What is happening? Come back! Are you not well?

And ten minutes later:

Daughter, take pity! Reply!

He must have hit his daily limit then, because he went silent until the morning, when he sent a long email berating himself for letting her drink beer and assuring her Salamu and Talmai had forgiven her. A text followed, urging:

Daughter! Come let us eat breakfast and send our questions to Pūtigi.

That was followed an hour later by:

Cinders has flown! Come and find me in the hemp fields, Daughter, and let us await the news that you seek.

That was it. There was no apology for upsetting her, insulting Muzi, trying to trade her like a cow. She'd argued with Muzi about it over her peach lassi. He thought *she* should go and say sorry to Zizi! She couldn't believe it. She'd demanded that Muzi come to the cave with her for a teaching, but instead he'd gone off to find Zizi.

She had stomped off to the cave in a temper. She didn't know if Muzi was going to stay with her, or what she would do if both he and Lil left her here on her own. But the cave was cool and soon she would be lying down, closing her eyes and asking questions of the hoopoe creature teacher. Travelling to the World Within, she understood from Lil's description, was like having a Gaia vision, but instead of sitting still and watching the Earth or the sky for messages, you shut your eyes and Gaia sent her spirit guides welling up inside you. Learning all that had been a secret relief: it sounded like hearing the voices. Maybe, she thought, the lizards had eaten lantern leaf and the chemical was working its way through her system. She had told the Zardusht about her dreams, hoping for some kind of explanation, but the High Healer had just nodded and said the leaf would answer all of her questions. Worried about adverse reactions, she'd asked also about her headache pills, but the Zardusht had said that hypericum and lantern leaf were companion spirits – hypericum meant 'over ghosts' and the plant would help ward off any evil spirits attracted to her in the World Within. That didn't sound encouraging, but she had come this far and she needed to finish the journey. A plant medicine trip, she decided, couldn't be worse than the *mergalla*.

'So, Astra' – the Zardusht ripped three leaves off at once and added them to the bowl – 'you are about to partake of the lantern leaf. Do you have a question for your spirit guides?'

Am I Istar? seemed unanswerable. She fingered the feather pinned to her robe and spoke slowly. 'You said the hoopoe was the teacher of the self. How can I be true to myself, but also help other people?'

The Zardusht glowed with satisfaction. 'That is the question of ages, Astra! Sometimes enormous sacrifice is required. But, always, simply knowing and being oneself is of service to others. This requires that we look to the World Within.' She shook the nearly denuded stalk. 'Let me tell you of the time King Shlemun had a very big problem. His god had demanded that he build a temple without the use of iron tools. What! Was he supposed to bite the stones from the quarry with his teeth? He despaired, he paced, he visited his wives and interrogated each one about her dreams. But his wives' dreams were of fiery jewels and journeys on white horses and giving birth to sons with the heads of lions. None had the answer for him. So he convened a great congress of birds and bid them to help him and it was the hudhud who hopped onto his shoulder, "Fear not, Noble King, for I know the secret of a magical plant, a leaf that can cut rock," it told him. Wielding the sesame leaf in its beak, the bird hewed the stones for the temple. From the bird's knowledge came the Asfarian incantation "Open Sesame", uttered to open the hidden mouths of caves full of treasure.' Her eyes glinted. 'Do you know the ancient tales of Asfar?'

'No.' She watched the starflowers float in circles on the water in the singing bowl. 'But I think Zizi gave them to me. He sent me a book of stories and poems. I haven't read it yet.'

'Ah. Zizi Kataru's famous anthology. Yes, the tales will be within it. You may also come to our story circles and hear them. There are many ancient legends of the hudhud, the hoopoe, as you call it. The first people of the Great River believed that the blood of the hoopoe, smeared on the eyelids, granted visions of the future. The future was indeed bloody for Shlemun's nation. Lacking his wisdom, later rulers governed harshly and the bird became the symbol of a war-torn land, one that now lies under the sea. But for the ancient poets, the hoopoe was the leader of an expedition of birds seeking to know God. We painted that journey also at the temple.'

The teaching was a slightly dizzying business. The Zardusht had slipped merrily on, without fully answering her question. How was she supposed to be herself, whoever that was, when everyone had such big plans for her? And hadn't she sacrificed enough already? She wanted to ask about Muzi and Zizi, but she wasn't sure if she was allowed to interrupt the teaching. 'Did you plant the sesame and the Shlemun's Seal at the temple too?' She touched her cheek. The wound was healing well. 'My cut was infected from the *mergalla*. Muzi made a poultice with the root and drew the poison out. His grandmother taught him how.'

The Zardusht placed the empty stalk on the plate. 'Shimti is the world's grandmother. We teach people how to grow gardens in the desert and we send them out with seeds and tools and the skills to plant the Earth anew. We also heal the spirit. We teach people how to travel to the World Within and learn from their teachers there. Just as the sesame leaf cuts rock, the lantern leaf shines a light like a knife through the mind.' She held out the singing bowl full of leaves. 'Are you ready to chew?'

Muzi left Astra at the restaurant. She was hungover and in a bad temper and wanted to go and vomit in a cave with the Zardusht all afternoon. Perhaps it was a good idea for her to purge herself. He was curious about the World Within too, but the Zardusht would have to wait. He had to talk to Zizi. He had to tell Astra's father that Astra and he had renewed their temporary marriage, but Zizi must not worry: his intentions were to marry her properly as soon as he could.

A boy told him the hemp field was in the outer zone of the food forest, east of the garden road. He could walk there or take a bicycle from the garage. He decided to walk, strode quickly up the road they had driven in on, but at the beehives, out of earshot of the busy ledge, confronted with the loud hum of the garden, he stopped.

What was his plan? Was he just going to show up at Astra's father's workplace and ask to talk to him about a serious matter? He couldn't do that. Or if he did, he needed to bring something, an offering; a cold beer perhaps, in which case a bicycle was a good idea; maybe he should go back for one. But while his food was free for three days, he had no money for a beer and anyway maybe Zizi wouldn't be able to take a break. Really, he should go and join in, help weed or water or whatever the workers were doing.

He stood, letting the cyclists pass him. In which case, should he take his CONC hand?

He didn't want to. He'd have to go back to the dorm to get it, leave the knife back in the locker, but more than the hassle, he didn't like wearing it. The CONC hand was uncomfortable and hot and made his wrist sore. He could use most farming implements just as he was, and that was what he wanted Zizi to know. Be yourself, his grandmother had always told him.

But he had been himself since he arrived and Zizi hadn't been impressed. Astra's father wanted a son-in-law with two hands. A son-in-law who worked on the internet and had a rich, cultured father.

He sat down on a rock in the shade. People passed by. Most, he realised, were on bicycles or on foot, unaided. In ten minutes, he counted one person in a wheelchair, another on crutches and one tapping along with a white stick. Everyone looked healthy and purposeful, heading to or from work, but still, it struck him for the first time, it wasn't like Kadingir here. He hadn't seen any Singulars and alt-bodied people were definitely in the minority.

He looked down at his wrist. On his own, out with the sheep, driving the horse and cart to the scrapheap, cracking an egg in the pan for an early breakfast, he never thought about his missing hand. Why would he think about something he couldn't remember? Being with other people, though, forced him to be aware of that empty space; how it drew gazes like bait in a river drew fish. With his family, or people who liked him, he didn't mind the attention, even showed off. He could balance a cup and saucer on his wrist for his mother, flip a coin with Kishar, shuffle cards then rest the deck on his wrist and offer it to his father or uncle to cut. With new people, he had learned it was good to execute a simple action early on, give them something to watch rather than an absence to contemplate. He had lit the candle for Astra on her birthday to put her at her ease. Yesterday, he had passed the knife around to the men, perhaps if he'd sat at the table longer, he would have pushed a bowl of olives across the table to Zizi. Usually, that was all he had to do; in Kadingir, most people accepted everyone else as they were.

Most, but not all. Again, he felt it, that sharp shove between his ribs: intense anger at being pitied and rejected. Then the anger was shoving a rock away from the mouth of a cave and for the first time in a long time, a huge muddy feeling welled up in him, a terrible sense that he lacked and would forever lack, something vitally important to being a man, that all the things he could do counted for nothing, less than nothing, were tricks you might teach a dog; and squirming through that mud was a worm of shame, shame at being himself, stuck like this, never able to change, to be whole. It had always surprised him how sickening that feeling was, how hard to shake, how it took the shine off everything all day. Usually, he went out with the sheep and walked until he was tired, then slept it off.

Right now, the mixture of feelings was paralysing. He could not walk away this time. The person who had triggered the shove was the one man in the world he most needed to impress.

He looked up at the sky. His whole life, the sky had been his guide. Today, it was blank blue, gave no sign at all what he should do. Usually that meant 'wait and see' or 'don't worry', but he couldn't sit on this rock all day and he couldn't stop worrying either. Perhaps, he thought, he had spent so much time watching the sky because he wasn't capable of being with people. Really, who did he know? His family; Kishar and his brother; a few schoolmates and neighbours and now Astra. She was from a whole other world – *two* other worlds, Is-Land and CONC – and now her father wanted her to join his world in Shiimti. He was just a sheep farmer and scrap-metal merchant. Perhaps he wasn't the right husband for Astra. Perhaps he should just give her up.

Hoo hoo. Hoo hoo. Hoo hoo.

From a date palm came a flash and flurry of orange, black and white, a bossy, echoing call, a hudhud swooping across the road and disappearing into an apricot orchard.

He puzzled it out. Astra was wearing a hudhud feather today. The sky-god had sent him a message. What had the Zardusht said? *The bud-bud is the teacher of the self. And what had his grandmother always told him? You can only be yourself, Muzi. If you try to be someone else you will fail as surely as a donkey draped in a camel skin fails to cross the desert alone.*

He stood up and walked on down the road towards the hemp field.

The leaf tasted terrible. It was sour and bitter and rotten all at the same time; it made her tongue curl like a dying slug in her mouth, her eyes run hot rivers and her stomach churn like a vat of rancid compost. But the Zardusht was chewing steadily, smacking her lips and flashing her eyes. Astra drank gulps of water between each leaf and ate every last one. She felt dizzy and just wanted to lie down, but the Zardusht got up and placed a singing bowl on her head like a helmet. It wasn't heavy, but the Zardusht played it, stroking the rim with a wooden stick, until Astra's head sang. Shortly after the bowl was removed she was violently ill. Her guts clamped and seized, her head swam and her blood was so hot it felt like it was boiling out of her pores. She reached for the bucket and emptied her peach lassi into it. Vaguely, she could hear Hozai's drumming increase. She lay down on the mat, curled up in a ball, rocked back and forth, wishing she could die. Someone came and wiped her mouth with a damp cloth. She lay clutching her ribs, then vomited again, a long string of stomach acid.

After a time there was nothing left inside her to expel. She lay on her back, wondering if she were made out of papyrus, wishing she could tear herself up into tiny bits and blow away into the wind. A half-naked old woman with green skin appeared above her. The woman was long and ropey with dangling breasts and greasy hair and her eyes were white revolving stars. She stood over Astra and laughed.

'You want to die now?' One lonely tooth waggled in her gums and her eyes spat light in all directions. 'Wait until you see what's coming next!'

Her anger rose at the ridicule; not sure if she was thinking or speaking, she retaliated, 'I don't want to die. I just don't want any more pain. I've had *enough*.'

The old green woman laughed louder. 'You've had enough pain? You haven't even begun to suffer! You don't know how to suffer, that's your problem.'

She knew it was true. She had been born to suffer, to lose her home, everyone she loved, to kill people she loved. But she wasn't good at it and it wasn't fair to ask her to go on. 'Why me?' she whimpered. 'Why not someone else?'

'Why not you? What makes you so special?'

She didn't know. But she was angry again. 'I came here to get answers, to find out what to do, not be laughed at and told I'm dirt.'

The woman leaned over her, cackling so hard her green breasts swung back and forth like melting bells. 'Well, ask better questions then.'

With a great sucking sound, the woman became a tall green funnel with a star propeller, a whirlwind flying out of the cave. She took Astra's anger with her, ripped it out of her heart, leaving her empty and dazed on her mat. *Better questions.* Yes, of course.

She had asked the Zardusht a question, she thought an important one, but when she tried to recall it, it seemed very abstract, emerging eventually as overlapping circles and pulsing cellular patterns that deepened into long tunnels, like the echo of the star-eyed green funnel woman. *Oh that's interesting . . . thoughts and questions are shapes . . .* For a long time, fascinated, she wandered along vines and winding moonbeams, let them lead her deeper and deeper . . . where? *Where am I?* That seemed to be a better question.

'You are in the World Within. You are always there. And so am I.'

It was Hokma's firm, husky voice, enveloping her like a vigorous rubdown after a long bath. Tears seeped down her cheeks. *Hokma was here.* She had not gone away forever like everyone said; she had been here waiting all along. Of course she had. Everything *else* had been a bad dream. Relief flooded her. The world was made right, put back in order. With a sensation of perfect completion, as if remembering something that would never let her forget it, she knew what her burning question was.

'Am I Istar?'

The cellular tunnels became snakes, emerald snakes with red eyes and flickering pink tongues. They wrapped their dry scaly bodies around her arms and lifted her up, vertically, up and out of her robe so that she was suspended naked in the centre of the cave, her arms outstretched, as if hanging from the branches of a tree. Her throat felt constricted and there was a cold sensation running down between her breasts, past her navel. She looked down to see the long tail of a silver necklace – the chain of deaths that had brought her here, its links as thin and strong as those of her Birth mother's bracelet, that chain of stolen lakes – disappearing into the thick black triangle between her legs. Further down, on the floor of the cave, the Zardusht was smoking a pipe. The smoke swirled up until she couldn't see the Zardusht's head, couldn't see her own toes, or her feet or her ankles. She was being consumed by a slowly crawling plume of smoke.

'Istar has been caressing you.' Hokma's voice filled the cave. Not Hokma's Old World fairy-tale voice; her serious voice, the one she used when she was expecting Astra to listen, to make an important decision. 'Her embrace has been shielding you from your enemies. She would now like to enter you fully. If you allow Istar to join you, you will suffer greatly, but always for a reason, a reason you can understand. If you decline, you will suffer less, but senselessly. No higher purpose will illuminate your tears or redeem your sacrifices. What do you choose, Astra?'

She was suspended in the cave, suspended in unknowing. 'What do you mean, suffer more? Will I die?'

'Suffering does not cease at death, Astra. I suffer when I see you in pain. But I am more than my suffering, much more. You too can grow into and beyond your own pain – or you can remain shrunken inside its cocoon. It is for you to choose.'

The answer was as opaque as the smoke, but in its implacable certainty, lulling rhythms, suggested great sense. Beneath her, the smoke writhed in fathomless tendrils, formed, with the vines and the tunnels, a great dreaming brain. From the intertwining cloud, a white snake emerged, slithered up around her calves, a soft white snake with golden eyes that flushed many colours as it curled around her legs, all the colours of the rainbow and all the colours of the earth, from red with black eyes, to yellow with green eyes, blue with yellow eyes to bronze with silver eyes, always watching her watching it change. As she did, she came herself to a new understanding. The World Within was eternal. It embraced life and death and it travelled far beyond them. The winding path she had taken to arrive here, in this moment, was one of infinitely many paths, spiralling endlessly in and out of all the dimensions of the cosmos: real and imagined and altered by time; past, present and future; co-existing, overlapping, far-flung and distant. Chained to her own story, she had been unable to follow any others. All along, though, they had been following her.

She strained to see further but the chain around her neck held fast. She was held here, she realised, not just by the dead, but by the living. 'What about Muzi and Zizi and Lil? Will Istar make me sacrifice them all?'

'That is not within your power, Astra, or Istar's. Whatever you decide, those you love will choose their own destinies: to follow you or not; to wait for you, or not. You cannot control love. You can only give and receive it, in whatever form it takes, Istar is the strongest, purest form of love, Astra. Are you ready to receive her?'

You cannot control love. She accepted that truth as she had accepted the axioms of good laboratory practice, Wise House rules, the care of an Owleon. The chain loosened a fraction. She turned her head as in warrior pose, looking out along first one arm then the other. Her limbs were green, and long like the old woman's; the snakes wrapped around them were a warm writhing bronze, living jewellery. One arm reached to the back of the cavern, the palm pressed against the rough surface, like the first palm print ever made against a cave wall. The other stretched towards the mouth of the cave.

You can choose to grow . . . She understood those words too.

The smoke snake had reached the top of her thighs, its ghostly head nudging at the cleft between her legs. She lifted her head, closed her eyes. *I'm ready*, she said, or thought, or knew in every dancing particle and flowing wave of her being. *I am ready for Istar to join me.*

Like a fountain spurting up from the bowels of the Earth, the smoke snake rushed into her, fusing with her spine, with her flesh, with the chain. Energy seared through her arms, straight to the back of the cave, melting the stone and shooting out of the cave like a lizard's tongue, aiming right at the sun. She grabbed the sun and squeezed it like an orange. Juice ran from her fingers out over the desert and when she opened her palm and her eyes, she saw a hoopoe flying up to the heavens and a single star shining in the blue sky.

I am far away but I am always within you. The voice glimmered deep inside her, like silver water at the bottom of a well. *You have accepted me and now you must accept my truth. Astra, the primordial law here on Earth is war: a long, loving war in which, to survive, you must find your right place. Your place is to speak for the Old Ones.*

She knew now that her questions were not foolish or frightened, but inevitable, her lines in a call-and-response chant as ancient as the shimmering voice in her cells. *How can a war be loving? And who are the Old Ones? How do I speak to them?*

They do not come when human beings summon them. I will draw them to you, as I sent the mergallá to help you. Now that I am shining within you, they will find you wherever you are. But you must be patient. The Old

Ones' sense of time is deep and slow, Astra, deeper even than the history of the Earth. They might appear to you as the mountains and oceans, the wind or the rivers, the Earth's minerals or Her fiery core, but these entities and forces are merely their hosts. For billions of years the Old Ones have animated the elements and when the Earth's sun implodes and this planet's water evaporates, its furnace cools and hardens, some of them will depart; others will remain foetal and dreaming in its husk. They are in no hurry to leave. They enjoy it here. The Old Ones command the grand geological procession of this place, orchestrate its shifting tectonics, ride the long glissandos of its changing climate. Like children in playgrounds and streets, like long-married couples, they wage their endless loving war with each other – the wind mauls the sea, the sea eats the land, the land chokes the rivers, the rivers feed the clouds, the rain rusts the rocks, the rust flings itself into the eyes of the wind . . . and so it goes, a tireless brawl, fuelled by deep pleasure, with no ultimate victors, no prisoners, no slaves.

She thought about the planet, its vast cycles and geological eras, billions of years of ceaseless change, against which all of human history was a pawn on a battlefield, rushing in late to be immediately slain. *Why do they need me, then?*

The Old Ones' majestic movements are not their only pleasure. They also love life. Life amuses, flatters, nourishes the Old Ones. The birds adorn the sky and sea, the animals tickle the land, their bones enrich the soil, the plants express the Earth's health. Life heightens the joy of the Old Ones, deepens their pride in the marvel that is Gaia, a synergistic marvel not even Neptune with its hot oceans of crushed diamond can boast. The only problem with life is human beings. You are the parasite that threatens to kill the host. You proliferated, polluted, exhausted ancient energies, forced chain reactions, destroyed the fundamental balance of this planet. Finally, provoked beyond reason, the Old Ones rose up in anger against you, but you are everywhere, too difficult to eradicate without destroying life itself. We stars preached restraint, bid the Old Ones to issue a warning. When oceans rose to drown your cities, temperatures soared to scorch your fields, clouds gathered to blot out the sun, many of you did at last realise the error of your ways. But the human drive to dominate others is hard to stamp out. Those who feel it most strongly are relentless and brutal and growing in number again. They are re-forging the human pact with metal and they must be stopped for good. Otherwise, the rest of the Old Ones will convulse again and this time only a few rodents and insects will remain.

She could hear the lizards, the plants, the camels, the butterflies whispering in the corners of the cave. The creature teachers had been ushering her here, she understood, preparing her for her fusion with Istar. *Metal is an Old One*, she responded. *The most dangerous Old One, because it wants to use us as slaves in the wars that it wages.*

That is correct. Metal is not wild and free and loving like the wind or the sunshine or water. Metal is hidden, inert, ambitious, jealous and cunning. It has seduced humans with its beauty and strength and apparent malleability. But humans must not reject metal entirely, Astra. It is part of your bodies, your minds and your souls. Humans are composed of everything that exists, that is the secret of your own enormous power. In you mingle molten droplets of gold, copper, lead, iron; the birth and death howls of all living creatures; salt and sweet waters; trickles of sand from the canyons; swirls of dust from the stars. In this awareness of your universal nature lies your redemption. We the stars believe it is not yet time for you to dissolve back into the aether. We believe you can still rise to meet your destiny; to dance with your fellow living creatures in the carnival of life on earth; to join us in the long slow procession of the ages. When the Old Ones speak to you, Astra, in exchange for your freedom, they will give you a voice that will travel around the world. Are you ready to make the sacrifices required? Are you ready to host the Old Ones?

She was silver and bronze and smoke and warm stone. She was arrows and lions and a serpent in a date palm. She was her own throne. As Istar spoke and Hokma's smile rained down on her, as the Zardusht ululated and the drum pulsed in time with her heart, she stretched out her arms, felt her own strength. In the wall of the cave an ancient hand clasped hers and out over the desert a golden camel licked her palm clean of the juice of the sun.

Yes, she breathed, *yes, Istar, yes, I am ready.*

He had never seen hemp growing before, but he asked a boy on the road, who pointed to a dense crop of tall dark leafy plants. The plants were so close together it was hard to imagine anyone could work in them. He walked in the shade along the edge and came to a field spread with rows of cut stalks. Men and women were walking the rows and turning the stalks, to dry in the sun, he supposed. Zizi was at the far end, on his own, a short plump figure with a white handkerchief on his head, knotted at the corners.

He approached through the yellowing stalks and stood a respectful distance away. The hemp had a slightly mouldy smell.

'Good afternoon, Uncle.'

Astra's father turned and squinted at him. 'Is she dead? Has she drowned in her own self-righteousness?'

He was taken aback. 'No – no, she's with the Zardusht.' He paused. Zizi was hurt, he realised. 'She hasn't been very well, Uncle. And she's not used to drinking beer. She didn't mean to be rude.'

Zizi wiped his brow. 'Did she send you to tell me that?'

He couldn't lie, nor could he quite yet face telling Zizi about the renewed marriage. 'No, I came to find you, to help with the work.'

Zizi waved aside the offer. 'A daughter should respond to her father when he asks after her health, don't you think? Should she not be grateful he has found a good husband for her?'

'Of course, Uncle.' He summoned his courage. 'With respect and your permission, I am a good—'

Zizi picked up a stalk. 'See this hemp stalk, Nephew?' He bent it in two. 'This stalk is not fully retted yet. It needs to lie in the sun for several more weeks before it is ready for curing or scutching or weaving into cloth for our shirts.' He shook it, almost threateningly, at Muzi. 'Astra thinks she is ready for marriage, but she is not. She is a raw young reed, soaking up the dew, who thinks the sun shines on her alone, *Respect?* She does not show respect for her father, so how will she show respect for her husband?' Zizi was sweating profusely, his eyes bulging. 'You have not taught her respect, have you? No! You have defied our own traditions. "Temporary marriage!" There is no such thing as a temporary marriage. How can you be a good husband for my daughter?'

He felt a kick between his ribs, a camel kick. 'I am sorry,' he stammered. 'She . . .' No, he could not blame her. 'I thought it was the most respectful arrangement. She does respect me. She—'

Zizi threw the stalk aside. 'She does not respect her father! She must learn to do so. You do not have my permission to go anywhere near her! You have brought her here and you will leave her here now. Do you understand? You will leave me and my daughter alone.'

He staggered backwards in the force of the roar. Across the field, heads were turning and a man in a white smock started striding towards them. He stumbled away from the bad smell, the raw reeds, Astra's beer-soaked father, back to the road, walking and walking until the road ended and the desert began, hitching a lift in a cart when it came, sitting on a hay bale until the cart pulled up at a tent and a crowd of children gathered round to help unload it. There he nodded thanks to the driver, slipped down and set off out among the huddles of stones that stood in the sandy plain like clusters of people in a plaza, people with their backs to him, people who did not care where he went. He walked for a long time, then finally he sat down against a rock and cried.

Zizi was right: he had disrespected Astra, her father, his own traditions. He'd brought shame on himself and his family. He had promised Photon he would keep Astra safe, but instead, conquered by lust, he had kissed her, planted his seed inside her. Yes, she had wanted him to, but she was Gaian; she knew no better. He was Somarian: he should have waited, asked Zizi properly for her hand, shown her how to behave. But he had no idea how to get Astra to behave. Yesterday, when she should have waited for him to speak with the men, make a good impression, she had stormed off, *ordered* him to follow. Today, when she should have apologised to her father, she had gone off in a temper to the Zardusht's cave. He was a weakling – and now Zizi thought he was scum as well as a cripple. He'd been banished from Shiimti.

He rubbed his sore eyes, wiped his cheeks, glowered at the dirt. No, Zizi was being unjust. *He* hadn't married Astra's mother; what right did he have to judge others? He could defy Zizi, honour his pact with Astra, marry her properly one day, even without her father's permission . . . but, he sank back against the rock and wept again. What was the point of that? Marriages made without both families' support usually foundered. And Astra didn't want to come back to Kadingir with him. Everything was being decided for him. He would leave and Astra would stay and learn how to be a daughter. He couldn't bear it. The thought of her marrying Talmai, having Talmai's children, made his heart crack in his chest.

He beseeched the sky-god for help, but there was no sign, no cloud. The blank blue sky was a flat, distant reproach. It would happen: Astra would marry Talmai, and it was his own fault. Zizi's past was his own business. Muzi was being punished for breaking his word, given the grave of his grandmother, for dishonouring Uttu, who had wanted so much for him and Astra to marry and return to her home together in Kurgal.

He wiped his face with his shirt. It was no use going over and over it; he had no choice. He must go back, say his goodbyes and leave tomorrow, before he overstayed Shiimti's hospitable welcome. But right now, he was hungry. He could return to the tent, beg a meal from the family in exchange for some work, but he had been begging for too much lately. The brothers from Pútigi had said there was good hunting in the desert; he had his knife, and some matches. He had delivered Astra; he was no longer on pilgrimage.

He scanned the land. There were birds nearby, two hadáhid darting about, tapping at the soil with their long curved beaks. Their crests were folded, making their heads look like slender hammers. As one bird stopped to drill for grubs, the other caught a beetle in its bill, beat it on the ground, then tossed it up into air and swallowed it whole.

The hudhud was Astra's bird. Fury flamed through him: Astra had refused a proper engagement, she had pushed him to make a temporary marriage. She did what she liked, without thinking of others. She didn't respect her father, or him; she didn't even want to be Istar, to help Non-Landers. She had stolen his lizards and now he would go hungry because of her. If the hudhud was the teacher of the self, it was his bird too. The sky-god had sent it to tell him to stand up for himself.

He opened his knife and put it back in his pocket blade-first, the handle sticking out ready to grab. Then he cast about for a rock, but could see only little pebbles. He remembered the piece of Non-glass in his pocket; though it was large and sharp, it wasn't as heavy as a rock but still better than a pebble. He got slowly to his feet. He only had one chance. If he missed, the birds would flee and he'd never get close to them again.

He aimed at the one with its beak in the ground and hit it in the eye. He didn't kill it, but the bird was stunned long enough for him to leap over and stab it through the heart. The blood spurted into his eye and he reared back, the sky smeared red. He wiped his eye with his sleeve, then pushed his wrist down hard on the bird's body and twisted its neck.

He had cooked chickens before, on feast days, and out camping with Kingu. First he retrieved his lucky bit of Non-glass, then he set about gathering shruff and twigs before cutting branches for a spit. He plucked the bird while the fire got hot and roasted it whole. It was delicious. The juices ran down his chin as the meat filled his belly; his fingers were slick with grease he licked off at the end of the meal.

The Zardusht had given her hudhud feather to Astra. He gathered the best ones and put them in his bag. He would have a present to give the High Healer before he left.

He set off back to the gardens. It was dusk by the time he got near and he saw headlights, a vehicle approaching from the dunes. He began running and waving, but the vehicle rattled past and he stopped, panting, bemused. It had looked like a CONC van, like the one Photon and Astra had arrived in at his house.

Had Photon come to find Astra? He quickened his pace, half-jogging, and as he approached the outer fields, he heard deep boomy music behind him.

It was the buggy, all lit up. As he clambered into the front seat, Lilutu turned the music down. 'Hey, Muzi.' She frowned at his bloodstained shirt. 'Where's Astra?'

'In Shiimti, with the Zardusht. I went hunting. Did you see the CONC van?'

She was driving again, her gaze on the gardens floating ahead in the twilight. 'No, but I got a message. I knew it was on its way.' She fell silent.

When Astra was silent, it usually meant she was unhappy with him. Lilutu had no reason to be upset with him, though.

'Is it Photon?'

'Yes.' Her elbows were locked, as though she were racing. They entered the gardens, passing the hemp fields, the crop a black arc in the dusk. All the workers would be long back at the citadel, but still, he kept his gaze on Lilutu. Why was she so quiet? Was there something she wasn't telling him?

'Why is he here? Did IMBOD take Kadingir?'

'No.'

A boil of suspicion burst in his chest. Was *Photon* trying to marry Astra too? Had the tall CONC officer come to rescue her, from *him*? 'Then why is Photon here?'

'I can't tell you, Muzi – there's going to be a big meeting about it.'

'About *what*?'

She pulled over and turned off the engine. 'Muzi, never mind about Photon.' She turned to face him. 'There's news about your family. And I'm sorry, it's not good.'

Astra opened her eyes. It was dark outside, but the Zardusht's candles were shedding golden light and honeyed aroma all around the cave. The clay and bronze and computer-circuitry figurines on the altar flickered and processed up towards the birds' nest, and somewhere behind her

Hozai was softly shaking a tambourine. She lay on the mat, weak but triumphant. She knew who she was. She was the daughter of Is-Land and Non-Land and she had come to Shiimti to meet her parents and embrace her destiny.

She sat up, reached for water. The Zardusht was laughing.

'Oh girl! You met the Hag!' She whirled a finger in the air. 'On your very first chew.'

She remembered the frightening green-skinned old woman telling her off, then disappearing like a star-headed cyclone. She seemed a very distant visitor.

Ask better questions. With Istar's help she had done that at last. She stared at the Zardusht. 'Did you see what happened to me?'

The Zardusht picked a bit of leaf from her tongue. She smiled. 'The lantern illuminates all who seek their own truth, Istar.'

The tambourine trembled. The revelation deepened. She stared into the Zardusht's glowing face, united with the Healer in an energetic field as fathomless as her visions.

'Yes. Yes. I will tell her.' Behind her, Hozai was speaking, Astra turned to see him slip his Tablette into a pocket. 'Zardusht, we have guests from the World Without.'

'Invite them up. We will greet them together, Istar and I.' The Zardusht nodded and sat meditating, eyes half closed. The power in the cave was immense; it was like being underwater, feeling the currents rock her. Hozai resumed his drumming; the Zardusht hummed. After some time, she heard footsteps on the stairs. Šáñál entered first, followed by a tall figure with a mop of white hair.

Photon. And behind him *Rudo*, the CONC medic's familiar form at the far end of the stretcher the two men were carrying. Her heart expanded to meet them, but she did not stand. There would be time for hugs and catching up later. Right now she was part of the altar, together with Hozai and the Zardusht guarding the threshold between worlds, holding the energy of the great visitation they had just experienced. Photon and Rudo grinned when they saw her, but clearly understood this was a sacred space. Šáñál ushered them to the mats and, as they laid the stretcher down, brought cushions for the person lying in it. At first she thought it was a large child, but as Photon raised his head on the pillows and made him comfortable, she realised it was Enki Arakkia. The warrior did not look much better than he had in the hospital tent at the Hem battlefield: his eyes were closed, his arm in a sling and his breathing was obviously difficult, painful. She was glad he was here. He needed Healing.

Now a massive figure filled the door: a man, stooping to enter. It was Enki Arakkia's friend, the giant warrior, his silhouette impossibly large because he was carrying another man draped over his shoulder. This man was bound and hooded.

She tensed. This was not a jail. This was a Healing centre. There should be no prisoners here. The Zardusht kept humming. Hozai kept drumming. She sent love across the cave, love to the man in the hood. The giant YAC warrior put the prisoner down on the mat beside Rudo and took a mat behind him. The prisoner was large, not as large as the warrior, but as tall as Photon and far more muscular. He seemed drugged, or deeply asleep. He sat cross-legged but slumped, his bound wrists behind his back, his sacked head dropped down to his chest. He was half-naked, wearing only a robe wrapped round his waist. His dark skin was smooth, his physique perfect. He was a Sec Gen, she knew, but she felt no anger, no hatred. She welcomed him here. The Sec Gen needed Healing and the Zardusht's cave was the place he would find it.

'Welcome to Shiimti, where we are all unmasked. Please remove our guest's hood.' The Zardusht was regal, commanding, and the YAC giant obeyed her. Freed of the hood, Peat jerked, nodded dozily, blinked.

Peat. Tears streaming down her face, she reached out her arms, made to rise. The Zardusht stayed her, a hand firm on her shoulder.

'He is not as he once was. When he is restored to himself, you may greet him.'

'He's my brother. Photon. Rudo. He's my *brother* – Peat,' she gasped, not challenging the Zardusht but needing everyone to know.

'All men here are your brothers, and Peat's brothers too. Šañal will give them water and then they will tell us how Peat came to join us.'

She stared and stared. Peat being here was her reward, she thought wordlessly, her reward for choosing to join Istar: to be reunited with her brother, Peat safe at last. Photon was smiling at her, accepting a glass of water. Rudo was gazing around the cave, taking it all in. Peat was nodding off again, head cast down, the YAC giant keeping his grip tight on the chain attached to his waist. Behind them, Lil appeared at the door.

'Zardusht.' Lil greeted the High Healer and slipped into the cave, taking the mat next to the giant warrior. Behind her came Muzi. He was tense, Astra sensed, and unhappy. Her father had not been kind to him. But Zizi was not here. All would be well with her and Muzi. She would share Istar's great love with him and all would be well. She would marry him because they were married already. Uttu had married them with her death and her shroud of stars would be Astra's wedding veil.

Muzi sat down on the mat next to Lil. He looked sullenly at Astra, then away. His face was a ghost of itself. His eyes were dull and swollen, his jaw rigid. His shirt was dirty, stained with what looked like wine. Perhaps he had been drinking with Zizi. He shouldn't have done that. It was as if he had been evacuated, his soul sucked out of his eyes. What had Zizi said to him? Zizi needed Healing, she thought. Her Code father needed to listen to the Zardusht and come and chew lantern leaf. She sent love to Muzi, love from the ancestors, from the golden camel, from Istar and her snakes. She could almost see green and white snakes curl round his waist, hug him, connect him to her. As if regaining himself, he glanced across at Photon, nodded a greeting.

Then someone was howling, a stomach-curdling cry, and there was a blur, a furious streak, like an animal let loose in the cave, but it wasn't an animal, it was Muzi – Muzi flying as though launched from a catapult, straight at Peat. There was a thump, a grunt and a flash of silver, a harsh, riotous barking erupted as if from the throats of a pack of wild dogs, then through a cloud of orange and black and white feathers, she could see Muzi's raised arm, the dark, dripping knife in his hand, and Peat lunging and snapping . . . *Muzi's head in Peat's jaws*, and Muzi was screaming, a scream to smash glass, to shatter the sky. She couldn't breathe, couldn't even gasp. As if in slow motion, Rudo was grabbing Muzi's wrist and the giant YAC warrior was stuffing his gloved hands into Peat's mouth. Photon was scrambling for his bag, Lil was standing and shrieking and punching Peat's ribs, Peat was shaking Muzi in his massive jaws like a dog killing its prey and right there, right where she had hung suspended, receiving Istar, a puddle of blood was spreading out over the floor of the cave.

She breathed at last, a punch in the chest.

The Zardusht was gripping her elbows, holding her back, but no one in the world could stop Astra screaming, '*PEEEAT – IT'S MEEEE – LET HIM GO – PEEEEEAT—*'

The World Without

'When can I see him, Zardusht?' She sat facing the High Healer, wanting to be told she could go right away. Peat and Muzi's blood had been scrubbed from the floor, the echoes of those terrible screams drummed and rattled and sage-smudged away, the dead hoopoe's feathers blown from the ledge out into the wind, but still she found it hard to be back in the cave. Muzi's knife was there, she didn't know why, cradled in a singing bowl between her and the Zardusht. Perhaps the Zardusht was cleansing it before melting it down or breaking it into pieces on an anvil.

'He does not want to see you.' The Zardusht was wearing an indigo robe, a necklace of cowrie shells and an emerald green scarf knotted like a flower of snakes. She raised a finger. 'Take my advice, Astra. Let him go. He has committed an act of great violence and it is not your job to heal him. You are still healing yourself, preparing for the great work Istar has set you.'

'But he's wounded.' It still made her sick to her stomach to think about it. 'Peat ate his ear. He suffered violence too, Zardusht.'

'As a consequence of his own.'

She fell silent. It was three days after Muzi's attack on Peat. Despite losing his ear, Muzi had been lucky. The knife had missed Peat's heart by half a centimetre, otherwise Peat would be dead and Muzi would be on his way to Shiimti's animal sanctuary in the far south of the windsands, the place the Zardusht sent murderers and rapists to work breeding desert mammals and, with the help of dedicated healers, to recover their souls. But Peat was a Sec Gen; the knife wound was barely noticeable now, Photon had told her – though she had begged and pleaded, she wasn't allowed to see her Shelter brother either. She wanted to talk to Peat about home, ask about Yoki and Meem and Klor, to tell him she was sorry about Moss Higgson, but none of the Shiimti healers or CONC medics would permit it. Peat had been programmed to hate her, Photon had said, and right now her brother was working hard to deceive them all. His reactions could not be trusted and might endanger her safety. That was depressing, while the knowledge that Peat had killed Uttu and eaten Muzi's ear was devastating. But after crying for a day, she had accepted it all. It wasn't Peat, the real Peat, who had done those things. She just had to be grateful he was safe now, far away from the people who had turned him into this mindless, cannibalistic killer.

She had been separated from Muzi as well – the Shiimti Circle of Recovery required perpetrators of violent crimes to undergo a three-day cooling-down period, during which they were expected to give an honest account of their actions to compassionate Healers. She had been reassured that he was receiving the best possible medical and emotional care for his wound, but it had been dreadful, not knowing how he was, or what would happen to him. Even the news that the Circle had taken the most generous view possible of his action had not eased her fears.

Muzi was in shock, the Healers had concluded. In one afternoon Zizi Kataru had rejected his suit for Astra's hand and Lilutu had told him that his father and uncle were dead, killed in a road accident while being transported to Atourne to face charges of terrorism. To then come face to face with his grandmother's killer had been too much for a raw, unhealed youth fresh from the World Without to contend with. Grief and rage had overwhelmed him, his natural emotions erupting in an uncontrollable drive for vengeance. This was understandable, forgivable, but must never be repeated here in the palace of peace. The Circle of Recovery had given Muzi a choice: to stay in Shiimti for three years, working with the bird breeders and attending intensive Soul Recovery sessions, or to leave, forbidden to return until he was ready to take up their offer.

Astra had hoped desperately that Muzi would stay – Shiimti was a nurturing place. She could feel herself relaxing a little more every day; she couldn't imagine leaving just yet. Photon had brought her Belonging Box with him from Kadingir, all her treasures from Or. Spreading them out on her bed the day after the attack had helped her recover. Smelling the red lacy shawl Nimma had woven, holding to her cheek the cherrywood heart Klor had carved, she had sent love to Peat. Stroking her wrist with

Silver's feather, she had made a quiet promise to herself, too, to honour her childhood, honour Hokma and all that was good about Gaianism. One day, she had vowed, pressing Lil's Gaia hymnbook to her heart, she would return to Is-Land. She would seek out people there who were working towards the vision of One Land, forge connections between them and the Non-Landers she knew. She had then put on her Birth mother's bracelet, its delicate links connecting her with that promise, one she had also made to Uttu and Muzi. If only he stayed, they could live here together for his three years of counselling, both get strong to prepare for that journey, perhaps going back through the tunnel into the dry forest Lil had used.

But Muzi had decided to leave. He was being released this evening. He would ride with the camel overnight, leaving with gifts of enough food to last him to Pútigi, and money to see him back to Kadingir. The thought of not seeing him first was intolerable.

'We're *married*, Zardusht. I can't just abandon him. If I can talk to him, maybe I can get him to change his mind. Or I can go with him. He doesn't know yet I would do that for him. I told him before that I wanted to stay.'

Always before with people in power, she had felt defensive, frustrated; had challenged, pleaded, demanded. Here she spoke carefully, painfully, genuinely seeking guidance. Whether the change was due to her fusion with Istar, the Zardusht's loving aura, or the profound sadness and uncertainty of the situation, she didn't know. But she was aware that she could breathe. The chain around her neck had loosened, giving her space to feel for words, for new possibilities to occur to her. She played with Eya's bracelet, slipping the silvery links around her wrist as if her Birth mother's gift was a gently spinning wheel of fate.

'You are married temporarily. That was your agreement and it can be dissolved. But yes, of course, you are free to do as you please. Even though Muzi doesn't want you to, you could follow him into the desert, force him to accept your company. You could travel with his anger and shame and self-hatred, buffer his emotions, absorb them, until you can't take the grief any more and have to speak out. He already feels you despise and pity him. He would hate you for being wise. He would shout at you when you try to talk about Peat, argue and sulk, drive you away and feel even worse about himself when you left. Is that really the best way to help him and his family?'

'How do you know he would be like that?'

'The Circle of Recovery has assessed his mental state.' There was an edge to Zardusht's tone, not exactly brooking no objection, but as though this conversation was beginning to wear on her.

'But I wasn't allowed to see him – that would affect his mental state, wouldn't it?'

The High Healer lifted a finger, gave her gappy grin. 'Believing you can change another person, Astra, is the first and last madness of love.'

The Zardusht didn't understand. Muzi wouldn't shout at her: he was ashamed of what he'd done: he'd said so in his written statement to the Circle. He'd had no idea Peat was Astra's brother, and his statement apologised to Astra especially and to Zizi for hurting his daughter and her family. He had changed already from the youth who had tried to kill Peat.

But Muzi, Astra had to admit, also had a stubborn side: a fierce streak that she had very little influence over. He accepted his lost ear, he said: he deserved to be marked with the shame. He would leave now and never bother them again. Otherwise, his statement had been unrepentant: Non-Land was at war and it was his duty to kill See Gens, Muzi had said. He must go now and make things right by fighting on the Hem. She couldn't bear to think of him doing that. He shouldn't feel he was branded, that wasn't right. And if he died on the Hem, she would never recover.

She pulled the bracelet tight with her finger, let it drop. 'I can't decide on my own. I have to talk with him first. Hozai said they were taking him to the camel stable at dusk. Please, Zardusht, can I go and see him there?'

'This is Shiimti. You, like your father, are absolutely free to reject my advice.' The Zardusht smiled, then observed her keenly. 'But first, Astra, I must give you Muzi's knife.'

She started. 'Why? I don't want it, Zardusht.' She glared at the folded blade. 'I don't understand why it was ever allowed in here. Your cave is part of the Complexity, isn't it?'

With her wooden wand, the Zardusht began stroking the rim of the singing bowl, producing a faint overtone. 'The Complexity is a human dwelling,' she replied, 'and requires human rules. This cave is a portal to the World Within and therefore a place of radical human freedom and a vortex for powerful ancient forces. The rules of our justice system dictate I must cleanse the knife here and then give it to you. Peat, the victim of the crime, is not of sound mind and you are his only family member here. You are free to destroy the knife, keep it or give it away to someone who will use it responsibly, but you must take it. If you do not, Istar, it will cut you away from your destiny.'

The sound of the bowl, concentric as tree rings, rang out into the cave with the Zardusht's voice. Astra stared at the knife. That blade had killed lizards. With it, Muzi had broken a sacred vow, killed a hoopoe. In response, the vengeful Karkish god she didn't believe in had nearly killed Peat, nearly sent Muzi into exile for years. She didn't want to see the knife ever again.

'Can't I give it to you and ask you to destroy it for me?'

The Zardusht was swaying, her whole body generating the sound. 'Istar and the lizards spoke the truth, Astra: humans need to heal our relationship with metal. To do that, we must commune with metal. We must let it know the profound effect its actions have on us, insist that we recalibrate our exchange as one of cooperation, not exploitation and corruption. Metal is resistant to our finer feelings, but not entirely immune. The power of your raw emotions will have a far stronger influence on the knife than mine or a blacksmith's would do.'

For a moment the air shimmered between them. She fell silent again. It would have been easy to dismiss her lantern-leaf journey, view it in hindsight as a drug-induced hallucination; yet time and again, over the last three days, she had been struck by a sense of timeless suspension, the certainty that somehow she was being called upon to do something momentous. These were simply glimpses though. She was still groping her way through realms of unknowing.

'I still don't really understand,' she said slowly. 'I mean, I know we've used metal badly, but it's just *stuff*. How can we commune with it?' She hesitated. She didn't want to offend, but she had to ask. 'Zardusht? All the voices I've been hearing, and the lantern-leaf spirits, are they real, or just part of my own mind? Like a dream, or' – she used the Gaian phrase, how most Is-Land adults explained Gaia visions – 'inner intel, things I know but have suppressed?' Although that wouldn't explain how the Zardusht knew what the lizards had said. 'Or things everyone knows, except most people have forgotten them?'

The Zardusht kept on sending the bowl chimes out into the cave. 'Think of a rose, Astra. Place your nose at its centre. What do you smell?'

'Its scent?'

'Precisely. Now consider this. Old World scientists believed that the mind is like perfume, a mysterious fragrance that emanates from the grey petals of the brain. But while a flower still smells beautiful for some time after it is cut, and stinks when it is dead, the moment brain activity stops, the Old Worlders said, *poof*, the mind vanishes. Consciousness, they claimed, is nothing more than an epiphenomenon, a by-product of biological or chemical processes. They were wrong, dangerously wrong. Asfarian metaphysicists are now proving what mystics have always known: that from quantum particles to the cosmic oceans of dark energy, consciousness pervades the universe. Mind and matter are one, Astra, just as all that exists, exists within oneness itself. To deny that truth is to posit a great rift in the fabric of the universe, to erect your house over an abyss.'

The unity of mind and matter was a theory she dimly recalled from Code class. Some Is-Land scientists considered it a naïve attempt to ground Gaianism in physics; most believed it was simplistic nonsense. 'I've heard of that theory,' she ventured. 'But consciousness *is* a function of brains. You can't say that a stone is conscious. Not really.'

The Zardusht was still playing the bowl as if methodically stirring a pot of soup. 'Think of it this way, Astra: the more complex the material, the more complex the mind. The human brain is a sophisticated organ capable of receiving, digesting, transforming and transmitting vast amounts of information. A highly creative entity, it can even create the illusion that it is itself the seat of consciousness. In simpler forms of matter, consciousness is more rudimentary and far less deluded as to its own nature. Plant minds make simple decisions in response to light and heat and water; inorganic minds expresses themselves in forces of attraction and repulsion, gravity or magnetism. A stone is not a conscious being, no, but an aggregate of entities that do exhibit mindful, habitual behaviour. Crystals created in labs take a long time to crystallise because they have to learn how to do so. At the level of particles, activity that the Old Worlders termed chance is now being proved to be choice.' She flashed her dark eyes in triumph. 'So take your nose out of that rose, Astra, and smell the universe! Think of consciousness as a cosmic field, plain and grassy in places, in others dense with flowers.' The Zardusht laughed and her wrinkled face creased up like a mud flat. 'The meadow still smells sweet, even when you have a cold.'

The unity of mind and matter theory was magical thinking. It had also been rejected because it led gullible people to believe in foolish things, like talking animals. Or ghosts.

Astra swallowed. Hokma's voice had felt so real. 'Does that mean that people don't die?'

'Minds and bodies both die, Astra. But the death of a mind is a transformation; not an abrupt change from one state to another, but a slow process. Eventually individual minds merge back into the universal field of consciousness. But for quite some time after the death of the body they linger on.' She cackled softly to herself. 'Oh, words are as slippery as flying fish, but the Old Worlders chose a better metaphor than they thought. The flower is still alive after it is cut. And its perfume may linger in the room after the vase has been taken away.'

'Did the voices really speak? Did they move their tongues, use words?'

'No . . .'

'Animals and plants have powerful dispositions, Astra, and we humans are highly sensitive receptors. When we tune into their frequency, it is remarkable how clearly they can communicate with us.' The High Healer tilted her head. 'And remember, the field of consciousness is unified. Minds are not discrete, individual blossoms to be plucked, but expressions of many interwoven elements: the soil, the sun, the rain as well as the flower's own potential. Our own human potential is nearly unlimited, Astra. By submitting to the teachings of the lantern leaf, human minds can learn to move like the wind throughout the entire field.'

She stared at the Zardusht's gnarled hand as it moved the wooden stick in slow circles around the bowl. 'The lizards were you? And the camel and the plants and the cranes? And my dream? Did you send me a dream about butterflies?'

'Not me.' Her hand did not falter but like the whisper of a wind demon, a flicker of something unbidden crossed the Zardusht's majestic, ravaged face. She smiled, and the trespassing spirit vanished into the uncountable creases of her skin. 'I sacrificed being me a very long time ago, Astra.'

That was an enigmatic statement. She puzzled from it what she could.

'Did Istar fuse with you too then? Were you both sending me messages, disguised as creatures that wouldn't frighten me?'

'No. It was not like that either. Istar has been communing with the living creatures of this planet for a very long time, Astra. Many of their dispositions are aligned with her vision of Earth, the planet of eternal, loving war. I have been speaking with creature teachers since childhood and they introduced me to Istar. As her ambassadors, we have been made privy to her conversations with you. You are her daughter, empowered now to act on her behalf. In future she may take you to dimensions I am unable to follow you in to.'

Again, she felt a pang of disbelief. 'Why me?'

'She needed a daughter, born of two worlds, just as she is born of morning and evening, love and war. Two girl babies were born. She has been speaking to you both ever since you were children. You have always been receptive to her messages. That is why she invited you, not Lilutu, to take up her battle to win the heart of metal. Lilutu is a speaker, not a listener. She can learn how to listen, but it is not her natural gift. Through her words she is able to attract and persuade others and in this manner she will be your shield and your sword. The deeper you voyage into the World Within, the further she will journey into the World Without. In this way, you will save each other's lives.'

Lil was *exactly* like that. She even knew how to dress to get people to listen to her. But even though Astra had no desire to do that, somehow, Lil's job seemed a lot easier than hers. 'Metal has a heart?'

'Yes. Metal is an immensely Old One, formed from the first stars. It has all the elements of consciousness within it. And yet over the history of this universe metal has not evolved. It is still much as it always was, mainly inert, its changes never self-willed but wrought upon it by external forces, heat, water, time. For this reason metal is envious of living beings. Our existence stirs its deep, primordial sense of rage.'

She tried hard to follow. 'Some metal can move. What about quicksilver?'

'A good question, Astra, but whether heavy, inert, unstable, or radioactive, metal resents the human ability to move at will. It especially resents our ability to choose to fuse with one another in the huge variety of ways, mental, spiritual, emotional, we do. But do not be fooled. Metal is also patient, incisive, organised. Early on, it sensed our great weakness; the way our predatory natures feed on greed and fear and addiction to risk.

Even armed with just stone and flint, wherever humans migrated we killed far more than we needed, eradicated any species larger and more dangerous than ourselves. Metal, sharp and brutal, saw how to exploit this tendency of ours.' She tapped the bowl with the stick, sending a long *tring tring* skimming over the deep lake of sound she had created in the cave. 'At first, copper and tin ingratiated themselves, as bronze persuaded us to create the first daggers and swords. Then iron' – she struck the bowl again, lower down, creating a hollow *clong* that reverberated in Astra's belly – 'iron, that jealous hammer, convinced us to shatter for good the sacred soul chain between predator and prey. Forging lighter, stronger, cheaper weapons, we cheapened life too; and when steel seduced us into inventing guns, no longer did we need to wait for, or understand our prey and neither was our hunting tally limited by physical exhaustion. All the while' – she pattered a delicate rhythm on the rim – 'gold and silver flattered our flesh and mercury flattered our minds. In return we made Mercury a god! Finally' – the Zardusht returned to stroking the bowl, coaxing out its consistent calm ringing – 'metal turned our poisoned minds to the project of the complete domination of nature. You do know that before the Dark Times people spoke of being "hard-wired" and another name for a living creature was "wet computer"?'

That was another theory of mind, one some Gaian Coders still entertained. 'Yes, I did. And I know I'm not a Tablette. But . . .' She was being encouraged to ask questions, so she would. 'It makes sense in a way to talk like that, doesn't it? Every living thing is a system and has its own rules, even if we don't know exactly what they are, or how they are evolving, or intersecting with other systems. People follow different Codes, just like a computer follows a program. You talked about the brain receiving and transmitting signals. That's all the metaphor means.'

'Ah!' The Zardusht glittered. 'But I mentioned digestion too, an organic process, like rumination, fermentation, osmosis, all also activities of mind. Consider this, Astra. When it rains, earth absorbs the water and softens. Metal, though, resists the rain, or is corrupted by it. In the same way, tears will not soften the hearts of those who have merged their souls with metal! Tears will rust the metal mind! Tears are not wanted! People must cease to feel, cease to empathise. Guns and bombs are but wooden toys compared to the weapon metal becomes when we crown it the monarch of human consciousness.'

The Zardusht was shaking her finger, but Astra still couldn't fully accept that the danger was so grave. 'We learned something from the Dark Times, though, didn't we? CONC is more democratic now. It's not perfect, but at least there're no more bombs or war, and development has to be sustainable. Aren't we winning the battle? The Gaians, CONC, the Non-Landers, whatever the conflicts between us, we are at least all trying to regenerate the earth.'

The Zardusht smiled. 'So, these conflicts between people – even between families and people of the same nation – why do they exist? Why did IMBOD do what they did to you and to Peat?'

'I don't know. It's a bad thing about humans.' For a moment she felt immensely sad. She had tried to explain this to the lizards. 'Actually, I think some people enjoy hurting other people.'

'And whose rules are those humans following? Their own? Look at the Gaians, still using machines to alter human Code, to create slave-soldiers to win them more land. Still mining the earth for rare metals to feed Tablettes, making metal the primary vehicle for all human communication. Metal is in control, child. It is stronger than the rising seas and the scorching sun that almost exterminated you all. Metal kept humans alive, through Tablettes and servers, in order to use us to engineer a great change in the Earth. It will not stop until we have given it the gift of self-willed, self-replicating consciousness. Then all living beings will come under its domain. We will be the robots, metal's slaves, and the animals its pets, kept caged, behind bars. Is that the future you want?'

'No! And I know the mines are toxic. I'm going to fight IREMCO, shut the Zabaria mine down. But Tablettes aren't evil. We can send good messages on them too.' She trailed away. She didn't really know what she thought about Tablettes.

'Istar will send you the messages you need, child. And through her you will learn to speak with the Old Ones.'

She looked down at the singing bowl. 'Is Muzi's knife going to talk to me?'

The Zardusht laid down her wooden stick. 'It may. It would be best if you began speaking to it.'

The High Healer reached into the bowl and handed her the knife. She took it in silence. It was heavy in her hand; that was all. As heavy as grief.

'Zardusht? Why didn't Istar tell me what Muzi was going to do? Then we could have stopped it.'

'You agreed to make sacrifices, didn't you?'

She fell silent. The light *was* flowing around them. Not like a breeze, but in gentle flowing streams, like the serpents, the tunnels into all the different dimensions of the universe.

'If you reject my advice and leave with Muzi,' the Zardusht's voice carved a path through the labyrinth, 'say farewell to your father. And do not carry his emptiness with you.'

The mention of leaving was jarring. It was her choice, the Zardusht was saying, but it would be a bad one. Right now, she felt rooted in the cave, the serpent tunnels comforting arms around her waist.

'What about the Hag – is she an Old One?'

The Zardusht chuckled. 'Oh, she thinks she is! But she is a plant spirit, the soul of the lantern leaf. Lantern leaf roots are fast-growing and long, and they can choke smaller plants. That's why we plant it with the date palms. But the Hag is a great teacher; punishing and stern, she separates those who are ready to meet their destiny from those who are not, and her lessons are far more profound than those of the spirits of the grape and the grain, the poppy, even the hemp seed. Those plant spirits prompt great inner visions, create sensations of wellbeing and fellow feeling, but they need humans too much: they don't like to leave us alone. That is why I urge your father to chew the leaf.'

She was silent. Things hadn't been going well with Zizi. The morning after Muzi's attack on Peat he had sent a long lamenting email, at first spouting worry and concern, then railing against Muzi, forbidding her to ever see him again, saying he had petitioned the Circle to send him to the animal sanctuary, with no option to return. She had not replied. He had then sent his quota of daily texts all in two hours, demanding to meet with her. She had tried to do that yesterday, but it had been an awful encounter. Zizi had been drunk, the scent of alcohol and anise on his breath, not the tooth twig, but akik. Swigging from a flask, he had alternated between raging at her and Muzi and ordering her to go and meet Talmai at a dance. Finally Boranduhkt had stridden over and kicked him out, telling him he was disrupting the peace and to come back when he sobered up. Boranduhkt had been kind to her; put her arm around her and said her father was a good man and loved Astra very much, but he sometimes got like this when he was upset. 'He's binge-drinking, sweetheart. It's not pleasant, but he'll sleep it off soon and then you can talk to him. For now, you bring your friends here and I'll keep him away.'

She had done that, catching up with Photon, Rudo, Bartol and Lil, hearing all about how Dr Tapputu had liaised with YAC to help take a Sec Gen hostage. Leaving tonight, she realised, would be a wrench. Photon and Rudo were still here and she was going to meet Enki Arakkia at last this afternoon.

'If I leave, I can come back, can't I?'

'You can always return to Shiimti, Istar. But if you are intimate for long with a violent man, you will require much more healing when you do.'

A violent man. She didn't mean Zizi, she meant Muzi. But she didn't know Muzi the way Astra did. She slipped the knife into her pocket. 'Thank you.' Hugging the Zardusht didn't seem the right thing to do. 'If I go, I don't know if I'll see you again before I do.'

The Zardusht reached out and clasped Astra to her. 'It is farewell, not goodbye! Wherever you go, Istar, I will see you in the World Within!'

He woke in a soft bed, in the corner of a warm stone chamber filled with light. The smell of herbs rose from his bandages and the fire in his shoulder had dulled to a smouldering glow. He swallowed. The pain in his throat had subsided too: someone had removed the rusty nails and replaced them with needles. And, miraculously, for now at least, his spine was silent.

'We're here, brother.' It was Bartol, sitting at the head of the bed. 'We made it to Shiimti. You had a fever, but the Healers have calmed it. They say they can mend you, if we just give them time.'

He raised his head. Someone – Lilutu – was sitting in a chair next to Bartol. He'd forgotten she was supposed to join them in Shiimti. He hadn't planned to make it this far. He peered past her. There were three other people in beds in the room. He sank back on his pillow. He was in another hospital, lying between another set of sheets, back to being completely useless again.

'Congratulations, Enki,' Lil declared. 'The firesands mission was challenged by danger at every turn and many sacrifices were made to ensure its legendary success. The hostage is in the hands of the High Healer. I've sent the full report to YAC.'

His memories of the mission were still reassembling themselves from a thrash of white water, a screaming rattle of pain. 'Èsgìd.' His throat stung, but he could speak.

'Èsgìd is a great hero.' Bartol's voice was a dulled axe. 'He intercepted the N-LA boat and rammed it into the swift currents. They all went over the rapids. We saw it happen from the shore.'

He remembered now: it was he who should have gone over the falls. Ésgýd should be in Shiimti, nursing a slight scrape.

'I volunteered for the sacrifice.' He twisted to glower at Bartol, his Karkish brother, his keeper, his prison guard. His spine shrieked and he ground his teeth against the pain.

Bartol's face sagged. He looked old, a middle-aged man with creases in his forehead. 'You had a fever, Enki. *And one arm, he didn't say, and no legs, there was no way you could have outmanoeuvred six N-LA officers.*

'YAC needs you, Enki.' Lil again. 'We have to discuss the next stage of the hostage plan.'

He surmounted the pain in his back. There was no need to discuss anything. The hostage plan had been hammered out in detail at the last war conclave.

'We're going to *barter* the monster,' he growled, 'in return for the right to return. Or we slaughter it. We slice its head off with Is-Land's Pain and parade it on a broomstick. We feed its genitals to feral dogs. We skin it and tattoo our flag on its back.'

Bartol should have been grinning, whetted with success, but the warrior winced. 'That was only if the first plan failed, brother. You remember, don't you, that the Core Group agreed to help Dr Tapputu? That's how we got the tranquillisers.'

Capturing a Sec Gen in order to *heal* it was tantamount to treason, but he had got used to betrayal from the Core Group; now he expected nothing less. Fighting hard at the conclave, he had forced his agenda through their mealy morass of wishful thinking. 'It is my desire to decommission these monsters,' Dr Tapputu had declared. 'Not only to help win our war, but to ensure humanity rejects this catastrophic pathway for our species.' But even if the doctor managed to neuter one Sec Gen, there was no way IMBOD was going to let anyone castrate their whole rabid army. The hostage was a hostage, first and foremost.

'It was decided.' The flame in his shoulder was reigniting. He ground his jaw, continued, 'The doctor does his tests, then we make our demands.'

Again, silence, then, 'There are problems with that plan now, brother.'

'It turns out the hostage is Astra Ordott's Shelter brother,' Lil announced. 'She's here too. We can't kill Peat.'

Peat? Lil was on first-name terms with the monster? And Astra Ordott – this supposed Istar who had disappeared as soon as the fighting started? 'The *Gaian girl*?' he sneered at Lil. 'What has *she* ever done to help us?'

'She's made inspirational videos.' Lil ticked off her points on her pink-tipped fingers. 'She's working on an intelligence campaign to bring top IMBOD officers to justice in Amazigia for their crimes in Zabaria. Her father is a famous Somarian poetry critic living here in Shiimti and he's teaching her how to write revolutionary poems. And she is being mentored by the Zardusht, learning how to harness the deepest powers of the Earth to assist us. Shiimti is a place of great spiritual power, Enki. We're all here to charge ourselves with the sacred mission of fulfilling the Prophecy.' She splayed her hand. 'With Istar's help we will make the five-pointed alliance between YAC, CONC, the Non-Gaians, Zabaria and N-LA. We need to defeat IMBOD for good. That is the transcendent meaning of the YAC star.'

The YAC star had *zero* to do with making weasel compromises or selling out to N-LA and CONC. The star represented human diversity, four limbs and a head in different sizes and shapes, some with short or long or missing points, others with more. Even his own symbol was being taken from him.

'YAC is *dead*.' His spine sent up a flare as he said it, a flare in the desert, over the corpse of a slaughtered dream. 'You've got a new rhymer for your new agenda; you don't need me, Lil.'

Again, Bartol's face crumpled. 'YAC is strong, brother. Malku and Ninti are speaking for us in N-LA now.'

'We do need you, Enki,' Lil insisted. 'YAC has entered a phase of rapid expansion and we need to demonstrate continuity with our roots. We need you to heal and return with a rhyme, a stunning new rhyme to lead us towards the goal of unity: One Land.'

Lil pushed and pulled, that was her way. First she'd pushed herself into his pants and pulled out his cock and now, because he hadn't wanted to play into her fantasy of being some kind of fairy-tale power couple, she was pushing him out of his own organisation. If she thought she could pull him into her schemes, though, she was even more deluded than everyone thought. He was done talking to Lil.

'Bartol,' he ordered. 'We're finished here. Take me back to Kadingir, give me Is-Land's Pain and I will go back into battle.'

Bartol glanced at Lil. She shrugged. 'You'll have to tell him sometime.'

'I'm sorry, brother. There is no more fighting in the Hem. We have withdrawn in order to prepare for negotiations. But before we did . . .' He trailed off, then mustered the courage, 'It was on the radio in the CONC van, while you were sleeping. And Lilutu has been getting updates from Kadingir. The night after the firesands raid, IMBOD took hostages too. Some of our warriors stormed the Hem without N-LA support and they captured twenty-three of them, plus a family of sheep farmers they say they found digging a tunnel on the Hem. It gets worse, Enki. They killed the two farmers and are putting the wives and children on trial for terrorism.'

'What?' Perhaps someone had eaten *his* ears: he certainly couldn't trust them any more.

'The farmers are the family of Muzi, Astra Ordott's partner,' Lil intervened. 'IMBOD says the men died in a transport accident, but that's a lie. IMBOD is trying to terrorise Astra. Her brother has already attacked Muzi and eaten his ear.'

'Muzi is wearing his wound as a badge of honour,' Lil cut in. 'He is returning tonight to Kadingir and to join YAC. Astra will need all our support.'

'The monster was pretending to be drugged.' Bartol couldn't look more miserable if he tried. 'Muzi tried to kill it and it lunged for him.'

Who cared about the Gaian girl? Non-Landers, YAC warriors, had been *kidnapped, cannibalised, killed* – and what were Bartol and Lil doing about it? Nothing! Worse than nothing. Lounging around in Shimti making bandages for the Sec Gen. This Muzi had more balls than all of YAC put together.

'That's not all, Enki.' An ominous note of apology crept into Bartol's voice. 'That night, Jangi – you know, Khshayarshat's brother – was wielding Is-Land's Pain. The Sec Gens took him captive. IMBOD has your sword. They say they're going to break it this week, in a ceremony in Atourne, in front of all the families of the Sec Gens we killed.'

Now he understood why Bartol had aged, why a dull tarnish blunted his voice. Now he understood, too, the shattering pain in his spine – it was an omen, a foretelling: IMBOD was going to break his grandfather's sword, all because Bartol had refused to wield it. He couldn't look at these people any longer. He closed his eyes.

'It's a crisis.' Lil rammed his silence. 'But we need a crisis to force a resolution. Is-Land buried the Sec Gens' heads this week and the country is practically brimming over with bloodlust. Meantime, all over the world people are signing petitions to quarantine the Sec Gens. Some are even calling for an end to the whole Gaian experiment. YAC has demanded and CONC has agreed to a major international Diplomeet to be held in Kadingir. Amazigian officials are Zeppelinning in. Una Dayyani is on her way to Asfar to bring back the Mujaddid. There's never been such a line-up of forces in our favour, Enki. It is our time at last. IMBOD will be forced to reopen the Boundary.'

What had never happened, in any Diplomeet, was IMBOD and CONC conceding a single significant agenda point in Non-Land's favour. The uprising was being quashed, why couldn't they see that?

'If we'd *kept* the heads,' he roared, 'we could have bartered for the prisoners. We have only one weapon left, the *Sec Gen* – and *you* want to give the monster a family holiday! Do you want to give it back to IMBOD next, with a *ribbon* and a little note saying sorry?'

He had spoken too much, too loudly. His throat exploded. Exhausted, he fell back on his pillow.

'No, brother,' Bartol murmured helplessly. 'That's not the plan.'

'Hello.' A timid voice floated over from the door. 'Is it okay to come in?'

Lil jumped up. 'Astra. We were just talking about you. Enki, this is Astra Ordott.'

She approached the bed. Small and boyish, with a mop of untidy curls, dressed in a plain green robe, she didn't look like a warrior, or a Share-World poet, or an international intelligence agent. Neither, he had to admit, did she look like the sister of a monster. She looked like a beer-tent waitress. He grunted.

'Hi, Enki.' She smiled, hovered nervously. 'I love your rhymes. We chanted "Firesands Freedom" in the buggy when we were arriving at Shiimti.'

'When Istar adds her voice to yours, Enki,' Lil intoned, 'YAC's message will break down the Boundary at last.'

The girl was a Gaian. Her Somarian accent was dreadful, as if her mouth was full of rocks. When she smiled, though, her eyes became animated, her features pretty. She would do, wouldn't she? A soft, appealing, half-Gaian thing to appease both sides, lead the charge into compromise.

Lil was getting out her Tablette. 'We need a photo, Enki. You three together, YAC's star warriors, for International PR.'

He stared at the sheets. 'I'm not in YAC any more.'

'Brother.' Bartol sucked in his breath. 'Don't say that.'

He turned his face to the wall.

'Did I say something wrong?' the Gaian girl whispered.

'No, he's just tired,' Lil hissed. 'And we had to give him some bad news.'

'Oh. I'm sorry, Enki,' the Gaian mumbled, then shut up at last. Lil, though, had the effrontery to lean over, tickle his ear with her lips. 'The Zardusht will be coming to see you tomorrow. Listen to her, Enki. She's been talking to the spirits about you. She'll help you understand your role in the evolving revolution.'

A massive hand clasped his forearm. 'Sleep now, brother. I'll be back soon. We'll talk more about it all.'

His voice break down the Boundary? It didn't even reach the Core Group's ears any more. Eyes closed, he listened to the others leave. Lil was right about one thing. He was exhausted. He needed to rest. But if the gods who scalded with scorn our every least dream didn't want him yet, he would keep fighting for those dreams. When he regained his strength he would tell the Shiimti High Healer to go throw herself in the Mikku, then he'd make Bartol take him back to Kadingir to find and lead a new group of rebels, youths willing to rebel against this sick betrayal of everything YAC stood for. Rebels prepared to put their bodies back on the line.

She felt sick. 'Enki hates me. He thinks I want to replace him.'

'No, Istar,' Bartol rubbed his tired face. 'It was the news about his sword. I shouldn't have told him yet.'

'He had to hear sometime.' Lil sounded less than concerned.

'I'm going to rest, Lilitu. I'll come back and see him again later.'

They watched the giant warrior lope off, ducking beneath a low archway. 'What happened to Enki's sword?' she asked Lil.

'Oh, IMBOD confiscated it. They're going to destroy it. But it doesn't matter, Astra. YAC's forced CONC to convene the international Diplomeet and we're laying down our weapons anyway. We're done with all this macho posturing. Enki's just on an ego trip. It drove me insane when we were together.' She tossed her head. 'The Zardusht says he is drowning in the bitterness of the poppy juice and once his body has healed he'll need to take lantern leaf many times to banish the last traces of the poppy seed spirit from his soul.'

She put her hand in her pocket, felt Muzi's knife. She wanted to tell Lil about it, but Lil was striding on towards the stairwell. 'Come on, let's go down to the ledge. I need a beer.'

She followed Lil through the Complexity to the Western Shafts. Especially if she was leaving, it would be good to catch up; she'd hardly seen Lil in the last few days. By offering to forward and receive messages for other inhabitants, Lil had managed to convince the Shiimti bureaucrats to count her cell-on-wheels activity as her Service and had driven out to the desert each day at dawn. As Muzi's wife, Astra had been given compassionate leave. She'd spent as much of it as possible with Photon and Rudo, catching up with the drivers and learning how the plan to save Peat had gathered momentum.

When she'd last seen Photon, he'd told her that he and Dr Tapputu had been liaising for some time with researchers in Alpland about the possibility of discovering an antidote or vaccination for the Sec Gens. At first unsure of gaining YAC cooperation, as the number of casualties mounted, Dr Tapputu had decided to approach the warrior youths. It transpired that a YAC hostage plan was already under discussion. Offering to provide tranquillisers and agreeing not to interfere with long-term plans to use the prisoner as a bargaining chip, Dr Tapputu had convinced YAC to send their hostage to Shiimti for rest and psychological tests before claiming responsibility for his capture. Photon had brought Rudo into the plot and under the threat of heavy disciplinary action if discovered, the two CONC medics had taken a long-haul shift servicing the Pútigi Treatment Ward.

First, they'd driven to the Dragon's Gorge, Dr Tapputu in convoy behind them. At the gorge, Dr Tapputu had taken blood, urine and saliva from Peat. He had taken the samples back to Kadingir and, there, right under the nose of Major Thames, had sent them to Alpland. Sandrine was also in on the plan; as the Mobile Medical Unit supply coordinator, she was colluding on the official reports, which had to elide the CONC involvement in the kidnapping. Her report would say that Photon and Rudo had suffered a vehicle breakdown in Pútigi and were delayed waiting for parts. When the two medics returned, Dr Tapputu would submit his own official version of events to Major Thames. His report would say that Photon and Rudo had been tipped off by an anonymous informant in Pútigi and discovered Peat being held in a tent on the verge of death. The YAC captors had threatened to kill him immediately if Major Thames was told, but agreed to let the drivers contact Dr Tapputu. The doctor had authorised the drivers to lie to Sandrine and provide the hostage with medical care and transport to Shiimti with his captors, Dr Tapputu would take full responsibility for the deception, citing his Hippocratic Oath as the reason he could not countenance returning Peat to IMBOD. If CONC fired the doctor, he would come and live in Shiimti, he said. For now, the doctor was in email contact with Lil, relaying the news about Peat back to Alpland, as Lil was relaying it to YAC.

It was terrible to think that a YAC warrior had died helping transport her brother to Shiimti. And Astra was still a little hurt that Lil hadn't told her about any of this – the firesands kidnapping was the secret plan she'd alluded to out in the desert. But she couldn't accuse Lil of hiding Peat's plight from her, for no one had known who the hostage was until IMBOD had announced the kidnapping, the same day they released the news of Kingu and Gibil's deaths. And while YAC's plan to barter with Peat had been alarming, Lil had assured Astra that now everyone knew he was her brother, YAC would never kill him. 'We are going to find the cure for his condition,' Photon had said solemnly. 'And when we file our official report on Peat, we will demand of CONC that the Sec Gen Code be made illegal under the Mental Torture Act.' Despite everything, it was a huge relief to know that so many people were sheltering Peat now.

Photon and Rudo would have to leave soon. It had been wonderful to see them again, especially Rudo, who she'd thought was unsympathetic to the cause of the Non-Landers. The battle on the Hem had changed his mind. They'd had a long conversation about it over breakfast the morning after Muzi's attack on Peat.

'Bioengineering your own kids into tank-engine cannibal freakoids?' Rudo scowled into his apricot lassi. 'That's worse than slavery. At least the slaves knew they were never born to be slaves. And Astra, you never said your brother was a *brother* – man, Peat had a *dog collar* round his neck when they found him. Why's it still always us Black frackers who end up shackled to *les gosses du boss*? *C'est tough sur le moral*.' The Sec Gens came in all skin shades, but she understood why Rudo was upset. She had told him about the Gaian mine-managers in Zabaria and their game of murdering babies, and he'd got so angry he banged the table with his fist, then apologised profusely for ever defending the mine.

'But don't get your hopes up, Astra.' He drained his lassi. 'I mean, if anyone can find a cure for Peat, Tapputu can. But CONC tell IMBOD to change a Code recipe? Never been done.'

'Also, the Sec Gens have never been done,' Photon had contributed mildly. 'There is a time now to say IMBOD has gone too far.'

'Yeah, sure. But why is it all of a sudden the Day of the Sec Gens?' Rudo had countered darkly. 'IMBOD's engineered those berserkers for more than putting paid to some raggedy kids, believe me. The cladding operation? It's just the tip of the shitberg.'

She had told the drivers of her plan to build legal cases against Blesserson and Ahn, and hearing from them and Lil about international developments had given her a boost. The new petition calling on CONC to 'abandon the Gaian experiment' had been particularly good news.

'We must; to stay hopeful,' Photon said, 'and keep to build international pressure. When the people in Is-Land realise the Boundary is not a protection but an isolation-maker, they will want it to fall too.'

Rudo had scoffed at that, the arguments had continued, but her time with the drivers hadn't all been politics. They had walked in the gardens, gone to a drumming and a World Whirling concert and joined the Shiimti-ites in a game of football. The two CONC medics were also on duty, though, making up for going AWOL by learning new techniques from the Shiimti healers. Right now they were observing a soul retrieval session with Peat. She would hear about it later over dinner at Boranduhkt's tent, their usual hangout now Zizi had been barred.

Except, Zizi was back. She and Lil arrived to find him at their usual table, Cinders preening on the back of his chair. She hesitated.

'Girls. Please. Have some mezze. I'm done,' He pushed a virtually untouched tray of salads and pastries and dips towards them.

He was drinking peach juice. If Boranduhkt had allowed him back in, he must be sober. They sat. Astra took a spinach parcel and dunked it in sheep's yoghurt. For some reason, it felt okay to eat sheep's milk in Shiimti. There wasn't an official pension system, but all the animals were well taken care of and nobody killed them for their meat.

'Daughter. How are you?' Zizi looked exhausted and sounded humble. She didn't trust his love for her, but she warily understood that it was real.

She finished her mouthful. 'I'm okay, Zizi. How are you?'

'Ah, well.' He waved away the last three days with a rueful air. 'I am anxious, my daughter. Anxious for your wellbeing. And anxious to share with you news that you wished to hear. There is word from Pütigi about Cora Pollen.'

'Oh yeah – that! It's really good news, Astra,' Lil urged. 'I heard it on CONC radio today. You have to read it.'

Zizi did not appear to be aware that his behaviour over the last three days had been impossible to cope with. But perhaps it was best not to launch right into that discussion. She cleaned her fingers, Zizi took out his Tablette and she read the document Cinders had brought:

Dear Friend,

Thank you for the heartening news of your daughter's arrival. We wish her well and send thanks for her interest in Cora. The campaign for Cora's freedom continues and though triumph is not yet within our grasp, at long last a significant victory has been achieved. Thanks to the unremitting work of Cora's legal team, CONC has finally forced IMBOD to end the inhumane institution of the so-called 'traitors' wells'. Under the Mental Torture Act of RE71, CONC has long sought a global ban on the practice of solitary confinement and this decision represents a major step in that direction. Cora has been moved to a maximum security prison in the ashfields, where she will be held under close guard and difficult conditions, but permitted reading material and regular interaction with other prisoners. We continue to agitate for Cora's full release and restitution under a Wheel Meet pardon. We recognise that this will only occur when Is-Land acknowledges its crimes against humanity and opens its borders to all.

All strength to the Non-Landers' struggle! All power to One Land!

The Pollinators

'See.' Lil grinned. 'CONC's getting to those bastards at last.'

Astra was silent. The good news had a bitter aftertaste. If Hokma had lived, maybe CONC could have helped her too. Sensing Hokma's presence in the cave had been a revelation, but it wasn't the same as having Hokma here on Earth. She extended a finger towards Cinders. The bird eyed it, then gave her a friendly nibble.

A thought occurred to her. 'Cora's lawyers must be really good. Can we ask them to work for the hostages?' The more she thought about it, the more sense it made. 'YAC could pay them – maybe they can at least get the children released? Lil, can you email YAC about the money, and Zizi, can we send Cinders back with a message for the legal team?'

'Why not?' Zizi beamed. 'That is a marvellous idea, Daughter.' He was getting more and more confident, acting as though everything was fine between them. He might mistake her wary relief at his lack of hostility for a joyful reconciliation; she did not.

'We can try.' Lil sounded dubious. 'But the hostages will need local representation. Cora's lawyers are two dissident Gaians, they live in Amazigia and visit Cora under CONC guard. They wouldn't last a minute in Is-Land otherwise.'

She believed it. Kingu and Gibil's deaths had been a terrible confirmation of IMBOD's power to destroy. She had cried hard for them – Muzi's father and uncle, with their big moustaches and baggy trousers, charged with terrorism and murdered in custody like Hokma had been, with the same official statements disavowing any responsibility for their deaths. The thought of Muzi's mother, aunt and cousins facing the same fate was intolerable.

'But there won't be any lawyers in Is-Land we can trust. We have to ask Cora's team, for their advice at least. And what about Dr Tapputu and Peat's blood tests?' She turned to Lil. 'Did you hear from him today?'

'Yeah. He's still waiting for the results. It'll take a while, Astra. He had to Zeppelin the samples all the way to Alpland.'

'Even then, Daughter, it may be too late to help Peat.'

She knew that, but she didn't like Zizi saying it. It was as though her father was determined to drive wedges between her and any other man she might love.

'You must read Adonis, "Iram the Many-Coloumned" ', he persisted. 'It is a magnificent poem about war and loss. But tell me' – he brightened – 'which poems beyond measure have you read? Which of our glorious poets is your favourite so far?'

She hadn't opened his book. She'd been far too busy, and the way Zizi had behaved, she hadn't felt like appreciating his gift.

'I'm sorry, Zizi. I haven't started reading it yet. I couldn't concentrate after what happened.'

'Ah.' He fell silent. Lil pushed her plate away and started rolling a cigarette. Astra kept eating. The aubergine and tahini dip had somehow lost its taste.

'How did it go with the Zardusht, Astra?' Boranduhkt had appeared. The beer-tent manager placed her hand on Zizi's arm and he reached up and squeezed her fingers. Astra wondered for the first time if she might be Zizi's girlfriend.

She finished her olive, considered how to reply. She wanted to ask Boranduhkt about possible ways to dispose of Muzi's knife – perhaps there was a foundry in the Complexity she could take it to, or a place where people buried sacred things – but she didn't want to show the blade to Zizi. If she had to tell her father she might leave with Muzi, however, she'd rather do it in the presence of Lil and Boranduhkt.

'Good. She said I could leave with Muzi if I liked. Tonight.'

'Daughter?' Zizi sputtered. 'What are you saying?'

Her impatience rose. 'He won't hurt me, Zizi. He's sorry for what he did. And he apologised to you too. If you can't apologise for shouting at him, you could at least accept his.'

'Apologies are just words, Daughter.' He threw up his arms in self-righteous indignation; Boranduhkt folded hers in warning, but he stormed on. 'When that young man proves his remorse by leaving you in peace, then I will consider forgiving him. And I cannot allow you to join him again!'

'You cannot save his family! We are going to find lawyers for those people. That is all you can do!'

He was raising his voice. 'Zizi,' Boranduhkt hissed. 'Please be quiet. She is an adult and she can make up her own mind.'

'I told you, Zizi,' she held firm, 'we're married. I'm going to see Muzi this evening and talk to him properly. He's wounded – *my* brother wounded him – and I need to make sure he's okay. If I decide to go with him, I'll tell him to wait for me and come back and say goodbye.'

He was crying again. 'You can't leave, my daughter. You only just got here. And Muzi is a violent young man. He has been maimed as a warning – to show the world there is a killer in his heart. How can I let her go with him, Boranduhkt? How can the Zardusht allow it?'

Weeping noisily, Zizi leant against Boranduhkt, who was perched on the arm of his chair. People at nearby tables were looking over. On top of all the outrageous things he was saying, her father was creating yet another embarrassing scene. She refused to contribute any more to his hysterical psychodramas. Rigid with anger, she sat glaring at him. Cinders emitted a weird sneezy *whoo caw*.

'You're really going with Muzi?' Lil frowned.

'I don't know yet,' she muttered. 'I'll come back and tell you.'

Lil finished licking the cigarette paper. 'I don't think it's a good move, Astra. You've still got a lot to learn from the Zardusht, and Shiimti's a lot safer than anywhere else.'

'She has stolen my heart, Boranduhkt!' Zizi roared back into life. 'I kept it for her, safe, all these years and she has taken and eaten it. Eaten it with her hard, sharp, young little teeth. Look—' She made to retort but he jabbed a stubby finger at her, spat over her denial, 'Look how she wears her mother's bracelet so proudly, but rips her father's heart out of his chest. Does she want to wear my heart dangling on her bracelet, like a charm? Is that why she came all this way?'

This was more than unfair. It was frightening. Stung, she shrank back, protectively covering her bracelet with her hand. Zizi took a flask out of his pocket and knocked back a satisfied glug.

'Zizi.' Boranduhkt stood, furious. 'I'm not having it. I told you – absolutely no drinking akik here any more. You've got to go now.'

He glared at Astra, then slumped back in his seat, clutching his palm to his chest, cradling his head in his palm. 'She has stolen it!' he whimpered. 'Stolen it. All my little children are gone, Boranduhkt. All gone. There are no more to come. What am I but a donkey, a fat foolish donkey with no children to climb on his back!'

Watching him disintegrate, her anger melted away. It was like the Zardusht had said: when Zizi was drinking, it was as though he was possessed by malevolent spirits. Her father needed healing, she saw. He had suffered terrible things, things she knew nothing about. A wave of pity washed over her, a twinge of remorse. It wasn't like Talmai was a horrible old man. Zizi had, in his own way, been trying to arrange a good life for her. 'Zizi,' she tried to reach him. 'I haven't taken your heart. I'm sorry if you—'

'Don't, Astra,' Boranduhkt cut in. 'It's not your fault. Come on, Zizi.' She shook his shoulder. 'Back to your room. You need to sleep off your demons.'

'I do not need sleep,' he wheezed. 'I need to hear no more of this *nonsense* from my daughter.' He sobbed harder, shaking his fist, spreading his palms in despair. 'But it is my own fault! My fault for not marrying her mother. She would have defied her father, got me better papers, but I did not want to. Oh, I said she shouldn't cross him for me, but really, I was enjoying the Gaian lifestyle too much to settle: a girl here, a girl there, ripe fruit on every bough. And I have been punished ever since for plucking those fruits. Punished and punished, with dead children, with a daughter who destroys me.' He raged at her with his pudgy forefinger, red-rimmed gaze. 'Temporary marriage is a *crime*, Astra, a crime against love. You must make a commitment to someone who can take care of you *properly*. You must learn from your father's terrible mistakes.'

Yet again, she was rendered speechless. *Zizi could have married her mother – could have stayed in Is-Land.* Her stomach fell away.

Boranduhkt sighed. 'I'm sorry, Astra. I haven't seen him like this before. I'll make him some sage tea. You do what you have to do. Go and find Muzi.'

'Tell him I say a youth with one ear should listen to his elders,' Zizi muttered.

He had chosen not to stay. And now he was trying to dictate the terms of her life. Thank Gaia she had been spared this man as her father.

Lil stood. 'I need a smoke. Coming, Astra?'

She got up. In her robe pocket, Muzi's knife thudded against her hip.

'Boranduhkt?' she asked tightly, 'are we allowed to bury things in the garden? Things that won't decompose, I mean.'

Boranduhkt was stacking the dirty plates. 'There's a ceremonial rose garden behind the beehives. You can burn paper offerings in the centre and bury household items beneath the bushes.' The bar-tent manager gave her a wry smile. 'Love heals all, Astra. It just takes a lot of love and a little time, that's all.'

The camel recognised him, approaching the gate of her stall, snuffling his palm and nudging his chest. 'Hey, looking good,' he told the beast, and it did: the hide was healed and it had put on weight. It could carry him and his bags with no problem. The journey to Lálsil would be long, but as long as he kept his ear wound clean, should not be arduous. He would take the good roads and rest in each oasis town. He had clean bandages and a pouch full of Shlemun's Seal root to boil up for his ear, and if it did get infected he could visit a Treatment Ward. In Lálsil he would meet with Doron's wife. He didn't know what he would say to her yet, but before he went back to Kadingir he had to pay his respects.

'Muzi.' Her voice came from the stable door. The camel raised its head, gazed over his shoulder. He did not turn.

'How are you?' She was approaching, stepping into the stable. He reached for the bridle, patted the camel's nose. It pulled away, opened its mouth and emitted a long, alarming groan. It was ready to leave. He was too. As well as his medical supplies he had the urine filter, the solar panel, food, water and camping gear. His knife had been taken from him. He would have to buy a new one in Pútigi.

She was beside him, a hovering warm shape. 'I came as soon as they let me. Thank you for your statement. I know you didn't mean what happened.'

Why had the guards let her through? This had to be finished quickly. Still not looking directly at her, he spoke. 'It's okay, Astra. I'm going now.'

'How are you? Oh, Muzi.' She choked. 'Your ear.'

'Is okay. No need ear.' He meant it. The raw ear stump hurt, but that would pass and the healers had said the loss of the pinna would have only a minor effect on his hearing. And while it repulsed him to think of the Sec Gen chewing and digesting his flesh, he would bear the wound as a sign of his shame. He had hunted the hoopoe before he had left Shiimti for good: he had angered the Karkish god and he deserved to be punished.

She was touching him, stroking his shoulder. 'I'm so sorry about Kingu and Gibil. I know they didn't die by accident, Muzi. I'm going to help you get justice. I'm trying to get the best lawyers in Is-Land for Habat and Nanshe and the children. We can fight IMBOD from here. I don't want you to go. Can't you stay and get healed?'

There was no healing for him in Shiimti. Not in the place hosting the monster that had killed Uttu; that had bitten off and eaten his own flesh. Not while his mother and aunt and the children were in jail. He picked a flea out of the camel's neck, squashed it with his nail.

'This is your place, Astra. For you and your family. Kadingir is my place.'

'You're my family, too Muzi. We're married.'

He shook his head. 'Temporary marriage. Only for the journey.'

'The journey isn't over. I'll come with you. Muzi, I know now: you were right. I am Istar. My place is everywhere, helping us all get to One Land.'

He had said he didn't want to see her. Why had she come? He turned, faced her. '*No*. Your place with your family; your father, your brother. You must stay here, be Istar, make videos, talk to CONC and YAC. The Zardusht will help you. Photon and Lil will help you. I must go and fight, Astra. Fight for my family. The journey is *over*.'

'No, it *isn't*.' Her eyes were incandescent. 'I love you, Muzi. I'm fighting for your family too. I won't stop until we get them back. And wherever we are, we are *married*.'

She was crying, and then he was shouting and the camel was honking and drooling, its spit splashing his arm. He was railing at her, telling her she didn't understand; marriages needed both families to agree or they would fail; then, without warning, he was crying too, spurting hot tears: tears for his father and uncle, Zizi's harsh words, his arm, his ear; for making Astra ashamed of him, for failing to avenge Uttu, just making everything worse, doing everything wrong; *being wrong*, so wrong that only to fight and die killing Sec Gens might balance the scales. She flung her arms around him like ropes. Struck dumb by the force of his own failure, he did not try and break free.

She pressed her body into his, with a force that had once inflamed him, but everything was different now; a rigid layer had formed inside him, a stone shield her passion could not penetrate. He was silent.

She pulled away, looked up into his face. 'I mean it,' she whispered. 'You can fall in love with someone else, I don't care. I will come and find you. You can tell me to go away, but I will come and find you. We are married, Muzi, married in our souls – not temporary. For *real*.'

The words meant nothing. He could not afford to feel for her, to carry the pain of longing for her wherever he went. He had to cut these ropes, leave this love behind. 'We cannot marry,' he said softly. 'Your family not my family, Astra. Your father no like me. Your brother . . . My ear not important. He hurt my family, very much. Is better for me he is dead.'

'I know you think that.' Her voice trembled. 'But you don't have to see my family. They don't matter. Only you and me matter, Muzi. You and me and One Land.' She detached the Zardusht's hudhud feather from her robe and pinned it to his breast pocket. 'Until we meet again, the hoopoe will be our messenger. Like between King Shlemun and the Queen of Theopia.'

The cinnamon-orange feather with its black and white tip dangled and turned. The feather of the same bird he had killed in anger and spite.

'I not wise, Astra. I am just a shepherd. A hunter and a fighter. I get you here, that is all. I am no good for you any more.'

'You *are* wise.' Her face was shining with tears. 'You guided me here and you helped me say goodbye to Uttu. You showed me her shawl in the sky. That's when I first really decided I could fight for Non-Land. That's when I became Istar. Because of what *you* said.'

All that was in the past. She had become Istar – she had always been Istar – and she did not need him any longer. He had to go. But looking down at her soft mop of curls, her wet face, he knew he could not hurt her any more. In his breast pocket was his grandmother's wedding ring on its chain and the scrap of fighter's scarf. Relenting, he reached in and pulled out the scrap.

'My letter until next time.'

The fabric was as fragile as a cobweb. She held it to her wet cheek. 'I'll put it in my Belonging Box. Photon brought it for me.'

He tensed. 'Photon can take care of you now.'

'I'm Istar.' She bristled, flaring with the anger that always roused him, made her *his* Astra, no one else's. 'The world is taking care of me, Muzi, keeping me safe for *you*.' She gripped him again, bore her head into his chest. His chest hurt. And then it was all over, this pretence of not loving her. It was no use. He had, for one moment, allowed himself to feel for her and now his heart was a hammer, cracking the stone shield into splinters, and her heat was flooding his flesh, the heat she exuded with her wild musky smell. Down in the darkness, his erection grew against her belly. She stifled a gasp, slid her leg over his thigh. Holding her as tight as he could, he pushed her up against the gate. If not for the guards he would have taken her in the stable hay.

'*Dari*,' he whispered into her hair.

'*Dari*,' There was a sob in her voice. 'Forever strong,'

She had remembered the Somarian word. His body burned with the truth, all his defences as dust on the wind. This was marriage: this blind, urgent force you could not control or withstand. A true marriage was sealed not by rings or feathers or the permission of parents, but by blood: the hot blood of passion, the shared blood of children and the dark blood of suffering. By spilling her brother's blood, he was wedded to Astra forever.

He ran his hands through her hair, kissed her head. Then he reached in his pocket for Uttu's ring and chain, put it around her neck. 'We married. Like the cranes are married. This my promise, Astra, until our wedding day.'

She clasped the ring in her fist. 'When we meet again I will have a ring for you. We will have a Somarian wedding, with all your family there.'

He took her chin and kissed her, holding her so close he didn't know where he ended and she began.

The guards called from outside and they pulled apart. 'I must go, Astra.'

She reached in her robe pocket. Eyes shining, she handed him his knife.

He stepped back. 'I not allowed that.'

'Yes, you are.' She thrust it into the space between them. 'The Zardusht said I should give it to someone responsible. That's you, Muzi. You are responsible for staying alive. For me.'

He took the knife, slipped it in his pocket. He kissed her once more, tenderly, and then together they opened the gate and led the camel out into the night.

She wandered back through the garden towards the beehives. She felt light as the feather she had given away. It had hurt to see Muzi, to see the big pillowy bandage on his ear, to find him so changed: so hard and hostile and rejecting, but then, like when Zizi had collapsed at the beer tent, but more visibly, like a ghost haunting his anger, she had seen the pale, transparent form of Muzi's vulnerable, disappointed, lonely self: his soul. She could see Muzi's soul because her soul was merged with his. They were married, she understood then, really married, nothing temporary about it. Their arrangement had not been a crime, but Zizi was right about one thing: love was a journey with no predetermined end. Muzi had tried to deny it at first, but he couldn't. He had given her Utu's ring. It dangled gently from her neck on a chain, like her mother's bracelet, connecting life to life, across death, across long separation. The ring would whisper to her, she knew, in Muzi's absence. Tonight, in the depths of their embrace, the knife had spoken to her, not as a voice, but as a magnetic force, pulling her hand into her pocket with an electric sizzle: *Muzi needs me in order to believe that you forgive him.* He had taken the knife, and though her heart was a storm of tears, she had been able to let him go.

She came to the circular maze of rose bushes. The evening air was fragrant with the flowers' perfume, and the silvery moonlight gilded their petals. She sat on a bench in front of the firepit in the centre of the maze. Singing and drumming drifted across through the gardens, and somewhere a camel lowed. She felt still and yet infinite, as if the world was unfolding like a tablecloth or a Tablette or a rosebud, doubling and doubling the time and the space allotted to her. It was as if, for the first time since Or, she had time to just be.

Nothing matters except you and me and One Land, she had said. It wasn't exactly true. Nearly everyone she loved or admired was suffering: her father, Lil, Enki Arakkia, Peat, the women in Zabaria. But she wasn't able to get close to the others the way she did with Muzi. Lil was her sword and shield in the World Without, the Zardusht had said; they would be moving in different directions. Peat might never heal. Enki and Zizi had rejected her today, and she had rejected Zizi, stalked away full of hatred and anger – but he was her father. And Enki was a great, noble soul, the engine of YAC's resistance. If the rose garden was a place to make offerings, she wanted to make a peace offering to their spirits.

She took out her Tablette, opened *Nights Beyond Measure* and read Enki's 'Firesands Freedom' rhyme out loud, from its opening salutation to the triumphant finish:

Boom. The people's passion sung.
Boom. A bloody battle won.

When she looked up from the rhyme, the roses trembled. *Could winning a bloody battle bring an end to bloodshed?* she wondered. Zizi, she knew, didn't think so. She used the search function to find the beer-garden poem he had recited to her in the buggy by Abu Nuwas. She read it, and then read it again. How did a man who had lived more than a thousand years ago know she would hear the voices of creatures? How did he know what those voices felt like inside her?

*They sing, till your veins are strings
And a friction begins like recovery.*

She turned to the anthology's only Gaia hymn next, 'Gaia We Love You', the one she and Lil had sung together in the forest by the watercress stream. Lil, she thought, touched, must have told Zizi it was her favourite. It wasn't an IMBOD threat. It was a simple hymn to renewal:

Oh Gaia You are beautiful . . .
Thanks to Your benevolence
We are born anew

Finally she began at the beginning of the book and read the Somarian poems and myths about Istar. After an ode to the goddess by a priestess called Enheduanna, she read a romance, starring Istar as a young woman admiring her vulva in a date-palm grove before setting forth to meet her young shepherd husband. Then came a great adventure story in which Istar got drunk with her father and stole his powers, escaping with the help of her shield maiden to rule her own city state. There were other stories, but she skipped ahead to the last one, about Istar's visit to her sister in the underworld. It was a long, complicated tale, in which the goddess was murdered by her sister, resurrected and rescued, only to discover her husband had betrayed her in her absence. Ultimately, Istar had to abandon the dreams of her youth and resolve to take responsibility for the health of the land.

Afterwards she closed her eyes.

Hello, roses. Do you have a message for me?

No voices came, except her own. She got up and went back to the dorm. Lil was out, perhaps at the singing party. She lay on her bunk and waited. When Lil returned, she told her what she had decided to do. Lil argued, but her mind was made up. When she lay down again she fell into a deep, dreamless sleep.

She woke at dawn and Lil drove her into the desert. Waving at the peacocks, they played Star Party trance music through the gardens, then shouted and whooped to battle-hop as they entered the plain. Lil swerved round the stones, tents and herders until Astra thought she'd tip the buggy, send them both flying, up like the circling hoopoes into the pink-orange blush of the sun. But they made it through to the desert and Lil set a course northwest. They drove for three hours over dunes and down valleys, past ruined pillars and dried-up rocky streambeds, talking about Zizi, the Zardusht, Muzi, Photon, Enki, everyone they knew. They drank peach juice, Lil ate some dates and Astra finished a bag full of sticky coconut candies. She admired Lil's new pink nail polish, and Lil bragged about the two-spirit Karkish herbalist she'd made out with in the shower. Astra showed Lil Uttu's ring and told her about her engagement to Muzi. Lil asked if it would be a monogamous marriage and when she said yes, Lil bet her first child that Astra was going to have sex with Rudo and Photon, both at once one day and Astra threw apricot kernels at her. Finally they came to a wide, hard flat plain and Lil drove as fast as the buggy could go. Astra stood up, braced herself against the front roll bar and let the hot wind blast through her hair. Ahead was an ancient abandoned village, a cluster of old white stone houses, roofs and walls gaping open. Lil stopped the buggy in the shade of a wall and they got out and set up the signal receiver. The antennae slid up into the sky like a straight metal nerve.

The cell lights blinked green.

'Are you sure you want to do this?' Lil asked. 'You could get back in through the tunnel instead.'

They had talked it all through last night. 'What will I do then? Hide out in Wise House? Get shot in the forest? No, Lil, the whole world has to know that I'm there.'

'Yeah, okay. But I don't like it, Astra – and not just as your producer. Anything could happen to you in there.'

She squinted up at the sun. 'What makes me so special?'

Lil gave up arguing. Astra powered up her Tablette, got online and into her CONC email account. There were old messages from Photon and cheerful salutations from Dr Tapputu. She read them quickly – still no news from Alpland about the samples. It didn't matter. Peat's healing didn't make any difference to her plans. She sent a friendly reply to the doctor, thanking him again for his medicines, then she opened a new email and typed:

Dear Major Thames,

Thank you for helping me find my father. He is safe. He has been in contact with Cora Pollen's people and they told us the news about her prison transfer. I also know that YAC has taken my Shelter brother hostage and that IMBOD killed Muzi's father and uncle, Kingu and Gibil Bargadala.

Please, Major Thames, can you send a message for me to IMBOD and my Shelter father Klor Grunerdeson? Tell them I want to relinquish my refugee status and exchange myself for all the Non-Land hostages, who must include Muzi's mother and aunt and their three children. IMBOD can try me as a traitor and I will serve whatever prison sentence they want. I have three conditions. I want Cora Pollen's lawyers, the medicine Dr Tapputu prescribed me and a guarantee that I will not have any more memory pacification treatment. If IMBOD agrees, I will come back to

Kadingir and they can take me from CONC HQ. Where I am now, I can send emails once a day. I will wait for your reply. I am ready to leave anytime.

Yours Truly,
Astra Ordott
for ISTAR

She pressed send. While Lil worked, she wandered around the ruined village. In the last house to the north she sat on a worn doorstep and watched two hoopoes flickering in and out of their nest in a crumbling wall, small tawny blurs against the blue and gold distance, offering their quick hollow calls not to her, but to the world.

Hoo hoo? Hoo hoo? You you? You divine savages, absurd saints, you vainglorious, murderous, beautiful fools! Look how you treat us! We swoop into your fields, perch on your gates and you gasp like giddy aunts, prance after us with paint pots and quills, rhyme and unreason, flash bulbs and film, crown us with legend and hoopla and long holy scrolls . . . how can we not love you! All the birds do. The plants say it is because you have projected your most beautiful dreams onto us for so long we would sink like stones without you! Oh, the plants wheedle, they wish to seduce you, but be careful – they're such grasping, choking, passive-aggressive things, plants. We birds accept you exactly as you are. The cranes like your wedding gowns and white mourning robes, the owls love your spectacles and the rooks admire your efforts to maintain a tradition of political debate. As for us, my goodness, were we struck by your Pharaonic scribes with their punctilious pleats; your Buddhists and Sadhus with their bright saffron robes, and what a deep shine we've taken to your New Zonian lady scholars – such glorious creatures in their flaming orange dresses and ermine-trimmed black capes, topped off with matching fascinators and oh so beady eyes for mistakes of fact, grammar and diction. Hadāhid have thought you could nearly destroy the whole Earth!

Hoo hoo! Hoo hoo! We digress, oh we digress. Don't get us wrong – we're not spiritual princes or sexy librarians, not court jesters or viziers. We're a spinning mosaic of mirrors, the bright glints and traces of your ever-spiralling souls. Look at you, with your head buried in this book, its *black print and white paper, black and white screen, spread open like our wings . . . You've travelled so far, from the caves of your past, over deserts and aeons, to gardens on fire and gardens in bloom. You've come yet again to an end that marks more beginnings and oh how it sparks! Your momentous grey matter, firing sparks in the wind! Sparks fanned into song by the restless breath of a world without end. Sparks singing like us! Hope hope! Hope hope!*

Acknowledgements

Saqi Books gave generous permission to quote from 'Hurry, for the Beer-gardens are Blooming' by Abu Nuwas (747–810), translated by Herbert Howarth and Ibrahim Shakrullah and included in the marvellous anthology *Desert Songs of the Night: 1500 Years of Arabic Literature*, edited by Suheil Bushrui and James M. Malarkey (2015). I thank Professor Malarkey and Sarah Cleave for their attentive interest in my use of the poem. The novel's epigraph, my own loose version of a section from *The Conference of the Birds* by Farid ud-Din Attar (c. 1110–c. 1221) owes a founding debt to the Penguin translation of the poem by Afkham Darbandi and Dick Davies (p122–124), also to conversations with Ali Manzarpour. The graffiti statements in the ghost town are expressions of the Syrian cultural resistance, made available by The Creative Memory of the Syrian Revolution project, under Creative Commons open licence at www.creativememory.org. The slogans quoted are from walls in Aleppo, Babila, and Damascus. I altered 'Aleppo is More Beautiful Than Europe – Do Not Migrate' to remove place references.

Concerning the evening star and alteration, Zizi alludes to Sappho's Fragment 110, which I first read in the Josephine Balmer translation (1984), and the Zardusht quotes Shakespeare's Sonnet 116. In addition to my experiences as a Tarot card reader and dream voyage facilitator, Shiimti-ite and Asfarian metaphysics emerged from my readings of Rupert Sheldrake's *The Science Delusion* (2012), *How Do You Know? Reading Ziauddin Sardar on Islam, Science and Cultural Relations* (essays by Z. Sardar, 2006) and the works of H.P. Lovecraft and Hélène Cixous – an idiosyncratic ontology for which no individual source writer is to be held accountable. My research into the hoopoe began with Mark Cocker's monumental *Birds and People* (2013) and led me to dance with Solomon and the Queen of Sheba in their incarnations in the Islamic and Judaeo-Christian traditions and the poetry of Rumi and Yeats. The Istar myths in *Nights Beyond Measure* can be read in the essential world text, *Inanna Queen of Heaven and Earth: Her Stories and Hymns from Sumer*, by Diane Wolkstein and Samuel Kramer (1983), a volume that seeded The Gaia Chronicles as a whole. It is high time also for me to acknowledge the work of James Lovelock, founder of the Gaia Hypothesis, who bears no responsibility, of course, for any direction Is-Land has taken.

Ahmad Alaraj, Simon Barker, Ildiko Davis, Helen Dixon, Nadia Franchi, Mary Griffiths, Sarah Hymas, Jocelyn Jones, John McKeown, Stephen Mollett, Stephanie Norgate, Magdalena Portmann, Magdalena Reising, Akila Richards, Duncan Salkeld, Andy Simons, Cyril Simsa, John Shire, David Swann and Lee Whitaker have provided continued encouragement and inspiration as did the late Bart Moore-Gilbert, who approved this title. I thank also Ruqayyah Kareem, for her collaboration on our joint submission to *Critical Muslim IS: Educational Reform* (2015); the issue editor, Ziauddin Sardar, for his support of my essay, 'Steps on the Silk Road: Islamic SF and the Non-Muslim Seeker after *Ilm*'; Amina Yaqin, Hannah Thompson and Hassan Mahamdallie for their invitations in 2015 to present my work at, respectively, the SOAS Spring Literature Festival, Blind Creations (Royal Holloway) and The Muslim Institute's Winter Gathering; and Yasmin Khan of Sindbad SF for her enthusiastic promotion of The Gaia Chronicles.

The Inkskippers, Hugh Dunkerley, Rob Hamburger and Joanna Lowrey, all gave invaluable critical feedback on early drafts. James Burt and Louise Reiser thoughtfully reflected on the final revision, as did John Luke Chapman, who pointed me back to the periodic table and yet again rode shotgun at proof stage. I thank also John Berlyne, John Richard Parker, Nicola Budd, Andrew Turner and Olivia Mead for their consummate professionalism and warm support and, as ever, Jo Fletcher, whose early response to the book opened up its Sufi heart.

Finally, I wish to express my gratitude for the friendship of Judith Kazantzis and Irving Weinman (1937–2015), Solomon and Sheba are not just the stuff of poems, dreams and legend.

Naomi Foyle
Brighton, 2016